YOU HAVE THE RIGHT TO REMAIN SILENT

MARK M. BELLO

8Grand Publications

4301 Orchard Lake Road

Suite 180-124

West Bloomfield, MI 48323

ISBN-: 978-1-956595-07-9

This book is dedicated to my wife, Tobye, with all my love . . .

Table of Contents

Prologue

Blood trickled from the man's mouth. He sat on a hard, concrete floor, back against a black basement post, naked, blindfolded, hands bound with zip ties, mouth gagged. Down below, blood spurted from an empty space in the middle of his body. The swift swipe of a large, sharp object had separated him from his private parts. He could not see the blow coming, nor observe the result, but the excruciating pain told him all he needed to know. He could feel blood oozing down both legs, trickling to his feet, onto the cement floor. He understood that if his blood continued to gush at its current level, he would soon be dead. He was terrified, mumbling pleas for his life—silently begging for compassion, mercy, or, if neither was forthcoming, a quick death. Was she seeking only to torture him or was she a sadistic killer?

Yes, his captor was a *woman*. The captive tried to calm down without success, to make sense of the past few hours. He attempted to recognize his captor, the location of his captivity—anything he could recall in case a miracle occurred, and he survived this torturous event. The room was secluded; the door was shut. The tightly bound gag over his mouth prevented him from calling for help. The frantic man couldn't know this, but the door was bolted shut.

What is this place? A basement? Where? Have I been here before? Who is this woman?

"Is this how you like it?"

She'd spoken in a whisper, raped him to understand the attraction, poured vodka down his throat to soften him up for the kill, and finally, sadistically, sliced off his manhood.

The scene was akin to the worst horror movie he could imagine, only this time, *he* was the star of the show. In a movie or on television, he might have survived this horrible ordeal, lived to tell his story to the authorities. People loved horror stories, didn't they? Perhaps he'd seek revenge in the sequel. Alas, this was not an imagined scene from a television show or a movie. It was real, and the tortured victim was about to take his last breath. His thoughts turned to the love of his life.

The worst part of this, my love, is being forced to leave you, to never fulfill the dreams we had or the plans we made. We will never have a child together, but you still can have a child. Move on with your life, my darling. Mourn me—don't forget me; but find someone who makes you as happy as I have been with you by my side. I will always love you and watch over you. I'm so sorry for my momentary lapse in judgment . . . my indiscretion.

He was in and out of consciousness, becoming somewhat impervious to the horror. Fear, anger, pain, and torment slowly gave way to a silent acknowledgment of his soon-to-come death. He had fought courageously, struggled mightily to survive—there was solace in the fact that he had done all he could.

Brad Crawford was a two-term congressman from Southfield, Michigan. His Fourteenth District encompassed much of the larger cities and suburbs northeast and northwest of Detroit. He wondered if his abduction and torture had political implications. Did his enemies hate him that much? What could he have done to enrage this woman, or the people she worked for, to earn this horrific fate?

Try as he might, he could not think of any issue he supported or opposed that might be that consequential. In his second term, he was a rising star in the Democratic Party, a liberal supporter of the new president, and sponsor of a highly popular twenty-first century infrastructure bill that would create high-paying jobs and improve the quality of life in his district. Could his support of President Belding's progressive-leaning policies be a reason to torture and kill him? He was a popular, even beloved, congressman to most of his constituents. This tormented him in his last moments—he was dying to know why he was bound, gagged, and bleeding to death.

Feelings of confusion and sleepiness set in. A door opened—he sensed a light come on beneath his mask. Someone spoke to him—he thought he recognized her disguised voice but could not comprehend her words. He felt beads of sweat trickle from his temples and armpits, much like the blood that trickled from his empty groin.

Someone fumbled with his restraints. His hands were freed but he was too weak to fight back or resist in any way. His gag was removed but he was too feeble to scream, protest his fate, or plead for a last second reprieve. His blindfold was removed. His vision was blurry—he could not focus. He searched the room for his captor and made out the shape of a woman. But the image appeared and disappeared in a flash. She touched his crotch, admired her handiwork, but he no longer felt pain or humiliation. It was as if the trauma disabled him, gotten bored, and transported into someone else's body.

He calmed, spoke to his version of God, cursed Him for his fate, and thanked Him for the good things in life—his terrific family, a wonderful woman, and a rewarding career devoted to public service. His tormentor continued to speak to him. Her voice sounded like multiple voices speaking simultaneously, unintelligible. Freed from his bonds and gag, he tried mightily to move and speak, but all he could muster was a soft moan.

He felt someone tugging at both his legs, his body straighten, and his head bang against the hard floor. He tried to cry out in pain but could only emit another fragile moan. He felt a sudden rush, a pulsating movement, vibration, or sense of exhilaration. His vision suddenly focused and he saw a stern, muscular, short-haired woman pulling him forward. He again tried to mount a defense, to call out or resist, but sounds were muffled, his vision blurred.

He felt the odd sensation once again. What was it? Just some last-gasp energy? Nothing made sense—he tried to suck in a deep breath, the kind that emits a gasp of relief, as if he just emerged from the depths of a swimming pool having stayed underwater for too long. But he could not breathe. He no longer had lung capacity—he was now a mere shadow of life. He felt himself break into a million pieces—*ashes to ashes, dust to dust*—his last conscious thought on this earth. The room became dark and quiet . . .

CHAPTER ONE

Mia Folger lay on the couch, reflecting on her surroundings. Some version of a couch was featured in many television and movie scenes set in a psychiatrist's office. *Do modern therapists typically use them for treatment?*

When she initially consulted Dr. Harold Rothenberg, her session was conducted in a different room—no couch. Once doctor and patient began to feel more comfortable with each other, therapy moved to the current room—the one with the couch.

The couch was a rather common prop for psychoanalysts, first introduced by none other than Sigmund Freud. Freud learned, and practitioners have uniformly agreed, that patient-doctor encounters benefit from being freed of the constraints and self-consciousness that comes from looking each other in the eye. A patient enjoys the freedom of being able to talk without critique. The therapist's office should be one in which a patient cannot see the reaction his or her statement elicits in the analyst—a judgment-free zone, so to speak. The couch facilitates more honest, heartfelt responses.

Mia Folger began psychotherapy with Harold Rothenberg because she loathed herself and began to disparage her husband, who, she insisted, she deeply loved. She sought treatment to understand and rid herself of these feelings. Several sessions into her treatment, Rothenberg switched her session location to the room with the couch. Mia now enjoyed her newfound freedom to speak her mind without witnessing Dr. Rothenberg's judgment.

"I am very self-critical," she opined in an early session. "I feel my mother's negativity, her unrelenting judgment toward everything and anything I try to accomplish in life."

At first, Rothenberg thought she was typical of most patients who complain about their mothers. While most complain and imagine their mothers were constant critics, internal pictures of patients' mothers are commonly darker than the reality. These men and women could usually be persuaded, in therapy, that the mothers of their imagination were far more fearful than their actual mother. But this was not the case for Mia Folger. Her mother *was* unrelenting, evil, judgmental, impossible to please, and a consistent negative force in Mia's life.

Mia was married, wanted to have children someday, but would never be a stay-at-home wife and mother. She was a radio talk show host and political activist. She planned and attended many political events. Mia first met her husband at one such political event.

Rothenberg thought he would encounter trust issues with Mia, that it would take multiple sessions to enable her to feel comfortable confiding her deepest and darkest concerns. To his surprise, Mia took to therapy almost immediately. By her third session, she emerged more free, less self-critical, and responded willingly and forthrightly to his questions. Most importantly, she seemed to appreciate his insights. Today, however, she seemed distant, uncomfortable, aloof.

"Do most patients lie on this couch?"

Rothenberg was surprised by her sudden change in attitude. He pondered an answer to her 'couch question' then told her it was a psychotherapy tool, one that relieved a patient from the burden of face-to-face treatment.

"Many patients prefer the couch for that reason."

He asked her whether she had any thoughts or memories that would be easier to talk about if she wasn't forced to look him in the eye.

Mia was conflicted. Although she appreciated Rothenberg's concern, she was somewhat ambivalent about revealing her deep-rooted feelings when it came to motherhood, fatherhood, and marital relations. Rothenberg was anything but judgmental, as she was about these subjects, but there were aspects of life she felt were private, feelings that caused fear and profound shame. Would the couch free her to discuss these things too; help to rid her of these feelings?

"Let me get this straight. On this couch, I can now reveal all matters I wouldn't feel comfortable revealing to your face? I don't like your shoes, or the way you always cross your legs when we talk. I would never say those things to your face."

"Not exactly what I had in mind, but you get the idea. What do you think? More comfortable, less comfortable, or no difference?"

"I'm not sure. I told you how I feel, though. Maybe there's something to this couch thing, after all."

"Whatever gets the job done and makes you feel more forthcoming. Therapy is about discussing what's bothering you in an open and honest manner. My intent is to reduce your inhibitions toward talking about what you are thinking or feeling. Anything specific on your mind today?"

"I love my husband. I'd love to slice him open and then turn the knife on myself."

Mia's husband was Bradley Crawford, a two-term congressman, son of Congressman Isaiah Crawford, the long-term congressman of the 13th congressional district, which included the city of Detroit. The younger Crawford was recently re-elected, in a landslide, to serve the 14th congressional district. He rode the coattails of a proverbial blue wave led by current president Louis Belding, made possible by the toxic, divisive presidencies of Ronald John and Stephen Golding. Rothenberg lived in the district and voted twice for the younger Crawford. He was impressed with the young man's rhetoric, was aligned with his politics, and considered him future presidential material. Crawford had solid credentials, came from good stock, and, by all accounts, was a wonderful human being.

Rothenberg was stunned by Mia's sudden admission of suicidal and homicidal ideations, especially as it related to her husband. *Is she telling the truth or just trying to get my attention?* As an experienced therapist, Rothenberg knew that most people with such thoughts never acted upon them. Rothenberg also knew Mia was depressed and angry, but he had not considered her a danger to herself or others. Had he missed something? After all, clinically depressed people are sometimes pre-disposed to violence. Depression, when coupled with weak impulse control, frustration, irritability, and rage, can often lead to violent acts. While their sessions revealed many of these personality traits, Rothenberg did not consider Mia a person with weak impulse control—quite the contrary. He decided to explore this further.

"How long have you felt this way?"

"A long time."

"How long?"

"Not sure. Couple of years, at least."

"How long have you been married?"

"Four years."

"Happily?"

"Yes, for the most part."

"What causes you to qualify your 'yes' answer?"

"I want to have a baby. Brad is more focused on his career."

"Is that a reason to kill him? After all, you can't have a baby with him if he's dead," Rothenberg rationalized.

"I agree. I didn't say I had a logical explanation for my feelings, only that I felt them."

"But would you act on them? And do you actually loathe yourself enough to consider suicide?"

"I didn't say I could or would act upon them. I said I'd like to."

"That's an important distinction."

Rothenberg also knew that a person with a history of past physical abuse or illicit drug use was far more likely to resort to acts of violence.

"Is there anything about your past I should know? Have you ever been abused, physically or sexually? Have you ever taken or abused drugs of any kind? Anything you tell me, as you well know, will be kept in complete confidence."

"No, nothing like that."

Rothenberg was happy to hear Mia say this, assuming she was being truthful. He decided to focus on impulsivity. Impulsivity correlates favorably with aggressive behavior. The more he probed, the less concerned he became. She took no drugs of any kind. There were no recent events in her life that would trigger any type of violent outburst. She appeared to have good impulse control, almost no rage, and exhibited little aggressive behavior. All drug and clinical tests were negative. There were no physical components or impairments. Testing for serotonergic deficiency was negative, as her 5-HIAA levels (the primary serotonin metabolite) were within normal limits. Rothenberg was also able to rule out any impairment of the prefrontal cortex, which is involved in executive function.

Mia had no history of aggressive behavior or serious childhood trauma (despite her mother's judgmental behavior), no impulsiveness, and no alcohol abuse. Rothenberg decided to note her comments and monitor her for signs of increased aggressive behavior or serious escalation of threats to commit hostile or belligerent acts. At the end of the day, he remained relatively unconcerned about her admission.

"How are you feeling right now?"

"I'm fine, thank you. How about yourself?"

"Funny, Mia. Are you trying to get a rise out of me?"

"No, not at all."

"Good. So, tell me, if you were going to commit suicide or kill your husband, what's the plan? How would you do it?" Rothenberg challenged. He knew that the absence of a plan was a sign his patient lacked the clinical intensity to commit the acts.

"I haven't thought that far ahead. I just get angry every now and then."

This was the response he hoped for. Suicidal or homicidal thoughts, to be considered serious, needed imminent risk, a plan, some intrusiveness, or frequency. None of this was present in Mia's responses.

"Well Mia, I'm glad you disclosed these feelings. This is a very important step in your treatment. Let's keep talking about them. Perhaps we can develop a safety plan together. I'd like to increase the frequency of your visits. Would that be okay?"

"Sure. I like talking to you."

"If you ever feel out of control, you'll call me immediately?"

"I will."

"Great. Let's get together in two days. Make an appointment as you check out today."

"Check out?" Mia laughed.

Rothenberg huffed and chuckled. "Right. Poor choice of words. How about, see you in two days?"

"See you in two days," she repeated with a grin.

CHAPTER TWO

Mia Folger knew Brad Crawford was at home, awaiting her arrival. He'd ask her about Rothenberg and therapy, wonder how she liked it and him. He'd be annoying. She had zero desire for the congressional third degree. In fact, she wished he'd get off his social justice platform, just one time, and be her loving, caring husband. Would they ever have a baby? Or would she divorce or kill him first? She shook the evil thoughts out of her head.

Instead of rushing home following her session, she stopped at Mr. Joe's, a Southfield Sports Bar. She sat at the bar alone, sipping on a Long Island Iced Tea, watching Bernie Smilovitz announce the latest coaching change for the woeful Detroit Lions. Mia was a football fan, but had long given up on the local team, choosing instead to root for the Kansas City Chiefs. Her rationale was that the Chiefs were in the AFC and did not directly compete with the pathetic Lions, who had recently traded their franchise quarterback and embarked on yet another "rebuilding plan." *If I owned a company and ran it the way the Ford family runs the Lions, I'd have gone out of business long ago.*

A couple of men tried to approach her. She shooed them away without a sound, just a simple flick of her wrist and hand. As they retreated, they grumbled, muttering something that sounded like 'frigid bitch.' Mia didn't care; she wasn't interested in any man but Brad. Bars were for drinking, not carousing with strangers. Mia Folger intended to drink. As word floated around the bar that the lady was not interested in a party, the men left her alone. She finished her first Long Island Tea and ordered a second, a concoction that consisted of shots of vodka, rum, gin, and tequila, among other things. She began to feel the soothing effects of intoxication, perhaps assisted by the medication she was taking, prescribed by Dr. Rothenberg.

She liked Rothenberg. He was direct, no nonsense, had an easy way about him, and a good sense of humor. His best quality was his patience; she had given him a lot of shit and he was virtually unflappable. *He's heard it all before*, she surmised. In addition, she didn't like the way she felt about herself and her husband. She needed help. She loved her husband. Despite his 'too busy' work ethic, she loathed herself for wanting to harm him, wanting desperately for Rothenberg to 'cure' her of these wicked thoughts. She'd continue to see him for as long as it took.

Mia ordered a third Long Island, downed it quickly, paid her tab, stood, and began to stagger out of the bar. The bartender came around from behind the bar, took her arm at the elbow, and asked if she wanted him to call an Uber.

"I'll do it, thanks," she stuttered, pulling her arm away and stumbling forward. Patrons looked on, laughing, enjoying the unusual spectacle of a female drunk. Once outside the bar, Mia took a deep breath and looked up and down Twelve Mile Road for a cab. She turned east, and checked Northwestern Highway, where a yellow cab was cruising in the right lane, heading north. Mia raised her hand. The cab driver made a sharp right on Twelve and another into Mr. Joe's parking lot. Mia pressed on her key fob. A horn sounded; lights blinked on and off from a parked Ford Explorer.

"I'll come back for it tomorrow," she slurred, as she got into the back seat. "I was just about to call an Uber," she continued. "How nice of you to show up when you did."

The dark-skinned cabbie wore a turban and a thin beard. He smiled and spoke in broken English. "I hate Uber—they're killing my business. Where to, Miss?"

"5000 Town Center," she mumbled, barely coherent.

Mia Folger and Brad Crawford lived together when Brad wasn't in Washington—almost never these days—in an upscale high-rise condominium community. The tower stood in a group of six high-rise, high-rent buildings, that included a hotel and four office buildings off the Lodge Freeway, the main freeway linking Southfield with Detroit. On a clear day, upper unit residents enjoyed a view of the Detroit skyline and Windsor, Ontario, twenty-something miles southeast. Detroit was one of the few American cities that was north of certain sections of Canada.

The 5000 Town Center complex had tight security and full, hotel-like services for the rich and famous. Congressman Crawford and his wife were a high-profile couple who craved privacy but enjoyed amenities. This was the perfect set-up. And tonight, the residence was only two miles southeast of Mr. Joe's.

There was no conversation between passenger and driver, who soon eased the cab into the complex. He pushed a button on the meter to lock in the fare, then turned to his passenger to collect her cash or credit card. Mia was fast asleep. A doorman approached the cab and opened the passenger side back door. Mia was leaning against the door and would have fallen out of the cab, had the doorman not caught her. She awoke with a start. *Where am I? What time is it?* The impatient cabbie wanted his money. The doorman looked from Mia to the driver, reached into his pocket, and pulled out a ten-dollar bill.

"Keep the change," he grumbled, handing the ten to the cabbie, while struggling to help Mia out of the back seat. He knew she was good for the money—it was a cash flow issue. Mia steadied herself and started to walk forward, stumbling a second time.

"Would you like me to get a wheelchair, Mrs. Crawford?" the doorman offered.

"No, Charlie," she slurred. "What if a disabled person needs it and it isn't here?"

"We have plenty of them, Mrs. Crawford. I don't think it will be a problem."

"How many times do I have to tell you to call me Mia, Charlie?"

"As many times as you'd like, Mrs. Crawford. I'm not permitted to call residents by their first names. You know that." He tried to walk her forward, but she continued to stumble with each step.

"Even if I expressly give you permission? Mrs. Crawford is my mother-in-law. Yech!"

"Can't do it."

"How about Ms. Folger, then? Call me Ms. Folger," she sputtered and emphasized the "F" in Folger, spraying saliva all over Charlie's pristine uniform.

"Folger it is. How about that wheelchair?" Charlie asked, wiping spit from his face.

"Is the press anywhere around? Busybodies with cell phones?"

"Never mind. I'll walk you up."

"Thank you, Charlie. You are the sweetest boy." She reached in her purse, pulled out a Benjamin, and handed it to Charlie. His eyes lit up when he saw the denomination.

"I can't take that, Ms. Folger."

"Folger . . . I like it, Charlie." She reached in her purse and pulled out another hundred.

"Put your money away, Ms. Folger," he urged, red-faced.

"Only if you take the first bill," she insisted.

"Okay, okay. See? Look, I'm putting it in my pocket." He folded the bill and put it into his right pocket. "Let's get you upstairs."

"Lead the way, my knight in shining armor," she chirped.

Charlie smiled and ushered her forward, propping her up, trying his damnedest to not make a scene. She was a physically fit, powerfully built woman—not heavy, but quite solid. The other doormen snickered at his predicament, but Charlie had the Benjamin. *Who's laughing at whom?*

They rode the elevator to the thirtieth floor and Charlie helped Mia exit. They staggered to apartment 3030 and Mia, half asleep, fumbled around in her purse, trying to locate her keys. She handed the purse to Charlie and gave him permission to look through it and find them, but there were none to be found.

"I must have left them at the bar or in the car," she babbled. "Hey! Did you catch that little rhyme? I'm the next Dr. Seuss. I do not like green eggs and ham; Sam I am . . ." she rambled on.

"I have security keys. I'll call over there in the morning," Charlie offered. "Want me to send someone to pick up the car?"

"That would be great, Charlie, but make sure they have the keys first. Otherwise, you're wasting your time."

"True that," Charlie mused. *How did she come up with that in her current state?* Charlie turned the key in the door and pushed it open. The place was in shambles, ransacked. Possessions were strewn around the living area, framed artwork smashed, chairs, tables, and a loveseat overturned. An area rug was stained with a rusty liquid, also seen in drag marks leading down the hallway to the bedrooms in the back of the apartment. A corner desk lay on its side, shattered printer and monitor on the floor, still tethered to a CPU where the desk once stood upright.

"What the hell?" Charlie grumbled.

"Brad?" Mia shrieked, suddenly sober, ignoring the mess. *Who did this? Where is my husband?*

"Congressman Crawford?" Charlie shouted, echoing the fears of his tenant. The building had tight security. *How could this happen?*

Together, they followed the rust-colored trail. The substance looked more and more like blood. They reached the master bedroom. Congressman Bradley Crawford lay peacefully on the blood-soaked bedspread. Crawford was naked, blood still oozed from an open wound at the center of his body. The room was, otherwise, untouched.

"No! God, please no!" Mia screamed. "Not my Brad! Oh, God!" She began to lose her balance.

Charlie grabbed her and turned her head away from the grisly scene, never taking his eyes off Congressman Crawford. Mia buried her head into Charlie's chest, sobbing uncontrollably. Charlie held her with one arm, took out a walkie-talkie with the other, pressed a button, and shouted "9-1-1—3030!" into the speaker.

"Let's get out of here, Mrs. Crawford . . . uh . . . Ms. Folger," he pleaded. He led her into the vestibule and out the front door. Mia needed to sit down somewhere, but television cop shows told Charlie not to touch anything inside the apartment until the crime scene was processed.

They staggered down the hall. A bench and two chairs sat opposite the elevators; a mirror hung from the wall. Mia was now in shock, delirious, rigid, almost catatonic, mumbling incoherently. Charlie was unnerved, shaking with fear. He'd never seen a dead body before. In fact, despite his quasi-security status at 5000 Town Center, Charlie had never even witnessed a crime.

The elevator ding sounded, the door opened. Two doormen and a supervisor exited the elevator.

"Simpson? What's going on? Why the frantic 9-1-1?" his supervisor demanded.

"It's Congressman Crawford, sir. He-he's d-dead."

"Dead? How?" The super was shocked. 5000 Town Center was a safe, quiet, secure place.

"I don't know, sir. The place is a mess, turned upside-down. He-he's in the back bedroom . . . blood everywhere . . . they cut it off, sir."

"Who's they, Simpson? Cut what off?"

Charlie began to sob. "Whoever killed the congressman, sir. Th-they c-cut off his penis. It-it appears . . . oh, my God . . . he bled to death!"

Mia abruptly stood, screamed, and collapsed to the floor.

***

A half-hour later, the place was crawling with Southfield cops. CSI was inside the apartment, processing the crime scene. The lead detective, Ed Schreiber, was talking to Charlie, trying to get a statement while events were fresh in the man's mind. Mia, unconscious or catatonic, Charlie didn't know which, had been carted off to Providence Hospital.

"I have no idea, Detective," Charlie continued. "No one checked in. There were no visitors. No one called in to schedule a visit. We checked the security cameras; nobody came in or out except our residents on different floors. We have camera shots of them coming in and going straight to their residences. I have no idea how this happened."

"What about Mrs. Crawford?"

"She was here earlier this morning. She went back out, came home late, drunk, and I was helping her to her apartment."

"What time was that?"

"About forty-five minutes ago."

"Where was she before that?"

"I don't know . . . getting drunk somewhere, obviously. A cab driver dropped her off. He'd probably know where she was. We probably have his cab on camera."

"That's good work, young man. Good thinking. Get me the tape, would you, please? Do you have any idea when Mr. and Mrs. Crawford left the apartment today? Did they leave together? Separately? Did they come back and go out again? I'd like to revisit all of the ins and outs of the day, okay?" Detective Schreiber commanded.

"She left this morning, sir. She said she had a doctor's appointment," Charlie offered. "I'm not sure about the congressman, when he left . . . if he left. All I can tell you is I found him, like that, in his bedroom."

"Like what?"

"Like what, what?"

"You said you found him like that. Like what?"

"Like in his bed, lying on his back, naked, bleeding."

"No one saw him come or go?"

"Who?"

"Congressman Crawford."

Charlie looked around at his colleagues, who shrugged. "No, no one saw him come or go. He may have left and come back when we weren't looking. That's possible. I can check the security footage, or you can have the drive."

"I'll take the drive, if you don't mind."

At that moment, a crime scene tech exited the apartment and approached Schreiber.

"Time of death, based on body temp and rigor, was between nine and eleven this morning. The victim died from exsanguination."

"English, please?" Schreiber bristled, shaking his head, nostrils flaring.

"He bled to death," the tech retorted.

"He cut himself shaving or something else?"

"Unless he cut off his own penis, he was murdered."

"He bled to death from a severed penis?"

"That's about the size of it, sir," the tech chuckled.

"Funny, smart ass. Next you're going to say something like 'size counts,' right?"

"You took the words right out of my mouth."

"Anything else?"

"Yeah. I don't think he was killed here. I think he was brought here."

"But what about the mess in the apartment?"

"Staged to look like a robbery or something."

"What about all the blood?"

"Don't shoot the messenger, but I have a theory."

"I'm all ears."

"This guy Crawford pissed someone off. This is a crime of passion. He wasn't killed here; he was killed elsewhere. The killer collected his blood and poured it on the floor before dragging the victim into the bedroom. He positioned him on the bed and poured the rest of the blood onto his crotch."

"Why the hell would he do all that?"

"I have no idea—you're the detective. You figure it out. I'm just reporting the science."

"Crime of passion, huh? Was this guy having an affair?"

"He's a two-term congressman, sir," Charlie interrupted. "It would be pretty stupid to have an affair. Besides, have you met his wife? She's a stunner, sir."

"Have not had the pleasure, yet. Doesn't matter what she looks like. You know the old saying about absolute power corrupting absolutely. I'll bet this guy could get any chick he wanted. Thanks for your help with all this. Sorry you had to witness such a grisly scene. I understand why you're upset. Unfortunately, shit happens. Where did they take the widow again? Beaumont?"

"No, Providence."

"Providence. My next stop."

CHAPTER THREE

Detective Eddie Schreiber was a grizzled veteran on the Southfield Police force. While Southfield had a small department and did not see anything close to the level of crime in Detroit, the city was not crime free, and its police force was never bored. Still, a grisly murder at the prestigious Town Center complex? This case needed to be solved, quickly and quietly. Hopefully, they were dealing with a crime of passion committed by someone the congressman knew. Schreiber's money was on the wife, Mia Folger, lying in front of him in her hospital bed.

Mia appeared to be sleeping peacefully. Charlie was right; she was quite attractive, even in this condition. She was very well built, solid, someone who spent many hours at the gym. Schreiber sat next to her, waiting patiently, reading, and swiping emails on his iPhone. Stakeouts and events like this one, where a witness was not yet ready to sing, were excellent opportunities to catch up on emails and social media activity. Suddenly, Mia stirred, mumbled something Schreiber couldn't make out, and became quiet again.

"Mrs. Crawford?" Schreiber shook her gently, hoping she was awake. Nothing. A nurse entered the room.

"You're wasting your time, Detective. She's severely traumatized, catatonic. Furthermore, she is heavily sedated. Even if she were able to converse, the medication would make her incoherent. The good news for you is that she isn't going anywhere. I don't think she's going to wake up anytime soon. Her therapist, Dr. Harold Rothenberg, will be in to see her tomorrow. Hopefully, he can shed some light on her situation, perhaps even coax her out of this delirious state she finds herself in."

"She's in therapy?" Schreiber inquired. This was a new revelation. *Why did she need a therapist?* "What's the doctor's name again?"

"Rothenberg, sir. Dr. Harold Rothenberg."

"Why do I know that name?" Schreiber wondered out loud.

"The case against the Church, where Zack Blake represented his now wife and stepsons in that clergy abuse case."

The lightbulb went on in Schreiber's head. "Of course, Blake's ticket to fame and fortune. Can't say that creep and those enablers with the Church didn't deserve what they got. Despicable pieces of shit, every damned one of them."

Schreiber was talking to himself, oblivious to the nurse who stood before him waiting, slightly embarrassed by his sudden tirade and use of foul language. Schreiber snapped back to the present. He and the nurse looked at each other; now both were slightly embarrassed.

"Are you okay, Detective?" The nurse broke their silence.

"Yes, sorry for the salty language. But that case and those perverts never sat well with me. I'm glad Blake took them to school and cleaned their clocks. They had it coming. Still doing that shit, still covering it all up, blaming the victims."

"No problem, Detective. I am right there with you. Mia's not waking up anytime soon, though. Dr. Rothenberg should be here around seven-thirty, eight o'clock tomorrow morning during rounds. Perhaps he can shed some light on the situation. Come back then?"

"That is a great idea, Nurse . . ."

"Rosenfeld, Cheryl Rosenfeld."

"Well, nice to meet you, Nurse Rosenfeld."

"Call me Cheryl. My friends do."

Is she coming on to me? "We're friends?" Schreiber asked.

"You seem like a good guy, for a cop."

He smirked. "If I had a nickel for every half-assed compliment I've ever received . . ."

"I didn't mean it that way."

"Oh? What way did you mean it? Everyone hates a cop, until they need one."

"I don't hate cops. I appreciate your service. I wasn't shaming you. But it's like with lawyers, you know, how you always feel like you're being cross-examined? With cops, you always feel like you're a suspect, or being interrogated."

Schreiber sighed and smirked, trying to keep his temper in check.

"I guess I can understand that," the detective backed off, acknowledging that the lady did not deliberately chasten him. "Say, if I may be so bold, what time does your shift end? Would you like to get a drink or something? I'm buying."

"Rain check? I've got the graveyard shift tonight. I just got on. In fact, if you get here first thing in the morning to see Rothenberg, I should still be here."

"And we can grab a coffee?"

"You are a persistent bugger."

"I promise not to interrogate you."

"It's a date."

"Great, see you in the morning."

"See you in the morning."

Eddie Schreiber practically danced away. He loathed the dating scene. He hadn't been out on a date for as long as he could remember. His ex-wife began dating and screwing around, even before the ink was dry on their divorce papers. She had been the love of his life, the only woman he had ever been intimate with, and her willingness to move on so quickly was quite hurtful. Eddie had a few awkward dates, but they were fix-ups by wives of his fellow detectives. He didn't have free will in those situations. They were forced upon him. This was different. He'd charmed his way into a date with Nurse Rosenfeld. *What was her first name? Cheryl.* She was sweet, sharp-witted, and had a beautiful smile. He was looking forward to the coffee.

***

The following morning, Eddie Schreiber drove an unmarked squad car a few miles south of headquarters to Providence Hospital on Nine Mile Road and Greenfield. He flashed his badge at security and was quickly passed through. He asked the guard how to get to the Psychiatric Unit. The guard pointed the way and gave him a visitor sticker to place on his chest. Schreiber took the elevator to the psych ward. Nurse Rosenfeld was seated at the nurse's station.

"Well, well, Cheryl," he chirped. "Ready for our date?"

"I get off in fifteen," she replied. "I could really use some coffee."

"Great. Is the doctor in with Mrs. Crawford?"

"Who?"

"Mrs. Crawford. You know, the woman we talked about yesterday."

"Oh. She was admitted as 'Folger', not 'Crawford'." Nurse Rosenfeld advised.

"Right." Schreiber made a note of that interesting point. He looked at his notepad for a name and spoke before he found it. "Is Dr. . . . uh . . . Rothenberg with the patient?"

"I believe he is."

"Did you let him know I was coming?"

"I did."

"Can we go see him now?"

"See, interrogation!" she exclaimed.

"It was not. I was just asking where the guy was," he pleaded.

"Gotcha!" She laughed.

"Okay, smart-ass. Keep it up and you'll be buying the coffee."

"Not if you want my company."

"Geez. You are one tough broad."

"And that is two strikes. I loathe that sexist, 1950's term."

Schreiber raised both hands and arms in surrender. "Sorry. I'll shut up. Can we please see the doc?"

"Right this way." She led him down the hall to a dark room. A tall, balding man in a white lab coat sat at the bedside of Mia Folger.

"Dr. Rothenberg? This is Detective Schreiber, the cop I was telling you about? Dr. Harold Rothenberg? Detective Eddie Schreiber."

"Pleased to meet you, Detective." Rothenberg stood, respectfully, and extended his hand. The two men shook.

"Likewise. How's the patient?"

"She enjoys doctor-patient confidentiality, but you must certainly see for yourself. She is not doing very well."

"Is this some sort of psychotic break?"

"Not the term I would use, but for our purposes, I would say yes."

"I understand, in talking to Nurse Rosenfeld, that you have been seeing her for a while."

Rothenberg shot Cheryl a hostile glare.

"Hey, I never told him anything of the sort," Cheryl snapped.

"You advised she was in therapy. True, Doc?"

Cheryl diverted her eyes, upset at her own breach of patient confidentiality. She hadn't recalled saying this, but Schreiber was reading from his notes.

"No big deal. Yes, she is in therapy. No breach in telling you that. Many people are in therapy, one way or another. What I can't share with you is *why* she's in therapy or anything we've discussed."

"Her husband is dead, and she seems to be the last person to have seen him alive. Does that count for anything?"

"Sure, it does. But it does not trump doctor-patient confidentiality, Detective."

"Can you tell me what kinds of things, generally, would cause a patient to clam up and suddenly become an emotional vegetable?"

"Emotional vegetable? Interesting choice of words. I'll have to remember that one."

"What would you call it?"

"A catatonic state, brought on, perhaps, by severe emotional trauma. I have not been able to communicate with her since the death of her husband, so I have no clue what happened. I can only surmise, since its onset was yesterday, that it was triggered, in some way, by her husband's death."

"Do you have any thoughts about what kind of trauma might trigger such a condition?"

"Finding her husband brutally murdered would certainly do the trick."

Touché. One question too many. "Could murdering someone cause someone to withdraw like this?"

"Hard to say. Witnessing the murder is more likely. There is a much bigger shock element. If you're the murderer, seeing the body a second time is not too traumatic. This is all hypothetical, of course."

"Oh, of course," Schreiber confirmed.

"I really can't tell you much, Detective. She is my patient. I have rounds, other patients to see. Will there be anything else?"

"Will you make your records available?"

"Not voluntarily. And even if a judge ordered their release, I would have to appeal such a ruling. I take patient confidentiality very seriously."

"I guess we'll cross that bridge when or if we come to it."

"I guess so. Zachary Blake is a friend of mine."

Is that supposed to intimidate me? "I know; Nurse Rosenfeld reminded me."

"I really have to go. It's getting late. If you have any additional questions, not saying I can answer them, but feel free to call my office and make an appointment."

"Will do. Thanks for your time."

"You're welcome." Rothenberg saluted and walked away, leaving Schreiber with Nurse Rosenfeld.

"Sorry I ratted you out," Schreiber conceded. "It wasn't deliberate."

"No problem. In retrospect, it was my fault, not yours. You were just doing your job."

"How about that coffee?"

"Can I get a rain check? I'm exhausted. This has turned into a fourteen-hour shift."

"You're not mad at me, are you?"

"Not at all," she quickly responded.

Too quickly, Eddie believed. He worried Cheryl was miffed at being manipulated and outed by a wily cop. He attempted to salvage the situation. Smiling, he said, "I'll let you off the hook if we can make another date, right here and now."

"I don't need your permission to walk away, Detective."

"Call me Eddie, please? Another day for coffee or drinks? Tomorrow? Tonight, when you wake up?"

"I'm off tomorrow. Tomorrow night, okay?"

"It's a date. Give me your number. I'll text you."

They exchanged numbers and went their separate ways.

CHAPTER FOUR

Doctor Harold Rothenberg was concerned about Mia Folger. Given what she'd told him about her husband, Rothenberg believed she might be a suspect in a murder case. Worse, she might be guilty. He picked up his phone and punched in a number.

"Zachary Blake and Associates, Kristin speaking. How may I help you?"

"Dr. Harold Rothenberg, Kristin. How are you doing?"

"Fine, sir, you?"

"Is Zack in?"

"I believe he is. I'll buzz his office."

"Thanks, Kristin."

"Not at all. Please hold."

Rothenberg was treated to music on hold for a short time. The line clicked.

"Zachary Blake. Harold?"

"How are you, Zack?"

"I'm fine, Harold. Is this about the boys?" Dr. Rothenberg was Zack's sons' long-time therapist, following their traumatic experience with an abusive priest. Harold was a family friend.

"No, Zack, it isn't. They're doing quite well. They're both adults. Can't tell you much. Ask them."

"I wasn't prying, Harold. I was just concerned the boys were the reason for your call. What's up?"

"I've got a patient who is about to be charged with murder."

"Murder? Who is it?"

"Does attorney-client privilege apply to this conversation?"

"No, Harold. The patient is not my client."

"Is there anything you wouldn't do for me if I asked a favor, Zack?"

"Nothing I can think of, my dear friend, unless it was illegal or immoral."

"I'd like to refer a client, and I'd like you to commit to representing this client, no matter which way the publicity winds blow. Would you do that for me, Zack?"

"Boy, Harold, you sure know how to push my buttons. Mental manipulation must be a specialty of yours," Zack chuckled. "Of course, I'll represent your client. You've done plenty for me and my family over the years. What's this all about?"

"One more minor issue, Zack. I don't know much about the client's financial situation. I know they are prominent citizens."

"Are you trying to get me to back off, Harold? I've got plenty of money, as you know, and I love pro bono cases, if it comes to that. Now, give. What's this about?"

"Are you familiar with the name Mia Folger?"

"The right-wing talk show host?"

"Her real name is Mia Crawford. She's the congressman's wife."

"Right! I knew that. Crawford—the guy who was just murdered. I contributed to his campaign."

"That's the one."

"Is Mia a suspect?"

"I believe she's about to be."

"What makes you say that?"

"As I was visiting her in the hospital this morning . . ."

"What's she doing in the hospital?"

"Have you taken the case?"

"Yes."

"But you have no retainer agreement or consideration."

"You owe me a buck."

"Huh?"

"Will you confirm, please, that you owe me a buck and will pay me the next time I see you?"

"Whatever."

"Not 'whatever.' I'm serious. Confirm you owe me a buck."

"I owe you a buck." Rothenberg shrugged.

"Great! I now have a legal and binding agreement to represent Mia Crawford."

"She goes by Folger."

"Why Folger? Why not Crawford?"

"Show biz reasons. Besides, you may assume they have a somewhat rocky marriage."

"Oh shit! Here we go! Harold, did you sandbag me?"

"Not exactly, Zack. May I tell you the story?"

"Please."

Harold Rothenberg spilled his guts about his sessions with Mia.

"Shit, Doc, your reading of the situation is correct. She will be charged, especially when the cops find out about their marital issues. Who else knows about these threats of violence?"

"Not sure; patients don't tell me everything. If she was candid with me, she may have been candid with other close friends or relatives."

"Do we know who those people might be?"

"No, not really."

"Okay, well, she enjoys a presumption of innocence. She also has the right to remain silent. I'll go talk to her at the hospital and see what's what."

"You can't do that," Rothenberg advised.

"Oh, why not? The right to remain silent doesn't apply to discussions between Mia and her lawyer. She can talk to me in complete confidence."

"That's not the issue, Zack. She's catatonic, in shock; she's not talking to anyone unless we have a breakthrough."

"Like . . . comatose?"

"Something like that."

"She can't participate in her own defense? She can't tell me what she was doing that morning? Where she was, who she was with, or who has a particular axe to grind with her husband?"

"Nope."

"Great. Any more good news?"

"There is a detective snooping around. His name is Schreiber—he's with the Southfield Police. He tried to get me to talk about her but backed off when I cited doctor-patient confidentiality. I'm almost positive he's going to try and obtain her hospital and medical records."

"I'm familiar with the guy. He's a friend to Jack Dylan." Dylan was a police captain in Dearborn. He and Zack clashed over a murder case back in the day. Arya Khan's case helped propel Zack's career and enhanced his notoriety as Detroit's 'King of Justice.' When Dylan found himself facing a murder charge up north, Zack came to his rescue. They were now good friends. Perhaps the friendship would come in handy when dealing with Schreiber.

"We'll cross that bridge when we come to it, Harold. Anything else?"

"Nothing I can think of. Hey, Zack?"

"Yeah, Doc?"

"Thanks for doing this. I really appreciate it."

"It's what I do, man."

"I know, but you don't usually do it pro bono."

"It's *not* pro bono," Zack grumbled. "You owe me a buck! You better pay up when I see you!"

"I'm good for it, Zack," Rothenberg chuckled. "Thanks again."

"I need to see those records, Harold."

"I know you do, Zack, but I have to get consent. Let me talk to some ethics people and find out what is typically done in these situations."

"Okay, talk soon."

***

The following morning, Harold Rothenberg returned to Mia Folger's hospital room. The hospital staff was trying to decide what to do with her. If she remained unresponsive, they would send her to a psychiatric hospital, probably Walter Reuther, in Westland, unless Rothenberg or Zack Blake could leverage her political status and get her into a private mental health facility. Rothenberg hoped for a breakthrough. Mia would regain consciousness and provide a perfectly logical defense to the coming allegations that she brutally mutilated and murdered her husband.

He looked into her eyes, half open, bluish green, staring into space. He waved his hand in front of her face. No reaction. Her shoulder-length brown hair was matted and tangled from lying in bed for days. She looked drawn and unclean, but he could plainly see she was a beautiful woman. With consciousness, solid food, a shower, make-up, and fashion, Mia Folger would be a head-turner. A cocktail of drugs currently helped to keep her sedated and calm. Saliva trickled down the side of her mouth, the main effect of an unconscious, medicated state. Mia Folger was mentally, a missing person. Rothenberg wiped the side of her mouth with a tissue. He decided to cease her medication protocol and let nature take its course. He penned instructions in her chart and walked out of the room, stopping at the nurses' station to deliver the chart and verbally repeat the instructions.

CHAPTER

FIVE

Detective Eddie Schreiber walked into the Southfield office of the late Congressman Brad Crawford. The lobby was small and elegantly furnished. A receptionist whispered into a telephone receiver on the other side of a partition that separated the lobby from the inner office. Schreiber waited patiently at the window. The receptionist finished her call, slid the glass window open, and looked up at her visitor.

"May I help you?" She smiled.

Schreiber flashed his badge. "Detective Schreiber to see Elyssa Naylor. I have an appointment."

Naylor was Congressman Crawford's chief assistant and sometimes bodyguard. She had called police headquarters the previous day and asked to speak to the person in charge of the Crawford murder investigation. She refused to provide details over the phone, so the sergeant made an appointment for Eddie to pay her a visit.

Eddie sat down in a lobby chair, rather comfortable for an office lobby. *People could fall asleep waiting* . . . As his eyes closed and his thoughts drifted, a door opened; a young woman muttered, "Detective?"

"That's me," Schreiber stood, shaking off sleep. "Detective Eddie Schreiber here to see Ms. Naylor."

"I'm Elyssa. Come on in. Sad to meet you under these difficult circumstances."

"Indeed. Hopefully, I won't take up too much of your time."

"Coffee, pop, water?" In the Detroit area, soda is "pop," thanks primarily to the Faygo beverage company.

"No thanks."

He followed her down a short hallway to the last office, a beautifully appointed space with mahogany walls and bookcases. Photos of the congressman with the president, senators, celebrities, and wealthy donors adorned the walls.

"This was his office," Naylor indicated, pointing to a chair on the opposite side of an elaborate, hand-carved, ornate, pillared desk. She sat down in a matching, oversized executive chair.

Our tax dollars at work, Eddie mused. "You called me down here, Ms. Naylor. What can I do for you?"

"Have you arrested Mrs. Crawford yet?"

"Pardon me?"

"Mia Folger Crawford. Have you arrested her?"

"And why would I arrest Mrs. Crawford?"

"Because she murdered her husband."

"That's quite a charge, Ms. Naylor. Did you witness this murder?"

"No, of course not, but she's the only person who hated Brad enough to kill him."

"Hate is a strong word. They were married. Most people I've talked to believe they had a pretty good marriage."

"Smokescreen, Detective. Mia wanted a divorce, but Brad thought it would hurt his career. He wanted to tough it out, lead separate lives, but stay married if they couldn't reconcile."

"And you know this, how?"

"I am . . . er . . . I *was* . . . Brad's right-hand person. I know . . . er . . . knew *everything* that went on in his life, including everything that went on in his marriage."

"Not getting along in a marriage is a far cry from murder." *She called him 'Brad.'*

"She hated the idea of pretending they were happy. She didn't want an open marriage. She despised him and the fact that he put his career ahead of her plans to have a family."

"Still a far cry from murder."

"I have texts."

"Texts?"

"Texts."

"What do they say?"

"See for yourself. I collected a bunch of them on this flash drive." She handed over a small, rubberized case containing a green USB circuit board with a congressional logo printed on its base. "I'm constantly amazed by what people will put in a text or email."

"How did you get these?" He pondered.

"Snooping," she admitted.

Snooping? She may have violated the law. "I'll check out the texts. Do you have the congressman's phone?"

"We haven't been able to find his phone. We've looked everywhere."

"Does it have GPS tracking or Find My Phone?"

"Probably, but we can't find the phone. Tracking must be turned off. Damn thing contains a lot of private, maybe even quasi-classified information, and important contacts."

"We'll do our best to find it. Have you ever witnessed the Crawford couple arguing? Her being violent?"

"I've seen them argue. We've all seen them. I wouldn't call any of the arguments violent, but these texts . . ." She trailed off, choked up.

"Anyone else I should talk with who can verify your account?"

"Anyone who was close with this couple, might be hundreds of people, can verify that their marriage was on the rocks and that Mia was very unhappy. Besides, check out the texts. You'll get a rather vivid picture of the relationship."

"Please get me a list of these 'hundreds of people'."

"Will do. Anything else? I have a funeral to arrange."

"Sorry for your loss. We will do everything we can to bring the killer to justice."

"Thank you, Detective. I'll be fine when I see that bitch behind bars."

Strong feelings for a legislative assistant. Something going on between her and the congressman? Schreiber penned a note in his pocket-sized notebook.

***

Eddie returned to headquarters, gathered his investigative team in his office, and popped the flash drive into his computer. The screen blinked off and on; the CPU made a whirring noise, and the screen came to life with a series of files to choose from. Eddie clicked on the first file and a series of texts appeared on his screen.

Crawford: "Sorry babe. Working late again. Don't wait up."

Folger: "Sure, sure. Think I was born yesterday? Which bimbo this time?"

Crawford: "Cut the shit Mia. No bimbo. I love you."

Folger: "FY-A"

Crawford: "Real mature. Signing off. Sleep tight."

Folger: "GFY"

"Kind of childish, but no overt threats of violence. What does 'FY-A' mean?" Jerry Kramer, Schreiber's chief assistant, wondered.

"'Fuck you, asshole'. 'GFY' is, of course, 'go fuck yourself'," Schreiber advised.

"I knew that one." Kramer shrugged. "One thing is clear—she's not very happy with him."

"Open another one. See if things escalate," Schreiber commanded.

Kramer clicked on the next series.

Folger: "Where the fuck are you?"

Folger: "Answer me, philandering whore! Want me to go to the press?"

Crawford: "C'mon Mia. Stop this. For hundredth time, not cheating on you."

Folger: "Lying sack o shit!" (The text was accompanied by a cartoon pile of feces)

Crawford: "Hilarious Mia. Home soon. Finishing up."

Folger: "Who is it this time? That iron-pumping Naylor? Bet she kicks your ass in bed. Like it rough? I can get rough-violent too. Handcuffs whips chains knives. How about we cut the little fucker right off-no more wandering dick? Wandering dickless."

Crawford: "Jesus Mia. Home soon. Calm down. We'll talk."

Folger: "What's to talk about? Field day for press. Career down the toilet."

Crawford: "Please stop Mia. Drinking?"

Folger: "Drunk. WTF you care?"

Crawford: "Care a lot."

Folger: "Sure you do. Get your ass home. We'll talk."

"Whoa!" Kramer exclaimed. "Did I read that right? Did she threaten to cut off his dick?"

"I believe she did," Schreiber sighed.

"Game, set, and match," Kramer declared. "Quite the coincidence. She threatens to do the very deed that killed him."

"Could be just that, a coincidence."

"You don't really believe that, do you?"

"From all accounts, so far, Mia Folger is a smart woman. Does it make sense she would kill him in the exact way she threatened?"

"Maybe she *meant* to cut his dick off; no threat. Maybe his *death* was accidental. She didn't know he would bleed out and die. Probably panicked."

"Possible. It's also possible that the real killer saw these texts. Naylor, for instance."

"What's Naylor's motive?"

"Same as Folger's. Hell hath no fury like a woman scorned."

"What scorn? Mia claims they were screwing around. Naylor would be the 'scorner', not the 'scornee' in that scenario."

"Who was Crawford married to? To whom did he go home every night? It wasn't Naylor."

"Got it, boss. So, we've got two suspects?"

"At least two. Let's open more texts."

The more texts they opened, the more they began to suspect Mia Folger of murder. Text after text contained vile thoughts, vulgar language, threats of suicide if Crawford did not stop 'screwing around', indirect and direct threats to Crawford's life. It was a tedious process, but they went through every text, cataloguing them by severity of the threat and language. By the end of the process, a clear pattern had emerged. Mia Folger had threatened to kill her husband; her rage increased as the texts continued, and she had a motive and the capacity to mutilate and murder her husband.

In Eddie Schreiber's mind, however, it wasn't enough. They needed forensics to back up Mia's electronic motive, opportunity, will, and personal call to action. He called the crime lab and asked to speak to his favorite crime scene investigator.

"Jim Sawyer, how may I help you?"

"Jim? Eddie Schreiber. What can you tell me about the Crawford murder? Blood? Fingerprints? DNA? What's the story?"

"I'm fine, thank you, Eddie. And you?" Jim laughed.

"Sorry, man. This case has me spooked. Mia Folger is in la-la land in a psych ward. I don't have a clue when she will be able to tell us anything. Her psychiatrist claims doctor-patient, won't give me shit. I got ahold of some texts—how they were obtained might violate federal privacy laws. Let's save that story for another day. The texts clearly indicate that Mia had both motive and means to kill her husband. And get this: She threatened to do the very deed that killed him. Please tell me we have forensics to back up these texts. With supporting DNA, perhaps I can convince a judge we have probable cause for a warrant for phone records and texts."

"I've got good news and not-so-good news. Which do you want first?"

"The good."

"There is plenty of DNA where we found the body. Multiple samples, a few different people, including Mia Folger and Brad Crawford."

"That's good. What's the bad?"

"Come on, Eddie. The congressman was found in his own bedroom. *Their* own bedroom. It follows that Mia's prints and DNA are all over the place. There were other samples and fingerprints. I'm trying to identify the other people. Want the *worse* news?"

"There's worse?"

"Congressman Crawford wasn't killed in their apartment. He was killed elsewhere and dumped in the bedroom *after* the murder. His tox screen detected slight traces of GHB. Rigor, lack of blood splatter, blood volume, and body temp all prove that the murder happened elsewhere. ALS and luminol indicate drag marks from the freight elevator to the front door, into the apartment, down the hall leading to the bedroom, and onto the bed. The damage to the apartment was a smokescreen to make it look like a break-in."

"Shit, Jim! Where did the murder take place?"

"I have no clue. I just completed these tests. We've got to process the elevator, and every floor from the basement to the roof until we identify the murder scene. I was just about to assemble a couple of teams when you called."

"Assemble your teams, pronto. Contact the building manager and tell him that the whole area around the freight elevator is a crime scene. Seal the damn thing. No one up; no one down. And no one near those lobby areas leading to the freight elevator. We may have to go door-to-door and search every apartment."

"Start at the top or the bottom?"

"Put one team on the roof and the other in the basement. They can work their way towards each other. Hopefully, they won't have to get very far."

"Will do, Eddie. Anything else?"

"Warp speed, Jim. But very carefully."

"In other words, the usual."

Schreiber chuckled. "Yeah, Jim, the usual. Thanks."

"You're welcome. I'm on it."

CHAPTER

SIX

Dr. Harold Rothenberg returned to Providence Hospital. Off the drug cocktail, Mia Folger was awake and alert. She looked far better than the borderline catatonic specimen he visited the other day. However, she was still unable—or refused—to speak to anyone.

"Good morning, Mia. It's a beautiful day, today. How are you? You're looking much better. You gave everyone a scare."

Mia said nothing, staring into space.

"You've been through quite an ordeal. Your situation is not uncommon. I hired a lawyer to represent you. You may need him."

Mia said nothing; a slight fidget led Rothenberg to believe she comprehended the news. This fidget, although almost indiscernible to the untrained eye, was a physical reaction, an encouraging sign, perhaps evidence of comprehension.

"His name is Zachary Blake. I've known him a long time, and I trust him. He's rather famous around here. Perhaps you've heard of him?"

Mia stared out the window, unable or unwilling to make eye contact with Rothenberg. She lay motionless on the bed, with her hands and arms to her side, devoid of expression. Rothenberg stared at her, willing her to acknowledge his presence—a shrug perhaps, a grunt, nod, wink, or grimace. He wondered what, if anything, she was thinking. Was she a murderer? Was she capable of murdering someone she obviously loved at some point in her life? Could someone so innocent looking castrate a man? *Who knows?*

The study of the mind was not an exact science. People think kind thoughts or evil thoughts from time to time. A healthy mind can distinguish right from wrong, good from evil, and restrain the body from converting evil thoughts into evil actions. *Does Mia Folger have a healthy mind?* This was the ten-million-dollar question; Rothenberg needed to penetrate her thoughts, the deep recesses of her mind, and connect her state-of-mind in the present with what she'd exhibited in previous sessions.

When he last saw her, she admitted being self-critical, feeling her mother's negative, unrelenting judgment of everything she did. *Nothing abnormal there; she was quite astute about her mother's personality and negative influence.* He recalled a pleasant patient, forthright and honest, trusting, appreciative in therapy sessions, except the last one, when she was distant and aloof. *Why?*

"I love my husband. I'd love to slice him open and then turn the knife on myself."

It was, in retrospect, a startling revelation. *Was she up to the task? Truly foreshadowing future events? Was she just trying to get a rise out of me? Just a strange coincidence? She will be convicted if her words are made public.*

He simply did not believe her capable of acting out this 'fantasy'. She was not a naturally violent person; clinically depressed, perhaps, but not violent. She did not have weak impulse control, nor had she been in an abusive relationship. There was no drug use. *Two and two does not equal five.* The couple's biggest conflict was her desire to have children clashing with his focus on a political career, hardly a reason for murder or suicide.

Was Rothenberg trying to rationalize his dismissal of her admission? No. She was lucid, cheerful, witty even, willing to discuss a safety plan. This was not someone who was about to kill her husband or herself. He was certain of that.

"Mia, do you remember the last time we spoke?" He reached down and took her hand in his. Her skin was cold; her arm was limp—there was no physical reaction to his question or his touch.

"Do you remember anything we talked about?" No response. He decided to take a risk.

"How's your husband doing?" No reaction.

He had no idea how to proceed. If things remained the same, he would have to gather insight and information from others or from Mia's non-verbal responses. Maybe, in time, she would be capable of some type of communication, even if she remained unable to speak. He felt terrible, powerless to help her when she needed him most. He wanted to reach out with both hands, grab her by the shoulders, and shake the doldrums out of her. Instead, he decided to sit for a while, silent, leaving her in conscious or unconscious peace.

***

Two days later, Schreiber and Kramer met with Jim Sawyer. The crime scene was quickly identified as the basement of the 5000 Town Center tower.

"Good to see you again, Jim. What do we have?"

"Forensics confirm the murder was committed in a secluded room in the basement of the 5000 building."

"Secluded how?"

"It's an unused storeroom. The basement runs the entire perimeter of the building and is partitioned. The maintenance office is down there. There are apartment storage units for residents to store stuff they don't need or can't fit in their apartments. People purchase storage lockers or cubicles, about five by seven. I'm guessing this room would be used if people required extra storage, which hasn't happened yet."

"Go on," Eddie prompted.

"I've got some pictures . . ." Sawyer pulled out a file, withdrew an array of photos printed on eight-and-a-half by eleven copy paper, and handed them to Schreiber.

"See," he said, pointing to a closed door. "It's non-descript. You would have to know it was there and empty. Only someone who worked or lived there would know the room existed."

"Or cased the joint." Eddie continued to study the pictures. "It's not used at all? Hard to believe in a building this size, they have a room no one uses."

"Yet, that seems to be the truth."

"Sorry, please continue."

"If Mrs. Crawford is your principal suspect, I'm sorry to report that there are no fingerprints. In fact, there are no fingerprints of any kind, other than those belonging to Crawford, building management, and maintenance people. We did elimination prints on those guys. Luminol and ALS confirm Crawford's blood all over the place. Blood spatter everywhere, high pool concentration tells me where he bled out." He pulled out one of the photos and pointed to the middle of the storeroom floor, against a post.

"Right there," he said, tapping on the photo. "Probably tied to that post. We found fibers consistent with the zip ties we found on the body in the bedroom. A couple of hair samples match Mia Crawford, but those could have come from the congressman's clothing. There are two other hair and fiber samples that remain unidentified."

"I did not find the murder weapon. The killer must have taken it. There were no signs of struggle. It looks like Crawford was subdued and brought down there without a tussle," Sawyer concluded.

"Anything else?"

Sawyer searched his notes and memory. "Oh!" he exclaimed. "Get this! Someone electronically disabled the cameras in the freight elevator and on the thirtieth floor. You've got to know what you're doing to do that. This was premeditated, clearly murder one. There are no cameras in the basement, by the way."

"So, the killer somehow gets into Crawford's room. Cameras should show Crawford or others coming in at some point, right?"

"Yeah, that's a mystery. No one tied to Crawford, in or out of the lobby, although we can't rule out neighbors. Crawford, apparently, was already there."

"We're going to have to canvas the whole building. Perhaps security can help us identify people coming in and out," Kramer opined, speaking for the first time.

"He never comes out of his room that morning, correct?" Schreiber wondered.

"Correct."

"So, as I was saying before, someone, somehow, gets up there, stays out of sight, and disables the thirtieth-floor camera. This psycho gets into Crawford's apartment without a struggle; maybe Crawford and the killer knew each other? The killer renders Crawford unconscious or otherwise incapacitated, takes him down the freight elevator where there are no cameras, does the deed, and escapes where? How does he or she do that?"

"We're not sure yet. Still processing. One more point about your hypothetical. If the killer is the wife, she doesn't need to 'get up there'. She's already there, which would explain why there are no signs of a struggle on the thirtieth floor."

"Right." Kramer agrees. "But here's the rub: If it's the wife, how in hell does she get out of the apartment without the camera picking her up?"

"The camera doesn't pick up her front door. It wouldn't have been easy, but it was *possible* to avoid the camera, especially for someone who knew it was there," Sawyer offered.

"Is that it, Jim?" Schreiber wondered.

"No. One more thing. There is a blood trail from the storeroom into the hallway leading to the lockers and the elevator. Luminol tracks a large pool of blood in the freight elevator. All blood belongs to Crawford. He was obviously killed in the storeroom, dragged from the room to the elevator, left bleeding on the floor of the elevator up to the thirtieth-floor, and dragged back into the apartment, where the scene was staged."

"And no one saw a fucking thing?" Kramer was astounded.

"No one saw a fucking thing," Sawyer confirmed. "Uniforms questioned everyone on duty that day. As I indicated, we need to question all the tenants, especially the ones who have storage rooms in the basement."

"Good thought, Jim. We'll take care of that," Eddie promised.

"No problem. Sorry I couldn't be more help."

"Not your fault. You've got to report the facts, ma'am; just the facts."

"You're showing your age, Schreiber."

"So are you, if you understood the reference." Schreiber chuckled. "How was my Jack Webb?"

"Wasn't it Broderick Crawford?"

"No, he was 'Highway Patrol'; Webb was 'Dragnet'."

"That's right. Not bad, Eddie. Not bad."

"Cops need a sharp mind and a good memory."

"Okay, fellas, that's a wrap. You'll keep digging, Jim?"

"You know I will, Eddie."

"Thanks, man. Something tells me the poop is about to hit the fan."

"In a good way, I hope." Kramer shrugged.

"Let's hope so."

CHAPTER

SEVEN

Zachary and Jennifer Tracey Blake were curled up on the couch watching an episode of "Law & Order: Special Victims Unit" when local news broke into the program with a special report.

"I was watching that!" Zack yelled at the screen. He turned to his wife. "I hate when that happens. They never return to the show at the point where they interrupted. Shit!"

"Quiet, Zack. Listen! It's about your new client," Jennifer admonished.

Zack sat up and glared at the television.

". . . reports confirm. According to a police spokesperson, Crawford, a two-term congressman from Southfield, was found dead in his apartment by a building manager and Crawford's wife, the right-wing talk show host, Mia Folger. According to sources close to the couple, Mrs. Crawford is currently hospitalized for an unspecified mental health issue. For all appearances, the couple had a good relationship and a happy marriage. Unconfirmed reports have circulated, however, that there are some rather racy text messages between the congressman and his wife. These texts suggest the couple may have been experiencing marital problems.

"The police have not yet identified any suspects or motive for the crime. The congressman was quite popular with constituents in his district and sponsored a series of infrastructure bills that brought much-needed federal funding to repair crumbling highways, surface streets and bridges, replace the area's inefficient energy grid, improve broadband and Internet speeds, implement a modern mass transit system, address climate change issues, and create hundreds of jobs.

"For the first time in history, grants awarded pursuant to the bill will consider both environmental justice and racial equity. Citizens credit Crawford with assuring that these requirements were present in the legislation's final draft. The congressman's tragic death means that this historic legislation will be his signature, final congressional achievement. May he rest in peace. We'll have more details at eleven and as more information becomes public. We now return you to your regularly scheduled program."

Zack hit the pause button on the remote and turned to Jennifer; they both uttered: "Text messages?"

"This can't be good news. And Mia can't explain herself in her current condition," Zack noted.

"She may snap out of it at any moment, sweetheart. Besides, we don't know what those texts say," Jennifer proposed, ever the optimist.

"If they helped her case, Channel Four wouldn't have broken into regular programming. No way these texts are a positive development."

"Not much we can do about it tonight. Want to see if Benson and Stabler get together?"

"It's been, what? Over twenty years? If they haven't gotten it on yet, it's never going to happen."

"But it might. That's what keeps us watching."

"Bullshit. It's the rape, violence, and sexual situations that keep people watching. And Mariska Hargitay." Zack flashed his eyebrows.

"Oh, is that right?" Jennifer pouted.

"What? Are you jealous? She doesn't hold a candle to you, my dear. You are the most beautiful woman on the planet." He snuggled up to her, face-to-face, and jiggled his eyebrows a second time.

"Sure, sure, why don't you fly to New York and wiggle your eyebrows at Mariska. I'm sure she's familiar with the King of Justice," she mocked.

"That's a local distinction. But . . . it's worth a try . . ." he floated the idea and smiled.

"Putz," she snapped.

"Your Yiddish has improved."

"Thank you, now give me a hug and turn the show back on."

***

The following morning, Zack was sipping a cup of coffee at Little Daddy's, a diner near his Bloomfield Hills office mansion. Micah Love, his favorite investigator, was supposed to join him, but Micah was fashionably late. Zack was one of the few people of his generation who liked to read the newspaper rather than get the news electronically on the Internet. Somehow, holding the printed word in his hands made the message more trustworthy.

He glanced at the headlines and almost spit out his coffee.

"EXPLICIT TEXTS MAKE WIFE PRINCIPAL SUSPECT IN CONGRESSMAN'S DEATH"

Someone leaked Mia's texts to the *Detroit Free Press.* Aside from Mia's current inability to cooperate in her own defense, pre-trial publicity was Zack's biggest concern. Zack hated the press, unless, of course, *he* was driving the narrative. He was quite skilled at using the press to advance his cases and his client's causes. But in many high-profile cases, the press did a hatchet job on the accused, declared her or him guilty, and poisoned any chance an attorney might have to assemble a fair and impartial jury.

Congressman Crawford had been an incredibly popular politician, especially in Democratic circles. He was widely considered the logical choice to run for Diane Stabler's Senate seat when she decided to retire. He was young, well-spoken, good-looking, energetic, effective, and African American. People compared him to Barak Obama. His murderer would be despised, vilified in the press and on the street. *If the press and the public decided Mia was the murderer, they would have her hung in a day.*

Zack looked up and around to see if Micah had pulled in or was approaching; there was no sign of him. He put down his coffee, grabbed the *Free Press* with both hands, and began to read the article.

Like the Channel Four report that interrupted SVU the night before, the article cited 'confirmed reports' about the congressman's death, the condition of the body, where it was found, and by whom. However, the *Free Press* article was far more detailed. Sources indicated that the body was mutilated; cause of death was listed as 'exsanguination.' The reporter spoke in glowing terms about the congressman, his political and legislative accomplishments. The article turned to Mia, her current whereabouts, and the now infamous texts. Mia was 'resting comfortably' in the psychiatric ward at Providence Hospital, apparently unable or unwilling to communicate with her doctor, nurses, hospital staff, even the police.

The police have already paid her a visit? I've got to notify them of my representation. Zack continued reading. The texts were printed in glorious black and white, redacted in parts, for language. Readers would, absolutely, be able to read between the lines.

"Who is it this time? That iron-pumping Naylor? Bet she kicks your a- in bed. Like it rough? I can get rough-violent too. Handcuffs whips chains knives. How about we cut the little f-er right off-no more wandering di-. Wandering di-less."

Shit! Zack continued reading, getting increasingly restless. *Does Harold know about these?*

"Don't ignore me, dammit. I get angry when you ignore me."

"I'm going to f-ing murder you."

"I'll enjoy attending your funeral."

Zack sighed. He hadn't met Mia Folger, but Harold Rothenberg vouched for her. He said she was incapable of murder, especially the murder of her husband. Harold's opinion was good enough for him;

although, for plea deal purposes, he had to consider her possible guilt. The texts were graphic and damning. If guilty, Zack hoped to convince a jury that Mia's crime was one of passion—a sudden impulse to kill—involuntary manslaughter, or, perhaps, negligent homicide. *Yes, I meant to cut his dick off, but I didn't mean to kill him.*

After reading the texts, and again, assuming Mia was guilty, Zack knew a good prosecutor could put forth a solid argument for premeditation. He continued reading.

"I can't decide whether to kill you or myself. I love you, but I can't take the lying and sneaking around."

"When you least expect it . . . I watch you in your sleep, you know."

"B--ch can't make love to a corpse."

"This is completely irresponsible," he muttered aloud. "No way Mia gets a fair trial with this kind of pre-trial publicity How can anyone assemble an impartial jury? I'm going to have to request a change of venue."

"Zack?"

"Huh?" Zack had been glued to the newspaper, muttering at the reporting.

"Snap out of it, bud. It's me, Micah."

Together—Zack on the legal side—Micah on the investigative, this dynamic duo had waged numerous justice system battles, emerging victorious each time. Their joint escapades were legendary in Detroit legal circles. Zack's cases made Micah a multi-millionaire, the most sought-after private eye in the Midwest. Still, he always dropped everything when Zack called.

"Micah! Shit! How long have you been standing there? Did you see this morning's *Free Press*?" Zack raged.

"About the bitch who murdered her husband, the congressman?"

"Exactly!" Zack screeched. Everyone in the restaurant turned towards the two men.

"Whoa, man. What's your damage?"

"Mia Folger, the woman you call the bitch who murdered her husband?"

"Yeah?"

"She's my client, Micah. She's innocent. We must prove her innocence. Do you feel me, bud?"

"Shit, Zack. I'm so sorry. I didn't know."

"She's the reason I wanted to meet with you today. We've got to investigate this and start changing the narrative around here."

"Anything you need, Zack. You know I'm here for you. But those texts . . ."

"What person writes down—in graphic detail, no less—what they're going to do and then goes out and does it?"

"I can't answer that, Zack, but they are pretty damning."

"Step one: We must find her phone. Confirm the texts came from her number. Get Reed Spencer involved. Can someone's text messages be hacked?"

"Good thought, brother. I would bet that any device, or *anyone*, for that matter, can be hacked these days. What else?"

"Talk to this reporter . . . what's this shithead's name? . . . Paige Gladsden."

"Flattery will get you everywhere. I'll handle it. Perhaps a little more diplomatically than you would."

"I want to strangle her. But I wouldn't act on it. See how you can threaten someone without really meaning to bring harm to the person?"

"Hey, man. I get it. You're preaching to the choir. Has Mia been charged? Where is she now?"

"That's the biggest problem of all, Micah. Mia Folger is in a psych ward at Providence Hospital. She's not talking."

"That's a good thing, exercising her right to remain silent, right?"

"No, Micah, not like that. She is *unable* to speak or refuses to speak to anyone, including me and you. She cannot defend herself or help us defend her."

"Fuck me! How did that happen?"

"According to Harold Rothenberg, it happened when she walked into her apartment and saw her husband's body."

"Well, that's a start. If she murdered him, why would she be shocked at seeing him dead?"

"I asked the same question, and it is a good place to start. The obvious response is that she's *pretending* to be psychotic."

"That's quite a stretch. Do *you* think that's the case? Do you think she's pretending?"

"I haven't met her yet. The important thing is that *Harold* doesn't think she's capable of murder or an elaborate cover-up, like faking psychosis."

"Good enough for me."

"Me too."

"Anything else you need from me?"

"Poke around the Oakland County Prosecutor's office and see whether they are getting ready for battle. Find out, if you can, who their anointed gladiator will be."

"Will do. Hey, may I suggest something?"

"Sure."

"Remember last year, while you were away, I helped Jason Peri with that paraplegia motorcycle case?"

"What about it?"

"The press coverage was terrible. The plaintiff was part of a motorcycle gang; he had tattoos up the wazoo, liked to drink and ride, hard-living womanizer. He was accused of riding while drunk when the accident happened, even though he was stone-cold sober. The woman who caused the accident was a *WASP* from Grosse Pointe Farms—

prominent, wealthy, two kids and a dog, picket fence, the whole nine yards. She claimed he cut her off, came out of nowhere."

"I remember. Why are you telling me this? You want me to refer the case to Jason? I can't do that, Micah. I promised Harold."

"No, Zack, nothing like that. Jason couldn't find his way out of a paper bag on a criminal case. Can't shine your shoes on a civil case, either. The point is that Jason was really concerned about the jury and the pre-trial publicity, just like you are in this case."

"Okay, I'm starting to understand where you're going with this. What did our friend Jason do about it?"

"Jason's a member of the American Association for Justice . . ."

"So am I," Zack interrupted.

"I know, Zack. Jeez o' Pete, will you let me finish?"

"Sorry."

"Jason attended a seminar on mock juries, jury selection, witness preparation, and jury consultants. The speaker was a sassy woman from New York, apparently one of the best consultants in the country. Jason was so impressed with her presentation, he hired her on the spot, at the seminar, to help him with the biggest case of his life. I investigated the accident, found out a few things that helped.

"Anyway, this woman comes in and wants to do my witness prep. I laugh at Jason when he confronts me and asks me to participate in her process. 'I'm Micah Love,' I tell him. 'I don't need no witness prep.' He sings her praises, talks me into it, and, reluctantly, I agree to participate.

"I've got to tell you, Zack. This woman is extraordinary. She dotted every 'i' and crossed every 't.' She made my testimony far better than it would have been if she wasn't around. She polished me up like a shiny silver dollar, cleaned up the facts, cleaned up the plaintiff and his family, created some terrific graphics, assembled and conducted a mock jury, worked out the kinks of the case, helped with jury selection—the works. As you well know, the verdict was twenty-nine million bucks."

"Nice verdict. I remember the case. What's the lady's name?"

"Shari Belitz."

"Jewish?"

"Absolutely."

"What's she like?"

"She dresses to the nines. Sassy, but very professional. Very good at what she does. She got her law degree, practiced for a while, went back to graduate school and studied forensic psychology to prepare for her career as a jury consultant. She's the real deal, Zack, a no nonsense, tough broad. She's quite accustomed to dealing with arrogant lawyers who think they're smarter than her or can do what she does better than she can. I'm here to tell you, first-hand; they aren't and they can't. Even you, Mr. King of Justice."

"High praise coming from you, Micah. I'm impressed. Where is she located again?"

"Her office is in New York City."

"Let me get this straight, Micah. You want me to reach out to a snooty, pushy, New York Jewish woman, who thinks her poop smells like rose blossoms, and who will try to take over my case. You think I need help *trying a case*, the talent that made me wealthy beyond anyone's imagination. The Michigan Bar Association honored me with a "Best in Class" award in trial practice, but I need this woman's assistance? Does that sum it up?"

"Well . . . when you put it like that . . . Yes! You are the best at what you do. I'll concede. But Shari is the best at what *she* does. I've witnessed this. Trust me, this case needs her. Besides, what's the harm in a telephone call or Zoom conference?"

"Jeez, Micah, Mia hasn't even been charged with a crime yet."

"Do you believe charges are inevitable?"

"Yes, unless we can prove her innocence before they charge her."

"What's the likelihood of that?"

"Slim and none. More than likely, if she's innocent, we prove it after she's charged or at trial."

"And I will do my absolute best to make that happen."

"I know you will, Micah."

"So, again, what's the harm in a phone or Zoom call?"

"None. Set it up." Zack sighed.

"Really?"

"Yes."

"I thought this would be more difficult."

"You want me to give you more shit? I can do that. I'm very good at giving people shit, especially *you*, as you well know," Zack grumbled.

"No, no, that's fine," Micah gasped. "I'll set it up. You won't be sorry."

"For your sake, let's hope not. I'll never let you hear the end of it."

"All the more reason you should trust me on this. Is there a step three?"

"What?" Zack had no clue what Micah was talking about.

"You reached step two in barking out my marching orders, and I cut you off with my jury consultant idea."

"Right. Step three is retracing the cops' steps. Re-investigate every part of their investigation. Leave no stone unturned. We've got to turn this around."

"I'm on it, Zack. Let's eat."

"Don't you want to get started?"

"You invited me to Little Daddy's! Did you think you were going to get away without feeding me? Besides, I can't work on an empty stomach."

Micah was a man of wide girth. His slovenly eating habits and ability to eat large quantities of food were legendary. Zack capitulated, as usual. Micah ordered corned beef hash with two eggs, over medium, full orders of Cinnabon pancakes and French toast, a cup of coffee, and a large glass of fresh squeezed orange juice. Zack was quite familiar with

Micah's eating capabilities but was still surprised Micah finished everything on his plate, drank two large glasses of orange juice, and four cups of coffee. *He's got a very big job ahead . . .* Zack mused.

CHAPTER

EIGHT

Eddie Schreiber sat at his desk, reading the morning *Free Press*. He was livid about the text leaks. He preferred to build his case against Mia Folger, assemble it, piece by piece, until there was no doubt about her guilt. The text leak made that impossible. The public would demand justice for its beloved elected official, and everyone would blame Mia Folger, guilty or not.

Schreiber had doubts about her guilt. If she intended to castrate her husband, watch him bleed to death, why would she broadcast her intent in a series of texts? She was a bright woman. She had to know the police would discover the texts. But that wasn't the only thing that bothered him. It was difficult for Schreiber to imagine a woman, even a physically fit woman like Mia, committing this unique crime in these sequential steps. How did she subdue her much bigger, stronger husband? Where did she learn to disable security cameras in two locations? How did she move him into the basement storeroom without detection? After the deed was done, how did she move him back to the bedroom and up on the bed, arranged so perfectly? In the middle of killing her husband in a fit of rage, she thought to trash the apartment to make it look like a robbery? Where was the murder weapon? Where was her bloodstained clothing? If Mia killed her husband, did she act alone or did she have help? Rage isn't planned.

All these unanswered questions cluttered his mind as he read the sordid newspaper account. Eddie's captain, George Clarkson, also read the morning paper and declared this an open and shut case. He ordered Eddie to drive to the hospital, arrest Mia Folger, charge her with Murder One, and place an armed guard outside her hospital room door. Eddie protested, demanding more time to build a solid case. He knew the dangers of a rush to judgment, but the captain's mind was made up.

"What more do you need, Schreiber? She's all but confessed to the crime."

"I know it appears that way, Cap, but things don't add up."

"Like what?"

Eddie ticked off a litany of issues that bothered him about the case.

"I get it, Detective, but if not Folger, someone else did each thing you claim she couldn't have done. Would you agree that slicing off a man's penis suggests a female perp? Ask John Bobbitt. So, if the murderer was a woman, who had a better motive or better access to Congressman Crawford than his wife? Arrest her! Now! She's not going anywhere or talking to anyone. Arrest her and build the case after the arrest."

"Aye-aye, Captain."

"Smartass."

After Captain Clarkson left Eddie's office, Eddie summoned Jerry Kramer to help him prepare for the arrest. To arrest Mia, Schreiber and Kramer had to obtain an arrest warrant. A warrant is an official document, signed by a judge or magistrate, that authorizes the police to arrest the person named. The warrant must identify the crime and must be accompanied by an affidavit of the arresting officer. The affidavit, Eddie's testimony under oath, had to recite facts that establish probable cause for the arrest.

Eddie felt trapped. This was his statement, under oath, and he had to make sure that everything he alleged in the affidavit was the truth. He wasn't satisfied they had enough evidence to convince a judge to authorize a warrant. Yes, he had the damning texts. They provided motive. But he had no witnesses, no murder weapon or knowledge of Mia's whereabouts during the day. For all Eddie knew, when Mia awoke from her daydream, she might alibi out or have a perfectly logical explanation for her texting escapades. The affidavit read: "Mia Folger Crawford murdered her husband, Bradley Crawford, in a fit of rage, after sending a series of texts in which she not only promised to kill her husband, but promised to kill him in the exact, unique way he was killed. Her DNA was found at both crime scenes."

Eddie thought the case, as stated, was weak and determined that probable cause was a fifty-fifty proposition at best. A better version might read: "Mia Folger Crawford murdered her husband, Bradley Crawford, in a fit of rage, after sending a series of texts in which she not only promised to kill her husband, but promised to kill him in the exact, unique way he was killed. The murder weapon, a serrated knife, was found at the scene, with the accused's fingerprints on the handle.

Her DNA was found at the scene and witnesses saw her running away." Now *that* was a solid arrest warrant.

While Schreiber prepared the arrest warrant, Kramer worked on a search warrant for multiple areas of the 5000 Town Center building and grounds. The apartment-condominium complex was the crime scene, and investigators had exigent circumstances without a warrant, but Schreiber wanted to buttress the arrest warrant with a search warrant for the murder weapon. Unless Mia disposed of the weapon elsewhere that day, it had to be somewhere in the basement, elevator, stairwell, or the couple's apartment.

When the two men finished typing the affidavit and warrants, they jumped in an unmarked and headed for the Oakland County Courthouse. When they arrived, they flashed their badges at security and skipped the metal detector. Judge Samuel Andrews was the chief judge of the circuit court. As chief, he was responsible for reviewing and approving all warrants sought by municipal or county police and sheriffs' departments throughout Oakland County. Andrews was a conservative, law and order jurist, a good draw for Schreiber and Kramer. In Eddie's estimation, the fifty-fifty increased to eighty-twenty. The men took a service elevator to the fourth floor. There were four courtrooms on four, and they quickly located Judge Andrews' chambers. They walked in, introduced themselves to the clerk, and Eddie asked her if she was a notary public. The clerk assured him she was. Eddie asked her to notarize his signature on the affidavit. She agreed, Eddie signed the document in her presence, and she notarized it with signature, stamp, and seal. Afterwards, she invited them to have a seat. A few minutes later, the judge emerged from his chambers and invited them into his office.

"What can I do for you two fine public servants?" Judge Andrews inquired.

"Your Honor, thank you for seeing us. We have a search warrant for the 5000 Town Center building and an arrest warrant in Congressman Crawford's murder case."

"Crawford, eh? What a shame! So young. Bright future. Too liberal if you ask me. Who did it, the wife? That's what those texts seem to suggest." Eddie was mildly surprised by Andrews' rush to judgment based upon newspaper accounts.

"We have solid evidence linking the wife to the murder, Your Honor. It's all in the warrant and the accompanying affidavit."

"Let's have a look." The judge extended his arm across the front of his desk, palm up. Eddie placed the paperwork in his open palm. The judge took it, donned his reading glasses, and began to read.

"Uh-huh . . . mm-mm . . . yes, everything seems to be in order. Compelling case. Do you get many cases where the chief suspect admits the crime in a text?" The judge asked as he signed the documents.

"No, sir, we don't. Good thing she did so in this case." Eddie was sorry the minute he said it. Kramer kicked him under the table.

"Oh? Why?"

Eddie was upset with himself but had no choice other than to answer the judge's question. "It would be a tough case to prove without the admission, Your Honor."

"How so?"

"We have no murder weapon or witnesses—at least, not yet. We hope to find the weapon after a thorough search of the building and grounds." Eddie waited for the hammer to fall. *Give me back that warrant and don't come back until you can hand me a solid case!* Eddie expected.

"Keep working the case. All the pieces will fall into place. The wife, what's her name? She's guilty as hell," the judge declared.

Eddie let out the breath he was holding. He silently hoped that if he was ever accused of a crime, Samuel Andrews would not be the assigned judge.

"We will, Your Honor, no stone unturned."

"I like that, Detective, no stone unturned. Well, gentlemen, good luck with the case. Hope you get a good draw on a prosecutor. I've got a courtroom full of people waiting for me to dispense justice. Have a wonderful day."

"You too, judge. Thanks."

Schreiber and Kramer exited Judge Andrews' chambers. They did not say a word or even look at each other until they were in the parking lot.

"What the fuck, Eddie?" Kramer finally grumbled, as they got into the unmarked.

"Freudian slip?" Eddie groaned.

"Indeed," Kramer chuckled. "No harm, no foul, I guess."

"Chances are Andrews won't be assigned to the case after the district court arraignment and prelim. Getting a warrant is nothing compared to proof beyond a reasonable doubt. We've got our work cut out—we've got to build a better case. A good lawyer will poke holes in this case and a *great* lawyer might even get her off."

"I agree. We're still processing and gathering. We'll get the goods on her. Where to now, boss?"

"Providence Hospital."

***

Eddie and Jerry arrived at Providence Hospital about twenty minutes later. They flashed badges at security and ambled to the psychiatric ward. Cheryl was on duty, sitting at the nurses' station, head down in paperwork. Eddie was embarrassed. He couldn't remember her last name. He didn't want to call her Cheryl in front of Kramer. The third degree would never end. *Rosen-something*, Eddie couldn't remember. He walked up to her, cleared his throat, and read 'C. Rosenfeld' from her employee badge. "Nurse Rosenfeld? Remember me? Detective Schreiber?" He pointed at Kramer. "And my associate, Jerry Kramer?"

Rosenfeld continued writing on a record of some type, and finally looked up, wearing a distracted half-smile.

"What can I do for you, gentlemen? I presume this is about Mia Folger?"

"It is, ma'am. We have a warrant for her arrest."

"She's in with the doctor."

"Would that be Dr. Rothenberg?"

"Yes."

"Please take us to her room."

"Right away, Officer."

"That's 'detective'."

"Right away, Detective," she smirked.

As they entered Mia's room, Rothenberg was quietly addressing Mia, almost in a whisper, trying to illicit a verbal or non-verbal response.

"Dr. Rothenberg? These men have a warrant for Mia's arrest."

Rothenberg turned in his chair, away from Mia and toward the three intruders. He looked visibly annoyed at the interruption. "She's not going anywhere, gentlemen," he whispered, ignoring Cheryl. "She's in no condition to leave the hospital and is no threat to anyone. What purpose is served by placing her under arrest now? Can't this wait?"

"I'm afraid not, Doc. The purpose is to arrest her, restrain her, and make sure she cannot lash out, violently, against herself or another person. We can set up a Zoom hearing to formally arraign her."

"She's not a danger to herself or others. I will vouch for that. This stunt is totally unnecessary," Rothenberg protested.

"If I intended a 'stunt', as you call it, Dr. Rothenberg, I would have alerted the press. Do you see any reporters?"

Rothenberg softened. He was grateful for Schreiber's non-public gesture. "Appreciated, Detective. Ms. Folger has an attorney. I will notify him of your visit."

Eddie was surprised by the news of an attorney. *How can a comatose woman retain an attorney?* "This is a murder warrant, Doc. I'm not sure what a judge will do, but it is my responsibility to protect the public. By the way, who is this attorney, and how could she possibly hire one?"

"The attorney is Zachary Blake. I hired him for Mia. He's a friend of mine."

"Zachary Blake, huh? He's the best of the best. She's going to need a lawyer of his skill and legend. We have her dead to rights," Schreiber blustered.

"We'll see about that, Detective. Well . . . get on with it."

Schreiber pulled out a set of handcuffs and gently secured Mia's limp hand to the metal bedframe. A uniformed officer entered the room, and Kramer introduced Officer Jennings to Rosenfeld and Rothenberg. Jennings would be the first of many officers to stand guard outside Mia's room.

Rothenberg was on his iPhone.

"Yes, Zack, I understand. They're here now. What? Now?"

Rothenberg held out his phone to Schreiber. "He wants to speak with you."

"Why?"

"Beats me."

Schreiber took the phone from Rothenberg. "Detective Eddie Schreiber, how may I help you?"

"Looking forward to seeing you at the arraignment, Detective. Feeling confident, are you?"

"If I didn't feel the evidence supported her guilt, I wouldn't have arrested her."

"We both know that's not true. You arrested her because of public pressure and because that's what your captain ordered you to do, right?"

How the fuck does he know that? What is this guy, psychic? "I make my own cases and my own decisions, Mr. Blake."

"Call me Zack. We're going to be good friends," Zack taunted.

"Don't know about the 'good friends' part. Let's keep things professional. I have a lot of respect for what you've accomplished over the past several years. However, we both have jobs to do. You do yours. I'll do mine. How does that sound?" Eddie countered. Zack got under his skin, probably the intent of this conversation.

"Understood, Detective. I appreciate your candor. Put the doc back on, please."

Eddie handed the phone back to Rothenberg. A short conversation ensued with Rothenberg saying "yes" three or four times, then disconnecting the call.

"Will there be anything else, gentlemen?"

"How is she doing?" Kramer asked. "Any communication of any kind?"

"None," Rothenberg advised. "She's been severely traumatized. Something literally shocked her silent, probably the condition of her husband's body when she discovered him."

"Thanks for the update. See you in a couple of days for the arraignment?"

"I will be there."

"See you then, Doc. C'mon, Jerry. Let's leave these fine people alone."

Schreiber and Kramer went into the hall and spoke briefly to Jennings. Kramer stopped an orderly, and the young man brought over a chair for Jennings to place outside the door to Mia's room. Mia Folger was now officially charged with murder in the first degree in the gruesome death of Congressman Bradley Crawford.

***

The following day, Detective Eddie Schreiber called a press conference to announce the arrest of Mia Folger on first degree murder charges. A large gathering of print, radio, social media podcasters, and television reporters attended the event. Schreiber—flanked by Kramer to his left, and Captain Clarkson to his right—stepped up to a makeshift podium in the lobby of the Southfield Civic Center building. The event was televised live in Detroit and multiple cameramen stood near the podium, videotaping the proceedings.

"Ladies and gentlemen, I've called this press conference to announce the arrest of Mia Folger Crawford for the murder of her husband, Congressman Bradley Crawford, of Southfield. I am not here to comment one way or another on the charges. I will say that this was a particularly brutal murder, committed by someone close to the congressman in an obvious fit of rage. The events of this murder and the circumstances leading up to it have been a focus of you all in the press and your reporting has the entire community on edge. I am pleased the perpetrator is in police custody, and any potential harm to other members of the community has been avoided. Our focus, going forward, will be to develop and process further evidence in this case, help the family of the victim to heal, provide all necessary services to them and the community, and, hopefully, deliver justice for Congressman Crawford and his family. We will also work to ensure that the criminal justice system operates properly and fairly in this case. We are optimistic that it will. I will be happy to take a few questions."

"Detective Schreiber, Nancy Stone, Channel Seven. You indicated an arrest for murder. What are the specific charges and what degree of murder?"

"Thanks for that, Nancy. Mrs. Crawford is being charged with one count of first degree murder. If you have read newspaper accounts of this tragedy, you know this was, obviously, an act of passion. While it is unusual to have these types of crimes reach this charging level, texts and emails recovered from the suspect's cell phone and computer suggest planning, or, at least, a level of premeditation that meets the criteria for the more serious first degree charge."

Eddie scanned the crowd, looking for anyone pro-police. He chose Anthony Kruger of the Oakland Press, pointing him out, calling out his name.

"Detective, will you please enlighten us on what led you to charge Mia Folger? She has been a suspect for a while. My understanding is that she is currently a psychiatric patient at Providence Hospital, is non-communicative, and a threat to no one. What evidence came forth that caused you to change course and bring charges at this time?"

Nothing, asshole. This guy is pro-police? "Excellent question, Anthony, I'm pleased to respond. I cannot yet comment on specific evidence found at various crime scenes. We are still processing the multiple locations at the 5000 Town Center complex. I will say that the texts and emails discovered in Mrs. Crawford's phone and computer helped us determine not only her motive for the crime, but also her specific intent to commit this brutal method of murder. Anyone else have a question? Yes, Priya?" Eddie called on Priya Vernon from Channel 4.

"Detective, do you anticipate taking this case to trial, or do you expect a plea in this case? Will you consider a plea to a lesser charge?"

"You would have to ask her attorney and the assigned prosecutor that question. My job is to present the case, not to negotiate pleas. Anyone else? Yes, Paige?" Paige Gladsden was a justice reporter for the *Detroit Free Press*, the reporter who published the texts.

"Detective, have you heard from anyone from Mia Folger's family or friends as to who her attorney might be? And which prosecutor has been assigned?"

"No prosecutor has been assigned, at least none that I know of. According to a source close to Mrs. Crawford, it is my understanding that Zachary Blake will represent Mia Folger Crawford."

Everyone stood and began shouting rapid fire questions at the announcement that the famous Blake would represent Mia. Schreiber asked twice for quiet and attention, but the uproar continued.

"Thank you, ladies and gentlemen. That's all for now. I will provide future updates," he hollered, stepping away from the podium and walking back to headquarters. No one in attendance heard a single word.

CHAPTER
NINE

The murderer enjoyed the press conference until Zachary Blake's name was mentioned. She was hoping the catatonic Mia Folger, whose assets were now frozen, would be represented by appointed counsel. Blake was a force to be reckoned with. Until she heard his name, everything was going according to plan. The frame was well-implemented and solid. Everyone believed Mia was a murderer—the only suspect—the only person even *considered* a suspect. *Not even Blake can get her a not-guilty verdict*, she reassured herself.

The murderer was confident that crime scene investigators would soon locate the murder weapon, carefully planted in the service elevator. The weapon contained fingerprints, *Mia Folger's* fingerprints. Everything had been carefully planned.

The murderer got the idea from Mia's texts. What a break! When she first read them, she knew exactly how to get rid of Brad Crawford. With Crawford gone and Mia on trial for murder, she would be back in the game. No one would suspect *her*. She had no obvious connection to any of the players—it was doubtful anyone would even look for a connection. Hell, no one even knew she was gay! To complete the ruse, she opened an account on the Tinder dating app, selected all the appropriate categories, and even went on multiple dates with men. One guy even referred to her as his girlfriend. *Disgusting!*

Mia is the gift that keeps on giving, discovers Brad's dickless body and goes batshit crazy! Her current silence is another wonderful break. She can't even profess her innocence. She was in therapy before the murder. The perfect set-up! Threatening text messages, a psych patient already, the congressman is killed exactly as she threatened? Must be divine intervention!

I'll bet she discussed doing the deed with her therapist. If I can get my hands on and leak those records . . . if the doctor is forced to testify and those records come in . . . game over! OMG! Could any murderer have envisioned a better set-up or patsy than Mia Folger? I almost feel sorry for her. Twice a victim. Better her than me.

***

Zachary Blake, Sandy Manning, and Micah Love watched the press conference in Zack's Bloomfield Hills office mansion. Manning was the firm's managing partner. The boss's acceptance of yet another case where the prospect of payment was 'iffy' annoyed the firm's money guy. Zack, however, was still the firm's founder and, by far, its largest fee generator. There was no close second, although the new immigration department was doing well. Everyone at Zachary Blake & Associates loved and appreciated everything Blake did for them over the past several years. If Zack chose to work for free every now and then, Sandy, although he felt obligated to protest, was powerless to stop him.

"So, what do you think?" Zack inquired of no one in particular.

"They've got shit, so far," Micah concluded. "My source at Southfield says all they have are the texts. Yes, they might certainly be read as a warning. I still say though, if you intend to kill someone, you aren't going to text a warning. They've got microfiber DNA in the basement and a lot more in the apartment, but it's *Mia's* own apartment. She probably used the basement from time-to-time. My two cents? Aside from pre-trial publicity, her being tried and convicted in the press, we have reasonable doubt up the wazoo."

"Sandy?" Zack turned to his partner.

"What he said," Sandy echoed, gesturing toward Micah. He paused, in thought. "But those texts, guys—I'm not the least bit surprised she's being vilified by the press. She's not talking much these days. The texts, if they get into evidence, might be enough."

"I see your point, although I have a different take on things. I'll share that in a minute. To Micah's point, though, how many killers would threaten to kill someone a certain way and actually commit the crime?"

"I don't know killers or killers' deepest, darkest thoughts, Zack. I'm a dollars and cents guy. You're the civil and criminal warrior, not me."

"How's the view from the cheap seats, Sandy?"

"Hey, I resemble that remark. I perform a valuable service to this firm. Try doing what I do, hotshot. In fact, there was a time . . ."

"I know, I know, I appreciate you, man!" Zack cut him off. "I couldn't do what I do without you. I was just kidding!" There was, indeed, a time in Zack's life when his rather unstructured career was in the toilet. He *needed* a Sandy Manning by his side. He could not be Detroit's 'King of Justice' without Sandy. Zack was a litigator, not a manager, and Sandy Manning was the glue that held things together and kept the firm's business humming. Sandy primed the pump. Zack turned straw into gold. They, and a solid group of lawyers and support staff, made the Blake firm the most successful law office in Michigan.

"To answer your question, unless they come up with something else, I don't think threats are enough. I'd prefer to have a communicative client, but threats alone do not a murder make. How many of us have threatened to do this or that and not followed through? When you consider a murder, especially a murder of someone you love or once loved, I think it's even more far-fetched," Sandy ventured.

"Micah, what else are you hearing from your source on the force? Hey, 'source on the force', see what I did there?"

"Yeah, you're a poet and seem to know it. They're continuing to work the scene. So far, nothing, just DNA and fingerprints you'd expect to find when the suspect resides where the murder took place. Now, if they find something else . . ."

"Do you think she's guilty, Micah?"

"I don't know, Zack, and I don't care. She's your client and they've got to *prove* her guilty beyond a reasonable doubt. Besides, I thought you said Doc Rothenberg doesn't believe it. He's closer to the situation than we are."

"True. So far, he's our star witness."

"Shit, I almost forgot, I reached out to Shari."

"Shari?"

"Belitz. You know, Zack, the jury consultant lady?"

"Oh, *that* Shari. And?"

"By sheer coincidence, she's going to be in Detroit for a Negligence Section seminar. It must be fate."

"When?"

"She'll be speaking later this week. Can you meet with her? Thursday or Friday, perhaps?"

"Shouldn't be a problem. Even if it is, I can move things around if you still think it's important."

"Come on, Zack, *everyone* thinks Mia is guilty. Shari is the queen of overcoming media bias."

"Yada, yada. I said I would talk to her. What more do you want? Better that she's here and I can meet her in person. Size her up a bit."

"You will like what you see, Zack. She's a pistol, that one. Almost as sassy as Jessica."

'Jessica' was Jessica Klein, Micah's long-time girlfriend and insatiable lover. They met when Micah worked Zack's case against the Church and its depraved pedophile priest. Until then, Micah was a sexually deprived porn addict. Now, he constantly complained of exhaustion. His sex life had never been like this.

"Like Jessica, huh? I guess I'll have my work cut out for me," Zack chuckled. "Let me know the final date and time."

"Will do. Anything else?"

"Yes, let's get back to the case for a second, shall we? I don't want you to forget about the *SODDIT* defense. If our working assumption is that Mia didn't kill her husband, based on her sessions with Harold, then some other dude did it, right?"

"I haven't forgotten. What else you got?"

"I've saved the best for last. I think we can get charges withdrawn at the arraignment. I believe Detective Schreiber jumped the gun and made a huge tactical error."

"Wow!" Sandy marveled. "That would save us a shitload of free, otherwise billable hours."

"Always about the money, isn't it? In this case, I'm glad I can accommodate you. We have a very good chance at making this go away early, at least temporarily."

"Care to share? Hey, see what I did there?" Micah snickered.

"Cheap imitation. I want to talk to Harold first, but I don't see how my strategy fails, at least, in the short term. If the charges are withdrawn, we will have more time to work the case, investigate, and develop a long-term defense. I'll do my job, Micah. Your job is to develop evidence that points in the direction of the real killer and away from Mia. Better yet, hit a home run and *identify* that person. What was his or her motive? Who hated Bradley Crawford enough to kill him, especially with this level of depravity? We must begin to compile a list of alternate suspects. That will be the principal difference between how the detectives approach this case and evidence and the way we do."

"On it, boss." Micah bowed, swearing fealty.

"Funny, asshole." Zack huffed.

CHAPTER TEN

Reporters, court watchers, attorneys, podcasters, and other interested spectators packed Judge Jordyn Bolton's courtroom in the Forty-Sixth District Court in Southfield. Bolton was once a plaintiff personal injury attorney, member of the Michigan Association of Justice, the trial lawyers' association. The Forty-Sixth was a three-judge court, and Bolton was a good draw for Mia's case.

Bolton was sometimes tough on crime, but fair, always following the law as written, rather than offering expansive interpretations. Zack was pleased with the draw. In fact, he believed Jordyn Bolton was the perfect judge for the argument he was about to make.

A typical arraignment is any defendant's first contact with the criminal justice system. It is always conducted at the district court level. First, the defendant is formally advised of the charges against her. Likewise, she is advised of the prospective penalty for those charges. Next, the judge will read a defendant her constitutional rights or a defendant might read and sign an 'advice of rights' form, which advises her of those rights. After the advice of rights, the defendant enters a plea, always 'not guilty'. Zack found the plea process amusing. Why offer a defendant the opportunity to plea in a felony case when no one ever pleads guilty? To Zack, it was like ordering a deli sandwich. The server asks: "What kind of bread would you like?" when the restaurant only serves rye. Next, the judge discusses the setting of bond and the conditions of bond. Finally, the next court date is set, or a defendant is advised that the next date will be determined and mailed.

George Bruch was the Oakland County Prosecutor's chief assistant. Bruch was a veteran attorney, a former sheriff's deputy who went to law school at night, hoping to land a job in the prosecutor's office. He was sick and tired of arresting criminals only to find that ineffective prosecutors helped set them free.

Once Bruch landed a job in the prosecutor's office, he quickly worked his way up the ladder to his current position as the prosecutor's right-hand man. Zack smiled to himself. He was not surprised Bruch landed the Mia Folger murder case. He admired George for his zealous anti-crime advocacy. But not every accused is guilty, and even the guilty deserve a fair trial. George, much like Zack, hated to lose. He was not going to enjoy what was about to happen.

Zack was already seated at the defense table to the left of the bench. Bruch entered the courtroom, shook hands with a few lawyers, and stopped to chat. Finally, he came through the swinging gate at the barrier that separated the gallery from the counsel tables and judge's bench. He approached Zack with an outstretched hand.

"Zack? George Bruch. Nice to finally meet you. Your reputation precedes you."

"Thanks, George. Nice to meet you, too. All set? Want to dismiss this and avoid the embarrassment?" Zack never missed an opportunity to unnerve an opponent. The strategy was not especially effective against the veteran Bruch.

"Pass, but thanks for offering. Those texts will be difficult to overcome."

"I try cases in court, George, not in the press. Let's see how things play out, shall we?"

"Always up for new challenges."

"You have one here," Zack boasted. Bruch flinched.

"All rise!" The clerk entered and shouted the traditional opening of proceedings. "Forty-Sixth District Court is now in session, the Honorable Jordyn Bolton presiding."

Bolton entered the courtroom and said, "be seated" before she sat down.

"Call the case of *People v. Folger*," the judge ordered. She was mid-50's with light brown hair, curled at the shoulders. She was small, maybe 5' 1", 5' 2", wore a judicial robe, which covered her pear-shaped body. "Today is the day set for arraignment. Is the prosecution ready?"

"Ready, Your Honor."

"Defense?"

"Ready, Your Honor."

"Please state your appearances for the record."

"George Bruch for the People, Your Honor," Bruch proudly proclaimed.

"Zachary Blake for the defendant, Your Honor."

"Where's your client, Mr. Blake?"

"She is currently a patient in the psychiatric ward at Providence Hospital, Your Honor."

"Mr. Bruch? Are you prepared to proceed without the defendant?"

"We are, Your Honor."

The judge very slightly raised an eyebrow and glanced at Zack, who made immediate eye contact. "Very well, Mr. Bruch, it is your rodeo. What's your pleasure?"

"May it please the court, Your Honor . . ."

"Your Honor, sorry to interrupt, but as you pointed out the defendant is not present in court today," Zack interrupted.

"Most unusual, Mr. Bruch," the judge agreed.

"Well, Your Honor . . ." Bruch began.

Blake interrupted him a second time. "Excuse me again, Your Honor, but I believe we can make short work of this hearing if you will let me speak."

"Mr. Bruch?"

"I would be happy to hear what the eloquent Mr. Blake has to say that would lighten our load today," Bruch smirked, motioning Zack to proceed.

"Well, gee, thanks, Mr. Bruch. Your Honor, we believe that any charges today are premature. I have Dr. Harold Rothenberg with me here today to testify that the defendant is not competent to stand trial. She is his patient, a patient at the psychiatric ward at Providence Hospital, and cannot participate in her own defense or understand the charges being brought against her."

"Your Honor, this was a particularly brutal crime. The defendant was consciously aware of what she was doing when she committed these heinous acts. Therefore, she should not be permitted to hide behind the guise of incompetence to avoid speedy prosecution, for the protection of our citizens," Bruch argued.

"Aren't you conflating competence to stand trial with an insanity defense, Mr. Bruch?" the judge inquired. "Mr. Blake is not arguing that she can't be required to stand trial when or if she becomes competent. He is arguing that she is not competent now."

"We believe she is fully competent, Your Honor, and that this is nothing more than a stunt to delay these proceedings."

"Your Honor, again, in deference to your precious time and your docket, I have an affidavit signed by Dr. Rothenberg attesting to Mrs. Crawford's current incompetence to stand trial. He's here in court. He can testify, but the affidavit speaks for itself and will save time. May I present it to the Court?"

"Mr. Bruch?"

"I'd like to read it, Your Honor."

"By all means!" Zack exclaimed, smiling, handing Bruch a copy of the affidavit.

Bruch scanned the document with a scowl.

"Would you like me to voir dire the doctor, Mr. Bruch, to determine if his testimony would be consistent with this affidavit?"

"No, Your Honor."

"Very well then, let's have a look." Zack walked up to the bench and handed a copy of the affidavit to Judge Bolton. Again, they made subtle eye contact. The judge was impressed.

"Ten-minute recess while I read the affidavit and prepare my ruling. Any additional arguments?"

"As I indicated, Your Honor, we are prepared to proceed," Bruch argued.

"And we would argue that an arrest warrant serves no purpose under these circumstances. You can't arraign her. She cannot participate in her own defense or understand the charges. You should laugh this ridiculous warrant right out of court, Your Honor," Zack decried.

"I don't think this is a laughing matter, Mr. Blake, but I catch your drift." She pounded her gavel, uttered "ten-minute recess," and left the courtroom.

Bruch immediately walked over to Eddie Schreiber and the two men exited the courtroom. Zack approached Harold Rothenberg and smiled.

"It looks like we are about to win round one. What do you think the prospects are that Mia wakes up anytime soon?"

"Hard to say, Zack. It could be any moment or years. Psychic trauma is a funny thing. Different people are affected in different ways.

Mia is a strong woman. If I was a betting man, I would bet on sooner than later, but there is no way to tell."

Reporters walked over to the two men and attempted to get a statement. They were greeted with a terse 'no comment.' A deputy sheriff walked over and motioned the press back to their seats. At that moment, an angry George Bruch returned to the courtroom, followed by a frustrated Eddie Schreiber. Zack was delighted.

The clerk shouted the familiar "all rise" command, and everyone returned to their appropriate places in the courtroom. Judge Bolton stormed in, commanded everyone to be seated, and took the bench.

"I have reviewed the affidavit. I understand that Dr. Rothenberg is in the courtroom?"

"He is, Your Honor." Zack turned and motioned for Harold to rise.

"Dr. Rothenberg, will you raise your right hand, please?" Rothenberg did as the judge commanded.

"You can stay where you are, sir. Do you swear that the testimony you are about to give will be the truth, the whole truth, and nothing but the truth?" Judge Bolton addressed Rothenberg.

"I do, Your Honor," Rothenberg swore.

"You prepared and executed this affidavit, Dr. Rothenberg?"

"I did."

"And, in your professional opinion, the affidavit reflects the current condition of the defendant in this case, Mia Folger Crawford?"

"It does, Your Honor."

"If you were to testify here today, would your testimony be consistent with the affidavit?"

"It would, Your Honor."

"Thank you, Dr. Rothenberg. You may be seated. MCL 33.2024 permits defense counsel or the court, for that matter, to raise the issue of the defendant's competence to stand trial. While MCL 330.2020 (1) presumes that a defendant is competent to stand trial, that defendant shall be determined incompetent to stand trial only if she is incapable because of a mental condition of understanding the nature and object of the proceedings or of assisting in her defense in a rational manner. The court shall determine the capacity of a defendant to assist in her defense by her ability to perform tasks reasonably necessary to her defense and in assistance of her counsel during his trial.

"It is obvious to this Court that Mia Folger Crawford is currently incapacitated as defined by 330.2020. According to Dr. Rothenberg's sworn testimony, Mrs. Crawford is not a current threat to the public. She is incapable of understanding the nature of these proceedings, and of assisting in her own defense.

"Furthermore, MCL 330.2022 states that a defendant who is determined incompetent to stand trial shall not be proceeded against while he or she is incompetent. While her period of incompetence exists, housekeeping motions that do not require the presence of the defendant may be made and heard. Furthermore, if there is essential evidence that may not be available at the time the defendant becomes competent, I will entertain arguments to admit and preserve that evidence. We'll determine timing and admissibility of this type of evidence as we go along.

"For the time being, I hereby order an independent fitness assessment. Proceedings are adjourned. During this period of assessment, I plan to visit with Mrs. Crawford and attempt to engage her in a question-and-answer session. If I am satisfied that she is not communicative, I will order an independent psychiatric exam to assess her mental acuity in a courthouse or medical setting. The independent psychiatrist will conduct his or her own interviews and make an assessment as to whether the defendant is fit or unfit to stand trial.

"Following this examination, the Court will conduct a formal fitness hearing, during which I will hear arguments from Mr. Bruch and Mr. Blake. I will also hear testimony from the independent medical examiner and the defendant's treating doctor, Dr. Rothenberg. If Mrs. Crawford is communicative at that point in time, the Court will also hear from her. Then, and only then, will I render my decision as to whether the accused is fit to stand trial. Do the attorneys have any questions about how we will proceed?"

"Yes, Your Honor. During this period, Mrs. Crawford may remain in the care of Dr. Rothenberg and be treated in whatever facility he deems appropriate?" Zack wanted to prevent the possibility of Mia's transfer to a state psychiatric hospital.

"I think the status quo is best for now. Mr. Bruch? Care to comment?"

"I'm fine with the status quo, Your Honor. Whatever gets her ready and able for trial."

"Very well, gentlemen. Mr. Blake, if you present an order consistent with my ruling today, I will sign it. We're adjourned."

The attorneys, cops, and Rothenberg exited the courtroom tailed by a cacophony of noise emanating from members of the press corp. Every person approached replied with a terse 'no comment'.

Zack and Rothenberg entered the hallway leading to the judges' chambers. Zack located a conference room, and the two men entered. Zack shut the door behind them.

"The best we could hope for under the circumstances, I guess," Zack began. "I was hoping the judge would dismiss the charges and force them to refile."

"Does it make a difference?"

"Not really, and, this way, she retains jurisdiction. I like her. We shared a moment."

"A moment?" Rothenberg was amused.

"An understanding, an informal agreement about what would happen and that it was the right thing."

"I must have missed your moment. I didn't notice anything."

"Just a little . . . moment. Hard to quantify or explain. She'll be a good judge for this case. Wait and see. How do you feel about an independent exam?"

"Depends on who performs it and why. Is it to rubber-stamp her competency or truly assess it? If the latter, I suspect the doctor will conclude as I have, unless he or she is a shill for the prosecution. The wild card, of course, is that Mia regains competency between now and then."

"Of course. The extra time, though, will help us to develop a case. I can meet with Micah's Belitz lady, strategize, perhaps convene a mock trial to see what a jury thinks of the current posture of the case. We would still have time to develop and present alternative theories that might resonate. Except for a dismissal, this is a great outcome. I've got to call Micah."

As Blake and Rothenberg were meeting at the courthouse, Schreiber and Bruch were sitting down in the prosecutors' conference room.

"What a shit-show, Eddie! I was embarrassed out there. And by Zachary Blake, no less, who cannot have a bigger ego!"

"I'm sorry, George. This wasn't exactly my decision. Captain Clarkson insisted."

"You should have pushed back! How can a catatonic woman assist in her own defense? This was a slam dunk for someone like Blake. We are not playing in the minors here, Schreiber. This is the major leagues!" Bruch pounded the table.

"There wasn't a whole lot I could do, George. When Clarkson makes up his mind . . ."

"I understand, Eddie. I'm just aggravated—sorry to take it out on you. The judge is going to visit Mia Folger. I presume she will determine that Mia needs an independent exam. I'll get a forensic psychiatrist ready to get to Providence as soon as the judge makes her initial determination. Although, she might decide to choose her own evaluator. In the meantime, you keep working the case. The more we nail Mia's ass into the coffin, the better. And Eddie?"

"Yeah, George?"

"Better decisions going forward. I don't like losing to arrogant ass defense lawyers like Zachary Blake. Politely tell your captain to go screw himself!"

"Uh . . . don't think so. You're welcome to tell him, George."

"Get the fuck out of here and get me more evidence than a bunch of texts."

"Aye-aye, sir." Eddie saluted him, rose, and sauntered out of the office.

CHAPTER
ELEVEN

The judge's decision on competency made finding the murder weapon and developing additional evidence imperative. Schreiber met with Kramer, Sawyer, and the CSI squad, and a new effort to scour 5000 Town Center with a fine-toothed comb was initiated. Techs swarmed the roped off areas of the building, annoying residents and building security everywhere they went.

On the third day of the blitz, two crime scene techs were unscrewing every screwed-in plate on walls and ceilings of the freight elevator when they made the discovery. Lodged in a small crevice in the ceiling of the freight elevator was a medium-sized, serrated, bloody, kitchen knife. The two techs alerted teammates, and a group of techs descended on the elevator, snapping photos and taping video footage of the bag and tag process. Soon, the knife was sent off to the lab for blood and fingerprint analysis.

Jim Sawyer notified Schreiber and Kramer, who were elated. Kramer contacted Bruch. Bruch notified Zack. The prosecution is obligated to turn over all discovered evidence to the defense. The purpose of the rule is to force the prosecution to turn over even *exculpatory* evidence, evidence which points *away* from a defendant's guilt. In this case, George Bruch was thrilled to turn over the evidence.

Lab analysis not only found Crawford's blood on the knife, but also found Mia's fingerprints on the murder weapon. This was the first and best evidence the prosecution had developed to demonstrate that Mia's texts were the opening salvo in an evil plot to murder her husband. The Southfield Police and the Oakland County Prosecutor's office firmly believed that the so-called 'bloody knife' conclusively proved that Mia Folger Crawford murdered Congressman Bradley Crawford.

Zack handled the news with remarkable stoicism. He demanded that George follow strict chain of custody protocols and make the knife available as soon as possible so that Micah's forensic team could do an independent analysis. He knew, however, that this was not good news for the defense. The prosecution now had independent verification that the texts were more than empty threats.

Bruch was far too ethical to leak the discovery to the press, so he arranged for the Southfield Police to leak the information. A whole new round of sensational press reports hit the print and broadcast media, declaring Mia's conviction a foregone conclusion—as soon as she regained consciousness and met minimum competency requirements.

Zack was livid. He filed two motions. The first demanded access to what the press melodramatically called the 'bloody knife', hearkening court watchers back to the O.J. Simpson trial and the infamous 'bloody glove'. The second motion asked for sanctions against the prosecution and an order to prevent future leaks to the press.

Judge Bolton granted both motions, giving Bruch one week to turn over the knife for testing and admonishing the prosecution for facilitating the leak.

"If there are any additional leaks in this case, Mr. Bruch, I suggest you bring your wallet and sleeping bag to the next hearing," she warned the prosecutor.

***

George Bruch's leak strategy, despite the judge's admonishment, worked like a charm. Reporters tried and convicted Mia Folger Crawford in the press. But the coup de grâce was a previously obscure podcast, *Slam Dunk*, hosted by a woman named Libby Curry. Curry created an enthralling mockumentary, suggesting evidence *conclusively* established Mia Folger as the murderer. In a quiet, soothing voice, broadcast live over all podcast streaming services, Libby aired her first of many podcasts about the Bradley Crawford murder case:

"Dear listeners, this is an unfortunate case of a scorned woman. Hell, it hath no fury, right? Mia Folger was an outspoken, frustrated woman whose husband, Bradley Crawford, was a busy and famous two-term congressman, whose politics were in stark conflict with her own. Crawford recently won re-election—Mia was faced with the prospect of days, weeks, and months of separation. Mia wanted to raise a family. Brad wanted to run for higher office. Mia was tired of competing with Brad's career. Or was it only his career? Apparently, dear listeners, Mia believed her husband was having an affair. It didn't matter whether her suspicions were true. They were true, so far as Mia was concerned.

"Mia became violently angry. She shot off a series of text messages, which won't be repeated here. You listen to this podcast; you've all read them, right? Suffice to say, they demonstrate Mia's intent to sexually dismember her husband. Mia decided if she couldn't have Brad the way she wanted him, no one could. Mia Folger would *never* let Brad Crawford leave her for another woman. Mia texted the world what she planned to do. She carried out her evil plan, drugging, kidnapping, and torturing her husband. Then, in her final act of revenge, she sadistically did exactly what she promised she would do.

"But Mia didn't count on the blood, lots of blood, spilling from a gaping wound. Did she care that Brad was bleeding out? Did she know he would die? Did she enjoy his suffering? Did she intend for him to die all along? Perhaps we will never know the answers to these questions. You see, Mia Crawford is now a resident of the Providence Hospital psychiatric ward, reportedly in a catatonic state. She cannot or will not communicate with anyone.

"Her condition did not stop the police from working the case. They found her texts. They worked the crime scenes and found fingerprints and DNA belonging to Mia Folger. But the most damning evidence was found yesterday, dear listeners. The police, after an all-out search for the murder weapon, found that weapon lodged in the ceiling tiles of a freight elevator leading to the ritzy apartment shared by Brad and Mia.

"The weapon is a serrated kitchen knife, one of a set found in Mia Folger's kitchen drawer. There are unconfirmed reports that DNA and fingerprints belonging to Mia Folger were found on the knife. Allow me to *confirm* those reports; my exclusive source in the Southfield P.D. tells me the police, indeed, have found Mia's fingerprint and DNA on that weapon.

"Despite this treasure trove of evidence proving Mia Folger is a murderer, she may not face justice anytime soon. Remember that catatonic state I mentioned? After extensive, often heated court arguments, Forty-Sixth District Court Judge Jordyn Bolton ruled Mia unfit to stand trial for murder. Judge Bolton has continued the hearing, ordered a personal question-answer session, an independent medical exam, and restorative psychiatric treatment to help Mia regain competency.

"You may ask, what does all this mean? I reached out to my legal sources—my personal legal gurus, if you will—and they tell me this is a very big deal. It may drag the case out for months, even years. In fact, depending on Mia's progress toward healing, she may *never* face justice. This is a stunning development and an appalling blow to the police community and Brad Crawford's family.

"You don't have to take my word for it, though, dear listeners. In the coming days, following my breaking news accounts on this *Slam Dunk* network, you will see all the local news stations and newspapers report exactly as I have.

"According to my expert sources in the psychiatric community, Mia Folger was fortunate she was not transferred to a state psychiatric center for the 'restorative process' I referred to earlier. Apparently, such a transfer is common in these cases where competency status is an issue. In yet another example of white privilege, Judge Bolton agreed to maintain Mia's.treatment protocol with Dr. Harold Rothenberg, her personal physician. Does the name Harold Rothenberg sound familiar, folks? He was an important player in another prominent legal case in our community. Dr. Rothenberg treated the Tracey boys, now young men, the two sons of Jennifer Tracey and adopted sons of her famous husband, Detroit's King of Justice, Zachary Blake. The boys were sexually abused by a priest in a very contentious case that served as a springboard for Blake to become, perhaps, the most famous attorney in the country. Apparently, in addition to a family, fame and fortune, Blake also found a friend in Dr. Harold Rothenberg. According to my sources, it was Rothenberg who secured Zachary Blake's services as attorney for Mia Folger—another startling turn of events in this case. Legal sources tell *Slam Dunk* that Blake is, at least for the time being, handling the case *pro bono*, which means he's doing it for free. Why? What does Rothenberg have over Blake? Our calls to Blake and Rothenberg have not been returned.

"Here's the bottom line: Mia Folger would be facing a trial right now, if it weren't for Judge Bolton's recent competency ruling. Was this a charade, orchestrated by Blake and Rothenberg? Do they have a connection to Judge Bolton? Undue influence on her decision-making capacity? Blake is a force to be reckoned with, as is his investigator, Micah Love, who, we understand, will be taking a deep dive into this case. What is there to find that hasn't already been reported, right here on this program? Is it nothing more than a smokescreen? We will be following developments closely in this case. Because, but for Judge Bolton's unfortunate ruling and the presence of Zachary Blake, this case would be a *Slam Dunk*. Have a great evening; let's talk soon."

***

"What the fuck, Micah? Who is this woman?" Micah Love and Zachary Blake sat in a booth at Little Daddy's on Woodward. Micah had just finished playing a download of Libby Curry's latest episode of *Slam Dunk*, featuring the Folger murder trial and Libby's declaration that Mia's guilt was a "slam dunk."

"She's a small-time journalist who couldn't get a job as a reporter and started her own podcast. It's a right place-right time story. She reported on and correctly predicted the outcomes of some high-profile cases and gained some traction. She gets a decent number of downloads every time she puts one of these hit jobs on the Internet. But this one . . ." Micah started to explain.

"These days, any idiot can be a reporter or an author on the Internet," Zack interrupted.

"True that, Zack. Get this: Reed Spencer told me this episode has been downloaded two-hundred-fifty-thousand times and counting."

"Shit, Micah! That's a lot of negative reporting in the hands of prospective jurors."

"It sure is, which reminds me, you've got a telephone conference set up for tonight with Shari Belitz. She'll be in town tomorrow morning for that seminar and your face-to-face is set for tomorrow evening at Andiamo."

"Are you sure about this, Micah? She doesn't sound like someone I would get along with. Clash of egos and all of that. I'm not going to cede strategy to some hot-shot psychologist from New York who's never tried a case."

"I don't think that's the case, Zack. Unlike most jury consultants, Shari practiced law before she became a jury consultant."

"I think I knew that, probably forgot."

"As I said before, if you don't like her, you don't have to use her. It's just a meeting. But this podcast and the news reporting of Mia's arrest, the competency hearing, and all the murder weapon chazerai is just the beginning of the publicity this case is going to generate. We need to rein this in. Shari is the expert's expert."

"I'm warning you, Micah. No case can stand more than one chief. I'm a one chief—multiple Indians kind of guy. I enjoy being the boss even though I don't like the title."

"But you delegate and concede investigation strategy to me. You concede and delegate technology to Reed. You concede and delegate immigration to Marshall and Amy. What's the difference?"

"Picking a jury is in my wheelhouse. It is a trial lawyer expertise. I'm very proficient in the art of picking a jury."

"But what have you really known about these jurors? Have you ever done a deep dive? Analyzed jury questionnaires and juror backgrounds? You don't handle that many criminal cases."

"Arya Khan and Jack Dylan turned out okay."

"Without verdicts, Zack! Our pre-trial work took care of those. Take the fucking meeting! Do it for me, okay?" Micah exploded.

"Sure, Micah. I never said I wouldn't take a meeting, did I?" Zack smiled, cat catching the canary.

"You just love to aggravate me, is that it?"

"It's such an easy task. Let's change the subject. Who is this Libby lady? I want you to check her out. Find out if there are any skeletons in her closet. I'm guessing Belitz will need this data, too."

"Why would Shari care about Libby?"

"My guess? If we want to turn public opinion, we are going to have to turn this Libby person."

"Wow! That's top-notch thinking for a lawyer. Maybe you don't need Shari."

"Told you."

"I was kidding. Take the . . ." Micah blustered.

"Meeting," Zack interrupted. "I'll take the meeting, alright? I'll take the meeting!"

"That's a good boy. Hey, Norma?" Micah took a spoonful of chili and called out to his favorite server, spraying chili on the table in front of him.

"Yeah?"

"Where are my Coneys? Don't forget the extra chili and make sure they're Kosher dogs."

"Yeah, yeah," Norma sighed. "Four kosher, extra chili," she shouted to the cooks.

"Four dogs? You're going to have a coronary, Micah. Why Kosher?" Zack wondered, amused.

"All meat. The other stuff is garbage," Micah rationalized.

The warped psyche of a chronic overeater—who can argue? Zack smiled.

CHAPTER
TWELVE

Andiamo at Telegraph and Maple Road in Bloomfield Hills is one of the Detroit area's many fine, upscale Italian restaurants. The restaurant has multiple locations and features made-from-scratch, fine Italian dining. Zachary Blake was friendly with Joe Vicari, the restaurant's owner. Zack appreciated that Vicari would always assure he'd receive a private table, if requested, great service, and fantastic food made fresh daily. Micah Love was a big fan of the delicious Italian pastries served at the elegant old dining spot.

The location has a somewhat dark history. It used to be called Machus Red Fox, the last place former Teamster's boss, Jimmy Hoffa, was seen, before he mysteriously disappeared on the afternoon of July 30th, 1975, never to be seen again. The running joke about the place was that if a couple of guys named "Tony" invited you to lunch at that location, politely decline.

Vicari might have considered ignoring this history, but Andiamo embraced it, naming one of its drinks a "Hoffa Old Fashioned." Zack, at his request, was escorted to a secluded table in a far corner. He ordered the Hoffa and waited, patiently, for his dinner guest to arrive. The Blake-Belitz relationship commenced with a telephone conversation the previous evening. As Zack waited, with growing impatience, he recalled the conversation.

"Hello? Hello! Speak up, please. I can't hear you. I'm headed up Sixth Avenue in an Uber. Hello?" A female voice shouted into the receiver.

"Ms. Belitz? This is attorney Zachary Blake calling from Michigan." Zack could barely make out what she was saying with all the traffic noise in the background.

"Zachary who? Michigan? Yes, I'll be there tomorrow. We can talk at the event, can't we?"

"I won't be at the event. I'm a friend of Micah Love. I understand he talked to you about our case?" Zack was becoming annoyed.

"I can't understand a word you're saying. Let me get this guy to pull over," Shari shouted in Zack's ear. A few more seconds went by—the traffic noise subsided. Apparently, the driver had obeyed her very loud instructions.

"That should be better. Now, who is this speaking?"

"Ms. Belitz?"

"Call me Shari."

"Shari, this is Zachary Blake."

"The hotshot from Michigan? Micah Love's buddy?"

"One and the same. Please don't tell anyone I'm friends with Micah," Zack kibitzed.

"Why?" Shari didn't get the joke.

"Never mind. I was joking."

"Oh? Well, Micah's an impressive guy. You should be glad to know him." Apparently, Shari only knew Micah professionally.

"You wouldn't say that if you ever shared a meal with him, but no matter, I'd like to get down to business."

"Indeed, I understand you've got a high-profile criminal case that might require my services."

"That's correct. I represent a woman whose husband was murdered. The details are unimportant at this juncture."

"Bleeding out from a severed penis is highly important, perhaps the *most* important aspect of your case. It's a gruesome way to die and makes for *sensational* headlines. It also suggests significant rage," Shari observed.

"Micah filled you in?"

"Somewhat."

"Sounds like more than 'somewhat'. So, what do you think?"

The traffic noise picked up again. "What do I what? Hey, asshole, watch where you're going!"

"What do you think?" Zack gasped, losing patience.

"She's been declared temporarily incompetent, correct?" Shari inquired.

"Correct."

"So, we have some extra time. After my seminar tomorrow, I have some time on my schedule. If you think we're a good fit, I'd suggest we use the time to our advantage. Assemble a mock jury, perhaps. Pose some questions. Find out what citizens of your community are thinking. Based on what Micah told me, initially, they are going to think she's guilty as hell. No worries. That's expected. What we want from them is their thoughts about what it would take to change their minds. The beauty of a mock is we can keep bringing the members new evidence, new theories, new suspects, and see whether any of it changes their mind. Get my drift?" The traffic noise continued to increase. "Hello?"

"I heard, Shari. I like it." A cacophony of horns began to blare in the background. "Hello?" All Zack could hear was horns honking.

"I'm so sorry. I just finished back-to-back trials. I'm on my way to my daughter's soccer game and I'm sitting in a fucking traffic jam. Hear all those horns? What the fuck, people? Move!" Traffic noise continued for a few seconds. Shari paused as traffic noise quieted.

"Okay, Mr. Zachary Blake . . ."

"Zack, to my friends."

"Oh, we're friends now? Good! So, we've got a Bobbit-style murder case. This shit is all over the press and social media, correct?"

"Correct."

"It's going to get worse. *People Magazine*, podcasts, local and national press, Gen Xers are going to go crazy for this stuff, especially everyone who remembers Lorena. Your jury pool is already tainted.

Your suspect-client isn't speaking. You have leaks up the wazoo, and you waited this long to call me . . . why?"

For one of the few times in his life, Zachary Blake was rendered speechless. *This is one ballsy woman! I love her!*

"Well . . . I . . ." Zack stuttered.

"Well, what?" Shari demanded, suddenly in charge.

"I-I don't know," Zack murmured.

"When can we get together?"

"Tomorrow night?"

"You've got my cell number. I know this because we are talking, and *you* called *me*. How about dinner tomorrow, after my seminar? Text me a location, time, directions, and I'll be there. Sound good? You definitely need me, Zachary Blake, even if you may be the best fucking trial lawyer in America."

"Sounds fabulous, Shari. I'll text you. See you tomorrow . . . hey, Shari?"

"Yes?"

"Thanks. Tell your driver to be patient and get you to the game safely. Safe travels to Detroit."

"Thank you, Zack. This may be the beginning of a beautiful friendship."

She hung up the phone. Zack sat back in his plush office chair and hashed over the wild conversation. *Movie quotes! What a woman! Brash, cocky, confident, knowledgeable . . . a female Zack Blake?*

Zack crossed his legs, eyes closed, smiling as he recalled the phone exchange. *Quite the character . . .* He heard heels clicking on the hardwood floor. He looked up to see a fortyish, dark-haired, attractive woman stop the hostess, who pointed toward Zack's table. The woman smiled, looked up at Zack, waved, and strutted toward the table. She wore tight, dark flare jeans, a Joie blouse, and a black leather jacket. The clicking sound came from high-styled black Chloé heels. Zack watched her saunter over, supremely confident. She reminded him of the actress, Jennifer Connelly. The woman reached the table and Zack rose to greet her.

"Shari?"

"Zack?"

"Nice to finally meet you." Zack walked around her and pulled out the chair opposite his.

"Such a gentleman," Shari marveled. "I'm not treated that way in New York."

"My mother's influence." Zack smiled, holding the chair until she was seated. He helped her pull the chair closer to the table. "So, how was your flight? How was your seminar?"

"Flight was annoying. A bunch of anti-maskers with pissed off attitudes and no masks boarded the plane. Delta had to send sheriff's deputies to escort them off the plane."

"Michigan's COVID numbers are high. People know there's a mask mandate for air travel. Why do these people even try this stuff? Kind of a dumb form of protest, don't you think?" Zack opined.

"Because they're *assholes*!" Diners' heads turned at the loud, vulgar retort. "In my business you see all kinds of stupid, from criminals to corporate types, attorneys, even judges," Shari chuckled. They made eye contact. She gazed into his eyes, sizing him up. He was immediately uncomfortable—like he was being profiled. Her eyes and diamond stud earrings sparkled in the dim restaurant lighting.

"Especially judges and attorneys, but don't tell them I said so," Zack laughed.

"Your secret is safe with me," Shari chuckled, continuing to stare.

"Are you profiling me?" Zack inquired.

"You have beautiful eyes. A gorgeous shade of blue, and those lashes. I'll bet you made the girls swoon back in the day."

"I had my moments. Most women preferred the taller athletes."

"Dumb. I always preferred the smart, handsome Jewish guys. In fact, I married one."

"I didn't say the athletes weren't Jewish."

"Duh-uh," she replied, scrunching her face.

Zack grinned. "My first wife was Jewish. Didn't work out, unfortunately. It was good while it lasted . . . until it wasn't. More my fault than hers." *Why am I telling her this? Is this some sort of psychologist witchcraft?* He changed the subject. "How was your seminar? I was going to attend, just to see you in action, but I had a scheduling issue."

"You would have been bored out of your mind. Besides, it was a civil presentation, not criminal."

"Big difference?"

"Not really, but this was more about the science of jury selection and how to think and talk about specific dollar amounts."

"Interesting topic. Civil cases are my bread and butter. What was the focus of the seminar?"

"Jury selection. If an attorney can't get a fair and impartial jury, the trial is sabotaged, and injustice is a virtual guarantee."

"Amen to that."

"The seminar focused on why it is essential and appropriate to tell the jurors what the verdict should be or to give the range of appropriate verdicts in voir dire and in opening statement."

"Makes perfect sense to me."

"You have to test the waters. I recommend that attorneys discuss each category of monetary damages and dollar amounts or ranges of dollar amounts if they truly care about getting a fair and impartial jury."

"In Michigan, a lot of judges have taken voir dire away from us."

"Then you have to persuade the *judge* to ask these questions. Threaten a mistrial or an appeal if he or she refuses. The best judges, those without bias or prejudice, will take you up on it, and thoroughly discuss different dollar amounts or ranges. They want to see if jurors have preconceived notions of justice or limits on damages. Whoever conducts voir dire must test the waters."

"You are preaching to the choir. Hopefully, there were some judges in attendance?"

"I was told there were. Maybe they paid attention. Enough about the seminar, let's talk about dinner. What's good here? What are you drinking?"

Zack raised a hand to his server, pointed at his empty glass and held up two fingers, silently ordering two more drinks.

"What was that?" She turned toward the server, now walking away.

"I ordered two more Hoffa's."

"What's a Hoffa?" She inquired, again staring into his eyes, leaning forward, seductively. Zack was uneasy.

"An Old-Fashioned; I sensed you were a Crown Royal type of gal."

"You sensed correctly." She nodded, then added, "Why Hoffa?"

"Oh! Of course, you don't know the history. This is the last place Jimmy Hoffa was seen alive. The restaurant had a different name back then, but this is the place where he disappeared."

"Cool," she remarked, looking around, soaking in the ambiance. Moving on, she picked up a menu and scanned its contents. "So, what's good here?"

"Everything, if you like Italian."

"I love Italian."

"Who in their right mind doesn't? I'll let you in on a well-guarded city secret: I love New York. Great town, great theatre, terrific entertainment, the city that doesn't sleep and all that, great food, but Detroit has better Italian food than New York. What do you like?"

"Salmon. Do they have a good salmon dish here?"

"Check out the *Salmone alla Griglia*. It's wonderful."

She studied the long list of choices and began to read out loud, her face hidden behind the menu. "Char-grilled Scottish Salmon . . . balsamic brussel sprouts . . . sweet potato-garbanzo beans hash . . . pomegranate agro-dolce . . . fennel slaw . . . That all sounds delicious!" she exclaimed.

"Hungry? Let's order and then we'll talk. Sound good?"

"It's your meeting, sir." She half-rose, curtseyed, and bowed.

Zack laughed. "You are quite the pistol, aren't you?"

"I've been called worse." Shari continued to stare at him.

"Are you still profiling me?" He continued to be discomforted by her glare.

"No. I'm so sorry. Was I staring? You have the most amazing eyes I've ever seen."

"So you said."

"I'll behave."

Zack called the server over. He ordered a *Carciofi alla Giudia* appetizer, *Salmone alla Griglia* for Shari, and *Pollo Olivia* for himself. Shari declined a glass of wine, preferring to wait for her Hoffa, which was delivered as they ordered dinner.

"What was that appetizer you ordered?" Shari was intrigued.

"Jerusalem style artichokes, fried in olive oil, garlic and sea salt. Homage to the promised land."

"Sounds delicious."

"To die for."

"Which leads us to your murder case," Shari giggled.

"Indeed," Zack agreed. "You read the materials I sent you?"

"Every page. Fascinating case."

"Hard to craft a defense when you have a catatonic client. What's your take on her, from a psychological perspective?"

"Dr. Rothenberg . . . is that correct? Rothenberg?"

"Yes."

"Is he Jewish, too?"

"Catholic, but the name does sound Jewish, doesn't it?"

"Well, either way, he's a better person to ask. In my opinion, though, a murderer doesn't go into shock when she comes upon her victim's body. Makes no sense. If she killed him, she wouldn't go into shock when the body is discovered."

"That's exactly what Harold said."

"Harold?"

"Rothenberg."

"Right."

"Let's size *you* up a bit, shall we?" He now stared her down, causing her to divert her gaze for a moment. "Tell me about Shari."

"What do you want to know?"

"Anything you are willing to share."

"Well, it's 1991. I'm wearing a flannel shirt, ripped jeans, and shoe boots. My hair is blonde."

"Blonde?"

"Well, blondish. How's that? Anyway, Nirvana is blasting in the background, I'm holding a Zima and a guy comes up and asks me out."

"Like, on a date?"

"Yeah. Amazing, huh? In that outlandish, hideous get-up, some guy actually asks me out! My roommates thought it was hilarious that someone would actually ask a girl out on a date in college. But, Zack, it was *Syracuse.* What else is there to do at Syracuse other than test drink weird beverages and go to smoky bars with no coat?"

"I wouldn't know. Never been. Continue, please?"

"I'm thrilled at the invite—the guy's a law student—he's boring as shit. But, I've got something I need to ask him."

"What was that?"

"If the judge instructs the jury to disregard something, hasn't the jury still heard it?"

"What was his response?"

"He says—'we are learning this exact point in *Evidence.*' A light goes off in my head. It has never dimmed—not for thirty years. The moment marks the beginning of my understanding that law and psychology are interconnected."

"Deep."

"Smartass! I have a decision to make. Am I getting a *PhD* in psychology or am I going to law school? I choose law school."

"Good decision? Bad decision?"

"Mostly good. I finish law school and choose a career in civil law on the defense side. I practiced law for several years."

"The dark side? Shame, shame. I can't picture you as a defense lawyer."

"I was damned good at it, used it as a springboard to go to grad school, two of my best choices in life. I would make them again in a New York minute."

"So, now you're in grad school and working at a defense firm. What happens next?"

"Life gets in the way. I wanted to have a baby."

"What difference did that make? This is the 21st Century."

"I had already decided to begin a new career in trial consulting, but the baby wouldn't happen. I needed fertility treatments."

"I see . . ."

"No, you don't see. You're a man! Do I begin my new career or pursue three years of fertility treatments with only a *possibility* of having a kid? I make the trade, postpone the career change for three years of fertility hell. I'd make the same choice again. I've got a beautiful daughter."

"Mazel Tov. I love happy endings. How long have you been doing this jury consultant stuff?"

"Since 2018. I worked for another company, then started my own company in 2020."

"And before that?"

"As I said, I practiced law for several years."

"How difficult was the transition?"

"It was the realization of that connection between law and psychology I told you about—1991, blondish hair, remember?"

"I remember."

"After the baby was born, I went back to school and took a shitload of graduate courses in forensic psychology . . ." The conversation continued with Shari recounting her course work and experience working with attorneys, mediators, and judges. Zack was impressed, more than satisfied he was talking to the correct expert.

"Do I pass?" Shari wondered.

"With flying colors," Zack raved. "Let's talk specifics. You've read the file, there's a boatload of negative press and public opinion. There's a podcaster who's getting lots of traction and downloads. As things stand today, selecting an impartial jury would be near impossible. In addition, based on our telephone conversation, I like the idea of a mock jury—finding out what different witnesses, pieces of evidence, or other factors would do to change a juror's mind and turn a potential guilty verdict into a not guilty verdict."

"That's a lot to unpack. It is still early in the game. The trial could be a long way off. You have a massive pre-trial publicity problem. We need to create a mechanism to change public opinion," Shari advised.

Zack studied her. The wheels were turning. "So, we assemble a mock jury and test the evidence and their media-generated bias?"

"Not so fast, hotshot," she cautioned, continuing to mull things over.

"I don't want to appear rude, Shari, but I thought a mock trial was the whole reason you were coming on board. Have you forgotten what we discussed on the phone?" Zack grumbled, with growing impatience.

"Look, Mr. King of Justice, I don't get the big bucks by forgetting things. Upon further review, I've determined we are too early in the game for a mock jury. We can do that later. The tool your client needs now is a focus group," Shari advised.

"I can do without the sarcasm. 'King of Justice' is what others call me, not that I haven't embraced it for publicity reasons. I would appreciate you taking this seriously. Mock trial, focus group, aren't these just different terms for the same thing?" Zack seethed.

"No, frankly, they're not. Everyone makes that mistake. They use the terms interchangeably and they are quite different. A focus group is done very early in the game. The group determines whether you have a leg to stand on. In a civil case, for instance, a focus group is done before suit is filed. We seek to understand the attitudes and perceptions of the community about your client, the victim, the media's reporting on the case, that podcast you told me about, publicity in general, whether the public trusts the media or the criminal justice system, and many other issues. It is critically important, especially if we want to move to change venue at some point.

"Mocks come later, after the case is more developed, perhaps even after the investigation is complete. For a case like this, with your client and her husband's celebrity status, and the huge media spotlight shining on them and the case, we will probably have to do a focus group *and* a mock jury trial," Shari decided.

"Sounds like a plan, Madam Consultant. What do we have to do to set up a focus group?" Zack was calming, becoming more comfortable with the rhythm of the conversation.

"Did you bring your file?"

"The nuts-and-bolts version."

"Hand it over."

"What?"

"You heard me, mister, let me see the file."

Zack turned it over. "That's not everything, but you'll get the idea. Didn't you read what I sent you?" He was becoming annoyed again.

"I will need *everything*. I look at *everything*. For focus group and mock jury purposes, I don't just look at a file, I dissect the fucking thing!" She groused. Heads turned again, sneaking a peek at the foul-mouthed crazy lady dining with Zachary Blake.

Shari was oblivious, totally focused on the task in front of her. "After I digest the file, I will write a neutral script summarizing every issue in the case. Then, and only then, will I assemble a representative focus group. Twenty participants will be read those parts of the 'story' I choose to assemble. Throughout my presentation, there will be questionnaires—my quantitative data, so to speak. At the end of the presentation, I sit with the participants in a room and begin asking them questions.

"Broad questions, initially. I inquire about their perceptions of various generalities of the case, then burrow into the guts. I constantly change things up, asking a series of 'what if' questions: 'What if you knew X?' 'Would it make a difference if you knew Y?' We do a deep dive into the issues and their answers, plus the post Q & A discussion, will comprise my qualitative data.

"I am especially interested in hearing details about what members hear in the press and how it affects their perceptions. I'm also interested in where they get their news, which news media outlets do they consume? Are they *FOX News* or *MSNBC* people? This is classic, early-stage jury selection."

She studied Zack's face. It displayed little expression. *He must be terrific in front of a jury. Even better at a card table!* She assumed he was a bit overwhelmed, then she softened the pitch.

"Let's consider an example: Everyone hates your client. They've heard horrible things. They watch *FOX News*, something we must know for jury selection."

"Whoa! Can't we try another example? I don't care for that one," Zack joked.

Shari was nonplussed. "Fine. They all watch *CNN*, read the *New York Times*, don't like your client because of her right-wing reporting, but think it's a stretch that she murdered her husband. Even if she did kill him, they wonder what provoked her. This is *also* extremely valuable information.

"I gather all the data, evaluate and analyze all sets. If the data tells us to change the venue, we will move to change venue."

"We can move for a change of venue, but I doubt Judge Bolton would grant it," Zack predicted.

"We'll cross that bridge when we come to it. Unfortunately, in a case like this, venue changes are difficult because the whole state of Michigan—shit, the whole *country*—knows about this case and is dissecting it and your client. We must lay the groundwork, though, and determine what the data is saying. Capisce?"

"I like the approach. Where do we get the participants? The trial, if it ever happens, would be here in Oakland County. How do you go about finding like-minded focus group members?"

"My recruiter is an expert at this. Your file materials and other technical factors I won't bore you with, allow us to screen for a representative pool of participants who closely model the demographics of this county. We also screen out anyone with a law enforcement or social service background, because these people would likely be bumped from an actual trial jury. We screen out people who are friends, family, or close acquaintances of any of the participants. You'll get a feel for how we do what we do as the selection process moves along," Shari explained.

"You obviously know what you're doing, Shari. I'm very impressed. But you haven't told me how a focus group might begin to change public opinion. It is crucial that we begin to turn the public around to at least considering that Mia might be innocent or that the prosecution cannot prove her guilty beyond a reasonable doubt. How do we begin to do that?"

"Zack, Zack, Zack. You are looking at this all wrong. You are looking forward; you must look back. You can't control the data; give it up! Relinquish control and let the data speak to you. It will guide and direct what you must do next. Can we control what people think? Do either of us have that power? While no one can control what they think, we can *know* what they think. And I mean a deep dive into what they're thinking and why. Maybe they're embarrassed to admit how they really feel. Maybe they're uncomfortable with people knowing. Maybe we're dealing with *unconscious* thought. The group members may not even be aware they feel a certain way. But it won't matter! We will know their deepest, darkest feelings, Zack, because the data will tell us. The data will whisper to me. I'm the data-whisperer—I will elicit everything I need about what they think through this focus group. Then I can make decisions about how you will present your case and select your jurors.

"Do you understand? I don't tell anyone what to think, *yet.* My role is to uncover what they *already* think. Data mining will get you the best jury possible. After we've got them, we pump them with case information and argument, telling them what to think. This is called theme development. We are not there yet; the focus group is first. We must focus, Zack. Focus first. Do you feel me?"

"I feel you, Shari." Zack smirked. "Clever. But can you give me a sense of timing? When and how do we transition from focus group to mock jury?"

"Sure. As I've outlined, we focus first. We get to know what our representative participant sample thinks about your case. The victim. The client. Lorena . . . er . . . what's her name? Mia, right? Mia, a severed penis, or anything else I want to know. Whatever they are thinking about whatever important issue is on their mind. If they're thinking it, I will know about it. We'll get two sets of data to analyze—quantitative and qualitative. Then we begin to develop your themes and your story. As the investigation moves along and more information becomes known, we can begin to test it on our mock jury. Evidence may come and go. Motions to exclude or suppress may be filed and granted. We will test every piece of admissible evidence on this mock jury. Every drop of testimony, every document or exhibit, all forensic evidence, alternate theories and suspects. Everything that might be presented to the trial jury will be presented to the mock. We just have to wait out the exclusion or suppression process." She took a large gulp of Hoffa.

"Back to focus groups and the change in venue motion, Shari."

"Yes?"

"As I said before, I don't see Judge Bolton granting that motion. Even if she *did* entertain one, this case has national implications. I don't think a change of venue will make much difference in the court of public opinion. If a focus group won't do it, can you walk me through how we might use a mock jury or any other tool in your repertoire to change public opinion?"

"Don't get bogged down on venue changes. What the hell difference does it make? Everyone in the whole fucking country knows about this case!" Again, heads turned toward the animated, 'crazy lady' dining with Blake. Shari continued to be laser focused, oblivious to their stares.

"Venue considerations are just one example where focus groups come in handy. The goal of this exercise is to tap into the thought processes of our representative citizens. What are they thinking? I understand you are a hard-charging, full steam ahead kind of guy, Zachary Blake, but you must start thinking backwards, like I do. We must work backwards to enable the correct moves going forward. Understood?"

"Loud and clear," Zack retorted, subtly referring to her public outbursts in the otherwise quiet restaurant. The appetizer arrived; they took time out from the conversation to help themselves to a portion. Zack, the gentleman, deferred to the lady, as he was taught by his mother.

Shari was as amused as she was touched by the gesture. She took a bite of the artichoke dish and remarked, with her mouth full, "This is delicious."

A bit of sauce dribbled off her lower lip, down her chin. Zack gestured with his napkin, and she lifted hers, shrugged, and wiped her mouth clean. Zack smiled. *No wonder she likes Micah!*

They resorted to small talk until the main courses arrived. The portions were huge. Shari commented that they should have shared a meal. Then, she proceeded to eat everything on her plate. As they ate, Shari shared her story about how she transitioned from lawyer to trial consultant.

"I started working at a firm in the late 1990s. In the summer of 2001, I was defending a products liability case in the North Tower of the World Trade Center. I took depositions there every day. On September 10th, I dropped files off on the sixty-eighth floor, admired the view, and decided I was the luckiest person in the world. Apparently, I was. The next deposition was rescheduled for the 12th. Tomorrow is promised to no one, Zack, whether she's rich or poor, young or old. I decided to study human behavior. I left the firm for an in-house job, went back to school at night to study forensic psychology and juries. People, Zack, at the end of the day, I engage in the study of *people.* And I need to do this, man. You know what I mean? I need to study people. Have you ever had a calling?"

"Same as you, Shari. I didn't miss 9/11 by a day or anything so dramatic, but I had some down years, some *terrible* years. With the help of a remarkable woman and her two kids, I turned my life around. Today? I am doing what I was *born* to do. So I know exactly what you mean by a calling."

"Wow. You'll have to give me the details one of these days. So, Mr. King of Justice, what do you think? Are we going to do some business together?" She gazed into his eyes again, this time, with anticipation.

"Micah Love done good, Shari. And I think you were correct."

"About what?"

"This *is* the beginning of a beautiful friendship." He reached across the table and shook her hand.

She was touched by his words, and immediately changed the subject. "I don't come cheap, Blakey baby. Micah told you, right?"

"He told me."

"I am also very straightforward. I hate companies who tell you their prices depend on this or that, bait and switch. I use flat fee pricing for my focus groups and mock trials, and my billable rate is quite reasonable for my trial services, witness prep, voir dire, or theme reports. My prices are firm, but fair. I'm not cheap because, frankly, I'm worth the money." Shari pointed out the various fees, then handed him a price list.

"What about travel expenses, an extended stay in Detroit, that sort of thing?"

"It's all in there." She pointed at the price list.

They continued to chat. Shari declared the salmon "the best I've ever tasted. You were right about Detroit and Italian food."

Zack summoned a server and ordered coffee. He asked Shari if she liked Reese's Peanut Butter Cups.

She groaned and said, "I can't eat another bite of anything."

Try as he might, he could not persuade her to try the Reese's Peanut Butter Cup Cannoli, so, to Zack's utter dismay, they passed on dessert.

Shari had taken an Uber from downtown to the restaurant. Zack booked her a room at the Kingsley Inn, in Bloomfield Hills, near his home and office. He offered to drive her to the hotel. "It's on my way." She accepted only for that reason. At the hotel, Zack and a valet helped her with her bag. Zack extended his hand. She took it and thanked him for a lovely evening.

"What time's your flight tomorrow? Do you have airport transportation?"

"Am I hired? I thought I would stick around and get things rolling. Who knows when that poor girl will wake up? I'd like to get started on a focus group."

"You're hired, Shari," Zack assured her.

"Good. Where's your office?"

Zack turned and pointed to a huge mansion, across Woodward Avenue, a little south of the hotel. "It's right there."

"Holy shit, Zack! That's beautiful!"

"Wait until you see the inside."

"Where do you live?"

"About a mile south . . . that way." He pointed down Woodward Avenue. He turned and faced north. "See that little diner across the street? Micah and I are having breakfast there tomorrow. Care to join us? We can plot strategy, go to the office, and I will have Kristin, my office assistant, set you up."

"Sounds good. See you tomorrow, Zack."

"Tomorrow, Shari. Welcome to Team Mia Folger."

***

The bellhop escorted Shari to her room at the Kingsley Inn. Her tip was enough to make him reply, "Wow, thanks lady!" She bid him good evening, unpacked her clothes, undressed, and showered. As the water cascaded down her slender body, she revisited her day.

I got what I came for. This is the high-profile case of high-profile cases. I should be damned excited about the assignment. Am I? According to everyone I've talked to, I just landed the big fish in Detroit—a huge pay day, no question. And Blake? He's something, all right, but he's damned lucky Micah Love referred me. He and his client need me, desperately. So, yes, maybe I did land the big fish, but more importantly, the big fish landed me.

I'm sure Zack's a great lawyer, as great as he thinks he is, but lawyers are not wired to do anything but lawyering. The money will be nice, well-deserved, but still nice. Should be a boost for my career, especially outside of New York. In the final analysis, though, this is not about Zack Blake or Shari Belitz. This is about exonerating Mia Folger. She is damned lucky to have Zachary Blake and Shari Belitz on her team.

Zack Blake, the consummate gentleman, asked pointed questions. He obviously knows his way around the courtroom. His best attribute? His willingness to defer to my expertise. Sure, there will be pushback or controversy over this process or that strategy. But Blake will be an asset to the process. Damned lawyers, such an arrogant breed, nothing but a hindrance sometimes. I don't believe that will be the case with Blake. Yep, Mia Folger is lucky to have him in her corner. I'm going to enjoy this assignment. Besides, Zack is very easy on the eyes, the most gorgeous baby blues I've ever seen. Cute tush, too!

After a long day, Shari Belitz crawled into bed and was soon fast asleep.

***

Zachary Blake exited the shower, donned a pair of boxers, and crawled into bed with his wife. She looked beautiful and sexy in her lace nightgown.

"How did the meeting go, sweetheart?" Jennifer asked.

"It was good. Shari Belitz is crazy talented, maybe just plain crazy, too. I like her, but she's an acquired taste."

"How do you mean?"

"She's extremely confident, cocky almost."

"Sounds like someone else I know and love." She leaned over, kissed his cheek, and rested her head on his chest. He immediately began to scratch her back, a Zack-Jennifer tradition.

"The thought occurred to me. I see the comparison. She's used to being the boss, getting her way. She's quite brash about it. You can only have one boss, and that's me. At the end of the day, I've got to do what's right for my client. I'm concerned that we will lock horns . . ." Zack drifted.

"I suggest you stay in your lane and let her do her thing. She was brought in for her expertise. Don't stifle her creativity. Let her work her magic."

"Good advice. She's also loud, exuberant, outspoken, and foul-mouthed. She turned heads at Andiamo. Reminded me of Micah. We even had an 'eating habit' moment."

"She's overweight and eats too much, too fast? What does she look like?"

"Very attractive and slim, actually. Nothing like Micah. Nice figure. Kind of a Joan Rivers personality in a rather beautiful package. Remember Joan? 'Can we talk?'" He did his best Joan Rivers impression.

Jennifer laughed. "What was the food thing?"

"She spit pieces of an artichoke appetizer at me. Sauce dribbled down her chin. I must have asked her a question just when she took a nice-sized bite."

"That's your fault, not hers."

"True. She ate a lot more than you would have. That's probably what reminded me of Micah."

"But not as much as Micah! Please, say it isn't so!"

"No, nothing like that. She cleaned her plate. Probably her Jewish upbringing."

"She's beautiful and *Jewish*? Should I be worried?"

"No. I'm madly in love with my *shiksa*." He turned into her and reached out for a hug.

Jennifer pulled away. "I hate that word."

Zack was taken aback. "I'm sorry, sweetheart." He was genuinely contrite. "It just means 'Christian woman'."

"I know what it means, and I know you don't mean anything by it. But religion is something we don't have in common, and that word is a constant reminder."

"I'll be more careful." He meant what he said and reached out again. "Hug?" He pouted.

"You are such a baby. Come to mama." He quickly moved toward her, and they embraced.

"More?" he whispered in her ear, lightly outlining it with his tongue.

"I love you, Zack Blake. I hope you get everything you need from this Shari woman," Jennifer cooed.

"Who?" His lips and tongue wandered from her ear to her neck and headed south.

Jennifer turned and flicked off the lamp.

CHAPTER THIRTEEN

The search warrant turned up nothing new. The following morning, Eddie Schreiber and Jerry Kramer were viewing interior and exterior security video from the 5000 Town Center building at various angles and locations around the site. The veteran cops focused on the day before, the day of, and the day after the murder. A 40-piece Snack Pack of Tim Horton's Timbits sat open beside them, 15 donut holes left in the box.

Jerry fast-forwarded the early evening outdoor footage at the back of the building for the day of the murder. No one in, no one out, for hours. The men were bored out of their minds. As dawn approached and the screen lightened, what could only be labeled a shadow suddenly appeared on the outside camera at the utility door leading to the basement. The two men were half-asleep when the moment came, but Jerry cleared the cobwebs, leaped to his feet, and shouted: "What the fuck was that?" He rewound the video and hit pause at the precise spot where the image first appeared.

"W-what?" Eddie stirred, rubbing his face with both hands. He sat up, glared at the screen, then stood, walked over, and looked closer. "The shadow of a person?" He wondered out loud.

"It sure looks that way."

"Keep rolling."

Unfortunately, there was no sound. The video continued with no activity recorded. The shadow did not re-appear and a minute and a half later—Jerry timed it with the stopwatch feature on his cell phone—the video cut out.

"Rewind to that shadow and pause it again. Get Jim Sawyer up here," Eddie ordered.

"Will do, boss." Jerry raced to a landline, hit a couple of buttons, and said, "Jim Sawyer, please?"

Sawyer came on the line; Jerry told him what was going on and Jim agreed to come right over. Three minutes later, Sawyer entered the squad room.

"Let's see what you've got," he prompted.

"Can you tell me, based on the surroundings, the approximate size of that shadow?" Eddie wanted to know.

"Whoa! Great thinking, boss. Why didn't I think of that?" Jerry exclaimed.

"Because I'm paid the big bucks . . . not." Eddie groaned. "Jim?"

"I'm looking. A dumpster about four feet away . . . a garbage can . . . hmm, should be able to give you some measurements. Tell you what. Make a copy of this for me. I'll send a team to measure, and maybe, just maybe, I can get you an approximate size."

"That would be wonderful, Jim. This might be one more nail in the proverbial coffin. If the shadow is petite, that will confirm our murderer is a woman—hopefully a Mia Folger-sized woman. How soon should we expect your analysis?"

"Give me a day or two. Anything else?"

"That's it for now, unless you've got something for me?"

"Actually, I do. We've got foreign fiber, like from an overcoat. Not a large amount, but I cannot match the fiber to any clothing or coats belonging to the Crawford couple."

"Are you able to date it? It could be from a visitor six months earlier, no?"

"We are trying to narrow that down. I'm not sure we can date the fibers, but we'll sure try."

"Are there different materials between female overcoats and male overcoats?" Jerry inquired.

"My gut tells me that wool and cotton are wool and cotton, but I'll check it out. Anything else?"

"Not on our end," Eddie concluded.

"Okay, I've got some work to do. Catch you in a couple of days."

***

As Eddie Schreiber and Jerry Kramer were making their video discovery, Dr. Harold Rothenberg sat at Mia Folger's bedside. Her file and history revealed little. He skimmed the file. She'd never tried to commit suicide and had no history of violence, other than her experience with her father. Attending nurses indicated that there was no change in her condition. All efforts to communicate with her failed, and she made no observable effort to communicate with the nursing or medical staff. She remained still, withdrawn, catatonic. In fact, to prevent decubitus ulcers, the staff had to place Mia on a regular turning schedule.

She might have been considered permanently brain damaged, except there were two markers of conscious thought. One, her eyes took in her surroundings. While she refused to make eye contact, Mia's eyes remained open, and she reacted to things, like a tray falling to the ground or a medical alert announcement. She also dreamed. Rothenberg wished there was a way to probe her dreams, bring them to life somehow, because her most animated moments came when she was asleep. She tossed, turned, displayed grim facial expressions, and mumbled incoherently. Staff tried desperately to make out words, to no avail. Rothenberg assumed she was dreaming about her husband, finding him and observing, first-hand, how much he'd suffered. Or was her unconscious mind reliving the events of a murder she committed and for which she now had remorse? Rothenberg was all but certain she dreamt of the former, not the latter, but he could not escape a lingering scintilla of doubt.

He leaned toward her and whispered, "Mia?" She stirred slightly, with no other conscious reaction. He tried again. "Mia?" Nothing. He opened his file and began scribbling notes. He needed a more aggressive plan of attack. Or, since trial and conviction for murder was likely if she regained consciousness, maybe he should leave things the way they were. *No, my first responsibility is to her mental health, not her legal status.*

His predecessor's file was in disarray. The man had not kept careful notes. Likely concerned about patient confidentiality. Rothenberg's own time with Mia was too limited to truly understand the depth of her anger and guilt. He desperately wanted to help her, understand her torment, and her relationship with her husband. Did she love him? Hate him? Something in between? Had he not been murdered would their marriage have survived? *So many unanswered questions.*

He wrote down: *Murderer?* He contemplated the question and wrote: *No!!*

He wrote: *Victim?* Followed by: *More than likely.*

Rothenberg leaned forward, attempting to establish eye contact. Every time their eyes met, she tilted, ever so slightly. *Conscious eye-contact diversion?* He wrote.

"Hello, Mia," he whispered. He tried re-positioning his head, this way and that, in a vain attempt to force eye contact. Her eyes were clear—she was not being medicated.

"How are you this fine morning?" He chirped. She stared straight ahead, past his eyes, into his soul. He became slightly unnerved. *What is she thinking?*

Over their past few sessions together, Rothenberg had worked hard to obtain her trust.

"Do you trust me, Mia? I really need you to trust me. I'd like to help you, if you'd let me."

Mia continued to stare past his eyes.

"I talked to Zack Blake today. Remember Zack? I told you about him. He's your lawyer. He has contacted a jury consultant. They're going to assemble a focus group to see what's what. They will test for media bias, determine whether you can get a fair trial here in Oakland County. Apparently, this consultant is very good at what she does. This is good news, Mia. Mia?"

No reaction.

"I'm sure Zack and his jury consultant would love to talk with you, Mia, hear your side of the story, fill in the gaps. They could really use your help preparing for your defense. No one knows more about what happened than you do, right? Other than the murderer, of course. Who do you think murdered your husband, Mia?"

Mia stirred, grimaced, but continued to stare straight through Harold Rothenberg. Suddenly, Rothenberg noticed her eyes water; a single tear ran down the side of Mia Folger's face.

***

That same morning, Zachary Blake sat in a corner booth at Little Daddy's, awaiting the arrival of Micah Love and Shari Belitz. Zack offered to pick Shari up at the hotel, but she opted for her morning exercise regimen, a brisk walk down Woodward Avenue toward Birmingham. Their conversation took place 90 minutes earlier, so Zack expected her to wander into the diner at any moment. Micah was rarely late for a meeting when the meeting involved a free meal.

Zack heard a commotion at the front entrance, and the two of them walked in together, engaged in animated conversation, talking fast, gesturing with arms and hands, as well as rather loud, boisterous vocals. Zack smiled at the scene.

Shari wore a black Lululemon hoody with matching, tight-fitting leggings that sported a biker design at the knees. Her hair was pulled back into a ponytail. She wore little makeup, if any, and colorful designer sneakers. Zack could not help but notice how attractive she was, even dressed down considerably from the evening before.

Micah was Micah. He, too. wore some sort of jogging outfit in a vain attempt to hide his wide girth. The outfit hung loosely. His comb-over was blown to the wrong side; apparently, it was windy outside. He looked like a homeless dude, nothing like an ace multi-millionaire private detective.

They were enjoying each other's company, chatting from the front door to Zack's favorite corner booth at the back of the diner. As they approached the table, Norma walked over and asked everyone if they wanted coffee. All three accepted.

Micah and Shari sat down, continuing their conversation, ignoring Zack.

"I still don't understand what difference it makes. Who cares whether you call it 'focus group' or 'mock jury'? We are looking to gauge public opinion, no? Take the pulse of our citizens?" Micah shouted.

"Yes, Micah, but there are qualitative differences between the two, as I explained to Zack last night."

"Good morning, guys." He waved his hands in front of their faces to alert them that he was sitting right there. "That's right, Micah, she explained these differences last night at Andiamo. Where were you? It's not like you to miss a free meal," Zack kibitzed.

"You'll have to talk to Jessica about that," Micah sighed.

"Who's Jessica?" Shari was curious.

"His insatiable long-time girlfriend," Zack teased.

"Oh? Insatiable, huh? He does look a bit worn out," Shari quipped.

"Can we please change the subject? The woman is going to give me a heart attack," Micah gasped.

"Well, nice to see both of you this morning, too. Yes, I'm fine, thank you. I'm just your principal benefactor. Ignore me; go on with your conversation. Continue to pretend I'm not here," Zack grumbled. "And you can pay for your own breakfasts, thank you very much."

"Someone's feeling neglected. Did you wake up on the wrong side of the bed this morning, King?" Shari retorted.

"I asked you not to call me that," Zack snapped.

"Sorry, I forgot," Shari apologized.

"Ha!" Micah chortled. "Don't apologize, Shari! Stay on him! His massive ego can't stand someone dissing him!"

"I can take a joke, asshole," Zack groused.

"All evidence to the contrary," Shari observed. "Shall we talk business?"

"Let's." Zack longed for a change in subject. "So, what are our next steps?"

"You mentioned your office mini-courtroom. Were you serious?"

Zack opened his mouth to speak. Micah interrupted.

"As a heart attack, Shari. That thing is too cool. A full jury box, gallery, judge's bench, soundproof, great mikes and speakers—state of the art, baby," Micah rambled. Shari glanced at Zack.

"What he said," Zack sighed, rolling his eyes.

"So, I am setting up shop there?" She wondered out loud.

"I don't see why not. There is a small office behind the judge's bench—his or her chambers, so to speak. You can work out of the courtroom and that office."

"Sounds impressive. I've never seen a law office with full focus group/mock jury facilities. I've heard of some, but I've never actually seen or worked out of one," Shari marveled.

"Only the finest for the Blake firm," Micah ribbed.

"Cut the shit, Micah," Zack bristled.

"Ignore him, Zack. My best psychological advice is to not let a bully get your goat."

"He's hard to ignore. Like a blister on the bottom of your foot when you're jogging."

Shari laughed out loud. "Let's change the subject—focus groups. I've scoured the file you sent earlier, the materials you provided last night. and I summarized everything for my screener to give to my recruiter."

"When did you have time for all this?" Zack wondered. "I dropped you at the hotel around ten— you went for a walk ninety minutes ago. Did you get any sleep?"

"I woke up at four AM. I don't sleep much when I'm working. Too focused on the project."

"Impressive. Carry on," Zack encouraged.

"Thank you, kind sir." She handed both men a report.

Zack scanned the document. "What are we looking at?"

"This is a demographic census of what Oakland County residents look like. Remember, we want a representative sample, but in no way do demographics automatically translate to how a juror will determine their verdict. *Attitudes* and *worldviews* determine verdicts. That said, we must cultivate a proper sample: no law enforcement employees, no social service workers, nobody who has been involved in domestic violence. We don't want amputees or their family members, doctors, nurses, x-ray technicians, or anyone else associated with the medical profession."

"But we can't always keep those people off a jury," Zack reminded her.

"True, but let's table that for now. We don't want anyone related to any of the parties or prospective witnesses. Anyone who has a personal connection to these people? Out!" Shari exuberantly signaled with her thumb, like a baseball umpire. "My recruiter has a list, and we will effectively manage this process.

"As for the publicity aspects of the case, we can't exclude everyone who knows about the case, because *everyone* knows about the case! We *can*, however, screen out for *bias*, and I wrote up a series of questions to ask so that we can effectively screen out potentially biased jurors or focus group members.

"My recruiter will take about three weeks to properly screen; two, if I light a major fire under her ass."

"Light her fire," Zack quipped.

"When the recruiter completes her analysis, we will have a solid representative sampling of focus group participants. While she's engaged in this process, I will be writing up scripts and questionnaires. By the way, does that courtroom office have a window? I've got to have a windowed office."

"You will have a window," Zack assured.

"Wonderful. I could never be a criminal because I couldn't handle prison," she digressed. "Interior rooms make me dizzy. When I visit a client in prison, I get dizzy looking through the bars. So, no interior offices. I have my trusty laptop and the files you provided. I will need a large supply of post-it notes, a *shitload* of post-it notes, as a matter of fact."

"You shall have them, my queen," Zack schmoozed.

"My queen? I like that! I will need an assigned paralegal or assistant, preferably someone assigned to this project, full time. I run things lean—I don't need a large staff. Point me to the coffee room and I'll even get my own coffee, thank you very much. No *coffee-bitch*, please? I don't ask people to do anything I can do myself. If my computer malfunctions, I will need immediate access to your tech guy, an example of something I don't have a clue how to do. No co-workers and clients wandering in and out of the courtroom, wondering what's going on in there—no one bothering me, got it?"

"Got it." Zack saluted. "Aye-aye, ma'am."

"Ha! I like that respect! Keep it up, Blakey. If you guys come up with new evidence or investigation results, I want up-to-the-minute reports. New stuff might change everything, and I will need to incorporate new developments into the focus group. And no *coffee-bitch!* Did I already mention that? Any questions, gentlemen?"

"I'm good. Let's eat!" Micah rubbed his hands together in anticipation.

"Micah! Mia Folger is catatonic. She's being fed through a feeding tube. Get with the program!" Zack scolded.

"But I'm hungry, man!"

"Is he always like this?" Shari wondered.

"Unfortunately, yes. But after we feed the beast, he is remarkably effective and valuable, the best private investigator in America. If anyone can exonerate Mia through investigation, it's Micah Love. There are none finer than Micah and his staff."

"Gee, thanks Zack. Can we eat now?" Micah pressed.

"That's good to know. So, if I order in food, and Micah is in the building, I should . . ." Shari began.

"Hide! Run!" Zack bellowed. Patrons turned their heads and laughed.

"Funny, Blake! Real funny. Such a comedian. Regular Seinfeld," Micah growled.

"I thought it was rather funny, Micah," Shari cackled.

"*Et tu, Brute*? Don't forget who introduced you guys."

"I'm forever in your debt, Micah." She bowed and turned to Zack. "Will you feed this man, please? He's a growing boy." Shari put out both hands and began to slowly spread them wide, simultaneously puffing her cheeks.

"You're no better than him," Micah whined. He raised his hand and shouted: "Norma?"

CHAPTER FOURTEEN

Jim Sawyer came through. The 'shadow' was almost certainly a woman, approximately 5'4", perhaps 120, 130 lbs. She could easily be Mia Folger, or millions of other women, but only a few of whom had any connection to 5000 Town Center or Congressman Brad Crawford.

Eddie and Jerry coordinated with building security to identify and interview all women living at the residences or visiting the residences that day. They checked and cross-checked alibis and schedules. The results of several weeks of digging into these women were that only seven fit the dimensions of the now famous 'shadow'.

The two men were now in the process of interviewing those seven, and one more—Elyssa Naylor, whose body type was close to, but somewhat larger than, the body type Sawyer estimated. Jerry did a deep dive into Congressman Crawford's legislative assistant and uncovered some interesting information and theories. She was close to the congressman, vocal about her disdain for Mia Folger. It was prudent to interview Naylor. After multiple scheduling difficulties with the busy legislative assistant, an interview was finally set up.

Elyssa sauntered into the station with an enormous chip on her shoulder. She was well-built, with a muscular frame and a butch haircut shaved thin on the sides, wavy curls on top. Eddie and Jerry were on the fence as to whether she fit the profile.

"Why are you wasting time with me? You should be out there searching for clues, looking for more evidence to make sure that evil, crazy bitch never sees freedom."

Eddie and Jerry glanced at each other and sighed. Jerry began to Mirandize her.

"You have the right to remain silent . . ."

Naylor exploded. "Why are you reading me my rights? Do I need a lawyer? What the hell?"

"It's standard procedure, Ms. Naylor. You can agree not to talk to us."

Naylor calmed. "No, it's fine. Sorry. Just a bit jumpy. Dealing with Congressman Crawford's office situation, constituents, and other not-so-fun things. Making plans for his replacement has been extremely stressful. Ask your questions. I'll behave," she promised.

"Thank you." Jerry finished Mirandizing Elyssa; she declined counsel, and Jerry began the formal interrogation.

"Have you been interviewed by any other member of the Southfield Police?"

"No."

"Have you ever been a witness to a crime or been interrogated by the police for any reason?"

"Of course not," she huffed. "Except for a brief conversation with this guy." She pointed at Eddie.

"Do you understand this interview is being recorded?"

"I do *now*," she snarled.

"And do we have your permission to record the interview?"

"Do I have a choice?"

"Yes. As I indicated. You have the right to remain silent. You can refuse to talk to us."

"No, it's okay. I will have to do this sooner or later, right?"

"Right."

They went through all the preliminaries and Elyssa began to calm. She'd been working for Congressman Crawford for four years. Before that, she was a legislative assistant for the Democratic Congressional Caucus. She completed high school, attended a technological institute, and got a two-year administrative assistant/paralegal studies certificate. She planned to get a degree at one of the local universities, Wayne State or Oakland. She was very busy making the congressman look good—her words—and making sure he was always where he was supposed to be, when he was supposed to be there. She not only kept track of his schedule; she planned his events, optimized his brand, and handled all public inquiries. To hear her version of events, Crawford was the child and Naylor was the mother who packed his lunch and sent him off to school. Brad Crawford did nothing and scheduled nothing without Elyssa Naylor knowing about it.

"What was his schedule for the day of the murder, Ms. Naylor? Did he have any planned events?"

"I don't remember. I would have to check the calendar."

"Could you do that now, please?"

"Now? I don't have it with me."

"Weren't you asked to bring all pertinent records?"

"Yes, but I didn't know that included his calendar."

"What did you bring?"

"Nothing, really. I didn't understand what 'pertinent records' meant. The backup was his phone which, as you know, is missing."

"Did you call the station and ask what to bring?"

"No." She was now defensive.

"Can you give us a sense of the congressman's typical day?"

"Sure. His day usually started at seven-thirty in the morning. He would prepare rough drafts of bills he wanted to place into law. Sometimes he had committee meetings, debates, or scheduled votes. He had generous office hours for constituents to visit, by appointment and drop-in. He did a lot of arm-twisting, lobbying with fellow congressmen and our two U.S. Senators. He had a close relationship with Senator Stabler. Because a congressman only serves for two years before the next election, much of his time was spent prepping for re-election."

"For all of the activities you mentioned, which are you involved in?"

"All of them. As I indicated earlier, he didn't do much without me scheduling it or him running something by me for conflicts in scheduling."

"What about his personal life?"

"What about it?"

"Well, did he leave time for a personal life or was he a workaholic?"

"I'm not sure how to answer that."

"How about truthfully?"

"He made time for a personal life with his wife, if that's what you're asking. Whatever time he set aside, and he was a very busy man, was not enough for Mia."

"And you know this, how?"

"He vented . . . a lot! He was frustrated. He could not make her happy. She hated the late hours he kept."

"Working?"

"What kind of question is that? Of course, working. What else would there be?"

"Was he the type to step out on his wife from time-to-time?"

Elyssa paused, red-faced. *What do they know? Who have they talked to? Do they know about Brad and me?*

"I'm not sure what that means, Detective." She finally responded.

"Yes, you do, Ms. Naylor. Was the congressman having an affair?"

"How dare you! These are very personal, confidential questions," she seethed.

"Take it up with the brass. These are the questions I have, and I warn you, it is a crime to lie to the police."

She hesitated, fidgeted, and asked for a glass of water. Jerry poured her a glass from a pitcher on a coffee cart in the interrogation room. She took a gulp.

"Would you repeat the question?"

"Yes, was the congressman having an affair?"

"How the hell would I know?"

"You told me you kept his schedule. You said he did nothing without you knowing about it. I'm guessing you know about this. Remember what I said about lying."

Elyssa Naylor took another swig from the water glass. She turned away, inhaled and exhaled, visibly unhinged. "Yes," she finally gasped. "Yes! The congressman was having an affair. He was having problems in his marriage. His wife was angry all the time. He was keeping late hours. She kept falsely accusing him of having an affair. This was very stressful for him. Finally, he decided: 'If I'm going to be accused of it anyway, I might as well relieve some of this stress.'"

"He said that?" Jerry exclaimed.

"Heavens no, that's my take on the situation and what he was thinking at the time."

"When was this? What was the timeline between him expressing frustration and actually having an affair?"

"How would I know, Detective?"

"Do you really want me to ask, Ms. Naylor?"

Naylor burst out crying. "What do you want from me?" she exclaimed, sobbing.

"The truth, the whole truth, and nothing but the truth," Kramer replied, folding his arms across his chest.

"Why must you embarrass me like this? Will this interview be all over the press? There are leaks! Cops leak like sieves. You're worse than politicians!"

"We'll do our best to keep this out of the press, Ms. Naylor, but we need you to answer the question."

"What was the question?"

"What was the timeline between him expressing frustration about his marriage and having an affair?"

"About six months."

"And how do you know that his frustration was acted upon as you describe?"

"You seem to already know."

"I need to hear it from you, ma'am."

"Because he was having the affair with me!" she cried. The door was closed. The interrogation room windows were thick, but her anguished reply turned heads in the squad room.

"About those leaks, Ms. Naylor," Jerry bore in.

"Despicable," she spat.

"Like Mia Folger's texts being leaked to the press?"

"No. Not the same thing," she countered.

"Why not?"

"The texts were important evidence. The public needed to know."

"How do you suppose those texts got leaked to the press?"

"I just *told* you! It was probably you damn cops."

"What did we tell you about being truthful? Let's try this another way, shall we? How many people had access to Congressman Crawford's private cell phone?"

"I don't know. Lots of people. He got around."

"But how many people knew the password to open his texts?"

"The congressman, obviously. Me, and probably his wife. Why?"

"The congressman is dead; his wife is comatose. That leaves . . .?"

"Okay! Fine! It wasn't the cops. It was me! Happy now? I leaked them. So-frigging-what?"

"Why did you do that?"

"Because she's a *murderer*! You guys weren't charging Mia. I was frustrated. The public had a right to know! You *did* bring charges soon after," she rationalized.

"Do you know what happened to the congressman's phone?"

"No."

"Did you have access to Mia Folger's phone? Know her password?"

"Absolutely not!"

Jerry waited for her to calm. "Let's change the subject. How tall are you, Ms. Naylor?"

"What the hell difference does that make?" she shrieked.

"Simple question. Please answer it."

"Five, four."

"Weight?"

"Didn't your mother teach you to never ask a lady her weight?" She dabbed her eyes with a tissue.

"Yes, but this is important. I'm sure she'll forgive me."

"One-hundred-twenty-five pounds."

Within the parameters, Schreiber noted. *Works out—a bit ripped for the profile. Butch hairdo's not exactly right.* He noted the file. *Gay?*

"How long did this affair last?"

"We've been friends for a long time."

"Friends with benefits?"

"Two months before he died."

"Did you make plans?"

"What kind of plans?"

"The kind that involved him leaving his wife and shacking up with you!" Eddie exploded, interrupting Jerry's interview. Heads again turned in the squad room.

"No, nothing like that!" Elyssa blurted, sobbing again. "Why are you treating me like I'm the criminal?" she demanded.

"Are you?"

"Am I what?"

"Did Congressman Crawford tell you he loved his wife and wanted to end his affair with you?"

"Never!"

"What would you have done if he had told you that?"

"I would have tried to talk him out of it. That right-wing bitch didn't deserve a man like Brad."

"You hated *both* of them, didn't you? Brad told you they were getting back together."

"No, that never happened."

"You killed him and framed her for it, didn't you?"

"No, absolutely not. This interview is over."

"That is your prerogative, Ms. Naylor, but I only have one more question." Jerry waited. He enjoyed watching her squirm.

"Ask your question," she finally grumbled.

"Where were you on the morning of April 16, between the hours of eight and eleven AM?"

Elyssa Naylor retrieved her phone and stared at the screen. The device came to life. She hit a few buttons to pull up her calendar. "Eight and eleven you say?" She sniffled. "Brad was not coming in until later. I remember thinking how unusual for him to have nothing on the schedule. I went to the gym with three local office volunteers from seven-thirty until nine. We had breakfast at the Original House of Pancakes on Ten Mile Road, until ten. Appointments with constituents at ten-fifteen and eleven, finished at noon. Why?"

Jerry didn't answer her. "Sorry, I know I said that was the last question, but I have one more. I promise this will be the last question. Were you having sexual relations with anyone besides Congressman Crawford at the time of his death?"

"That's none of your fucking business!" she exploded. "I'm out of here." She rose, marched to the door and turned the knob. It was locked. She turned to the two detectives. "Unless I'm under arrest, open this fucking door and let me the fuck out of here! Any further questions can be directed to my lawyer!"

She crossed her arms and waited for one of them to do as she requested. Schreiber rose and slowly walked to the door, just to piss her off, glaring at Elyssa the entire trip. He pulled a key out of his pocket, opened the door, and stood aside. She brushed by him and stormed out of interrogation, into and out of the squad room. Those in attendance watched as she strutted across the high-gloss floor and out of the building. Everyone then stood and gave Eddie and Jerry a rousing standing ovation.

***

Eddie and Jerry spent the rest of the day checking out Elyssa Naylor's alibi. The veteran detectives were still fixated on Mia Folger as the murderer, but Elyssa Naylor was now a viable suspect. Either she was the murderer, or Zachary Blake could make her look like one. If they could not confirm the alibi, they would reconsider their original conclusion. Eddie was still troubled by Mia's reaction to her discovery of her husband's body. *Why would the murderer go into shock at seeing the body?*

Eddie didn't like the smug Naylor woman. He was silently wishing her alibi failed to check out. But it *did* check out. Elyssa's gym and breakfast companions, as well as her constituents, confirmed her whereabouts at the time of the murder. She could not have committed the crime. Mia Folger remained the number one suspect.

"Surprised?" Jerry asked.

"Not particularly. Disappointed is more like it. I don't care for the woman. You did a great job getting her to reveal her true colors. The unmitigated gall of the 'other woman' resenting the wife she's helping to cheat on. What a sanctimonious bitch!"

"Agreed. Thanks for the compliment, but she made it easy."

"Who's next on your potential witness list?"

"Couple of neighbors who fit the shadow profile."

"Will you be needing me? I'm not feeling too hot. I think I'm going to cut out early."

"No problem, my man. Have a good night. I've got this."

"Thanks for having my back, Jerry."

"Always."

CHAPTER

FIFTEEN

Following a flurry of activity surrounding the arrival of Shari Belitz and her takeover of the mini courtroom, the Blake law firm settled back into its normal routine. The firm was extremely successful, with clients constantly coming and going for new case interviews or deposition testimony, to complete interrogatories, or just to receive updates from their lawyers. Teams of paralegals were also in and out of the office in firm owned SUVs, making new client house calls and hospital visits. Civil trial lawyers with large caseloads ran back and forth to courtrooms all over the state of Michigan, returned to the office, and dumped large quantities of administrative and secretarial work on already busy staff members. File management, status and settlement conferences, motions, depositions, mediations, mandatory case evaluation summaries, and trials kept everyone swamped.

The new immigration department was a big hit; Marshall Mann and Amy Fowler more than pulled their weight. While they could not achieve big settlements or large verdicts like their brother and sister trial lawyers, they generated steady firm income, and immigration clients were excellent sources of new cases for the personal injury and civil practice. The place was humming, as Sandy Manning liked to say.

The only attorney in the office with the prerogative of handling whatever cases in whatever volume he wanted was Zachary Blake. Arguably, the most successful trial lawyer in the country, Blake's level of success permitted him to pick and choose his cases. The Mia Folger case made the firm no money. Worse, case expenses and the addition of Shari Belitz and her focus group team were costing a fortune. None of this mattered to Zack. If Harold Rothenberg felt, in his gut, that Mia Folger was innocent, then Mia Folger was innocent. Zack would devote time and money to proving Harold correct. And he wanted to do so regardless of whether Mia Folger ever regained full consciousness.

One key element to his client's pre-trial exoneration was Micah Love's investigation. The other was Zack's pre-trial advocacy, his ability to put pressure on the prosecution to honor its ethical responsibilities to turn over evidence in a timely manner. Zack was constantly in George Bruch's face, demanding test results, coroner reports, DNA evidence, crime scene investigator reports, photographs, witness lists, witness statements, and anything else the Southfield Police or the Oakland County Prosecutor's office developed. Bruch resisted, claiming the evidence was still being processed and would be turned over as soon as possible. Zack was forced to schedule a motion to compel discovery, a legal term for 'give me the damned evidence!' Zack knew he'd get nothing from Bruch until Bruch was ordered by Judge Bolton to release the evidence. He fully expected what is known as a document dump. Zack would win the motion; Bruch would rent a 16-foot U-Haul and have a driver dump thousands of files in the Blake firm's lobby.

Zack detested the gamesmanship. He was the type of lawyer who would honor a deal on a handshake or written on a napkin. A prosecutor's duty in criminal cases is different than the duty of the defense. The defense represents the best interests of the criminal defendant, guilty or not. If the defense team uncovers evidence of its client's guilt, it is not required to disclose the evidence to the prosecution. The defense cannot suborn perjury or knowingly permit a client to give false testimony, but it does not have to turn evidence of a client's guilt over to the prosecution. By contrast, it is the prosecution's job to promote and uncover the truth. If prosecutors discover evidence of a defendant's innocence, they are ethically and duty-bound to turn that evidence over to the defense. If the evidence proves a defendant's innocence, they are required to dismiss charges. The prosecution represents the 'People,' not the victims. The defense's only duty is to the person charged with a crime.

That morning, after the last of several contentious motions came before Judge Bolton regarding the development and availability of evidence, the usually patient judge finally blew her stack. She recognized bullshit when she saw it, and ordered Bruch to turn over all case materials, DNA results, fiber and blood results, documents, witness statements, and any other evidence compiled by the Southfield Police, 'forthwith'—right now. She also levied a fine of $2,500.00 against the prosecution and threatened to go to the Michigan Bar Association with a charge of prosecutorial misconduct. Bruch knew he would eventually be ordered to turn over the evidence, but he deliberately withheld it until ordered to do so by the judge. Why? Because dumping all the evidence at one time made it extremely difficult to sort through. It was time consuming and just plain annoying.

Bruch didn't care about the fine; the taxpayers would foot the bill. Zack found Bruch's ethics appalling but not surprising. While a document dump was challenging for the average firm, it was no challenge at all for the Blake firm. Zack unleashed an army of paralegals, law clerks, investigators, file clerks, and administrative staff, and assigned them to divide, conquer, sort, file, index, supplement, categorize, and, finally, produce detailed memoranda explaining it all. Everything was then neatly packaged and summarized for Shari Belitz's focus group and Micah Love's investigative teams.

George Bruch was a frequent flyer—he used the document dump strategy as often as possible. The only times he did not dump evidence was when the occasional judge or lawyer would not tolerate it and quickly put a stop to it. Zack didn't move to stop the misbehavior because he knew two important things about George Bruch. One, if George had to turn over an isolated exculpatory piece of evidence, evidence that might exonerate a defendant who George believed was guilty, the evidence might get 'accidently' destroyed or simply disappear. George would never let a silly thing like 'evidence' get in the way of a guilty verdict. Two, if there was any chance that George Bruch would turn over exculpatory evidence, it would be in a document dump, a needle in a haystack, a diamond buried in a pile of shit so deep that George was satisfied the defense would never locate it. Zack did not want to do anything to discourage the potential release of exculpatory evidence.

With a document dump, George assumed Zack and his team would be sifting through boxes of evidence for months. Perhaps Mia Folger would regain consciousness well before the Blake firm could make heads or tails of all the information. George was not the first prosecutor to employ this strategy against Zack Blake and his clients. He also wasn't the first prosecutor to underestimate the skill, determination, and resources of Zack, his professional and administrative staff, and retained experts like Shari Belitz. Zack, Micah, Shari, and their respective teams had the document dump indexed, analyzed and ready for the focus group in less than three weeks, or before the focus group was even assembled. And Micah Love's team was already working the investigative pieces of the puzzle, full tilt.

***

Shari Belitz wasn't shy. She took over the mini-courtroom and ran the focus group project as if she had been a member of Blake's staff for years. Zack made it easy for her, assigning one of his best paralegals to Shari's team full-time, while instructing other staff members to cater to Shari's every wish. The consultant never had it so good.

After the document dump, Shari's team poured through the evidence, assigned tasks, and went about the business of recruiting the focus group. Shari studied and summarized census data for her recruiter, Lauren Conrad, so that Lauren would have an accurate representation of juror demographics for Oakland County, Michigan. Lauren reviewed Shari's findings, and the two consultants compiled a list of potential names for service on the focus group. Any person who knew a party, the victim, the defendant, witnesses, or any member of this grouping was screened out. Likewise, anyone with ties to the law enforcement community, violent crime victims, victims of domestic abuse, or anyone who had formed a definitive opinion from media reports were also cut from the list. Shari and Lauren identified and eliminated people who worked in the media or the legal, medical, and mental health professions. It was Lauren's job to identify questionable candidates and bring them to Shari's attention.

"We've got a twenty-three-year-old true crime fanatic who's a criminal justice major at Madonna College. She really wants to be a part of the focus group, thinks it's good training for her career."

"Dump her ass," Shari ruled.

"Twenty-six-year-old grad student at University of Detroit. He's getting a masters in ethical and social responsibility."

"What the hell does that mean?"

"I'm not sure."

"Is it related to social work or psychology?"

"Again, not sure."

"Dump him. It's got to be related to one or the other."

"We've got a fifty-five-year-old finance guy who lost two fingers in a fireworks accident when he was a teenager."

"Out." Shari signaled with her thumb. "I should have mentioned that during the selection criteria process. We can't have amputees in this case, the guy was 'Bobbitted', remember?"

"Shit, of course! This guy's history—the no-amputee criteria will exclude a couple of other candidates, too," Lauren advised. "What about people who have suffered cuts or other serious injuries?"

"Not sure. I guess it depends on the injury and the circumstances. Let's see how many candidates are left standing at the end. If we have enough without people who fit that profile, let's eliminate them. I would rather err on the side of elimination than acceptance."

"Aye-aye, captain."

"Funny. If this were the service, I'd be a general, wouldn't I?"

"That would be Blake."

"Not on this project, it wouldn't. Zack delegated the whole exercise to us."

"So, in the chain of command, he's a four-star and you're, maybe, a two-star?"

"That's somewhat better, I guess. Moved up in rank quite quickly," Shari laughed.

The process continued. Lauren, who'd been working for Shari forever, had her complete trust. Still, Lauren's military background compelled her to respect the chain of command. Back and forth they went, eliminating or accepting potential candidates, qualifying or disqualifying them for this reason or that. Like George W. Bush, Shari was the ultimate 'decider'. At one point in the exercise, Shari decided there were too many millennials on the accepted list.

"We need more Gen Xers," she concluded. "Millennials don't remember Lorena Bobbitt. We need people in their fifties who remember the case. The media is making the comparison. We need to flesh this out. Get me some middle-aged or older people. The country has plenty, doesn't it? Are they all in Florida or something? Why are there so many millennials?"

When the number of acceptable candidates reached fifty, Shari addressed the group.

"Thank you for your interest in our focus group. I am an opinion researcher. The reason we recruited you for this exercise is to discuss and obtain your opinion regarding an incident that's been covered by most of the major news networks, one that occurred right here in Oakland County. The incident may be quite familiar to you; it may not be at all familiar to you.

"We're going to ask a lot of questions. Some may be very general. Some may be very specific. I may decide to probe a particular news item, something you've heard in the media, and ask what your thoughts are as they relate to that news item—maybe in accordance with a fact pattern I provide. If you've had a particular response to the item when you originally heard it, would this alternate fact pattern change your response or solidify it? Understand?" The group members nodded in acknowledgement.

"You have signed a confidentiality agreement. Everything we discuss must be kept strictly confidential. Please feel free to ask questions or answer questions posed to you. There are no stupid answers to questions or questions to answer. This is not the place to be shy. Your opinions, in fact, *everything* you volunteer will be helpful to us, one way or another. One more thing to note. Our primary focus is to see that justice is done. The fair administration of justice is a serious matter. You are to be commended for doing your part and volunteering for this exercise. Thanks again for being here."

***

The murderer was as frustrated as she was livid. The two lead detectives ran around taking witness statements from inconsequential people. *Idiots! I handed you this case on a silver platter. Concentrate on MIA, damn you, her motives and moods! She texted her intent—it is logical she acted upon it, isn't it? Like that podcaster said: SLAM DUNK!*

God, I wish this was over. I must move on. Back to life as it was before it happened. Move on to new opportunities now that he's gone. Get back together. If something happened to Mia, if she suddenly croaked of, say, 'natural causes', would the cops conclude their investigation? Something to think about. How would I get to her? Too risky? The thought is invigorating!

Crime scene techs found the murder weapon, as planned. The crime lab identified one set of fingerprints on the knife, belonging to Mia Folger. The cops had her texts, exhibit number *one* on the issue of motive. Witnesses were being shuttled in and out of the squad room or visited at their homes. *Does anyone consider me a person of interest?* Perhaps it was time for another bold move.

She couldn't appreciate her level of callousness, or bizarre sense of entitlement when completing the dastardly deed. To her, Brad Crawford was in her way, Mia Folger was a convenient mark. *Serves them both right!* was her prevalent thought process. She was initially nervous about crossing the line from model citizen to murderer. Would she be up to the task? Once she planned and carried out the premeditated murder of Brad Crawford, however, she felt damned powerful, exhilarated. She was shocked, validated, and relieved by how easy it was to dispense of him. She felt anxiety, sure, but more related to her fear of getting caught and spending the remainder of her life in prison.

The murder was righteous, intoxicating, like getting high, or having the best sex of her life. It was a rush to watch Crawford suffer, bleed, desperately cling to life. She reveled in the process, watched him grow weaker as blood oozed from his body, celebrated his last breath. She enjoyed the control, the agony and timing of his death, his pleas for mercy, those final moments when he convulsed involuntarily as death overtook his consciousness. Her feelings were borderline orgasmic.

The murderer was more than a woman scorned, she was unremorseful, someone who had removed a minor annoyance, like a mom backing out of the garage who first had to move her kid's bike out of the way. She couldn't care less that Brad Crawford was someone's husband, son, brother, or friend. There were no nightmares about the event, only peaceful dreams of a more pleasant future, with that stubborn obstacle removed from 'behind her car'. She felt no pain, disappointment, sadness, self-loathing, or guilt. She was a pure psychopath and, so far, most importantly, she remained invisible.

CHAPTER
SIXTEEN

According to Shari Belitiz, a focus group consists of several people, possessing certain characteristics, assembled for the purpose of providing qualitative data in a focused discussion.

When Shari Belitz defined a focus group, all Zack heard was 'jury'. This definition, Zack concluded, effectively described his ultimate focus group, a trial jury. Through the voir dire process, Zack rationalized, a jury is assembled to evaluate the quality of evidence applying to a civil plaintiff or defendant, or a criminal defendant or prosecutor. Shari's focus group was far more informal than an actual jury trial, or even a mock jury, but all three served the same purpose—to evaluate the facts and circumstances surrounding the case and come to a conclusion.

Until the 1930's, the type of research and analysis employed by social science researchers like Shari Belitz was focused upon a single subject, using closed-ended questioning. Psychologists began to worry that this method resulted in skewed data. What makes perfect sense to this person, makes absolutely no sense to that one. Researchers began to realize that a qualitative grouping of representative citizens answering open-ended questions permitted subjects to apply reason, elaborate, and explain their thought processes. This shift in research technique was the beginning of what is today referred to as a focus group.

In the beginning, these focus groups were used to study motivation and morale of the military during World War II. After the war, researchers began to use these research techniques in marketing fields. Gradually, researchers realized that focus group concepts translated quite well in helping lawyers select juries or evaluate potential courtroom strategies and arguments.

Shari's main purpose in assembling what was now a 20-person focus group was to evaluate whether people in Oakland County had sufficient bias to make a change of venue appropriate. In addition, Zack was not yet certain whether the eventual circuit court trial judge would permit him to conduct his own voir dire. Or, if a judge decided to conduct his or her own voir dire, was that jurist open to the broad use of strategic questions to root out potential jury bias?

If Mia Folger regained consciousness and was put on trial for murder, Zack and Shari both wanted to develop questions, for focus group purposes and for future voir dire, that revealed whether a prospective juror was an asset or a liability. In other words, should Zack keep or strike that juror? What were the main weaknesses of Mia's case? If reframed, would these weaknesses be less damaging? Shari was confident that the focus group she and Lauren assembled would provide Zack with solid intel as to how a cross-section of Oakland County citizens would respond to these vital questions and more.

She avoided using pure demographic models, even though they were highly predictive to an expert of her skill. She knew, however, that these models were useful in venues where courts severely limited voir dire to questions like the type of work a prospective juror did, whether he or she knew parties or witnesses, or, too broadly, whether he or she could remain impartial. Shari brilliantly combined demographics and stereotypes to create her selection criteria. She was confident that she would be able to provide Zack with the information he needed to give Mia Folger the best possible defense from the beginning, jury selection, to the end, closing argument and verdict.

Shari worked closely with Zack to develop what she called a 'unifying theme'. Because defense lawyers have multiple opportunities to influence a jury, theme development was quite important. Shari explained that focus groups were great tools to help identify themes that would resonate with a broad cross-section of Oakland County citizens. As such, the two professionals discussed using the focus group to test language and compelling, consistent themes for use in his opening statement, direct and cross-examination of witnesses, and closing argument. Shari was also fond of the strategy of utilizing catch phrases to hammer home central themes. Johnnie Cochran's famous "if it doesn't fit, you must acquit" line in the O.J. Simpson case was the ultimate example of a 'sound bite' or 'catch phrase'. Shari encouraged Zack to think about such phrases in Mia's case, especially as it related to her shock at seeing her husband's bloody corpse. "A guilty woman does not go into shock at the sight of her victim's corpse," she insisted.

Perhaps the most important function of the focus group would be to help determine how different socio-economic or cultural groups in the county viewed the case. Would a person's life experience skew potential case results? Mia and Brad Crawford were a high-profile, wealthy couple. Would citizens of different races, religions, or economic circumstances decide the case differently? Shari promised that the focus group would help shake out these uncertainties, as well as reveal preexisting biases and prejudices in those groups. This is the reason Shari wanted more Gen Xers on the focus group. A more diverse group would not only weed out cultural and economic bias, but biases related to personal responsibility, or hostility toward the legal system or accused criminals.

The focus group was also a great place to test the evidence and discover the strengths and weaknesses of the case. If, for instance, a focus group member had an intense reaction to the murderer severing the victim's penis, the focus group format would help probe the reasons for the reaction and help develop alternate viewpoints or methods of delivering the facts to assuage the member's negativity. Conversely, Shari considered Mia's catatonic state and reaction to discovering her husband's body as overwhelming evidence of her innocence. The focus group would help develop presentation methods, language, and theories to make the impact of this argument as effective as possible. Shari could also test the flow of the evidence, whether there were confusing elements of proof or gaps in the presentation.

On the evening before the focus group was to begin its work, Shari Belitz and Zachary Blake met for dinner at Pita Café in Birmingham. Shari called for a meeting to update Zack on the progress made by her and her team, the timetable, and the many issues and themes the group would be asked to consider.

"We have a diverse representative group, Zack. Lauren did a great job recruiting them, and I culled this group very carefully. We will dissect this case and its unique issues. I am certain this group will yield very helpful information for use when or if you are required to try this case," Shari reported.

"Good to hear, Shari. Everyone in the office has been impressed with your team. We see how hard you guys are working. As firm head honcho, I want you to know how much I appreciate the effort."

"Thank me when your client is exonerated."

"Amen, sister."

"As of now, the group will meet from eight AM to five PM daily, with a few small bathroom and refreshment breaks and a one-hour lunch break. Please clear your calendar; we will record the discussions, and it is imperative that you watch the entire thing. Your role is limited, but watching it live will allow you to pose questions.

"I'll devote the first day to pre-trial publicity. 'Who knows what from where? Does it influence your opinions and possible decisions?' 'How much coverage have you seen and from what news sources?' I'll also ask about Lorena Bobbitt to see who remembers the infamous case. Do those who remember the case remember details? Are they tainted as compared with those too young to remember?

"Since it's very early in the process, I plan to present the group different pieces of the case and have them answer questions, category by category. I'll change things up during the questioning, give them a fact pattern, then ask: 'What if you knew X?' 'Would it change your opinion of Y?'"

"You like those 'X-Y' questions, don't you?" Zack kibitzed.

"Someday, you will learn to appreciate my 'X-Y' questions, smartass," Shari countered. "Would you prefer calling them 'what if' questions? What if there is an alibi?"

"I'm working on that."

"I know you are. I'm rather certain the focus group would react very positively to that news. What if there is an alternative suspect? What if Crawford repeatedly beat Mia prior to his murder? What if this turns out to be a case of self-defense? Develop your theories, my friend."

"I will. I see your point."

"The first questions, though, even before 'what if' scenarios, will be the bias and media influence questions. After we've established an effective roadmap, which this process is intended to do, we can use this same group to prepare Harold Rothenberg and other expert witnesses, adverse witnesses like the cops, the Naylor woman, and other lay witnesses. The possibilities to test the various aspects of your case are virtually endless."

"I'm beginning to understand, Shari. This stuff is amazing. It's hard for me to look forward to any important trial and not consider the use of your service."

"Except that there has to be an economic reality test. Not every case can afford or requires this level of support."

"True, but it will be difficult to pick and choose going forward."

"Thanks, I think . . . that's a compliment, right?"

"Absolutely. What case would not benefit from a pre-trial test of all elements?"

"When you put it that way, it is hard to disagree."

"So, talk to me. Mia's *misfortune* seems to be our *good fortune.* Time is on our side, for now. What's the timetable, and what other parts of our case can we test?"

"Aside from rooting out pre-trial bias and prejudice, developing themes, and testing evidence, we can also use the group to prep witnesses and determine how their testimony will be perceived by a jury. This will allow us to tweak the testimony."

"Suborn perjury?"

"Not at all. Maybe a witness conveys unusual non-verbal signals—an annoying voice inflection, body movement, or mannerism that can be altered. Maybe outward appearances need work. Maybe we need to have a witness look jurors in the eye. We don't *have* to do a thing; we certainly don't want to pound a witness into submission. But the focus group can identify these quirks. Whether or not you wish to massage or eliminate these will be your prerogative."

"Makes perfect sense. What else?"

"We can develop trial strategy, test the order of proofs, the strength and weaknesses of the presentation, issues and evidence that resonate in positive and negative ways. We can also test any demonstrative evidence you may want to admit—timelines, photographs, video, those awful text messages, other text messages that may minimize the bad ones, voice recordings—you name it, we can test it. The idea is to determine how to present all of this in the best possible light favorable to the defense."

"And when you're done, you will try the case for me, too?" Zack quipped.

"Ha! My trial days are over, mister. But I would be happy to be part of the trial team if you want me there," she offered.

"You've earned your seat at the table. I would be honored to have you there."

"Thank you, kind sir." Shari bowed her head and continued, "Much later in the process, if you're willing, we can use the group to hone your trial prep. You can try out your opening, voir dire and closing, the manner or order in which you present exhibits and other evidence."

"Remember our dinner at Andiamo?" Zack recalled.

"Delicious. Detroit has the best Italian food, better than New York," Shari sighed.

"No, no, that's not why I brought it up. This kind of feels like that did, where I felt you were sizing me up, psychoanalyzing me."

"I was."

"I know. Having a focus group analyzing my every move pre-trial—I don't know that I love that idea."

"I offer the service to produce improved trial results. You have the right to take or leave the advice. You're the boss; you're paying the bill, your choice. I highly recommend you get over it, though. Focus groups have been very effective in these situations."

"I'll consider it. What else?"

"One last thing. You've been very quiet out there. Rumor has it that Zachary Blake *loves* the media and will typically win reporters over to his side. Consider this: A focus group may be used to test your public relations strategy. Want to announce the possibility of an alternate suspect? Test the news on the focus group. Will the news help or hurt your client? If it's not a net positive with the focus group, you may not want to call that press conference. Get my drift?"

"Absolutely. I love this stuff. Where have you been all my life?" He smiled.

"Like I said when we first spoke: What took you so long?"

"One last question. We are going to be disclosing a great deal of privileged information to these folks. Is this protected by attorney-client privilege?"

"Great question! Grey area—I'm not positive. That's one reason why each member signs a confidentiality agreement. If the other side finds out you've assembled a focus group, goes to the judge, and the judge orders release of the group's records . . ." She left it there, allowing her words to sink in.

"I would fight the release all the way to the Supreme Court and win," he blustered.

"I like that macho, blowhard attitude. By the way, I *agree* with you. Focus groups are part of trial prep, part of your client's confidential files, and you should have the right to assert the privilege. Anything else you want to discuss?"

"Yeah, I'm starving. Let's order."

"Detroit has the best mid-eastern food, too? Better than NYC?"

"Can't say for sure, but this place is great."

The rest of the evening was spent eating, discussing Detroit and New York cuisine, Zack, Jennifer and Shari's favorite Broadway shows, and what it was like to practice law and jury consult in America's busiest city. For a couple of hours, they enjoyed each other's company, and the looming trial was temporarily forgotten.

CHAPTER SEVENTEEN

Micah Love began his investigation by taking a deep dive into the social media and Internet worlds of Congressman Bradley Crawford and Mia Folger. The former subject was more difficult, because Crawford was a public official, thus the recipient of classified information. For all things cyber, electronic or on-line communication, Micah's office guru was Reed Spencer. Reed, an ex-con, once served seven years of a ten-year sentence for cyber-fraud. His specialty, back in his criminal days, was stealing the identities of the rich and famous and using them for his own economic gain. His own arrogance caused the demise of a lucrative criminal empire. He was captured after creating a password that included his dog's name and the numbers 1-2-3. He was convicted of hacking into the American Express black card database, extracting account information, selling accounts to other criminals, or using the higher limit accounts to buy hundreds of thousands of dollars in goods and services. He served his seven and was released for good behavior.

Reed left prison a bitter man. His own stupidity cut down a well-conceived, extravagant life of crime while he was still in his prime years. After his release on parole, locals in Detroit area law enforcement and the FBI recruited Reed to help investigate and capture cyber-criminals.

In Reed's professional opinion, cops and feds were stupid, knew little about cyber, and were unworthy of his expertise and assistance. Instead, he accepted a position with Love Investigations, Micah Love's company, as head of the firm's newly established cyber-crime division. Reed relished all opportunities to make police forces look foolish.

Because of his intense hatred for the men and women in blue, Reed was thrilled when Micah came to him with the Mia Folger case. The cops were relying heavily upon Mia's text messages in trying to prove her guilt. These lazy assholes believed the texts overwhelmingly demonstrated motive; prints on the murder weapon demonstrated participation in the murder. Had they done a deep dive into *all* the Internet accounts of *all* the parties and key witnesses? He was reasonably certain that the cops had not done so, even more certain they ignored the accounts of other potential suspects like Elyssa Naylor.

Police investigators are limited to investigating Internet abuses by legal means, another solid reason why Reed had no desire to work for them. The inability to access online intelligence rapidly and without detection, is a huge barrier to local police or federal law enforcement cyber investigations. Access to this type of information is crucial to exposing cyber-criminals who use electronic means to engage in criminal activity. Identity theft, Reed's old stomping grounds, or other crimes like drug and gun sales, as well as sex trafficking, are prime examples.

The Computer Fraud and Abuse Act is law enforcement's main computer crime statute. It was last revised about 10 years ago, and severely hampers discovering, investigating, charging, and arresting cyber-criminals. Reed was under no such statutory restriction, at least in terms of proving Mia's innocence. If Zack wanted evidence he could present in a jury trial, that was a whole different matter. In court, the evidence had to be admissible—it had to have come via legal means and could not be the so-called 'fruit of the poisonous tree'.

Reed decided to take dual paths—one kosher, one not-so-kosher. If he discovered something using illegal methods, he would double back and re-investigate using legal means and methods. He correctly calculated that neither the judge nor the prosecutor had the requisite expertise or inclination to discover questionable, parallel paths.

Cyber-investigation was a daunting task. Almost everyone uses the Internet, one way or the other. Thus, the sheer volume of information to sort through was mind-boggling. Americans have frequent contact with some type of digital device in almost every facet of life. However, this digital habit can also be a blessing for investigators—we believe our interactions are private. *Law enforcement will be too busy to notice, won't they? Won't the sheer volume of information on-line camouflage our innocuous criminal behavior?* That was Reed Spencer's secret sauce—his sweet spot, so to speak. He relished finding illegal needles in multiple legal haystacks.

Micah instructed Reed to begin his investigation into Mia Folger and Brad Crawford, but Reed quicky added Elyssa Naylor to his to-do list. None of the three ever worked in technological fields; none had criminal records. Thus, it was fair to assume that misbehavior, if any existed, would be found in on-line user personal or business computers, tablets, or cell phones. Reed knew that automobile navigation systems, video game consoles, and other networked devices might contain vital data, but he decided to put those on the back burner until the others bore enough fruit to prompt a broader technical investigation. The auto navigation system, for example, would be vital in tracking a suspect's movement, once Reed established that person as a suspect using more conventional cyber tools.

Reed paused to consider when any of his three subjects might have made use of the dark web, which provides greater, almost total anonymity for conducting crime. Hacking, drug or human trafficking, pornography, data breaches, or hate crimes flourish on the dark web. The good news for Reed, and especially for law enforcement officials, is that the sheer volume of criminal activity on-line made it necessary for officials to create user-friendly tools to safely navigate the web to identify crime and criminals, especially unsophisticated cyber-criminals. Reed began with the presumption that Mia Folger was not guilty. Someone set her up. The level of sophistication and planning required for the set up caused Reed to decide to begin his investigation using the dark and deep webs.

At its core, the Internet is a large collection of data. Reed knew the web contained levels or layers, all of which differed in the types of possible criminal activity, and in the way an investigator might access that activity. Want to improve your golf game? Watch a YouTube video. Want information on a business or industry? Google the industry or business. What Reed was looking for, however, was the huge amount of information on-line that cannot be discovered using conventional search engines. While every layer of web content is relevant to an investigator, not all content is easily discoverable or legal to access.

Since his investigation was primarily focused on email and text communication, Reed decided to skip the surface web—the layer that billions of people navigate daily, all data publicly available and indexed on the web. If you can find it on Google, it is considered 'open'. But the surface or open web comprises only ten percent of all web content. The surface web is fair game for investigators. Public or private investigators may utilize the open web to find any content relevant to their investigation, legal or illegal, without a warrant. If police are engaged with an active shooter, for instance, they may access public social media sites to pull up offensive posts, maps of the location, or evidence of planning. Thus, Reed's only interest in perusing the open web was to access and closely examine his subject's social media accounts. Perhaps he could track intent, whereabouts, relationships, or other valuable personal information from social media interactions.

The so-called 'deep web' consists of non-indexed pages and contains almost ninety percent of all web content. Two examples of this type of private, password protected information, are texts and emails. There are also discussion sites for those offering to engage in criminal behavior for a fee, and those seeking to employ their services. Reed intended to search unindexed adult classified ads to see if Elyssa Naylor, for instance, sought the services of a hit man to end the life of Brad Crawford.

The anonymous version of the deep web is the 'dark web'. It is used, almost exclusively, to conduct illegal activity in total anonymity, except to highly skilled investigators like Reed Spencer. If you planned it or shopped it on the Internet, Reed Spencer will find it and you, even when you use the *TOR* network. One prime example of this skill was found in Reed's work on another Zachary Blake case—the trial of Jack Dylan, a Dearborn cop falsely accused of murder—and was instrumental in freeing Dylan. Reed liked Dylan, the lone exception to his "I hate cops" philosophy.

TOR browsers route internet traffic through so many random servers, it makes them nearly impossible to track the origin unless you have the skill of a Reed Spencer. Reed liked to use the library analogy in explaining these concepts to Micah and Zack. The open web is the library—alphabetized, using the Dewey Decimal System, professional shelving, and a librarian to help you navigate. With the dark web, the shelves are turned over, the labeling is removed, and the investigator's job is to find the book he's looking for somewhere in the mess on the floor. And while the good guys are looking for that book, the writer or publisher might publish and release a new edition.

Seeking information on the deep or dark webs was not only difficult and time-consuming, it was also potentially dangerous. Reed was a professional. Unlike a novice, he did not have to worry about potential traumatic content, but he *did* have to worry about his own safety. When you are tracking people or information on the deep or dark web, evil, dangerous criminals may be tracking you.

Here again, Reed had to begrudgingly acknowledge the assistance of law enforcement. As criminal activity increased on the dark web, law enforcement officials had to find or develop efficient and safe tools to conduct searches and navigation. The law enforcement community teamed with private technology companies to develop methods of searching for and discovering relevant information on the deep and dark webs. Because Reed worked for a multi-millionaire investigator with tremendous contacts in the law enforcement community, this state-of-the-art technology and a team of tech investigators were accessible and purchased by the unflappable Micah Love.

First, Reed purchased and installed a virtual private network or *VPN.* Then, he navigated to the *TOR* project and installed *TOR*, without maximizing the browser on his screen. He used a website called Darknet Live to locate relevant websites and links and purchased a dedicated, secure email account to register on dark web sites, markets, and forums that required login information. He utilized the email service's random username and password generators to create his handle. He was now ready to search the dark web.

***

Dr. Harold Rothenberg walked into Mia Folger's room, a regular stop on his morning rounds. Nurse Rosenthal was with her, stroking her arm, speaking in a low, soothing voice. Mia was asleep but demonstrating visible signs of having a nightmare. Cheryl was trying her best to calm her without administering medication. Rothenberg stopped at the door and took in the scene.

"Mia, calm down, honey. It's only a dream."

Mia's face contorted. Her cheeks rose. She crinkled her nose and furrowed her brow. Her face registered only one emotion; pain.

"Mia, wake up. You've been sleeping almost fourteen hours." She gently shook Mia's arm.

Mia groaned and continued to contort her face. "No," she suddenly uttered, clear as day. "Brad?" In the form of a question.

Cheryl turned toward the door and saw Rothenberg standing there. Rothenberg motioned with his hands, encouraging Cheryl to continue the conversation.

"He's gone, honey. But we can talk about him, if you'd like," Cheryl prompted.

"Gone?" Mia moaned.

"Yes, Mia. Brad passed away. You remember, don't you?"

"Passed away . . ." Mia murmured, drifting off. Rothenberg noted two words, 'conversation' and 'comprehension' and encouraged Cheryl to continue.

"He's dead, Mia. You remember. He was murdered." Rothenberg shuddered. He would not have taken the conversation in this direction. *Will she withdraw?*

"Murdered . . . blood . . . everywhere . . . terrible," Mia groaned in agony, tossing, turning, her face contorted. Suddenly, she stopped moving. She lay on her back, eyes wide open, staring up at the ceiling.

"Mia?" Cheryl inquired.

No answer.

"Mia, honey?"

No answer, no movement.

"Mia?" Rothenberg chimed. "It's Dr. Rothenberg. Wake up, Mia." Would a new voice prompt a continuation of the discussion?

No answer. Mia Folger retreated into a catatonic state.

CHAPTER EIGHTEEN

Shari Belitz convened day one of the focus group and, again, addressed the entire group.

"We will begin today by reviewing a paragraph about media publicity and criminal prosecutions." She dimmed the lights, pulled down a white screen, and turned on a laptop computer and projector. Printed written words appeared on the screen. Shari read them out loud from the projected image:

"*TOPIC ONE: PRESS & PUBLICITY*

"The first of several stories you will hear about today is one featuring a wealthy Democratic congressman and his Republican celebrity wife—a right-leaning talk show host. In this story, assume the husband has been brutally murdered and multiple issues and facts have somehow been leaked to the press. Assume the press has run with the story, writing numerous accounts of the murder and has declared the celebrity wife the main suspect. Multiple sources have even declared her guilty.

"You will be completing a questionnaire about this story. After you've completed the questionnaire, I will pose a series of questions aimed at getting your opinions. All opinions are welcome and valid.

Nothing is off limits. The only rule that applies to this exercise is that you must respond honestly. We need your true feelings, an open and honest exchange of opinions. All information is valuable, so please hold nothing back, either in providing responses to the written questions or in your verbal responses."

Shari walked over to the group, seated in Zack's private jury box, and handed out the questionnaires. The group spent the next half-hour answering the questions in writing. After all questionnaires were turned in, Shari again addressed the group, much as a lawyer would approach a jury box in a courtroom or in a courtroom scene on television.

"In general, how accurate or truthful do you believe the press is when it reports a news story? Do you feel that certain networks report items more accurately than others? Do you think newspapers or television add their own 'spin' to increase readership or viewership?"

A group member raised his hand. "Number four?" Shari called out. Number four was an elderly gentleman in his seventies, a resident of Waterford, Michigan.

"There's no question the press spins these stories. Sales and readership are the name of the game, true? Who wants to read a boring story with no speculation about the outcome? At the end of the day, television news and newspaper publishers are in business for profit. They tell interesting stories, perhaps told in more compelling ways than their competitors, maybe with a different slant on things to appeal to their typical viewer or reader, right? They want to make the story as juicy as possible. So, yes, I believe they spin these stories."

"Number five, do you agree with that assessment?" Shari turned and surprised an otherwise unwilling member. The member was a young woman, a college student at Oakland University, majoring in Sociology. She lived in Royal Oak and commuted to the campus, some fifteen miles up I-75. The woman was initially startled to be called upon, like a student being selected from a professor's class list. She quickly recovered her composure.

"Absolutely. I do. I remember studying the concept of 'yellow journalism' in a history class. This goes all the way back to Hearst and Pulitzer and their famous press wars, where one of them said: 'You provide the pictures and I'll provide the story,' or something similar. So, yes, the press has been sensationalizing stories forever."

"Number two?" Shari called out. A middle-aged African American woman raised her hand. She lived in Southfield, the same town where the murder occurred.

"I one hundred percent agree. Newspapers and television have been declaring black folks guilty of crimes before their trials for a very long time. We call this 'arrested, tried, and convicted in the press.' Reporters, with very little information, rely on inside sources or leaks, and report this stuff as 'news', when it's only one source's interpretation of the evidence. It's not fair to the person accused, nor is it fair to the victim. We want to get this right, don't we?"

"Thank you, Number two. Anyone else have an opinion?" Shari scanned the group.

Number six called out without raising his hand. He was thirty-something, dressed in a power suit, hair neatly combed, manicured fingernails, and a two-day growth of beard. Shari noticed the younger females in the group were doting on him.

"I don't agree at all. Just because you do what you do for profit, doesn't mean you don't try to do it well and get it right. These guys swear an oath, don't they? They are duty bound to have integrity and report the facts. They are professionals, after all. I don't think they spin articles, and, even if they do, the reporting is still honest and accurate."

The questions and answers continued throughout the morning. Shari asked a series of follow-up questions. The group started slow, staring at each other, waiting for someone, *anyone* to provide the next response. As the questions continued, group members relaxed, became more forthcoming, and Shari no longer had to call on anyone to obtain the responses she coveted. She continued to probe opinions on the concept of whether the press sensationalized stories to increase readership, listeners, or viewers. She wondered whether the group felt that people like to read stories about the downfall of others, especially public figures. She advanced the term *Schadenfreude* and asked the group if they were familiar with the concept.

"Yes." Number seven, a twenty-year-old Wayne State University college student from Ferndale, responded. "We learned about this in my Journalism class. There are many different versions and contexts for the term, but the main point is that people seem to derive pleasure or self-satisfaction from learning about the troubles, failures, or even the *humiliation* of others, especially the rich and famous."

"And what do you think, Number seven, or anyone else? Do you think the press or public gets off on the public humiliation of a public figure or even a regular citizen?"

The group chuckled at Shari's dumbing down of the concept.

Number Seven continued, "Honestly, I think it's a mixed bag, and it depends on the story. If you look at the O.J. Simpson case, for instance, his race may have been a more important factor than his fame. In President Ronald John's case, it was a mixed bag. His fame kept him out of serious trouble for a while, but when his crimes were made public, fame didn't hurt or help him. The same was true for Oliver Wilkinson, the Supreme Court candidate. At the end of the day, Zachary Blake brought both these guys down because he had the truth on his side. *Schadenfreude* aside, these men were brought down because the truth of their evil, overreach, and criminality was exposed. I think we may enjoy bringing famous people down, but not under false pretenses."

"Interesting observation, Number seven. Does anyone else want to comment?" Shari encouraged. The discussion continued throughout the morning, moving on to other questions. "Do you think the media portrays these events accurately for the most part? Where do you get your news? What is your favorite media outlet? Television? Radio? The Internet? Newspapers?" These questions elicited a robust conversation and varied responses, which Shari recorded for Zack and Mia's benefit.

After a lunch break, during the afternoon session, Shari moved on to case specifics.

"Show of hands, how many of you are familiar with the name Mia Folger?" she inquired. Over three quarters of the participants raised their hands. When Shari reminded everyone about the case of the murdered congressman, almost everyone knew the case, even if they did not remember Mia's name. Once Mia's identity and case were established, Shari went to work on the specifics. What media source did they use to reference the case? How obsessed were they—how often did they read about the case and from how many different sources? Did they form any opinions from what they read or what they already knew about her? Was she a nice person? A bad person? Did they like or dislike her politics?

"I'm not a fan," replied Number one. "She does not seem to be a nice person. These right-wing rabble-rousers are very divisive elements, and I don't like their politics. I've listened to her show, and she is very rude to anyone who dares to disagree with her. Nothing she says rings true; it seems she says things to get a rise out of people. She doesn't really believe what she says. For her, it is more about fame, fortune, and publicity, not about telling the truth or helping to make the country a better place. I sense she is someone that doesn't handle criticism well and would punish anyone who disagreed with her. She probably resented her husband's popularity and poll numbers."

"Does anyone else have a comment? Agree or disagree with Number one?" Shari wondered.

"I wholeheartedly agree with Number one," Number two chimed in. "She's a right-wing nut."

"I could not disagree more," Number ten exclaimed. He was a mortgage broker from Clarkson. "I despise these political labels. Right-wing nut . . . rabble-rouser . . . why? Because she disagrees with her husband on the issues? Because she disagrees with the president? Not every Republican is in bed with Ronald John, Stephen Golding, or Oliver Wilkinson.

"I'm a proud Republican and I despise what these guys have done to our country and our party. Mia Folger, if you listen to her show, is hardly a 'right-wing' nut. She slants conservative, sure, but she's not dishonest or radical. Her views, if you stop to listen, are quite sensible: She supports a balanced budget. She opposes out-of-control spending and refuses to support any government program that is not fully funded. She supports limited abortion rights but doesn't believe it should be used as a form of birth control. She does not want to see *Roe v. Wade* overturned. She supports the right to vote and does not believe there is widespread voter fraud. She supports limited government and regulation; she is not a tax and spend liberal."

"It sounds like you know her quite well," Shari suggested.

"I listen to her all the time. We have similar political views."

"If you were a juror in Mia's case, would your feelings effect your ability to determine her fate in court?"

"No."

"Why not? You like her, right?"

"Yes, I like her. But I have sworn an oath to do my duty as a juror. I would listen to the arguments, follow the evidence, and make my determination based solely on what was presented in court."

"Interesting," Shari noted. "Anyone else?"

Number four spoke up. "I don't think people should prejudge anyone, especially based on politics or what the person does on television. Who knows whether it is all an act to get ratings? Let's get real, shall we? She's obviously educated and ambitious. There's nothing wrong with that. She's successful. Should she be punished for that? Is this another one of those 'successful woman' stories where white men cannot handle a woman of ambition and power? Would she be treated this way if she were a man? I would give her the benefit of the doubt and let the cards play out in court." Shari noted the response, quietly surprised it came from an elderly, conservative male.

An interesting day of opinions and evaluations continued. Shari asked the panel if they were all aware that Mia Folger was married to Congressman Bradley Crawford. Every hand shot up. What did they think of Crawford's politics? Was Crawford their congressman? Did they vote for him? These questions sparked another round of vigorous debate, all carefully observed and recorded by Shari Belitz. Shari was quite detailed and continued to compile data based on members' answers to a host of questions.

The day was getting late, but Shari had only allotted two days for the focus group and was determined to finish on time. She decided to move on to another topic, knowing it would elicit a whole new round of debate and discussion. She handed out, waited, and then collected a second questionnaire. Shari stepped back and addressed the group.

"Thank you for a vigorous and meaningful exchange on our first topic of the day. Let's move on to our next topic. It is getting late; we may be here into the evening hours. Does anyone have strong objections about continuing or have somewhere else to be this evening?" The panel was engaged, enjoying the exercise. Not a single focus group member objected to continuing the discussion with a new topic. Lauren had recruited well.

Shari displayed the next topic on the screen:

TOPIC TWO: THE SCENE

"I want you to assume the congressman, a married man, has been discovered dead in his home. He appears to have been murdered. His penis has been severed; there is evidence he was restrained, bound and gagged, tortured, and his death ruled a homicide. While his home has also been ransacked, the police have determined that the murder took place elsewhere—namely, a storage room in the basement of the congressman's condominium complex. Assume all evidence indicates that after he was murdered, the victim was transported to his apartment, which was ransacked, remember, and the body appears to be staged, placed peacefully on the bed in the master bedroom. Assume also that security video identified a shadow at the rear entrance to the building and have calculated that the shadow is either a woman, or a very slight man. Got it, everyone?"

Shari scanned the focus group. Everyone nodded affirmatively, glancing at one another, wondering what other members were thinking and doing.

"Great, here is my first question related to topic number two. What's the first thing that jumps out at you about this story?"

"Du-uh," Number eight blurted. "The severed penis. *Hello?* Who could ignore a severed penis? It is terrible and gruesome, like the Bobbitt case, years ago. Only John Bobbitt didn't die. Cutting off a guy's manhood? That is just disgusting, cruel, and sick!" Number eight was a salesman from West Bloomfield. His questionnaire listed him as a moderate. He considered himself an independent, voting for the *person*, not the *party*.

"Number seven? Agree or disagree?" Shari turned to the young college student.

"I'm not familiar with the Bobbitt case. I think it happened before I was born, but I agree that this is a cruel act. It probably qualifies as torture, no?"

Everyone began talking at once, animated, talking over each other. Shari shouted, "One at a time, please?"

One by one, all members of the focus group agreed that this was a cruel, barbaric and tortuous act.

Shari continued, "What do you think the feelings were of the person who committed this act? Have you read media coverage of the act itself and comparisons to the Bobbitt case? What do you think happened here?"

Again, the answers were as diverse as the focus group. Most responses agreed that the person must have been extremely angry at the congressman for one reason or another. To Shari's surprise, the group was split along political lines about whether the perpetrator knew the congressman well or had feelings for him. 'Anger' was the prevalent motive proffered by the group, followed by 'hurt'. All agreed that anger did not require an intimate relationship with the congressman, while hurt required more intimacy or feelings. Shari was quite surprised by this development and noted it accordingly. One member responded with 'fear' as a motive for the crime, but no one offered her encouragement. Shari noted the response as statistically insignificant.

Shari moved on to the staged scene, the ransacking, the police investigation, and trust for law enforcement. "Do the police lie?" she inquired. "Do you think they ever tamper with evidence? What do you make of the ransacking of the apartment? Staged or rage?" she queried. "If staged, by who? The cops or the perp? Have any of you had any negative encounters with the police? Was there one perpetrator, or more than one?"

"The cops lie and plant evidence all the time," one member shouted.

"That's a stereotype and an overstatement from someone who watches too many crime shows on television," shouted a conservative member.

"Defund the police!" shouted a liberal, laughing.

Shari asked them to calm down, identify themselves, be respectful of one another, and speak one at a time. She noted each response for Zack.

The group almost unanimously agreed that the apartment was not ransacked out of rage, but the scene was staged to make the incident appear like a robbery. No one believed a burglar would murder and dismember his or her victim. A few scoffed at the possibility that the cops staged the scene. Number two pushed back a bit.

She referenced and compared the possibility of a staged scene to the phenomenon of being pulled over for 'driving while black' and having 'the talk' with her sons. While she had not yet had any personal experience with these well-known, cop-citizen interactions, she recalled the city of Cedar Ridge and Zachary Blake's famous headline-grabbing case that resulted in a substantial award for the family of a deceased victim of a racist cop.

"If cops can pull over a law-abiding citizen for driving while black, they can easily stage a crime scene." She believed.

Her opinion sparked another long debate about the integrity of the police. Once again, Shari smiled and noted it all.

Finally, the group began to discuss the possibility of more than one perpetrator. If the perp was a woman, she would have to be extremely strong to pull this off. "Did she transport the lifeless or almost lifeless body herself, or did she have help?" Shari wanted to know.

"Were there luggage carts in the basement?" One member wondered.

Almost all participants decided that a strong woman could have committed the act alone, but that two perpetrators or a pushcart was far more likely. Shari paused, troubled. At this stage of the focus group's analysis, a majority of members were clearly wondering: 'Did Mia do this herself or did she have help?' Shari sighed. *Tomorrow is another day!*

CHAPTER
NINETEEN

As Shari Belitz was completing day one of her focus group, Reed Spencer and his team of cyber-wizards were completing a day at the computer monitors, deeply engaged in traffic on the deep web and dark web and hacking into email, cell phone, cyber, and social media accounts of the various players. The cyber-team's new principal target, per Micah Love's instructions, was Elyssa Naylor. In addition to Reed's team tracking and pinging Elyssa's various online accounts, Micah's follow team also established surveillance on the legislative assistant.

While Reed's team focused on social media and email accounts, Reed explored her three mobile phones, especially telephone calls received and sent, and text messages back and forth. Reed wrote proprietary software to discreetly monitor these communications. He probably could have marketed these inventions. However, by the time he realized there was a private and public market for this technology, others had already flooded the market with similar products.

Companies wishing to track corporate espionage, parents seeking to keep an eye on their children or keep them out of trouble, distrustful spouses trying to catch a cheating spouse—all looked to use this or similar technology. Law enforcement used similar, more advanced software, but were required to monitor communications legally, usually requiring the issuance of a search warrant. Reed's software was also an advanced product, akin to that used by law enforcement, but Reed enjoyed a significant advantage over law enforcement officials. He did not need to worry about warrants and other similar legal tools to conduct electronic surveillance. In situations where his results were to be introduced in court, he strived to keep surveillance activities legal.

In the case of Mia Folger and the hack on Elyssa Naylor, Reed and Micah, with Zack's permission, determined that keeping surveillance legal was unnecessary. If George Bruch received concrete evidence of Mia's innocence and Naylor's guilt, Bruch would be duty-bound to dismiss all charges against Mia, regardless of whether dismissal evidence was obtained illegally. Besides, if Reed discovered incriminating evidence of Naylor's guilt, they could simply bring the evidence to Bruch's attention and duty would require Bruch to obtain a warrant to legally obtain the information himself.

Reed named his sophisticated software *Spytext.* He was proud of his invention. It was equally effective for all iPhone and Android models and permitted remote access and ability to monitor a phone, without having possession of the phone. Reed could also clone the phone of his choice and create an exact duplicate. He could monitor current and future calls and texts, or review and capture historical use. He had recently upgraded *Spytext* and could now download an app for his phone to create a remote internet connection with the phone he wished to capture.

Accessing Naylor's government phone was difficult, but Reed's search did not focus on that phone. He doubted Naylor would use a government issued phone to conduct private business anyway, especially a clandestine affair with her boss. Reed was mildly amused that she had a personal iPhone *and* an Android model, but given her unethical behavior, he decided that ownership of two phones was not that surprising.

The best feature of *Spytext* for this investigation was its unique ability to extract past and present texts and iMessages, even after they had been deleted. Another important feature was that the target phone's owner—in this case, Elyssa Naylor—could not detect that her phones were cloned or hacked. Any activity was captured and uploaded silently. The software enabled Reed to obtain texts, calls, or GPS information. In other words, if Naylor was the murderer and carried a phone in her purse, her GPS would place her at the murder scene, whether or not she used the phone at the time of the murder. Since these phones were also able to send email and access social media, Reed could also double check the efforts of his team members to make sure no data was ignored.

Reed focused on the month before, time of, and month after the murder. He began his search by extracting all calls and texts made to and from both phones. He planned to access social media and emails, if necessary, at a later date.

The search produced a treasure trove of information. There were multiple texts between Naylor and Crawford, including naked pictures of Naylor texted to Crawford. The congressman responded with a harsh rebuke, warning that these accounts could be monitored. He demanded she delete them immediately. While Naylor complied with Crawford's demands, Reed's software was immune to the delete button. All texts were recoverable regardless of current status. In addition to recovering what could only be called evidence of 'sexting' between the boss and his number one employee, Reed found similar texts between Naylor and a third party. Naked pictures were exchanged, salacious conversations between Naylor and a mystery woman were uncovered. *Elyssa Naylor swings both ways, interesting . . .* Reed made note of mystery lady's phone number, and a further note to discover her identity, monitor and clone her phone.

Reed yawned and rubbed his eyes. He'd been in front of a computer screen for over fourteen hours. Just as he decided to call it a night, Naylor's cloned iPhone pinged. A text sequence appeared:

Where the fuck are you?

Answer me, philandering whore! Want me to go to the press?

C'mon Mia. Stop this. For hundredth time, not cheating on you.

Lying sack o shit! A cartoon picture of a brown pile appeared next to the words

Hilarious Mia. Home soon. Finishing up.

Who is it this time? That iron-pumping Naylor? Bet she kicks your ass in bed. Like it rough? I can get rough-violent too. Handcuffs whips chains knives. How about we cut the little fucker right off-no more wandering dick. Wandering dickless.

Jesus Mia. Home soon. Calm down. We'll talk.

What's to talk about? Field day for press. Career down the toilet.

Please stop Mia. Drinking?

Drunk. WTF you care?

Care a lot.

Sure you do. Get your ass home. We'll talk.

Reed recognized the sequence immediately. This was the text sequence between Mia and Brad Crawford that was leaked to the press. How did the sequence get in Naylor's phone? Did she clone Mia's phone and manufacture the texts? *This could blow the lid off the whole case!*

Suddenly wide awake, Reed dialed Micah and told him what he found. Micah conferenced in Zachary Blake and filled Zack in on current developments. The three men began to discuss the find.

"Reed, you are frigging amazing! That software of yours is incredible!" Micah crowed. "Slam dunk indeed! We should leak this stuff to that podcast bitch!"

"Leaking this stuff might be a solid idea for the public. However, it may not have much probative value in court," Zack cautioned.

"How so?" Micah didn't understand.

"Can we verify it came from Naylor and not Mia? How do we know that Naylor didn't do the same thing Reed did, but with less sophisticated software?"

"You think she hijacked Mia's phone?"

"I don't know, Micah. Reed? It is at least *possible*, isn't it?"

"Yes," Reed conceded.

"Is there a way to determine where the texts originated?"

"Yes," Reed brightened. "We can do that."

Zack was getting a germ of an idea. "I'd like you to verify the origin of the texts before we decide on a course of action. At the end of the day, I'm not sure it's going to matter who created or sent the texts. As far as I'm concerned, the more important information right now is this mystery person. Who is she? Who is she to Elyssa Naylor? This might be a turning point in the case. Identify her. I want to know who she is and what she looks like. Where does she live? How does she fit into the equation? Get me whatever information you can. I need to talk with Bruch."

"Now? Or after we identify mystery lady?"

"Now, I think. I've got to mull this over a bit, sort things out in my mind, but I think I have a potentially winning strategy."

"Care to share?" Micah wondered.

"Not just yet, guys. For now, please get me whatever you can. I agree with you that if it turns out Naylor set Mia up with the texts, it is damning stuff, but it does not prove Mia didn't commit the crime."

"But it might create reasonable doubt, which is all you need."

"All we need for a *trial* victory, but not a *dismissal.* For a dismissal, with prejudice, we need Bruch to agree that our evidence exonerates Mia. I don't see that yet."

"If you say so, Zack. It sure seems compelling to this trained investigator's eyes," Micah grunted.

"It may be enough, Micah. But it isn't a slam dunk," Zack decided. "As to whether we want to leak the information to the podcast lady and start to change public opinion, let me run that by Shari."

"This Shari person is running your case now?" Reed was astounded.

"She evaluates public opinion better than any lawyer I have ever known. I haven't known her long, but I trust her judgment on these publicity issues."

"Your client, your coin, your decision, Zack. Be careful with this woman. As you say, you haven't known her that long. Maybe this is junk science," Reed warned.

"I have seen her in action, Reed. You should see how she conducts these focus group sessions. She's incredible. Trust me, man," Zack assured.

"You know I do, Zack."

"Get me the goods on this mystery woman, ASAP. Anything else for tonight?"

"No, boss; that's about it," Micah sighed.

"Reed? Great work, young man! Micah? Don't call me boss."

"Sir, yes sir," Micah joked. Zack did not respond.

"Zack?" No answer.

"Where did he go?" Reed wondered.

"The son of a bitch hung up on us."

***

A preliminary examination is a mini version of a trial. There is no jury. A lower court trial judge—in this case, Forty-Sixth District Court

Judge Jordyn Bolton—determines whether the prosecution has produced enough evidence to move forward with the case. Under Michigan law, any criminal defendant, charged with a felony, has the right to have a preliminary examination. At the prelim, also known as a probable cause hearing, the prosecution must show a crime has been committed and that it is more likely than not that the defendant committed the crime.

A preliminary examination does not require proof beyond a reasonable doubt. Instead, a far lower probable cause standard, 'more likely than not,' applies. Following a preliminary examination, a defendant is almost always bound over for trial. The number of witnesses called at a prelim are at the discretion of the judge, usually smaller in number than a witness list at trial. In many cases, the only people called are the arresting police officer and a crime victim.

Zack planned to ask Judge Bolton for an expanded witness list. During the hearing, the prosecution presents evidence first. The defense has the right to cross-examine all witnesses called by the prosecution. The defense may also call witnesses, even hostile ones, and the prosecution gets to cross-examine those witnesses. After both sides present evidence, the judge rules whether there is probable cause—more likely than not—that a crime was committed and the defendant committed the crime. The judge may rule in favor of the defendant and reduce the charges or dismiss the case entirely. If the judge rules in favor of the prosecution, the case is immediately transferred to circuit court, where a new circuit court judge, selected by blind draw, would be assigned the case for trial. Zack knew that a preliminary exam was an absolute right of any criminal defendant and George Bruch was powerless to prevent it from occurring.

The day after his telephone meeting with Micah and Reed, Zack Blake telephoned Bruch's office. Bruch's long-time receptionist buzzed him to advise that Blake was calling.

"What does he want?" George inquired, more to himself than to the receptionist.

"He didn't say, sir. Defense lawyers like Zack Blake do not typically share telephone strategy with lowly receptionists," she cracked.

"Funny, Wilma," Bruch sighed. When Wilma hung up the phone at her station, Bruch's phone began to ring. The veteran prosecutor was surprised to hear from his hotshot opponent. He wondered whether Mia Folger regained consciousness. The phone continued to ring. If he didn't pick up, the call would automatically transfer to voicemail. Bruch finally picked up the receiver.

"George Bruch. How may I help you?"

"George? Zachary Blake here."

"Zack? How the hell are you? More importantly, how's Mia Folger? Is she awake? Ready for trial?"

"No, she's not. Thanks for asking, though. I appreciate your concern." Zack waxed sarcasm; Bruch took him seriously.

"Whether she's guilty or not, and I believe she is, her situation is awful," he groaned.

"Yes, it sure is, George." Zack shook his head in disbelief.

"What can I do for you, Zack?"

"I'd like to schedule a preliminary exam."

"What? I thought Mia was still catatonic. Can she suddenly contribute to her own defense?"

"No."

"Then why in hell would you want a prelim?"

"I'd like to test the evidence, even if she cannot yet contribute. Perhaps I can get a district judge to dismiss the case."

"Fat chance."

"Then you have nothing to lose, George."

Bruch paused. *What the fuck is he up to?*

"What's on your mind, Zack? Spill!" Bruch demanded.

"Nothing, George. We're still going over all those documents and exhibits you dumped at my office. I'll disclose that there were a couple of interesting needles in that haystack you provided, but nothing special in your disclosures."

"Then what's it all about?"

"As I indicated, I'm not sure you've got enough, and I want to test the evidence."

"Bullshit, Zack. Tell the truth."

"Look, George. This is a courtesy call. I don't need your consent to schedule a prelim. I can go to Judge Bolton. You can refuse to stipulate—I'll file a motion. She'll grant it. You know she will, and she'll be pissed at you. Can we stipulate or not?"

"She could deny the request based on Mia's medical condition."

"I suppose she could. I doubt it, but I suppose it's possible. Don't you have confidence in your evidence?" Zack goaded. Bruch took the bait, as Zack knew he would.

"I have absolute faith in our evidence. Mia Folger is guilty and we will prove her guilt beyond a reasonable doubt."

"Then why oppose a preliminary exam? At a prelim, you only have to prove it is more likely than not that Mia committed the crime. Like that podcast lady, Libby what's-her-name, this should be a *slam dunk* for a seasoned prosecutor like yourself."

"I won't oppose the request," Bruch decided. "Send me the stipulation and order and I'll execute it."

"You'll have it in five minutes, George. Get me some dates and I'll coordinate a hearing with Judge Bolton."

"Okay, Zack. I look forward to kicking your ass."

"It's a prelim, George. Besides, slam dunk, right? You *should* kick my ass."

Bruch could not shake the feeling he was being set up, but there was little or nothing he could do about it.

"Okay, Zack. See you in court. Anything else I can do for you?"

"Dismiss the case?" Zack proposed.

"Funny, Blake. Real comedian."

"My wife and kids think I'm funny."

"Hanging up now, Zack." The phone clicked. Zack heard a dial tone.

"Was it something I said, George?"

***

After being silent for a long period of time, Libby Curry finally posted a new podcast, shortly after Blake's agreement with Bruch:

"Dear listeners. We have not chatted for a while. Information about the Mia Folger situation has been hard to come by but, as most of you know, I am a very persistent journalist. After a long period where no leaks were forthcoming, suddenly, both sides are leaking like sieves. *Slam Dunk* has recently learned Judge Jordyn Bolton will hear arguments that may pave the way for a preliminary examination hearing, despite Mia's catatonic condition.

"It is unclear, at this point, who initiated the request for a hearing, but sources tell *Slam Dunk* that a hearing is a foregone conclusion. According to my legal gurus, the standard of proof to bind someone over for trial is a far lower standard than that required for a guilty verdict. A guilty verdict requires proof of guilt beyond a reasonable doubt. A preliminary examination or probable cause hearing requires it be more likely than not that Mia Folger murdered her husband. I don't know about you, dear listeners, but unless Zack Blake can pull a rabbit out of his hat, that low standard should be easily met by the prosecution. This suggests to me that it was Bruch, not Blake, who moved to conduct a preliminary examination.

"My legal sources report some additional interesting news. Zachary Blake has enlisted the support of a top-notch jury consultant from the Big Apple, New York City. Her name is Shari Belitz, and rumor has it she has assembled a citizens' focus group to test various elements of the Folger case evidence and expected testimony. While we do not have participant names, or the subject matter being tested, we do know that Belitz is highly regarded in her field and usually works for large insurance companies. According to her company website, Belitz specializes in focus groups, mock juries, witness and trial preparation. Blake and the high-fashioned Belitz have been seen dining together at various restaurants around town. *Slam Dunk* has reached out to Zachary Blake and his firm for comment. Our calls have not been returned. Mouths are also zipped tight at the NYC office of Shari Belitz—*Slam Dunk* was greeted with a terse 'no comment'.

"I have also learned, dear listeners, that a private investigation into the facts and circumstances of Congressman Bradley Crawford's death is being conducted by Love Investigations, including an electronic investigation of some sort by Micah Love's shady cyber guru, Reed Spencer, who once served time for cyber-fraud. *Slam Dunk* is working diligently to obtain details of both investigations.

"I must say, dear listeners, what once looked like a *Slam Dunk* before Zachary Blake entered the picture is looking more and more like a fifty-fifty toss-up. We'll have more as additional details are released or leaked. That's all for now. Have a great evening. We'll talk soon."

CHAPTER
TWENTY

The evening before the second day of the focus group. Zachary Blake took Shari Belitz to dinner at Ocean Prime in Troy. He briefed Shari on the newly discovered electronic evidence and his demand for a preliminary examination. Shari, in turn, shared the results of the first day of the focus group.

"The group is providing some terrific feedback, Zack. Lauren did a marvelous recruiting job. There have been robust political and philosophical exchanges. I think you'll find that the members replicate your potential jury quite well," Shari advised.

"I read your preliminary report and I have to agree, Shari. The findings are fascinating, especially the left-right, back and forth political swing. You're going to have to educate me on the subtleties of this going forward, not just for this case, but in many future cases. I always thought right-left was easy. Right is out, left is in. Your data suggests otherwise."

"Considering your record of success, Zack, I am pleased you feel I can teach you something. That is high praise indeed."

"You deserve it. So, what's next?"

"We continue to do what we're doing. I have another day, two more topics, and a shitload of questions to ask so that you have a clear picture going forward. I could not be more pleased with the participation and makeup of this focus group. Your case will benefit from the data. How goes the investigation? How's Mia? Any change?"

"Mia's been having nightmares. She has spoken in her sleep—not much, just a little. Most of her words relate to her husband, but Harold hasn't been able to make anything of it, yet. As to the investigation, we have a viable alternate suspect, and we are about to do a deep dive into her electronic footprint. What does the data say about an alternate suspect?"

"The emergence of a viable alternative to Mia will be, hands down, the number one reason for a not guilty verdict, Zack. I was quite surprised by the responses to the unique circumstances of the crime. The average member did not feel that the dismemberment angle required a personal connection between perpetrator and victim. The group determined that 'anger' was the prevalent emotion for the perp. 'Hurt' came in second but was not necessary. That surprised me. I thought they'd figure that the victim and perpetrator would have to know each other well. This is wonderful news for Mia. The alternate perp could be a virtual stranger and still have committed this gruesome crime, assuming Crawford made the person angry enough."

"So, we need to find someone who was angry with Crawford, even short term, and not necessarily someone who was *involved* with Crawford?"

"Exactly. Interesting development, no?"

"Yes, and very helpful to Mia."

"I thought so."

"What are the topics for tomorrow?"

"Perfect timing, actually. Tomorrow we'll look into the principal suspect and the victim, as well as the viability of alternate suspects. I have dozens of questions that should get you to the promised land."

"Wow, Shari. It's almost like fate is moving things in a positive direction. I'm also working on playing out a . . . *hunch*, I guess you would call it. I've been mulling a theory around in my head, and I have decided to test the evidence and see whether my hunch pays off."

"Test the evidence? I told you, Zack, it's way too early for a mock jury."

"This isn't a mock. I'm going to test it at the preliminary exam. I goaded George Bruch into it and will need your help with witnesses and testimony. With the right breaks, I believe I can persuade Judge Bolton to dismiss this case."

"Care to share?"

"Not yet, but you are going to play a big part in the process. Are you available to stick around after the focus group is over tomorrow?"

"I've got lots to do, but I've got a great staff. Besides, you pay by the hour and pay well."

"Money talks and bullshit walks? That sort of thing?"

"I don't do everything for money. This is a fascinating case and I've believed from the start that Mia is innocent."

"How can you be so sure?"

"It's like I keep saying, the murderer does not go into shock at the sight of a body she dismembered. Her reaction to his body is the truest emotion in this case. She's innocent, Zack. I'd stake my career on it."

"Let's keep working the case. You on the psychological end and me on the legal. If my plan comes to fruition, I have a real shot at getting the charges dismissed."

"From your mouth to God's ear, my friend. I'm hungry. What's good here?"

***

Focus group members arrived early, ready for another interesting day. Shari was quite satisfied with the group's comments on the various topics, and answers to questions related to those topics. Members were fully engaged, happy to be there, had different views on the various issues, and were very representative of people Zack might expect to find on Mia's jury.

The second day began as a near duplicate of the first. The topic was different, of course, and the group was far less tentative than they were the day before. Shari turned on the projector, and words from her computer filled the screen. Shari read the words aloud:

"*TOPIC THREE—VICTIM & PRINCIPAL SUSPECT*

"Assume the victim is a two-term congressman. He is handsome, charismatic, popular in his district and well-liked by his constituents. Assume he was working on a controversial infrastructure spending bill, opposed by most conservative Republican legislators and citizens.

Assume he received angry emails from people opposed to the legislation and supportive emails from those who liked the legislation. Assume that he was having some marital difficulties and was guilty of infidelity." Shari paused, letting the idea that the popular congressman was actually a sleaze who cheated on his wife sink in.

"Assume the principal suspect is the wife of the deceased. She is attractive, wealthy, an outspoken critic of her husband's policies. She has a right-leaning talk show on radio. Assume she suspects her husband of cheating on her. Assume she is accused of authoring and transmitting a series of text messages accusing him of infidelity and threatening to kill him in the exact manner of death he ultimately suffered. Assume that the principal suspect was in therapy at the time of the murder and her therapist will testify at trial.

"Does everyone understand the topic? Any preliminary questions?" Shari inquired.

"No questions, Shari, but I would sure rather serve on the Folger jury than in this focus group," Number five, the Oakland University student cracked. The room filled with laughter. People began chatting with neighbors, agreeing with Number five.

"Quiet, please. Can we please settle down? We've got a lot to cover today and I'd like to get started. Cute, Number five. Way to get things rolling in the right direction," she acknowledged.

"Let's start with a broad question. Do any of you know anyone who has committed marital infidelity? Let's start with Number five—payback is a bitch." Everyone laughed a second time.

"As a matter of fact, my parents are divorced because my mother cheated on my father," she disclosed.

"That's tough; sorry that happened to you, Number five. Was the split amicable or nasty?"

"It was nasty at first, but things calmed down. My father decided that my mental health was more important than his anger and feelings of betrayal."

"If their relationship had turned violent, would that have surprised you or would you have expected it?"

"Surprised, without a doubt. My parents loved each other. Deep down, my mother regrets her lapse in judgment."

"Anyone else? Number eleven?"

Number eleven had her hand raised. She was a forty-something female artist with a home-based business.

"I've just received my final judgment of divorce. My husband left me for his paralegal."

"Ouch," Number four responded with a scowl.

"Yeah, it was surprising and painful. I thought we had a good marriage. The split was very tough on the kids. They're teenagers."

"Was the divorce amicable?" Shari inquired.

"Not really," Number eleven revealed. "His betrayal broke my heart. I wanted him to pay. The welfare of my children was lurking in the background, holding me back from being a total bitch."

"If you had no children, you would have been even 'bitchier' to use your word?" Shari probed. The other members chuckled.

"Probably. In fact, much bitchier," she admitted.

"Violent?"

"Heavens no! I'm not a violent person, but I was deeply hurt by his behavior."

"Whether or not you've ever been violent in the past, do any of you think that marital infidelity could push you to the brink?"

"I believe you have to have violent tendencies to begin with," Number eleven continued. "The thought of physical violence against my husband never occurred to me."

"Do all of you feel the same way? Is someone who has never committed an act of violence capable of violence at the height of betrayal?" Shari probed.

Almost everyone in the group agreed that a person would have to have a violent nature to begin with. The lone exception was Number four, the seventy-something man from Waterford. He believed that a person with no violent tendencies could be driven to violence with the right motivation.

"Everyone's different. People who lash out, even kill people, have their first experience with acts of violence at some point in their lives. They weren't necessarily violent to begin with," he observed.

"Does anyone feel the parties' different political views had an impact? Do most couples have similar political views?" Shari posed.

"Today's politics can drive anyone to violence," Number eighteen bristled. He was an investment advisor from Troy. "All I have to do is tell a lefty that I voted for Ronald John and he's ready to kill me! I don't think it's a stretch to believe that people could harm each other over political differences."

The discussion continued throughout the morning. Number eighteen's position was a distinct minority, at least as it related to violence. The focus group agreed that political differences could easily contribute to marital tension, but members' clear position on the issue of marital and political violence was that any spouse, especially the female, would be highly unlikely to commit violence against the other, even if they had stark political differences. While all members acknowledged domestic violence, all believed that the splits in those cases were typically based on domestic abuse or previous violence, not on infidelity.

Shari moved on to other questions. Mia was in therapy at the time of the murder. Did anyone know anyone in therapy? Must a person have deep-seated mental issues to seek therapy? Is seeking help from a therapist a sign of weakness?

The group felt that there was, indeed, an unfortunate stigma attached to therapy, but the fact that someone seeks help was neither a weakness, nor a sign of deep-seated mental problems. The group wanted more information, but Shari could not give them what they wanted. Mia's sessions were confidential, and Shari had no access to Rothenberg's treatment or records. Most members felt that past or present violence disclosed in treatment or contained in medical records would impact their opinion on the question of marital or political violence.

Shari moved on to the topic of threats. She did not mention the text messages—her question was more general.

"If someone threatens someone, do you believe the person will always act on the threat?"

The group unanimously responded "No."

Number seventeen, an event planner from Southfield, summed up the group's opinion on the issue. "Most threats are idle bluster and very few people would ever carry these out, especially if the threat is completely out of character or is conduct the threatening party has never engaged in before."

Shari moved on to the congressman and his political work. Did the panel believe Crawford had political enemies? Might they be more or less likely to harm him than his betrayed spouse? What did they think of politicians in general? Were they all liars and cheaters? Does absolute power corrupt absolutely?

The group had no love for politics or politicians, right-leaning or left. Most members believed politicians were power-hungry liars and cheaters who put self-interest ahead of constituents and country. When asked how they felt about Bradley Crawford, they split along party lines. This finding had little or nothing to do with Mia's guilt or innocence, but Shari found the split fascinating. Politicians were all liars and cheaters, unless they were the panel member's own representative, from the member's preferred party, and a politician the member voted for.

Every member believed violence, especially murder, was an extreme act, required a particular personality type, and was unlikely to be triggered by political discord. They doubted that some "political enemy" would have committed this murder, as the type of murder was not typical of an assassination.

Shari noted the responses and moved on. The next set of questions related to the act.

"As you well know, the congressman died of exsanguination, from a severed penis. Do you believe the murderer intended to kill the congressman, or just harm or humiliate him?"

This question went to the crux of the matter. It was far more believable that Mia intended to punish his cheating with violence short of murder.

"Chopping off someone's penis is an extreme, angry act, but not necessarily something done to commit murder," one member voiced. "I'm sure it has happened more than once, but only one case, the Bobbitt case, reached a level of notoriety. This is quite unusual, would everyone agree?"

Everyone agreed. The member continued.

"I could see Mia Folger cutting off Crawford's penis as punishment for cheating, especially if she didn't mean for him to die." Everyone agreed with this statement.

The response and consensus meant the group determined that Mia might be the killer, perhaps guilty of a lesser criminal charge based on her lack of intent, but a murderer, nonetheless. Shari noted and contemplated the impact of the responses. *Could Mia be convicted if Bruch is wise enough to argue that she didn't mean to kill him?*

She would have to discuss this finding with Blake. From what little she knew of Bruch, he would prosecute Mia, full tilt, arguing murder in the first. Shari's take on Bruch was that he wanted to beat Zack Blake on the original murder charge. She didn't doubt his ability; she doubted his wisdom, motive, and strategy. She penned a note to discuss options with Blake.

Shari Belitz was a brilliant forensic psychologist. She was already two steps ahead of the group. While the average jury consultant might be concerned with the groups' consensus response to the question of accidental death, Shari had studied the investigators, CSI, and medical examiner reports closely. Crawford's murderer was someone capable of *torturing* the congressman. She apprehended and subdued him, carried him down to the basement, slowly tortured him to death, and carried his lifeless body back to the apartment for staging. Those horrific acts required a criminal mindset. *Could Mia do all those things to someone she once loved?* In addition, when Mia first observed the body, she went into a catatonic state. *Why? If she was the murderer, she knew the condition of the body. Could her condition be a pretense? Could anyone fake a catatonic condition for this length of time?*

Shari laid all of this out for the focus group, and the possibility of Mia's guilt was utterly and completely vanquished. Not a single group member believed Mia Folger was capable of torturing and transporting Brad Crawford in the manner perpetrated by the murderer.

"This took considerable planning, don't you think?" a member wondered out loud.

"Could someone of Mia's size and strength secure and transport someone as large as Crawford?" asked another.

"Could she have hated him enough to torture him for hours? She loved him once, didn't she? In fact, she might still love him, which makes this type of long-term torture even more unlikely," offered another.

"What kind of anger or hatred does an act like this require? For cheating? I don't buy it," claimed another.

"Mia has been catatonic since this happened? How does an untrained person pull that off? Wouldn't the doctors be suspicious? Isn't there a way to confirm she's faking? And, if she's not faking, how could she be the murderer? What's so shocking about encountering a body you dismembered? Sorry doubters, but this stuff doesn't track," argued still another.

"What was the message here?" another member inquired. "The killer is obviously angry at Crawford. What could have caused such anger? What's the profile of such a murderer? I agree with the others. It can't just be infidelity."

"What do *you* think the message was?" Shari demanded.

"That Crawford lacked the courage of his convictions? Perhaps he sold someone out? Excuse my French, but he's 'dickless' now, get my drift? No spine or courage," a member suggested.

"That could imply someone who is angry with his voting record or politics, right?" Shari reasoned.

"I can't see that," offered a member, without further comment.

"I agree, this seems far more personal," another offered.

"A lovers' triangle?" another posited.

"Interesting theory," Shari commented. "Please continue."

"How about the person Crawford was cheating with? Maybe Crawford decided he loved his wife. The killer reacted violently to the news," the member expounded.

"Hell hath no fury like a woman scorned," another chirped.

"But that applies to Mia, as well," someone warned.

"True, but Mia wasn't a dishonest cheater, the other woman was. Perhaps she's already morally compromised. Murder is less of a stretch for someone like that, isn't it?"

Shari was delighted with this turn of events. The existence of a viable alternate suspect was the best chance Mia had. The lawyer-turned-psychologist noted every response.

"Did everyone read the text messages?" Shari moved on. "What do you think?"

Number six, the young conservative, raised his hand and began speaking at the same time. "I'm quite familiar with Mia Folger. I listen to her show. I know many of the people in this room disagree with her politics, but dumb, she's not. She's extremely bright, knowledgeable, and well-informed. If we are to assume she's a murderer, which from the many responses I'm hearing, many of us do not, we would also have to assume she's an idiot. Only an idiot would send a text promising to do exactly what was done to the congressman. This is either an amazing coincidence, or someone is setting her up."

"Setting her up, how?" Number two prodded.

"Perhaps someone hacked her text messages, saw this one, and decided to harm both Mia and the congressman at the same time. The woman Crawford was cheating with, if Crawford decided to return to his wife, would have hated them both. Doesn't that track better?" Number six proposed.

Everyone agreed it did.

"At this point, I'd like to see a show of hands. How many of you think Mia Folger is guilty?" Shari inquired. Two hands shot up.

"The rest of you think she's innocent or are there still some people who are undecided?"

"Undecided," shouted Number four.

"Ditto," Number two agreed.

"We have sixteen not guilty, two guilty, and two undecided, correct?" Shari calculated. Everyone nodded affirmatively.

"Mia was in therapy; we discussed that. How many think the therapist's testimony is important?" Shari moved to the next question. She looked at her watch. *Time for lunch.*

"It depends on why she was in therapy and whether the judge has the power to make the therapist disclose confidential information.

Shari, you are an attorney. Does a judge have that power?" Number three inquired.

"This is a question for Zack Blake, not me, but since he's not here and I am, I would file a motion for a protective order or a motion to quash the subpoena," Shari advised.

"What the hell does that mean?" Number four laughed.

"Sorry." Shari smiled. "It means, no, I don't think a judge can make a psychologist or psychiatrist violate doctor-patient privilege. This is true in Michigan and most states. There are exceptions and variations, but none of those would apply to this case. Generally, the psychologist has a responsibility to maintain confidentiality and to assert the privilege. A client can waive the privilege, but that is not likely in this case. And, as many of you know, the release of records would probably violate HIPAA," Shari advised, referring to the 1996 Health Insurance Portability and Accountability Act, which protects medical records and prevents release without patient consent.

"Psychologists and psychiatrists have ethical and professional obligations. They cannot just comply with a subpoena, like ordinary citizens who have no such obligations. While they are required to give truthful answers, just like any other witness, ethical boundaries may require them to refuse to answer certain questions."

The conversation continued until the group broke for lunch. The consensus of the group was that while they would prefer to hear from the therapist, the fact that Mia was in therapy and the possibility the doctor would refuse to testify, did not weigh heavily in their decision making.

One topic remained for the afternoon session. Shari would take a deep dive into the notion of an alternate suspect. She believed this was the ultimate issue in the case. A viable alternate suspect created reasonable doubt. Would the focus group agree?

CHAPTER

TWENTY-ONE

Zachary Blake and George Bruch sat together in the gallery of the Forty-Sixth District Court in Southfield. This was a cattle call morning. Multiple citizens appeared pro bono to fight traffic tickets. Other citizens had arraignments or minor civil actions. District court in Michigan was a court of smaller case jurisdiction, including small claims cases. Because of the publicity associated with Mia's case, Judge Bolton decided to clear out the other litigants before calling *State of Michigan v. Folger*. Blake, Bruch, and a large contingent of reporters waited patiently for the judge to clear a rather mundane docket. As he waited, Zack wondered why any lawyer, especially a talented female attorney like Bolton, would want to be a district court judge. *Boring!* Because Bolton was once a trial lawyer, Zack was ticked that he and Bruch did not receive a courtesy call advising them to show up after eleven instead of wasting two-and-one-half-hours listening to district court garbage. A high-profile arraignment was one of the few 'big-ticket' hearings conducted in the lower court. Zack privately wished Bolton could retain jurisdiction for the trial.

The purpose of the hearing was to place the stipulation and order for the preliminary examination on the record. The order was already entered; the hearing should have been unnecessary, but the two veteran lawyers were unable to hash out ground rules without judicial intervention. *Folger* was the last case on the judge's morning docket. The clerk called the case and the two lawyers stepped to their respective podiums.

"Sorry to keep you waiting, gentlemen, but I felt it was prudent to hold this hearing in an empty courtroom," the judge began.

Zack almost laughed out loud. Still seething from the wait, Zack turned to the gallery. It was packed to the gills with members of the press. Bolton accomplished nothing with her decision to call the case last.

"I understand you gentlemen are having difficulty agreeing on protocol?"

"Two sticking points, Your Honor," Zack responded, nodding toward Bruch for a moment.

"And they are?"

"Obviously, we must proceed without my client. She is still in an unconscious state. Mr. Bruch wants you to issue an order that the preliminary exam may proceed without her. He does not want to stipulate."

"So ordered." Judge Bolton replied, without hearing from Bruch. "What's the other sticking point?"

"The number of witnesses, Your Honor. We want to be able to call as many rebuttal witnesses as necessary, enter exhibits—the whole nine yards, depending on the People's presentation."

"Mr. Bruch?"

Bruch was suddenly formal, in stern prosecutor mode. "May it please the court, Your Honor, George Bruch for the People. The hearing will be a prelim, not a trial. The standard of proof is more likely than not. We don't need a parade of witnesses to meet the threshold. This is a waste of the People's and the court's time."

"I don't mind," Bolton chuckled.

"Can we get a ruling on the number of rebuttal witnesses and a disclosure of the defendant's proofs?"

"Mr. Blake? What about it?"

"There is a reason it's called rebuttal, Your Honor," Zack argued. "The defendant must respond to the People's evidence. I have no idea how we will respond, how many rebuttal witnesses we will need, or how long our presentation will take. I can't agree to some arbitrary cut-off of exhibits or witnesses. I'd like you to dismiss the case, but only after you see the full picture and are confident that no jury would ever convict Mia Folger."

"Fat chance," Bruch repeated his frequently used epithet, loud enough for everyone to hear.

"If that's how you feel, Mr. Bruch, why the problem with the defense's request?"

"Can we go off the record, Your Honor? Approach the bench, please?"

"Step forward, gentlemen."

The attorneys left their respective podiums and walked up to the judge. Bolton cut her microphone and chirped, "What's up, George?"

"Jordyn, I could care less what you order here, but I'm not the Oakland County Prosecutor. I'm just a lowly assistant."

"The chief assistant is hardly lowly, George, but if I'm reading between the lines, the boss has *ordered* you to oppose this motion?"

"In a hypothetical manner of speaking, yes."

Bolton turned her microphone back on and said, "Step back."

The attorneys returned to their podiums.

"Thank you, gentlemen. The preliminary examination will proceed next Wednesday morning. I will set aside two full days for the People to present its case and another two for the defendant. If more time is needed, we will adjourn and reschedule. Mia Folger is facing life in prison without parole, and any inconvenience caused to the People by expanding the scope of the hearing is miniscule in comparison to what Ms. Folger is facing. I will place no material restrictions on the defendant's proofs for this hearing. I will sign an order to that effect. Anything else, gentlemen?"

"No, Your Honor," Blake and Bruch replied in unison.

"We'll adjourn for lunch. Court will resume promptly at one-thirty PM. Good to see you, gentlemen. We'll reconvene *this* case bright and early on Wednesday."

Zack and George walked out together.

"Thanks for stipulating to this, George. I appreciate it."

"I really didn't have much choice. Any change for Mrs. Crawford?"

"No, not really. She's started to dream, a good sign, but has not regained consciousness."

"If she's still unconscious, why are you doing this? Why not wait until she's competent?"

"Because I believe I can get the charges dismissed."

"Like I've been saying, fat chance!" Bruch repeated.

"We'll see," Zack warned. "May I have your list of witnesses and exhibits for the prelim by Monday morning?"

"I'll see what I can do. This is very last minute."

"A woman's life is at stake. Please do the best you can."

"You have my word. See you Wednesday." Bruch turned and walked away. Zack watched him as he exited the double doors.

"Sanctimonious prick," Zack grumbled out loud.

***

The murderer effectively hid in the back of the courtroom, obscured by the press mob. She wondered what this new development meant. Mia was still comatose. Why push for a preliminary exam? Who pushed the hearing? Was it Blake? *He is such a slippery bastard!*

She was satisfied with the evidence. Mia helped immensely with those text messages. The murderer's original plan was to shoot Crawford in the head, make it look like a political assassination. Mia's texts made it possible to stage a crime of passion and kill two birds with one stone. *I hate that right-wing bitch, anyway.*

The murderer reminded herself that she was not a suspect, or on anyone's radar. The Southfield Police and the Oakland County Prosecutor's office were fixated on Mia Folger. George Bruch was confident in his case—she heard his 'fat chance' remark. The wild card was Blake and that investigator, Love. Those overweight police detectives completed their investigation, but Blake and Love were just getting started. *What can they do? Nothing! I was too careful. All evidence, including her own electronic words, point to Mia. The text messages, the location of the crime, the fingerprints, the DNA, all point to Mia. Can't touch me.*

She wondered what Blake was investigating at this point. The more evidence the cops found, the more it pointed to Mia as the murderer. Yet, Blake seemed convinced of her innocence. Worse, his smug arrogance in court was troubling. *What does he know that I don't?* She wondered.

The murderer knew Blake and that psychologist, Rothenberg, were buddy-buddy. Mia wasn't providing alternative facts—maybe it was the psychologist? *Those guys keep meticulous notes, don't they? Maybe the answer is in Mia's medical records. Should I chance it or leave well enough alone? Rothenberg's office is in Birmingham . . .*

***

That same afternoon, Shari Belitz conducted her final session of the focus group. The words on the white screen were:

TOPIC FOUR: ALTERNATE SUSPECTS.

Shari asked the focus group to once again assume that a woman was having an affair with the deceased.

"This woman has emerged as a potential alternate suspect in the murder. She is physically fit and is an adverse witness to the suspect." She further asked the group to consider and assume the existence of additional alternate suspects. Who might they be? What motive might they have?

Shari began the afternoon *Q & A* by asking whether this so-called 'other woman' had a motive to kill or harm the congressman. The answers came swift and furious, much to the delight of Shari Belitz.

"If you add one more presumption, she is just as likely to be the murderer as Mia," Number seven, the Ferndale student, suggested.

"What presumption is that?" Shari inquired, knowing the answer, but wanting it published for the group.

"What if the affair was over and Crawford was returning to his wife?" she floated.

"Yes?" Shari sensed she had more to offer.

"If Crawford communicated this decision to his now former lover, *she* becomes the jilted lover. *She* is furious with Crawford. *She* becomes as viable a suspect as Mia."

"Thank you, Number seven. Anyone else?"

"I completely agree," Number two concurred. "You're tried and convicted in the press and the cops ignore what's right in front of their faces, a person with the same motive and means to kill the congressman."

Shari pushed back. "But Number seven's so-called 'jilted lover' didn't shoot off a text message that she wanted her lover dead."

"Who knows if that was sent by Mia Folger? And even if it was, it's quite stupid to kill someone in the exact same way you threaten. As I indicated earlier, Mia is anything but stupid," Number six observed.

"Show of hands. How many of you think that Mia was set up?" Shari requested. About three quarters of the group believed in this theory.

"How many of you believe the texts are fake?" Only one quarter of the group raised their hands.

"How many of you believe the real murderer somehow leaked the texts to the press?" Again, three quarters of the group believed the murderer was responsible for the leak.

"Interesting . . ." Shari noted, as she wrote something on a legal pad.

"Most of you are willing to entertain the possibility of Mia's innocence. Most believe she was set up. A few believe the texts are fake and most also believe that the real murderer leaked the texts to the press. So, let's explore this a bit further. Is it possible to expand the alternate suspect base? Who else besides Number seven's jilted lover had a motive to murder Congressman Crawford?"

"A right-wing nut?" shouted Number one. The comment prompted a vigorous and heated political exchange between right and left leaning group members. The left believed that a political motive was, at least, possible. The right dismissed the idea. Shari brilliantly bridged the political divide by raising the dismemberment issue.

"Those who believe the congressman's death might have been political, do you also believe that the murderer was cunning enough to devise this particular method of murder to make it look like a crime of passion? If this is a political hit, why not just shoot him in the head? And why frame a right-wing talk show host for the crime? That's quite a diabolical leap, is it not?"

These questions diffused a rather sharp political divide and brought the panel back to evaluating suspects with more personal reasons to murder the congressman. This tactic was unusual for Shari. She didn't typically steer focus group conversations. Jury consultants monitor independent thinking. Shari also knew, however, that Zachary Blake was convinced this was a crime of passion not politics. She saw no value in having the panel continue a divisive right-left debate like those happening all across America.

"So, who besides a jilted lover might this person be?"

"An angry constituent?" someone shouted.

"Political and diabolical," replied another.

"Some lobbyist who spent a lot of money only to have Crawford vote the other way?" A member suggested.

"Still too political," came the response.

"A second lover?" Number five suggested.

"Interesting," Number two replied. "Might he have been cheating with more than one person?"

The group spent several minutes discussing multiple possibilities.

"What do we know about this sexual partner?" A group member finally asked.

"You may assume she is Crawford's legislative assistant," Shari advised.

"Can you describe her?" Another inquired.

"Hang on, let me make a phone call. Please continue chatting about this." Shari left the courtroom and called Zack Blake.

"Shari? What is it?" Zack knew she was in session.

"The focus group wants a physical description of the side piece."

"Side piece?" Zack was not familiar with the term.

"Crawford's girlfriend, his lover on the side."

"Oh! Side piece. Cute, Shari. New York slang?"

"Jesus, Blake. You need to get out more. It's common slang. Do you have a description? Everyone's waiting."

"Sorry. Yes, she's either a light-skinned black woman or mixed race, very well-built—works out, if you ask me—with a muscular frame and a butch haircut shaved thin on the sides. She's got wavy curls on top. Kind of nice looking, if you like the type."

"Thanks, Zack. Talk soon." Shari started to disconnect the call until she heard Zack's voice.

"Wait! Anything else? Something I can do? How are things going?" He sounded desperate.

"You're so cute, Zack. Can't stand not being the center of attention, can you? Nope. Nothing you can do. Dinner tonight? It's my last night."

"I need you to stick around until Thursday. I've got us a preliminary examination hearing on Wednesday, and I need you to do witness prep."

"I've got other business. How's this? I go home tomorrow, catch up, and come back Monday. You line up all the witnesses."

"Works for me. Thanks, Shari."

"You're welcome. May I go now, Your Highness?" she quipped.

"You are excused, subject."

"Subject?" She groused.

"You started it," Zack retreated.

"Hanging up now, juvenile."

Shari returned to the group and provided the description. Everyone agreed the woman was the perfect murder suspect candidate. The person who killed Crawford had to be a very strong woman or the whole woman theory was wrong.

"Excuse me if this is not politically correct, but her description makes her sound like she's gay," Number four suggested.

"You sound homophobic, but you may have a point," Number five responded. Everyone laughed.

"If she's gay, why would she carry on with the congressman? And why kill him? It couldn't have been anything more than a harmless fling. Maybe she came on to him just to see how the other half lived." Number six believed.

"Wait! This may be way out there but hear me out. I've got another idea for a suspect. Are we still looking for alternatives to the alternative?" Number five inquired.

"Absolutely," Shari encouraged. "The more the merrier."

"Here's what I have in mind . . ." The group discussed this alternative suspect and the more Number five talked, the more sense the theory made. The group talked through the afternoon and into dusk. When the last comment was made, Shari walked to the front of the courtroom and addressed the group.

"Thank you so much, ladies and gentlemen. This concludes our little two-day conclave. Feel free to exchange contact information and stay in touch. Follow the case—your theories and conclusions will likely play out in real time. Your time has been appreciated and your input quite valuable. Remember your signed agreements. Everything that has happened over the last two days is confidential. You may not discuss group sessions with anyone. Does everyone understand and agree?" The group nodded its assent.

"As to our last topic and final discussion, I am going to bring these ideas straight to Zack Blake. Wouldn't it be cool if your theories turned out to be more than mere theory? Do any of you have any questions before we wrap this up?"

"I have a question." Number seventeen raised his hand. "Is there any possibility we will be called back in?"

"Thanks for that question. No, I'm afraid once you've been seated and released, we can't bring you back. If we need an additional group or a mock jury, we must start all over again," Shari advised. "Anyone else?" She scanned the room.

One member began to applaud, then two, three, and the whole group began to applaud and shout "Shari" in repetition. Shari smiled, bowed, and thanked everyone. Lauren re-entered the courtroom. "Lauren will handle your checks and tax paperwork. I've got to meet with Zack. Thanks again everyone," Shari acknowledged, as she edged toward the exit door.

The group again applauded and began chanting her name as Shari Belitz exited the courtroom.

CHAPTER TWENTY-TWO

Mon Jin Lau, or "House of Ten Thousand Jewels," in Troy, was Zachary Blake's favorite Asian restaurant. It was owned by the Chin family, in business since 1969, and now operated by the family's third generation. Zack wasn't alone in his praise of the restaurant; it was one of Detroit's premier dining destinations, featuring a wide variety of traditional and contemporary dishes and a diverse contingent of chefs from all over the Asian continent to prepare them.

Zack and Jennifer sat in their favorite booth, waiting for Shari Belitz to arrive. Jennifer was excited to meet the superstar jury consultant. She rarely heard Zack carry on about anyone the way he did about Shari.

The couple was also excited to be at Mon Jin Lau. They hadn't dined there in quite a while. Zack loved their General Tso Chicken and Jennifer could not wait to order her favorite sushi rolls. Zack offered to pick Shari up at her hotel, but she declined, saying she had to finish a conference call and would join them as soon as possible.

"Where is she already?" Zack checked his watch. "I'm starving!"

"Is she usually late? You've shared a lot of meals these past few days," Jennifer commented.

Zack studied her. They gazed into each other's eyes. Jennifer was the only woman for Zack. He adored her. She kept him grounded. In his eyes, she was as beautiful now as the day they'd met, with platinum blond hair, gorgeous blue eyes, and a peaches and cream complexion that never wrinkled or aged. *Is she jealous of Shari?*

Jennifer blinked. "What?" she asked.

"Are you jealous, Mrs. Blake?"

"Jealous? Heavens no! What gave you that idea?"

"Your comment about the meals we've shared."

"I was kibitzing." Jennifer smiled.

"Yiddish? Great pronunciation. I'll make a Jew of you yet." These days, Jennifer was a non-practicing Catholic. Aside from her two boys' encounter with a pedophile priest and the lawsuit that followed, her marriage to the Jewish lawyer who handled the case caused friction with her parish.

At that moment, Shari entered the restaurant, walked up to the host, and asked for Zachary Blake's table. The host pointed to Zack and Jennifer and Zack stood and waved. Shari walked over, ignored Zack completely, and addressed Jennifer.

"I can see why Zack raves about you. Has anyone ever told you that you're gorgeous?" Shari giggled.

"That guy, all the time." Jennifer pointed to her husband.

"Whatever possessed you to marry a trial lawyer? Does he cross-examine you at home?"

"Yes!" Jennifer exclaimed. "How did you know?"

"All the good ones do that to their spouses or girlfriends. They can't turn it off."

"It's annoying. He does it to the boys, too."

"I love your outfit. What is it, St. John?"

"Why, yes. How did you know?"

"I love fashion. After all, I'm a New Yorker. Besides, the designer is very distinctive."

"I hate to break up this love fest. Do I need to introduce you two? Shari, Jennifer; Jennifer, Shari. Do you guys want me to find another table?" Zack teased.

"This guy cannot stand it when he's not the center of attention! Have you noticed, Jennifer? Nice to meet you, by the way."

"I *have* noticed. With success comes *ego*. Know what I mean?" Jennifer winked. "Zack, I love this woman! We should have been having lunches and dinners during her visit."

"Sorry, ladies. Work got in the way. Besides, she would have *billed* me for her time at lunch. She carries around a mini cash register and hours calculator."

"Cut the shit, Blake. I've been very reasonable, and I haven't billed for *any* time not related to the focus group."

"Give it to him, Shari. If he misbehaves in any way, you give me a call."

"Ladies, ladies, can we look at menus, please? I'm starving."

"What's good here?" Shari muttered, studying selections while hidden behind a menu.

Zack opened his mouth to speak, but Jennifer exclaimed "the sushi is terrific," which led to a discussion about the freshest sushi restaurants in Detroit and New York.

"May we order please?" Zack was exasperated.

"Absolutely, I'm hungry. How about you, Shari?"

"Starving. All I do is work around here."

"That's bullshit and you know it," Zack grumbled.

"Gotcha!" Shari laughed.

The server came over and the two ladies grilled her about the best and freshest sushi rolls. Zack was, again, forced to wait out the conversation. After a five-to-ten- minute exchange, the ladies ordered six sushi rolls, agreeing to split them equally. Zack was finally able to order his General Tso Chicken. He also ordered a bottle of 2016 Moraga Estate Sauvignon blanc for the table.

"Fancy schmancy, as my mother used to say. Drink it slowly, Jennifer."

"He can afford it. He's got a few bucks, you know."

"I've heard."

Off they went again, talking about Zack, his work, his causes and generosity, and his advocacy, as if he wasn't seated at the same table. He rolled his eyes, smiled, sighed, and gave up trying to engage. The food arrived. Jennifer and Shari dove right into the sushi, chatting back and forth about this roll or that, suggesting that each try "this one" or "that one" while Zack quietly devoured his General Tso.

The two began chatting about where Shari might find a blowout bar. She confessed that in New York City, she and every other Jewish girl she knew went to one of these two to three times per week to get their hair blown out. Jennifer offered to take her to the salon she frequented. "We can go together," Jennifer suggested. "When would you like to do it?"

When the two women finally had their mouth's full at the same time, Zack found his opening.

"So, Shari, you remember why we're here? Tell me about the focus group. What do I need to know for next Wednesday and what marching orders do I need to give to Micah Love and Reed Spencer?" He knew Shari loved talking about her work. He also surmised she would relish the opportunity to discuss her sessions with the focus group and plot strategy for the preliminary exam.

"What an interesting experience, and such a great group of people. Outspoken, a wide cross-section of ages, lifestyles, political and social justice views. You will be pleased to know that most group members believe your client is innocent, despite the physical evidence."

"That *is* interesting. Did they share why they felt that way?" Zack asked excitedly.

"Almost unanimously, they do not believe that someone would send a text like that and kill in the way they promised. They also do not believe that a woman has a psychotic break at the sight of the body if she is the murderer."

"I've been saying both things all along," Jennifer chimed in.

"We all have, sweetheart," Zack advised. "It's nice to have those suspicions validated. What else can you tell me?"

"The group believes the so-called 'other woman' may have committed the murder. They almost unanimously agree in the alternate suspect theory."

"Elyssa Naylor?"

"I only told them that the congressman was having an affair and that one candidate was his assistant. On their own, they came up with the theory that Crawford may have decided to end the affair and go home to his wife. Would that create enough anger to commit murder? As much as a deceived and bitter wife, they said."

"Wow. This is good stuff, Shari."

"There's more."

"Let's hear it already!" Jennifer exclaimed. She leaned forward, face-to-face with Shari.

"Naylor's physicality was discussed. She's well-built, buff even. She works out, probably strong enough to secure Crawford, subdue him, and move him from place to place. She's also smart. She would have thought to disable the security cameras."

"You were right, Shari. This is terrific news." Zack raised his arm to the server and requested the dinner check by imitating the signing of a receipt.

"I'm still not done. You haven't heard the best part."

Zack sensed what was coming. He had been thinking about it for a while. But he was not about to burst Shari's bubble. Besides, if she was about to say what he thought she was about to say, he was pleased that his suspicions were validated by the focus group.

"Not the best part?" Jennifer looked surprised. "What could be better?"

"Jennifer, in a million years, you would not have come up with this one. It shocked even me."

"Give, Shari. The suspense is driving me crazy!" Jennifer pleaded.

"The group asked whether Elyssa Naylor's sexual orientation was in question."

"What? Why?" Jennifer didn't understand.

"They knew Naylor had an affair with Crawford. Someone raised the issue of her butch appearance and asked if she might be bisexual."

"Why would that matter?" Jennifer asked. Zack was silent, knowing what was coming.

"Everyone agrees the murderer was a woman, right?"

"Right," Zack agreed.

"What if Naylor *is* bisexual and her affair pissed-off a lesbian lover?" Shari dropped the bombshell Zack had been waiting for.

"Huh? I still don't get it." Jennifer remained confused.

"Naylor has a long-term, same-sex relationship with a woman, a buff woman, someone she met at the gym, perhaps. Perhaps she's built like Naylor. Strong, physical. Naylor tosses her to the curb and takes up with Crawford. Who's going to be just as pissed as Mia Folger Crawford?"

"Oh my god! Shari! Oh my god! Zack, did you hear? That makes perfect sense. The other woman is another woman!" Jennifer exclaimed.

"Interesting way to say it, honey, but yeah, it does make sense," Zack mused.

"You don't sound too surprised, Zack. I was floored when one of the focus group members raised the possibility. She walked all of us through the scenario and the more she talked, the more sense she made."

"I'm very pleased."

"But not surprised?"

"Honestly? I've suspected the other woman for quite a while."

"Why didn't you say something?"

"Because I didn't want to taint your process. You told me to stay away, so I stayed away. Considering the outcome, I made a wise choice."

"You did indeed, Zack. Thanks for trusting my process and respecting my boundaries. Not many lawyers I've worked with could have restrained themselves."

"That's my Zack, Shari. Be he ever so humble."

"Funny, Jennifer. Humble and Zack in the same sentence? Ha!"

"What do we do with this, Shari? I've got to get this theory over to Micah and Reed. They need to do a deep dive into Naylor and find this mystery woman. Maybe Reed can identify her through Naylor's phone and computer. He's already working on Naylor's electronics."

"That's Micah's, Reed's and your job, Zack. My job was to pull viable alternate suspects out of the focus group. One caveat I must warn you about, though."

"What's that?"

"The group's opinion changes somewhat if Bruch were to consider lesser charges."

"Noted. I don't think he will ever consider lesser charges."

"Neither do I, but I had to bring the finding to you."

"Thanks, Shari. Oh! I almost forgot. I've got a new job for you."

"What's that?"

"I need a psychological profile on Naylor. I need to know her, inside and out. I must prepare trial questions that tap into the profile and make her uncomfortable, pry out details of what has been, up to now, a private relationship. I'm not even sure anyone in her political circle knows she swings both ways. I've got to break her on the stand. Are you up for that? That's why I wanted you to stay for witness prep."

"I've actually got some ideas on that score."

"Forget the check. Let's order dessert and talk about those ideas. Is that okay with you, Jen? I can take you home and Shari and I can work out of the home office, or we can go to the law office, if you prefer," he offered.

"Dessert or no dessert, you guys aren't getting rid of me. This is beyond captivating! I could listen to you two all night. You were right, Zack. This woman is *amazing*!" Jennifer gushed.

"Okay, let's get out of here," Zack started to rise.

"Hold the phone, Blake." Shari stood her ground.

"What?" Zack asked, suddenly impatient.

"Dinner was fantastic. Zack was absolutely correct about Detroit cuisine. Tell me, Jennifer. How are the desserts here?" Shari asked.

"To die for," Jennifer giggled. "They've got a Sanders Hot Fudge Cream Puff. Sanders is a Detroit exclusive. You've never tasted hot fudge like this in your life. They've got a great carrot cake and an out of this world chocolate layer cake, but you can get those in New York. Sanders Hot Fudge is *legendary*."

"The hot fudge cream puff it is, then. Hard to pass on such a glowing recommendation."

"Can we get one and share?" Zack pleaded. "I'm stuffed."

"Do you promise to behave?" Jennifer scolded.

"What does that mean?" Shari grinned expectantly.

"He's famous for his 'I'm not hungry' routine. Dessert comes, and Zack devours it before anyone else gets their share," Jennifer tattled. Zack scowled.

"I thought that was Micah," Shari laughed.

"It is. With Micah it's *everything*! With Zack, it's only sweets," Jennifer explained.

"Alright ladies, enough already!" Zack was embarrassed.

"I suggest we get two and share," Shari proposed.

"Great idea," Jennifer agreed, signaling for the server.

They ordered the cream puffs. Zack ate one, the ladies split one and made fun of Zack the whole time.

Zack and Shari dropped Jennifer off; the two women embraced as if they had been friends for years.

"Come back soon, Shari. We can have a girl's day. First, we'll go to the salon. I'll tell you everything you want to know about Zack. Afterwards, we'll have you over. I'll make you a home cooked meal," Jennifer offered.

"Take her up on that, Shari. Not the gossip part, the dinner part—she's a wonderful cook," Zack praised.

"I'll be back Monday. I'll take you up on that," Shari laughed.

"Monday? Really? That's great! You're on! See you then."

Zack watched Jennifer go up the walk to the front door. He waited until she opened and closed the front door, then drove off into the night. As they headed toward the office, Shari turned to him.

"What a lovely evening, Zack. Jennifer is special. You're a lucky man."

"I pinch myself every day. I was heading into the deepest hole of my life. I firmly believe I would never have climbed out. I met that fantastic woman and her two boys, and my life has been a fairy tale ever since. 'Lucky man' is an understatement, Shari. I am the luckiest man alive."

"Don't let this go to your head, buster, but she's pretty lucky, too."

"That might be the nicest thing you've ever said to me."

"You're okay, Blake, for a *trial lawyer.*"

"Thank you, I think."

"Let's get to the office. I've got some ideas for Wednesday."

"Thanks for everything, Shari. I could not have done this without you."

"The job is not over yet. Let's keep Mia out of prison."

"Amen, sister. From your mouth to God's ear."

CHAPTER
TWENTY-THREE

Shari Belitz planned on taking a Metro Car from LaGuardia Airport to her Manhattan office. As she exited the plane and walked to the terminal, she observed a man holding a sign that read 'SHARI BELITZ.' She approached him with caution.

"I'm Shari, what can I do for you?"

"I drive a limousine; I have orders to take you wherever you'd like to go, courtesy of Mr. Zachary Blake."

Shari smiled and shook her head. *What a class act this guy is!* The driver helped retrieve and load her luggage into the limo, which was first class all the way, fully stocked, free WIFI, and a wide screen satellite television setup. Airport transportation would never be the same. She called the office and confirmed her return in approximately forty-five minutes, assuming normal weekend traffic. Lauren assured her that the staff was assembled to tackle backlogged assignments as well as Shari's cross-examination prep for the Mia Folger case.

Shari arrived at the office a bit tipsy from a morning mimosa generously provided by Blake, along with a continental breakfast and coffee spread. As she entered the office, everyone wanted to know about the limo and hear Shari's first-hand account of her dealings with the focus group, the latest news about the investigation, the looming hearing and her interactions with the famous "King of Justice" from Detroit.

"Is he as good-looking as they say?" someone asked.

Shari opened her mouth to answer, but Lauren interrupted. "Yes, he's a hottie. And those eyes! He has bedroom eyes!"

"Shari? Do you agree?" Another wondered.

"What she said." Shari nodded toward Lauren.

"How about his body?" A third woman inquired.

"He's a little on the short side, very well-built and very nice looking," Shari replied, searching her memory as she spoke.

"Very well what?" Someone snickered.

"Very funny. This was a *business* trip, as all of you know. Mr. Blake was a perfect gentleman. Get your minds out of the gutter."

"Any sparks between you and *Mr. Blake*?" Another teased. The others turned to Shari, anticipating her response.

"Sparks? He's very happily married and, as all of you know, so am I. I've got a young daughter. You guys have had your fun; now we've got work to do."

"Come on, boss! He's handsome, well-built, filthy rich, you must have felt *something*."

"In another time, another life, I suppose I could fall for a guy like that. Aside from the looks and riches, he's Jewish, brilliant and, despite all his success, down-to-earth and a very nice guy. Wouldn't you agree, Lauren?"

Lauren wiggled her eyebrows in agreement. "His wife, Jennifer, is a great lady. They are a wonderful couple and fortunate to have found each other. Neither had an easy time of things before they met. They both deserve their good fortune. If you had spent time with Zack and Jeni, you'd realize that this conversation is ridiculous. Now, I've answered all your prurient questions. Thanks for the great welcome home. I need you guys to get me up to speed on the Radcliffe and Fink cases. Their trials are only three weeks away. I need a few of you to help me prepare for my return to Detroit on Monday. I've got to prepare some sensitive, hot-button cross-examination questions. Can we please get to work?"

The party broke up and Shari divided the staff into groups of three and four to work on the three cases. Shari, Lauren, Randi, and April began work on the cross-examination of Elyssa Naylor and Judy Hoffman. The telephone sounded; the building front desk was calling. Lauren hit the intercom at her desk.

"Yes?"

"Lauren? This is Rodney downstairs. There's a delivery for Ms. Belitz."

"Shari? Delivery for you."

"What is it?" Shari inquired.

"What is it?" Lauren asked Rodney.

"It's a surprise, the guy says," Rodney replied.

"It's a surprise," Lauren repeated.

"Did Rodney inspect?" Shari wondered.

Rodney could hear her question over the receiver and replied, "I inspected. You will enjoy this delivery."

"Send the guy up," Lauren advised.

A few minutes later, the front door buzzer sounded. Two Uber Eats delivery men carried breakfast for fifteen from Barney Greengrass. Carafes of coffee and orange juice, bagels, lox, cream cheese, a large bowl of scrambled eggs with cream cheese and chives, smoked fish, sable, and creamed herring, and a generous supply of fresh baked goods for dessert.

"What the hell is this?" Shari exclaimed. "Who's responsible? This must have cost a fortune!"

"Breakfast courtesy of . . ." the driver checked his notes. "Mr. Zachary Blake."

"Oh my god, Shari! Leave your husband and marry this guy!" An assistant exclaimed.

"I told you guys—he's quite amazing," Shari marveled. "In another life, another time . . . For today only folks, pleasure before business. Let's eat!"

Shari offered the driver a generous tip. He declined, advising that "Mr. Blake was very generous."

"I'm sure he was," Shari shook her head in wonder and muttered out loud: "Zack, you are something else." With that, she walked into the conference room to join her co-workers for breakfast.

***

As Shari Belitz was returning to her Manhattan office, Reed Spencer was implementing his marching orders. His electronic investigation and surveillance would now concentrate on Elyssa Naylor and her mystery lesbian lover. *Assuming she has one.* Reed wasn't convinced such a woman existed, but he was not the man in charge. Zack Blake believed the theory, and Blake was the straw that stirred the drink.

Digital evidence is no different than any other type of evidence. Aside from his *TOR* research and electronic surveillance of current communications in real time, Reed now searched for evidence that might place Naylor or her mystery girlfriend in a place and time that established guilt or created a likelihood of guilt. For all Reed knew, the crime was carefully planned. Therefore, he decided to investigate periods months before the murder. Likewise, the cover-up was brilliant and might be ongoing, with exchanges of electronic communications or location trackers through today's date. The easiest and most effective methods to obtain data were not completely kosher. Reed, Micah, and Zack decided, long ago, that finding the evidence was the important thing—admissibility of uncovered search materials was a problem for another day. Apparently, 'another day' might have arrived sooner than later, as Zachary Blake recently demanded concrete evidence to introduce at a scheduled preliminary examination hearing.

The most obvious first device for Reed's search was Elyssa Naylor's cell phones. If Naylor had a girlfriend, she would likely telephone, text, or email the woman with one of her cell phones. Assuming Naylor did not turn off location services, Reed could also track her movements, so long as she carried her phone from place to place. The combination of these searches might yield a phone number or address which, in turn, might yield a name and a person. Voice messages or Facetime calls might permit identification of suspects by voice or facial recognition.

Reed was quite fortunate to work for someone as successful as Micah Love. Performing digital forensics is an expensive proposition involving state-of-the-art equipment and significant personnel. Micah had unlimited resources and permitted Reed to run his department as he saw fit. Reed purchased the latest equipment and had a dedicated team of digital forensic analysts conducting in-depth investigations on all Naylor's devices. The team was extensively trained, not only in acquiring the evidence, but also in preserving it. A Faraday bag was used to protect recovered data from being damaged by radio frequency interference or electromagnetic pulse. These clever devices prevented RFI or EMP from passing through its material.

Reed expected the investigation to yield a treasure trove of data and material obtained from Naylor's electronic devices and cloud-based services. Digital forensics, Reed knew, would likely provide significant leads or concrete evidence of an alternate suspect. Once that suspect was identified, the group would do a deep dive into her electronic footprint.

To assure that the evidence was secure, Reed had an 'eyes only' policy. Only those investigators who were working on the project were granted access to the information. While the team would ultimately report to Micah and Zack, the boss and his lawyer client had no immediate access to data. They were, essentially, kept in the dark. Data was stored in a secure location, backed-up in multiple locations, and chain of custody was thoroughly documented and limited, again, only to investigators on the team.

The hardest part of the investigation was its 'needle-in-a-haystack' character. People use electronic devices extensively, for a variety of business and personal reasons. An innocent sounding personal or business call might lead to the person the team was searching for. The investigators knew that every crime had some digital artifact or footprint that would be useful to the investigation. Thus, they meticulously combed though Elyssa's location finder, email, text messages, and call log, attempting to capture digital information that might otherwise have been ignored.

The Fourth Amendment to the Constitution protects against unreasonable search and seizure. But it only applies to *governmental* authorities. For the government, a warrant is required to examine cell phone contents. Not so for Reed and his team. They worked in shifts, twenty-four/seven, to sort through the vast storage room of information contained in these small electronic devices. Considering how effectively the murderer committed and covered up the crime, Reed was surprised the data was even available. He expected Naylor to use a remote command or timed security lock to delete or deny access to data. Apparently, Naylor's precious data was more important than her freedom or committing the perfect crime.

The other tricky part of the investigation was in identifying where the information was stored. Aside from the devices themselves, data might be found on a server somewhere—many counties, states, or even countries away. Hacking into stored data on a remote cloud, somewhere, was far more difficult. There were also challenges relating to relevance. Were these harmless communications or relevant to the commission of a crime. People sometimes communicated in 'code' or language only the participants understood. The team carefully preserved what they considered a relevant communication and was careful to avoid contaminating the information. They did not want to risk being accused of tampering or altering evidence. Storage, handling, and access were key to chain of custody and evidence verification issues.

Each investigator had his or her own sub-specialty in digital evidence extraction. Extraction modes differed depending upon the type of device. Evidence collection was truly a multi-faceted challenge, requiring different technical training, capability, and expertise. Manual techniques, for instance, involved using standard inputs built into a particular device, such as touch screens or keyboards. Logical extraction incorporated external computer equipment to provide commands through code to the targeted device. Specialized processing options, like micro read, were highly technical activities and required advanced digital evidence extraction training.

To make things even more difficult, recent models of Apple or Google mobile phones now had operating systems with improved security, preventing even the manufacturers from unlocking phones. Password protected photos, messages, email, contacts, call history, and other personal data were virtually impossible to recover without a password. Password bypass efforts were further complicated by the fact that different types of devices required different expertise.

Reed sought permission from Micah to hack into the congressman's networked devices. He suspected that Naylor may have used government computers and electronic devices for some personal communications. Zack and Micah decided this was too dangerous and denied his request. Reed would have to obtain the data he needed from Naylor's personal devices.

The team's search was concentrated in three main devices or categories, Naylor's cell phones, computers—both desktop and laptop—and Internet browsing history. Reed's primary focus was Naylor's cell phones and tablet, because she used them so often. There was also a wealth of digital information on her desktop and laptop computers, especially since sites visited often maintained internet files, cookies, and browsing histories for long periods of time. This was especially true of email providers.

A secondary search category was message boards and chat rooms. Reed surmised that if Naylor was a closet lesbian looking for same sex romance, she might have visited a chat room or posted a discreet message on one of these communication websites. These searches were technically difficult, because the site developers built in technology to hide identities and locations of individuals accessing or sharing such information.

With a Wednesday morning deadline looming, the team worked furiously, day and night, capturing and analyzing data that might be related to the murder or a same sex relationship. They searched for communications with people and tracked every person or name they could identify. They also searched for incriminating emails or texts that might have acted as an admission to criminal activity. Finally, they tracked Naylor's movements, and pinned various locations on a map, hoping to capture addresses and identities of property owners. Reed purchased and used the latest software, explicitly designed to facilitate temporal, spatial and network analysis of large troves of digital evidence. One investigator was even responsible for obtaining video surveillance from cameras near places that Naylor visited, hoping to capture evidence of criminality or companionship on video. Triage tools were employed to reduce skill thresholds for certain types of digital evidence, which helped speed up the search.

As the investigation wound down and bore fruit, reporting specialists were required to receive the evidence, maintaining strict chain of custody protocols and handoff the evidence and prepare reports for Zack and Micah. These reports were vital to helping Zack understand what each communication meant and prepare to use the information in court, assuming a judge might admit it into evidence. It was Zack's job to effectively communicate the meaning of the evidence to a judge or jury. The hope, again, was that the evidence would never be required to meet admissibility standards in court. Zack hoped the effort would uncover evidence to persuade George Bruch to dismiss the charges. It was an open question whether any of the evidence uncovered by Reed's team would meet the *Daubert* standard of admissibility in court. *Daubert v. Merrell Dow Pharmaceuticals* was a now famous case that established five criteria for the admission of scientific evidence. Considering the back-handed way the evidence was acquired, Zack doubted it would be admitted under *Daubert*. If a trial was necessary, he hoped to either sanitize the evidence for future admissibility or get some or all of it in as rebuttal to the People's case-in-chief. Zack hoped to never have to cross that bridge.

On Sunday evening, Reed's entire investigating team met with Zack, Micah, some administrative staffers, associates, and partners in the firm, in the main conference room of the Blake law office. Shari Belitz attended via Zoom. The room was stunning, with mahogany walls and a huge marble table surrounded by sixteen executive chairs. An ornate buffet table featured the offerings of Zack's gourmet chef, who'd prepared multiple entrees, salads, and sandwiches for the meeting participants. Micah, of course, was first in line at the buffet table, piling huge quantities of food on two large plates. Dinner meetings at the Blake law firm were his favorite activities.

After everyone was fed, Zack pounded on the table and called the meeting to order.

"For those of you who haven't met Shari, the beautiful lady on the widescreen is Shari Belitz, jury consultant extraordinaire. Shari is to jury consulting what Micah Love is to investigations, without the healthy appetite," Zack cracked.

"Hey! I resemble that remark!" Micah exclaimed, spraying food as he spoke. Everyone at the table laughed. "Ditto on Shari. She's the best."

"Hi, everyone. I think I met most of you during the focus group," Shari said.

"Reed? I understand you and your team did electronic device deep dives into Elyssa Naylor and Congressman Bradley Crawford. Micah tells me you retrieved some interesting digital information," Zack indicated.

"That is true, Zack."

"The floor is yours. Please tell everyone what you found."

"Thanks, Zack. We concentrated our search on their main devices, business and personal cell phones, desktop and laptop computers, and tablets. Naylor is the late congressman's legislative assistant. As you might imagine, they have a robust communications history, both personal and business. We also used these devices to track their movements at or near the time of the murder. Those movements confirm a close business and perhaps personal relationship between the two, at all hours of any given day. There are probably mobile or text communications, but, as you know, Congressman Crawford's cell phone has not been recovered."

"Excuse me; Reed, is it?" Shari interrupted.

"Reed is fine, Ms. Belitz."

"You may call me Shari. How do you distinguish between personal and business for these communications . . . how do I characterize . . . get-togethers?"

"I don't believe we could characterize a two-to-three hour visit to a hotel on the other side of town as a business meeting. And why would the congressman spend hours at Ms. Naylor's home? If you read our report and review the electronic evidence, it becomes quite clear that

Mia Folger's suspicions were correct. Crawford and Naylor were far more than boss and employee. They were having an affair."

"Sorry for the interruption. Please continue," Shari prompted.

"We can also confirm that Elyssa Naylor was nowhere near the 5000 Town Center condominiums on the day of the murder. Location tracking software rules her out as a suspect." The attorneys and law office staff were surprised by this, and a brief commotion followed the revelation. When they quieted, Reed continued.

"We were also ordered to track the communications and movements of Naylor, Crawford, and any unknown person who had frequent interactions with Naylor and an interaction with Crawford on the day of the murder. Does everyone understand?" Reed looked around the table; everyone was nodding their heads and talking with the people around them. Again, Reed waited and continued only when things settled.

"One person had both frequent interactions with Naylor and was at 5000 Town Center on the day of the murder." Shari expelled a loud gasp. She was excited her focus group members helped establish this vital link.

"Are you okay, Shari?" Reed asked.

"Yes, I'm fine. My focus group efforts bore fruit—*that's* exciting. These people did a marvelous job of smoking out the possibility of a third suspect. I'm really proud of them."

“Me too,” Zack agreed. “While I had a similar suspicion, the focus group’s confirmation of my suspicion is what led me to add this component to Reed’s search.”

“It appears that both you and the focus group got this dead right.” Reed pressed a button on a remote control in his hand. A wall opened and a white screen emerged from the opening. A projector came to life and flashed an image of a light-skinned, well-built black woman. She strongly resembled Elyssa Naylor—same coloring, haircut, and body type. The woman clearly worked out, with a body builder’s physique.

“Meet Judy Hoffman. *This* woman clearly had the physical tools required to murder Congressman Crawford in the unique manner he was murdered.”

“What’s her motive, Reed?” Sandy Manning, Zack’s law office managing partner explored.

“I’m glad you asked that question, Sandy. We recovered a treasure trove of texts and emails between Ms. Naylor and Ms. Hoffman in the year before Crawford’s murder. Location services prove they worked out at the same gym. Cell phone and tablet communications revealed a robust sexual relationship. They also did a lot of sexting.

“All this activity stopped about two months before Crawford’s murder. During that two month period, there were multiple texts sent by Ms. Hoffman that were not answered by Ms. Naylor. At first, the texts read as inquiries. ‘How are you?’ ‘Where have you been?’ ‘Please text me back,’ that sort of thing. As time passed, they became more desperate. ‘I’m dying to hear from you.’ ‘Have I done something to offend you?’ ‘Please get in touch. I miss you.’ Finally, they became threatening. 'I will not be cast aside like common trash.' 'Who are you screwing now, whore?' 'How dare you treat me like this after all we've meant to each other?' And more. Hoffman, if she's the murderer, would have had the same motive as Mia. She was Naylor's jilted lover. Location services place her at 5000 Town Center on the day and time of the murder."

"Wonderful news, Reed. It may not conclusively prove she's the murderer, but it creates reasonable doubt for Mia. Both ladies made threats, both ladies were at 5000 Town Center on the day of the murder. Mia lived there. I presume Hoffman did not?" Zack wondered.

"She did not," Reed confirmed. "She lives in Novi."

"I don't want to be a spoilsport, but how was this evidence obtained?" Amy Fletcher, a firm associate inquired. "Is it admissible? What about chain of custody and Fourth Amendment issues?"

"Chain of custody had been preserved throughout. Multiple investigators can testify to clear adherence to chain of custody protocols. The Fourth Amendment only applies to the government. The cops must surveil and gather by the book. Private citizens have no such restrictions. I think we'll be okay, but that's more a question for you attorneys in the room. I'm not a lawyer, although I do have considerable experience as a criminal," Reed joked. The room exploded in laughter.

"Amy, I'm glad you asked that question," Zack advised. "I do not plan to introduce electronic surveillance into evidence. I plan to use it to rebut testimony at the preliminary examination hearing or at trial with either Elyssa Naylor, Judy Hoffman, or both on the stand. I am reasonably confident that Judge Bolton will allow the data to be used for impeachment. What we must do now is carefully prepare for cross-examination of both women. That's where Shari comes in. She'll be providing a detailed psychological profile for both women. With the right sequence of questions . . ."

The conversation continued into the evening. Shari was provided with specific assigned tasks for when she returned to the office. She excused herself to pack for her early morning flight to Detroit, promising to return with a cross-examination roadmap for both women.

The one unanswered question was whether Naylor was complicit in the cover-up. Did she suspect Hoffman? Was she willing to allow Mia to take the rap, despite those suspicions? Or would the emergence of Hoffman as a suspect be a complete surprise to Naylor? Time would tell. Zack, for one, couldn't wait until Wednesday.

CHAPTER
TWENTY-FOUR

After a work-filled weekend, Shari Belitz returned to Detroit. Again, a limo and driver greeted her at the airport, almost a carbon copy of her New York City homecoming experience. She called Zack from the luxurious vehicle to scold him for his ridiculous and wasteful extravagance.

Zack's long-time receptionist, Kristin, answered the phone and transferred the call.

"Shari! So glad you're back. We've got much to talk about. My digital surveillance team has almost conclusively determined that Hoffman was at the scene on the day of the murder. We already know that Hoffman and Naylor were lovers before Naylor's affair with Crawford. Did you and your team come up with an effective approach for the witnesses and the judge?" Zack's excitement was so contagious, Shari forgot she had called to scold him.

"I think you will be pleased with what we came up with. There's no time to test it, except on staff members, and I'm sure you've got some great ideas, too. We've got a good start on a solid approach to a dismissal."

"Great news, Shari. Did you enjoy the limos? You deserve to travel in style, you know."

"And the Barney Greengrass breakfast? Jesus, Zack, how much did this shit cost? How did you know about Greengrass? You are so out of control!"

"And you love me for it?"

"And . . . I love you for it. My office staff, for sure, loves you. They ate like pigs. It made them very productive."

"That was my secret plan."

"Well, your secret plan worked like a charm. There is now nothing my people won't do for Detroit's King of Justice. They are in love with you!"

"Glad to hear it. I've got a team waiting for you here. We need to put all of our ducks in a row for Wednesday."

"I should be there shortly. Oh, and Zack?"

"Yes, Shari?"

"No food! I've probably gained twenty pounds between Friday and today."

"Too late."

"Zack, dammit. Zack?" The line disconnected.

***

Shari arrived at the Blake office mansion about forty minutes later. Kristin escorted her to the large conference room where there was, *of course*, a large breakfast spread. She greeted everyone, poured herself a cup of coffee, and went right to work. She brought copies of sample questions and scenarios for Wednesday's hearing. Zack's professional staff put together similar documents after receiving a report from Reed Spencer and his electronic surveillance team. Reed, Shari, and Zack worked tirelessly, day and night on Monday and part of Tuesday, to put together a rebuttal argument, exhibits, and witness protocol for Wednesday's hearing. It was made quite clear that Zack wanted no less result than a dismissal of all charges against Mia, and a viable suspect to prosecute so that George Bruch could dismiss the case and still win a trial that took a murderer off the streets.

Tuesday evening, Shari and others on the preliminary examination protocol team were Jennifer and Zack's guests for dinner before Shari and Zack retired to Zack's home office to put the final touches on the rebuttal. Zachary Blake had a terrific staff of attorneys and investigators. But never in his life had he worked with anyone who understood how the justice system worked like Shari Belitz. Her questions and hearing protocol were spot on. If tomorrow was successful, Shari Belitz and Reed Spencer would be major non-lawyer contributors. Zack could never admit this to Micah, because Micah brought both of them into the fold and would never let Zack forget it.

Jennifer cooked a feast fit for royalty. Shari complained, once again, how much weight she'd gained since meeting Zachary Blake. She asked Jennifer about the dishes and recipes.

"These are old recipes from both sides of Zack's family. We had various members of each clan locate and forward recipes, some of which are over a hundred years old. We put it all together into a cookbook we call 'The Blake-Lewin Family Cookbook.'"

"May I see the cookbook?" Shari requested.

"Sure. Lots of old Jewish recipes from the old country on both sides of my family," Zack chimed in. "If you like it, I'll have one made up for you."

"I would *love* that!" Shari exclaimed. "Tell me, Jennifer, what did I eat tonight? What family member is responsible for each recipe, and on what page in this fabulous book do I find each recipe?" Jennifer went through the various appetizers, salads, soups, main courses, and side dishes—while Shari looked each one up and noted who the relative was and what generation the recipe emanated from. They were having a fabulous time.

Zack chatted with the others at the table, thanking them for their contributions and hard work. He watched Shari and Jennifer go at it about the cookbook, pleased they had become friends, and pleased that Shari enjoyed the meal and the recipes.

Jennifer paused her conversation with Shari and announced: "Who's ready for coffee and dessert?"

"Dessert from the cookbook?" Shari wondered. "Oh my God, Jennifer, I'll bet they're to die for!"

"I made three of my favorites from the cookbook. Aunt Tibby's Trifle, Aunt Bettie's Mandel Bread, and the dessert of all desserts, Great Grandma Pearl's Cookie Dough Apple Pie. Wait until you taste these, Shari."

"I couldn't eat another bite."

"Just wait. You will eat those words, with these desserts."

Everyone enjoyed the desserts and the conversation. Shari remarked that the apple pie was the best she'd ever tasted.

CHAPTER TWENTY-FIVE

The following morning, Zack retrieved Shari at the Kingsley Inn and the two drove what Zack called the scenic route to the Forty-Sixth District Court in Southfield. Zack took Woodward to Cranbrook and drove through a neighborhood of stately mansions. A few miles south, the road became Evergreen, and took them directly to the Southfield Civic Center, located across from the Town Center complex where the murder took place.

A mob of reporters awaited the arrival of the famous lawyer. Bruch was already inside. As Zack exited his car, the mob descended, shoving microphones in Zack's face, asking for strategy and predictions. "Is this the jury consultant lady . . . Belitz?" someone shouted. "What did the focus group have to say?" "Has Love's investigation come up with anything?" "Do you really believe Mia's innocent?" Zack's response to all these inane questions was a terse "no comment." Shari never said a word.

They edged closer to the door and finally pushed it open. Zack and Shari walked into the municipal building followed by a mob of reporters in hot pursuit. The mob followed into Judge Bolton's courtroom, still shouting out questions, making far too much noise. A court officer picked up the judge's gavel and slammed it down, several times, scaring the hell out of everyone.

"Members of the press. You are present today because Judge Bolton believes in a free and fair press. However, if you abuse her invitation, she will have it revoked. There will be order in this courtroom before Judge Bolton takes the bench. I will order more deputies to stand guard and eject anyone who violates courtroom decorum, if that's what it takes. I expect you to behave like someone's life depends on this hearing, because, as we all know, it does. Does everyone understand?"

The reporters nodded in unison and settled down. Two or three minutes later, Eddie Schreiber, Jerry Kramer, and Jim Sawyer strolled into the courtroom. Bruch rose to greet the witnesses and invited them to sit in the front row behind the prosecutor's bench.

Zack walked over to Bruch and asked to see the witness and exhibit lists he was promised. As Bruch was preparing to give another lame excuse, the court officer called, "Forty-Sixth District Court, the Honorable Jordyn Bolton presiding." A door behind the bench opened, and Judge Bolton assumed the bench with a smile.

"Be seated, please. Zachary Blake, attorney for the defendant and an officer of the court, reports that he has not been provided with a witness list, the witnesses' expected testimony, an exhibit list, and the exhibits. Is this true, Mr. Bruch?"

"We had an unavoidable, bureaucratic oversight, Your Honor. I apologize to you and brother counsel. The record should reflect that I am handing the witness and exhibit lists to Mr. Blake."

"Mr. Blake? We can adjourn this hearing and provide additional time to prepare, if you prefer. And, of course, Mr. Bruch would be responsible for all court costs and expenses associated with this hearing."

"Not necessary, Your Honor. Looking at this list of witnesses, it does not contain anyone we haven't prepared for. I would only ask that we be given the same courtesy when we present our rebuttal."

"You shall have all benefits of doubt, Mr. Blake; isn't that correct, Mr. Bruch?"

"Yes, Your Honor," Bruch sighed. His deferential tone resembled a dutiful husband muttering 'yes, dear' to his wife.

"Are we ready to proceed, then? Any other last minute snafus or games?"

"No, Your Honor," the two lawyers replied.

"Mr. Bruch, please call your first witness."

"The People call Detective Edward Schreiber to the stand."

Schreiber rose, approached the witness chair, and was greeted by the court officer.

"Raise you right hand, please? Do you solemnly swear, under penalty of perjury, that your testimony will be the truth, the whole truth, and nothing but the truth?"

"I do."

"Be seated. Please state your name and occupation for the record."

"Edward Schreiber, I am a senior detective for the Southfield Police Department, Homicide Division."

Bruch skillfully took Eddie through the investigation. The gruesome murder scene, type of weapon, the method of murder and his professional opinion that this was a crime of passion or extreme anger at the congressman. They discussed breaks in the case, the discovery of the text messages, finding the murder weapon, lifting only Mia's fingerprints from the serrated kitchen knife, and finding only Mia's DNA at the scene. Zack made a note to ask Schreiber whether he was lying or mistaken about the DNA issue.

Eddie was a veteran cop. He knew how to testify in court and his testimony was compelling. As he completed direct examination, almost everyone in the courtroom, except perhaps Shari and Zack, believed Mia would be bound over for trial on first or second-degree murder charges.

"No further questions, Your Honor," Bruch concluded an effective direct examination. "Pass the witness."

Zachary Blake rose and approached Detective Eddie Schreiber.

"Before we begin, Detective, I want to remind you that you are under oath today."

"Objection, Your Honor! Badgering." Bruch rose and growled.

"I haven't even asked a question." Zack shrugged, not a care in the world.

"It is condescending to ask a veteran cop if he knows he's under oath," Bruch pontificated.

"Overruled. Cut the nonsense, Mr. Bruch. Proceed, Mr. Blake," Bolton prompted.

"Yes, I know I'm under oath," Schreiber conceded.

"And you will listen very carefully to my questions and answer them honestly, correct? My client's life depends on it."

"I certainly will."

"Deal. Let's talk about the beginning of your investigation, shall we?"

"Sure."

"Your investigation started with a 9-1-1 call from building security at the 5000 Town Center, correct?"

"Correct."

"Who placed that call?"

"One of the managers or security people at the building."

"Did this person tell you what prompted him or her to call 9-1-1?"

"Yes. He said he discovered the body of the congressman in the congressman's apartment."

"What was he doing there and how did he get in?"

"I learned later that he had escorted the congressman's wife, Mia Folger, into the apartment because she was intoxicated and needed assistance. They entered the apartment together, and, as I said earlier, discovered the apartment appeared to have been vandalized. They observed a trail of blood, and followed the trail to the congressman's body,"

"And to be clear, the 'they' you are referring to are this security person and Mia Folger, correct?"

"Correct."

"For the record, the security guy-doorman's name is Charlie Rogan, does that ring a bell?"

"Yes, that's the guy."

"Suppose I told you that Charlie will testify and tell the court that Mia let him into the apartment that day, would you agree?"

"That's what he told us."

"Did he also observe Mia's reaction to the condition of her apartment?"

"He said she was shocked—screamed her husband's name, as I recall."

"Screamed it how? Was she angry, surprised, wondering where he was or if he was hurt, what?"

"Objection, Your Honor. Calls for speculation," Bruch interrupted.

"It calls for the results of portions of the detective's own investigation. I'll allow it. Objection overruled," Judge Bolton ordered.

"As I said, she was shocked about the condition of the apartment and seemed to be concerned about her husband's well-being and whereabouts."

"Especially with the blood on the floor?"

"I couldn't say."

"I understand, from talking to Charlie and from your earlier testimony, they followed a trail of blood to Congressman Crawford's body, is that correct?"

"Correct."

"Did Charlie report Mia's reaction to finding her husband's body?"

"She screamed; I can check my notes. It was something like: 'No, not my Brad—oh my God, no,'" Schreiber deadpanned.

"As I understand it, she screamed, sobbed, and went into shock. Charlie held her, tried to shield her eyes, and ordered the 9-1-1 call. Isn't that correct?"

"Correct."

"After that, and Charlie will testify to verify this, he led her to the vestibule, and sat her down. She was still in shock, sobbed uncontrollably, became delirious and rigid, mumbled incoherently, and became what Charlie and others have called 'catatonic', is *that* correct?"

"Yes."

"Detective, I will probably be calling you back to the stand later in our rebuttal presentation, but here are my last few questions for now. I again remind you that you are under oath, sir." Bruch stood to object, but Judge Bolton sat him down with an arm gesture, while never taking her eyes off the witness.

"Did Charlie ever suggest to you that Mia Folger's reaction to discovering her husband's body seemed phony or manufactured?"

"No, he never mentioned that. He was concerned about her."

"And, in your many years of experience, you've investigated many murders, correct?"

"Correct."

"More than ten?"

"Yes."

"More than twenty?"

"More than fifty?"

"Yes."

"More than one hundred?"

"Yes."

"Lots of experience at murder, right?"

"Right, unfortunately."

"Amen to that. Tell me, please. How many murders have you investigated where the killer leads you to the body, is shocked at the condition of the scene, sobs uncontrollably, and goes into catatonic shock upon the discovery of the body?"

"Objection, Your Honor. Assumes facts not in evidence."

"Overruled. The witness will answer."

Eddie Schreiber squirmed uncomfortably, appearing to search his memory.

"Detective?" Zack prompted.

"None," Eddie whispered.

"I'm sorry, Detective. Could you speak up? I could not hear you."

"None," Eddie groaned.

Zack appeared to have completed an effective cross-examination. He turned his back on Schreiber and began his return to the counsel table. He suddenly turned back to the witness who had risen and was now exiting the witness chair.

"By the way, Detective, you said earlier that the only DNA you recovered was that of the defendant and the victim, is that correct? Did you say that?"

Eddie Schreiber sat back down.

"Yes, I said that."

"But that isn't the truth, is it? I'm going to give you a chance to rehabilitate yourself."

"It is the truth."

"But it's not, Detective."

"Objection, argumentative."

"Sustained. Mr. Blake, Mr. Bruch's objection is technically correct. Would you please stop toying with the detective and get to the point? There's no jury here. Where are you going with this?" Bolton admonished.

"Indeed, Your Honor. I apologize. A report was buried in a mountain of documents dumped on our office by the prosecution. I don't know if this was deliberate or not, but I would invite the detective to review his own file for *all* DNA findings, not just those that support his theory of the case. Detective, would you do that for us, please?"

"Sure." Eddie opened and began reviewing the file. He pulled out Jim Sawyer's DNA report and began to casually scan the document. He paused, looked closer, and glared at the words. He had forgotten and neglected to follow up on this extraneous finding. He glanced at Bruch, who shrugged. The assistant prosecutor had no idea what was going on. Eddie raised his eyebrow, obviously considering his response.

"Detective? Would you like to amend your testimony?"

"Apparently, I would."

"In what regard, sir?"

"The DNA."

"What about the DNA?"

"We did, indeed, find DNA that was no match for either the victim or the defendant." A loud murmur was heard in the press gallery.

"Whose was it?"

"Unknown, Mr. Blake. Cotton fibers from an overcoat."

"Male or female?"

"Impossible to tell, sir."

"Your Honor, I would respectfully request a gag order preventing the release of information about this coat until a search warrant is executed at the location where the coat is currently."

"So ordered. Members of the press—remember, you are here as my guests. I hereby grant the defense's motion for a temporary gag order about the existence of this jacket, and any DNA recovered from this jacket, pending further investigation. I am not saying you can't report on it; I am saying you can't report on it *yet*. Anyone caught violating this order will be in contempt of court, subject to harsh penalties. Understood? Please signify by raising your hands." Every hand in the room shot up. Bruch stood at the prosecution counsel table, mouth wide open, glaring at Schreiber.

"No further questions, Your Honor." Zack concluded with a sly grin. The war was on. First battle won by the defense.

***

The murderer had no press credentials or connections. For the first time since Mia was indicted, she was completely in the dark about the status of the case. Could she reach out to Elyssa? What would she think? Up to now, she hadn't attempted contact, afraid Elyssa would put two and two together. *If Elyssa knew I was the murderer, would she protect me or turn me in? How much did she love Brad Crawford?* That's what the decision came down to, and the answer was clear. *The bitch preferred Crawford.*

How was the preliminary examination going? Was it the slam dunk that the podcast lady said it was? Why hasn't she reported on the proceedings? Does she have press credentials? Maybe I should pay her a visit.

Would Mia's doctor testify? Could they make him talk? *There is no doubt she threatened to emasculate Crawford. Should I leave well enough alone? Mia's losing, isn't she?* Judy was almost convinced that not even the great Zachary Blake could wiggle Mia out of the mess she made for herself.

The mess she made for herself. True, she didn't commit the murder, but her behavior was so reckless that she set herself up to be the patsy. Could a frame have been any easier? That cold, hard fact was on Mia Folger. Bruch was a very experienced prosecutor, and the level of proof necessary to bind Mia over was slight. *Perhaps we maintain the status quo.*

***

George Bruch called crime scene investigator, James Sawyer, to the stand. He still felt the pain of Blake's cross of Schreiber. Bruch could not believe he'd overlooked the DNA finding. Worse, he could not believe that Blake's team found the needle in all the haystacks George dropped in the document dump. He would make up for his shortcomings with Sawyer. If he had stopped to think about the circumstances, it wasn't any *person* that came up short. It was the *evidence.* Where George Bruch went wrong was in caving to public pressure to solve the crime and expose the murderer to the public. Cops and prosecutor both were lured in by various press reports and, ultimately, those text messages.

As Bruch did with Schreiber, he presented a compelling direct examination of Sawyer. The pair methodically presented cause of death, murder weapon, motive, timeline, opportunity, text messages,

DNA, fingerprints, and location tracking evidence to make a compelling case for Mia as the murderer. Zack and Shari whispered to each other throughout direct examination, tweaking cross-examination ideas based on Sawyer's now-live testimony. Bruch completed his direct examination and passed the witness. Zack Blake jumped to his feet and immediately began his vigorous cross-examination of crime scene tech Jim Sawyer.

When was Sawyer first called to the scene? How many techs investigated under his supervision? Were any of them inexperienced? Did he maintain control of the scene and the evidence throughout? Who collected DNA, fingerprints, and blood samples? Were any contaminated? He bore in.

"DNA can often prove a crime, isn't that correct?"

"Certainly. That's why we collect it."

"But not in this case, correct?"

"I'm not sure what you mean. Yes, in this case and all other cases. DNA, blood, and fingerprints led us to Mia Folger."

"Well, I'm sure you didn't come here to lie, Mr. Sawyer, but that statement just isn't true, is it?"

"Objection! He's badgering the witness."

"I'll allow it. I believe defense counsel is about to explain himself," Judge Bolton ruled. She knew exactly where Zack was leading this witness.

"Isn't it true, Mr. Sawyer, that Mia Folger's blood was nowhere to be found at the scene. All blood found belonged to the victim."

"Well, yes, but how does that make me a liar?"

"Would the court reporter please read Mr. Sawyer's answer to my question: 'But not in this case, correct?'"

The court reporter pulled on her scroll of paper, trying to locate the question. After a short time, she stopped searching and said: "Quote: I'm not sure what you mean. Yes, in this case and all other cases. DNA, blood, and fingerprints led us to Mia Folger. Closed quote." The court reporter read from the scroll and repositioned herself to continue. Zack politely awaited her nod to move forward.

"That isn't true, Mr. Sawyer, is it?"

"Sure it is. I don't understand what you're talking about." Sawyer was totally confused.

"Let's try this a different way. Did you find Mia Folger's blood anywhere at the scene?"

"Well . . . uh . . . let me check . . ." Sawyer began to search through his file. "Uh . . . let me see . . . no . . . I guess we did not find Mia Sawyer's blood at the scene."

"Your statement that you relied on DNA, fingerprints, and blood evidence was not true?"

A light bulb went off in Jim Sawyer's head.

"Oh! Now I follow! Yes, you're right! Mia Folger's blood was not found at the scene. But her fingerprints were the only ones on the knife and her fingerprints and DNA were all over the apartment."

"And in your world, the presence of DNA and fingerprints— to quote your previous statement— 'led you to Mia Folger' and every other murderer you've investigated. Is that correct?"

"Correct."

"But this case is different, isn't it?"

"Again, Mr. Blake, I don't understand."

"What was the murder weapon, Mr. Sawyer?"

"A serrated kitchen knife."

"And where did you find all of this DNA and fingerprint evidence?"

"At the crime scene."

"This is like pulling teeth, Mr. Sawyer. Are you deliberately trying to be evasive?"

"Objection, Your Honor. Badgering." Bruch scowled.

"Sustained. Mr. Blake, move along."

"I'm getting there, Your Honor. The witness is making this more difficult than it should be, but the technical point is quite important, as you will soon discover."

"Get on with it, please."

"Where was the crime scene, Mr. Sawyer?"

"The victim's apartment at 5000 Town Center in Southfield."

"And who lived at that location with the victim?"

"His wife."

"The defendant, Mia Folger, correct?"

"Correct."

"The apartment was Mia's too? And the kitchen and the kitchen knife, true?"

"True."

"So, I'm going to ask you again, sir. The presence of DNA and fingerprints in one's own apartment is no surprise, right?"

"Right."

"So, how could the presence of fingerprints and DNA, and *no blood*, in the defendant's own apartment lead you to the conclusion that she was guilty of murder?"

Sawyer paused. He really had been *that* clueless. He was so accustomed to the presence of DNA and fingerprint evidence proving guilt, he forgot to consider that the crime scene was the defendant's own residence. *Of course, there is DNA and fingerprints! I'm such an idiot!*

"I guess, by itself, it wouldn't, but considering where we found the knife, the nature of the crime, and the text messages, it is additional evidence of guilt." He tried to recover.

"That's absurd, Mr. Sawyer. It is evidence that she *lived* there. Nothing more. Let's move on, shall we? We can agree now, can't we, that the presence of Ms. Folger's DNA is expected in her own apartment, right?"

"Right."

"What about the presence of foreign DNA?"

"Pardon me?"

"Wouldn't the presence of foreign DNA be more unlikely, and, if present, more suspicious?"

"I suppose."

"It is more likely, if we can identify the foreign DNA, that whoever that sample belongs to is the murderer?"

"If you are referring to the overcoat, I don't think so. It could be anything."

"Fair enough." Zack decided not to belabor the point. Sawyer would never admit it, anyway. "You would agree, though, that you found no such overcoat in the apartment belonging to either Congressman Crawford or Mia Folger, correct?"

"Correct."

"Thank you, sir. No further questions." A second battle won by the defense.

***

Shari Belitz and Zachary Blake stood outside Judge Bolton's courtroom discussing the hearing and the two witnesses.

"That was great fun, Shari. Cross-examining witnesses with psychological triggers built into the questions is an amazing experience. It never occurred to me how much psychology and the law merge in these situations. You predicted where these questions would lead, and they led exactly where you predicted. You are a wizard!"

"Thanks, Zack, but everyone contributed, and any courtroom success depends on a terrific lawyer to execute the plan. You executed beautifully and those audibles you called created even greater success. We are clearly winning," Shari encouraged.

"In my humble opinion, and I know you agree, we can't win at this level, with this low proof threshold without the *SODDIT* defense coming into play."

"In this case it is *SOWDIT*, no?" Shari smiled.

"Huh?"

"Some other w*oman* did it."

"Right, Belitz, cute. For us to pull this off, some of our assumptions must be true. For instance, we are only *assuming* the coat belongs to Hoffman. What if it doesn't?"

"If it doesn't, we still have reasonable doubt at trial. This is a great test of the state's evidence. It is almost an official mock trial. The prosecution is losing, and you are creating reasonable doubt up the wazoo."

"The downside is that Bruch will have plenty of time to correct these mistakes for trial. I agree with you, Shari, but winning now and winning decisively must still be the goal. That coat belongs to Hoffman and that's all there is to it."

"How do we prove her ownership and keep it quiet at the same time? For the plan to work, we have to do both." Shari was dubious.

"Leave that to me. I've got a few tricks up my sleeve."

"Care to share?"

"I will, but not now. I've got to get back in there."

***

The afternoon session went much like the morning. Bruch called the Southfield Police's equivalent of Reed Spencer, a tech nerd with a cyber-stalking record who served his time and went to work for the police, preventing crimes like those he used to perpetrate.

Alvin Magid testified that he verified, one hundred percent, that the now famous texts came from Mia Folger and Mia's computer. There was no doubt in his mind.

Zack suspected that Mia, indeed, sent the texts. He believed Alvin but could not resist having a bit of fun. Besides, Shari's psychological profile made him easy prey on cross-examination.

"Alvin, may I call you Alvin?" Zack began.

"Sure."

"Alvin, do you have the skills to make a text seem like it's coming from person A when it is actually coming from person B?"

Alvin readily took the bait. After all, he was a tech nerd. To admit you can't do something is taboo. "Of course, I can," He boasted, as Zack and Shari suspected he would. "Piece of cake."

"I presume others of your skill level could do the same?"

"Not many have my skill level," he crowed.

"Understood. Are you familiar with Reed Spencer from Love Investigations?"

"Yes, I am, very talented guy."

"Does he have the skills to do what I described earlier?"

"He does, one of the few," Alvin conceded.

"That makes at least two of you that can make a text look like it came from someone else. Correct?"

"Yes, and from *somewhere* else."

George Bruch wanted to run up to the witness chair and strangle the bastard. *He didn't ask you that question, moron!*

"Whoa, Alvin! You mean you can not only hack a text, but you can make one look like it came from somewhere else?"

"Yes."

"Here's my question. You testified that you were one hundred percent certain that the texts were written by Mia and sent from Mia's computer. True?"

"Yes, I said that, because it's true."

Zack shook his head in mock bewilderment. "I'm confused. First you say it's impossible; then you say it's possible. Which is it?"

"It's impossible for a lay person to do the twofer."

"Twofer?"

"Hacking a phone and making the text look like it came from that person's phone when it actually came from another person or phone."

"I see. And in this case?"

Bruch listened intently. He wanted to crawl under the table. His arrogance about meeting the low 'more likely than not' threshold of guilt or innocence standard for a preliminary examination, caused him to underprepare his witnesses. Zack Blake was making him pay for his arrogance, one witness at a time.

"In this case, the participants do not have the requisite expertise. I fully investigated all of the people involved and none of them had the skills." He folded his arms and adopted a smug expression.

"How many people out there have similar expertise to you and Reed Spencer?"

"I'm not sure, but it would be a small number."

"Maybe one percent of the population?"

"Maybe. Probably less," he bragged.

"Half a percent? We have people like you working for most police departments, right?"

"Right, but not all of us have the same skill set. Half a percent is probably a good number."

Zack poured it on. Bruch was powerless to do anything. The judge was amused. Only Alvin Magid, self-professed tech genius, could not see where this was going.

"Great, Alvin, let's go with half a percent. But I will concede that the number is even less. Most of that half-percent work for the FBI, the CIA, or the police and other law enforcement communities, right?"

"Right. I hadn't thought of that. It's an even smaller number." He now looked confused, trying to compute the number in his head.

"Let's knock it down to a quarter of a percent of the population. Sound good?"

"Sure."

"And those would be people in the private sector, correct? Available, perhaps, to create firewalls or anti-hacking equipment for your home or office computers."

"Oh, yes, those guys are quite good," Alvin gushed.

"And available for hire?"

"And available for hire."

"To fix your computer, cell phone or tablet, or protect them from hackers, right?"

"Right."

"And they would also have the skill to hack into these devices, create a text, and make the text look like it came from the person who owned the device, also correct?"

"Sure."

"Okay, Alvin. You've been very patient with me and very forthcoming. I appreciate it. I only have one more question."

"Fire away," Alvin replied, confidently.

"If a person wanted to hack into someone's device, create and send a text, and make it look like the owner sent the text from his or her own device, couldn't he just hire one of the seven hundred fifty thousand people in America with that level of tech knowledge?"

"Seven hundred fifty thousand?"

"Actually, it's more than that. I estimated our population at three hundred million, and it is truly three hundred *thirty* million. But one quarter percent of three hundred million is seven hundred fifty thousand."

"So?"

"Please answer my question."

"I don't remember the question."

Zack had the court reporter read back the question. As he waited, arms folded, he turned toward the courtroom exit door. The door opened, and Elyssa Naylor entered.

"Could they have hired a talented techie to do the hack and make it look like the text came from the owner of the machine?" Alvin repeated.

"That's my question, Alvin."

Alvin sat in silence, clearly working things out in his head.

"Yes, Mr. Blake," he finally admitted, still not realizing the impact of his testimony. "And there are, according to your math, seven hundred and fifty thousand people he or she could hire."

"Thanks for pointing that out, Alvin. I have no further questions."

The judge suppressed a laugh. Bruch was furious. Shari was euphoric; the defense pulled off the trifecta, winning the first three battles of the war. Judge Bolton called for a brief recess. Bruch headed for Naylor, and Zack and Shari headed out the door.

CHAPTER

TWENTY-SIX

"Bruch will use this recess to sand Naylor. He'll tell her they are getting their asses kicked and how much they need her testimony, what a tricky bastard I am. He will prepare her better than the others," Zack told Shari as they headed out the door.

"It won't matter if we stick to the script. According to my psychological profile, she will fold like a tent," Shari reassured.

"I like the strategy, Shari, don't get me wrong. I just wish Naylor went first rather than fourth."

"Stick to the script."

"I will."

***

Inside the courtroom, Bruch was pleading with Naylor. "We are taking a beating in here. Blake has diffused every witness we've presented, from the cop to the CSI to the tech expert. I am beginning to get concerned that Mia will not be bound over," Bruch confessed.

"She's a murderer. How can this be happening?"

"I need you to tell the judge what you told me. You must be candid about the affair. Tell the judge what Mia's reaction was when she found out her husband was cheating."

"Isn't that hearsay?"

"Technically, yes, but it may be an exception to the rule. I'll worry about whether it is admissible. You worry about testifying, telling the story you told me."

"What about Blake? Any tricks up his sleeve?"

"Probably, any other skeletons in your closet I should know about?"

Naylor thought about Bruch's question. She was so careful about the affair. *Mia only found out because Brad wasn't careful. Who else could have done it? Everyone loved Brad, except for that bitch, Mia Folger.*

"Not that I can think of."

"If there are any, you may assume Blake knows about them."

"Again, I can't think of anything."

"Okay then, let's play it by ear . . . see what happens. I sure hope you're not holding out on me."

***

"All rise! The Forty-Sixth District Court is back in session, the Honorable Jordyn Bolton presiding," shouted the court deputy.

Bolton rushed in and sat down. "Be seated," she commanded.

"Back on the record in *People v. Folger*. Mr. Bruch? Please call your next witness," Bolton ordered.

"The People call Elyssa Naylor, Your Honor."

Naylor was sworn in and Bruch positioned himself to the right of the witness chair. He leaned on the ledge, like a neighbor chatting with Elyssa on her front porch. According to Naylor, Crawford was terribly frustrated with his wife's public declarations of disagreement with his politics. While a political odd couple relationship may have worked for James Carville and Mary Matalin, it was not working for Bradley Crawford, primarily because he was a current congressional officeholder and not a political pundit.

He hated Mia's show, and her constant bitching about policies and bills he was strongly in favor of. He tried to discuss his discontent with Mia, but she laughed it off, arguing that the public enjoyed the show. The more frustrated Crawford got, the more he turned to Naylor for support. One thing led to another and they fell in love—at least—that was Naylor's take on the relationship.

Elyssa wanted Brad to get a divorce. She argued that a public repudiation of Mia and her politics would advance his career. She also believed, if he divorced her, there was a more harmonious future for Naylor and Crawford together. Brad wasn't quite ready to commit to a divorce, but then he got Mia's text messages. He couldn't believe how vicious and vindictive they were. "Would she really do something like that?" he asked Naylor, more than once. Naylor concluded that Mia *would* do something like that. She warned Brad to watch his back.

Zack listened to her testimony and smiled. This was all self-serving hearsay, but he didn't care. He was about to dismantle Naylor 's testimony with one simple question.

Bruch continued the direct examination.

"How did Brad Crawford react to your warning?"

"He assured me that Mia was just blowing off steam. She loved him and would never do anything to hurt him. Obviously, he let his guard down."

"How well did you know Mia Folger?"

"As well as any legislative assistant knows the wife of her congressman. She was a nasty right-wing pundit who seemed to revel in making her husband angry. Sometimes I thought she took positions contrary to his just for that reason. She is a vicious human being. It doesn't surprise me that she killed him, nor am I surprised by the way she committed the crime. She wasn't satisfied with merely political emasculation. She had to *actually* emasculate him!"

Zack stood, still quite relaxed. "Your Honor, I've been very patient. Ms. Naylor's self-serving hearsay testimony is one thing, but her over-the-top speculation is another thing altogether. I must strenuously object. Suddenly, Ms. Naylor is a gossip *and a therapist*?"

"Your objection is sustained; Ms. Naylor's last few remarks will be stricken from the record. Move along, Mr. Bruch. And please try to ask questions that will lead to admissible answers at trial," Bolton chided.

"You are convinced Mia knew about the affair, is that correct?"

"Yes, Brad told me he got a few texts from Mia accusing him of cheating."

"Did Mia know you were the other woman?"

"She did. She confronted me in the gym."

"You worked out in the same gym?"

"Yes."

"What happened during the confrontation?"

Zack started to rise. Mia was not there to defend herself. He realized this woman would say anything, make up any story, to make Mia look guilty. He stayed in his seat because he was powerless to prevent the testimony. It was admissible—Mia's unavailability was his fault, not Bruch's. It was Zack who chose to move forward with the hearing.

"She shoved me into a corner. She was out of control angry. And she was so strong! I could not believe how strong she was. I'm not a lightweight; I work out, but I was no match for Mia. She got in my face, stuck a finger right at my eyes and accused me of sleeping with her husband. She told me if I wanted to stay healthy, I would stay away from Brad. I was really scared." Elyssa Naylor began to sob. She took a tissue out of her purse and dabbed her eyes. Zack wanted to applaud her performance.

"Two days later, Brad was dead. There is no doubt in my mind she killed him."

"Your Honor." Zack rose. "Objection, speculation. Please strike the last response."

"So ordered."

"Ms. Naylor?" The judge began to chastise her.

"No further questions, Your Honor," Bruch nipped it in the bud.

"Mr. Blake, cross-examine?"

"One moment, Your Honor." He leaned away and spoke to Shari, a quick conversation about whether anything they just heard altered the script. Shari assured him it did not. Zack rose and approached the witness.

"Ms. Naylor, you don't like Mia Folger much, do you?"

"No."

"And according to your testimony, she didn't like you very much either, correct?"

"Correct."

"And that was because you are a dishonest person, correct?" Pushing buttons.

"No, that's not correct."

"No? Do you consider sleeping with a man behind his wife's back the act of an honest woman?"

"We were in love . . ."

"You told us earlier, but that doesn't answer my question. Is sleeping with a man behind his wife's back an honest act?"

"I suppose not."

"So, we can agree you are dishonest."

"I don't think a single act of infidelity defines a person, Mr. Blake," Naylor groused.

"Maybe not, was there only one?"

"I don't know what you mean."

"How many times did you sleep with Brad Crawford, once or more than once?"

"More than once."

"More than five times?"

"Yes."

"More than ten?"

"Yes."

"And who stole a glance at Mia Folger's text messages, copied them, and leaked them to the press?"

"I-I-I'm not . . ."

"Be careful, Ms. Naylor. You are under oath."

"I did."

"And that wasn't an honest act, either. I will ask you again, can we now agree you are a dishonest person?"

"Your Honor, he's badgering the witness. I object."

"Overruled. She has brought this on herself. The witness will answer the question," Judge Bolton ruled.

"I suppose we can," Naylor finally admitted.

"Your testimony, before our little discussion, might be tainted as well, correct?"

"I am under oath."

"Do you promise that everything you say in this courtroom from now on will be totally truthful?"

"Yes, absolutely." She folded her arms and glared at Zack, resolute.

"Excellent. Who is Judy Hoffman?"

Elyssa Naylor was stunned by the question. *How did he find out about Judy?* Sweat began to form on her temple.

"Ms. Naylor? Judy Hoffman?"

"She's a friend. Actually, a former friend."

"You promised to be totally truthful. I will ask you again, who is Judy Hoffman?"

"I told you, we used to be friends."

"You were more than friends, weren't you?"

"I don't know what you mean."

"You have a terrible time being totally truthful, don't you?"

"Objection, Your Honor," shouted a frustrated Bruch. Blake was destroying yet another witness. "Badgering."

"Overruled, Mr. Bruch. The witness's evasive answers are creating her current situation. Proceed, Mr. Blake."

"No, I don't," Elyssa finally answered. "These are very personal questions."

"I'm sorry I have to invade your privacy like this, Ms. Naylor, but like the judge says, you brought this upon yourself. You are a bisexual woman and Judy Hoffman is your former lover, isn't that true?" The press began to murmur about the shocking revelations. The judge pounded her gavel and called for order.

Elyssa was stunned silent. She never expected her secret to be revealed.

"Ms. Naylor?" Zack prompted. "Your answer, please?"

"Yes, we were lovers," she blurted.

"And you ended the relationship when you took up with Congressman Crawford, true?"

"Yes."

"How did Ms. Hoffman handle the news?"

"She was very confused, sad, and angry. She kept calling and texting. She wouldn't leave me alone. She could not accept that the relationship was over and kept threatening to out me to Congressman Crawford or his wife."

"Do you know whether she did that or not?"

"No, I swear, I don't."

"Would you consider Judy Hoffman a jilted lover?"

"Yes, I guess I would."

"Many people have referred to Mia Folger as a jilted lover. They have determined that was her primary motive for murder. Would you agree that in this tangled web woven by you and Brad Crawford, Judy Hoffman has just as much motive to murder Brad Crawford as Mia?"

"I never thought about it. I suppose that's true."

Bruch was self-flagellating at the counsel table.

"In fact, if you think about it, she has greater motive. Crawford stole her woman, and she had no feelings, other than, perhaps, hatred for Crawford. Mia Folger was a less-likely candidate because she *loved* Brad Crawford, correct?"

Naylor had given up. "Yes, that's true."

"That's all I have." Zack turned away from Naylor, but quickly turned back. "Wait, one more question. Does Judy Hoffman have a beige overcoat?"

"I'm not sure. I don't recall."

"Your Honor, may we approach?"

The judge motioned the two lawyers forward and turned on a sound machine to drown out their conversation.

"What's up, Mr. Blake?"

"Your Honor, I would like Mr. Bruch to join me in a motion for dismissal of all charges against Mia Folger. Even if she may be guilty, she cannot be proven guiltier than Judy Hoffman."

"Mr. Bruch?"

"No, Your Honor. No way. With the lower "more likely than not" standard, we have made our case for Mrs. Crawford to be bound over. Besides, we have not finished presenting our case."

Zack and Shari planned for this response. Shari Belitz predicted every single occurrence thus far. "Your Honor, may I make a proposal?" Zack began to argue.

"I would like to invite Mr. Bruch to assent to the issuance of a search warrant. There is foreign DNA and fibers from a beige overcoat that the defense believes belongs to Judy Hoffman. We would like this search warrant to be executed in secret. If the coat is found at Ms. Hoffman's residence, it shall be seized and tested by Jim Sawyer to see if it matches the foreign DNA and fibers found at the murder scene. Neither Ms. Folger nor Congressman Crawford knew Judy Hoffman, so the presence of her coat fibers and DNA in the Crawford's apartment would be compelling evidence of her guilt. If we do not find the coat, we will continue with this hearing."

"George?" The judge turned to Bruch. "Sounds reasonable to me. I will sign the search warrant if you request it."

"I want to get a murderer off the streets. If that murderer is this Hoffman woman, I have no objection," Bruch conceded, just as Zack expected.

"Two more issues, then, Your Honor. You must admonish the press, a second time, that a gag order on what they just heard is in place and the facts and circumstances may not yet be reported. More importantly, we must make the same demand on Elyssa Naylor. She must be ordered to avoid all contact with Judy Hoffman. She must not warn her in any way, until the search warrant is executed, the coat is recovered, and Ms. Hoffman is brought to court to testify," Zack insisted.

"So ordered. Anything else?" Judge Bolton inquired.

"I think that covers it."

"I hope you're right, Zack. Unless the coat is found and tested, we will always have two viable suspects and I'm not sure we can convict either one of them under those circumstances," Bruch admitted.

"Step back, please. Ladies and gentlemen of the press. I am compelled to issue another gag order and this order also applies to you, Ms. Naylor." Judge Bolton turned to the witness, made eye contact, and obtained her silent assent via a head nod.

"The testimony about Judy Hoffman, her DNA, and coat fibers, must remain confidential until a search warrant can be executed for the Hoffman residence. If the coat is recovered, it shall be seized and tested by the Southfield Crime Lab under the direct supervision of Jim Sawyer. If fibers and DNA from the coat match the DNA and fibers Mr. Sawyer's team already has, I will issue a subpoena for Ms. Hoffman to appear in court. Does everyone understand what is happening, and your own responsibility under this order?"

Everyone, including Naylor, nodded their assent. The judge, however, was not satisfied. "I am going to ask all members of the press in attendance today to retire to the jury room. My secretary will draft non-disclosure agreements for your signatures. Ms. Naylor will wait in the courtroom with Mr. Bruch and will execute a similar NDA. Is that understood?"

Again, everyone either nodded or voiced consent. All in attendance understood the stakes and wanted the court and the law to get this right.

"Mr. Bruch? I am signing the search warrant right now. Will you please have your second chair deliver it to Detective Schreiber and have him or Detective Kramer execute the warrant? If the coat is recovered, and Ms. Hoffman is present at the residence, I hereby order her detained and transferred to my courtroom pending the results of DNA testing. Have I covered everything?"

"Yes, Your Honor," Bruch agreed.

"Mr. Blake?"

"Satisfied for now, Your Honor. Hopefully, you will soon see clear to dismiss the charges against my client," Zack suggested.

"Cart before the horse, Mr. Blake. We are adjourned. I am informally making all of you officers of this court. I expect full compliance with these orders, and severe penalties will be meted out if I discover any violations. Thank you, everyone."

The judge slammed down her gavel. The court officer led members of the press into the jury room. Bruch sat down with Naylor. His second chair exited the courtroom with the search warrant to deliver to Detective Schreiber. Zack approached Bruch and thanked him for his cooperation with the plan. George graciously indicated that he only wanted to get a murderer off the streets and if that murderer was Hoffman, he was happy to participate. Zack and Shari exited the courtroom, walked through the lobby of the municipal building and out to the parking lot. Once outside, Zack turned to Shari, beaming.

"I've tried a lot of cases, had lots of success, but I have *never* experienced anything like that! This hearing has been conducted like a maestro conducting a symphony. Every note follows the next in perfect harmony, executed flawlessly by the orchestra. Shari, I cannot thank you enough. You played both the prosecution and witnesses like finely tuned instruments."

"I followed the science, Zack. You executed the plan, brilliantly. Thank you. I have thoroughly enjoyed working with you. It's not over, though. Let's hope we recover a coat and that it's a match!"

"Amen. Let's pick up Jennifer and get something to eat. I think we're done until, at least, tomorrow. Perhaps you and Jen can have that blowout day at the salon."

"I would *love* that! I mean, look at my hair." She pulled out a make-up mirror and began to primp. "Thank you, Zack."

They got into the car and drove north to Bloomfield Hills. For the moment, all was right with the world of Zachary Blake.

***

After lunch at Val's Deli on Orchard Lake, Zack returned to the office, and Jennifer and Shari headed to Salon Edge for their girl day. In addition to a blowout from Roland, Jennifer's favorite stylist, Jennifer arranged a facial, mani and pedi, from Vivian, her favorite manicurist. The ladies enjoyed being pampered and each other's company.

Jennifer was uncomfortable chatting about Zack and her boys in front of Roland and Vivian, but in moments where the two ladies were left alone, Jennifer was more forthcoming. For some reason, Shari was very easy to talk to, and the women carried on like two teenagers discussing adolescent flirtations at the mall.

"What's Zack like at home? Is he able to leave the office behind?" Shari wondered out loud.

"Most of the time. However, when he's involved in a big case like this one, we know he will be preoccupied and just wait out the process."

"He told me he was in terrible shape when you guys met. How did he pull out of it?"

"It's true, he was. I didn't know him very well back then. The man I now love was buried deep inside that guy he had become. I guess you could say my kids and I resurrected him. Our case became the first crusade of the man you see now, and we have never looked back."

"But how did he get there in the first place? He's so strong—a freak of nature, if you ask me," Shari marveled.

"A bad marriage, a partnership break-up, some bad investment decisions, bad breaks, *life*, you know what I mean? It wasn't just one thing. All I can tell you is that those times were the worst of his life and drive him to always be the best he can be."

"What's he like in the sack?"

"Shari!" Jennifer turned red. She turned her head this way and that, making sure no one heard the question. "That's rather personal, wouldn't you say?"

"Just two friends chatting. Want to hear about me and my husband?" Shari offered.

"No!" Jennifer suddenly looked like she'd baked in the sun for hours.

"Jennifer, you're blushing! Zack told me you were a prude, but I didn't believe him."

"I'm not a prude. Some things are just . . . I don't know . . . private."

"How are your boys doing? Rothenberg seems like a great guy. He's helped them a lot?"

"The boys are great. I have Harold and Zack to thank for that. Their money is in a trust fund. They enjoy the trappings of Zack's success, but we try to keep them grounded. They went through rough times, but they are doing well in school and socially. How about your life?"

"My husband's a wonderful guy. Very understanding and accommodating. My business takes me all over, sometimes for days at a time, and he's terrific about it."

"Children?"

"I have a daughter. Her favorite activity is soccer and getting hurt. She just had a tooth knocked out."

"Zack told me. Is she okay?"

"She's fine, tough, like her old lady. So, Jennifer, give! How's Zack in the sack?"

"Shari!"

CHAPTER

TWENTY-SEVEN

Harold Rothenberg visited with Mia, unaware that Zack's cross-examination of Elyssa Naylor resulted in a new suspect, one even more compelling than Mia. Rothenberg watched her restless sleep—tossing, turning, mumbling incoherent words, clearly reliving past trauma.

"Mia?" He gently shook her awake.

She gasped, opened her eyes, and surveyed her surroundings like a scared child. She made eye contact with Rothenberg, her first eye contact with anyone since the day of the murder and the discovery of her husband's mutilated body.

Rothenberg tried to hold her gaze. "Mia?" he repeated.

Tears rolled down her cheeks, she began to cry out loud, sobbing, grimacing, in obvious pain.

"Mia, it's me; Dr. Rothenberg, Mia. Please, tell me how I can help you."

Mia stopped sobbing and wiped her eyes with her hospital gown sleeve. She again made eye contact with Rothenberg. She motioned with her free hand, imitating a hand writing something. Harold looked around, found a legal pad and pen, and handed them to Mia.

Mia took the paper and pen and began writing. She turned the pad around to show Rothenberg.

How long? Two words written on the first page of the legal pad.

Communication! "It's been several months, Mia. What do you remember?"

Mia again wrote frantically on the legal pad.

Brad?

"He's gone, Mia. He was murdered. You found the body, remember?"

Yes, she wrote. *Awful.*

"Mia? Are you able to talk?"

Mia cleared her throat, opened her mouth, and struggled to find words or sound. She could mumble her dreams when unconscious but could not find words while awake. Rothenberg soothed her, told her that her voice would return in time, and recommended she get some rest. He was buoyed by this sudden eagerness to communicate. She was coming out of her catatonic state.

"Doc?" Mia cooed out loud, clear as day.

Rothenberg was ecstatic that she had uttered her first words. He pulled out his cell phone and texted Zack Blake:

Mia is awake and communicative. Get to the hospital ASAP!

Rothenberg turned back to her, ready to offer encouragement and congratulatory words. Mia, however, was fast asleep.

Rothenberg texted Blake again:

Never mind. Fast asleep.

***

Eddie Schreiber and Jerry Kramer knocked on Judy Hoffman's door. A buff, muscular, young woman opened the door and stood before them. She reminded the men of Elyssa Naylor, only bigger and far more muscular.

She could easily kick my ass, Schreiber concluded.

"May I help you?" Hoffman inquired.

"I'm Detective Eddie Schreiber and this is my partner, Jerry Kramer. We're here under court order to execute a search warrant. Step aside, please, ma'am."

"I will do no such thing," she advised. "What's this all about?"

"Again, ma'am. Please step aside. We have a warrant to search these premises."

"Not until I call my lawyer."

"You may call your lawyer, but we are searching these premises, now! Either get out of my way or you will be arrested."

Hoffman stood in the doorway, feet spread apart, arms folded under her breasts.

"Detective Kramer, arrest Ms. Hoffman."

Kramer pulled out his handcuffs and approached the woman. She stepped forward, daring a confrontation. Kramer looked to Schreiber. Eddie pulled out his cell phone and called headquarters, requesting a squad car and strong uniformed officers.

"Strong, sir?" the dispatcher repeated, confused by the request.

"Yes, someone who works out."

"Will do, sir. On their way."

For the next five minutes neither Kramer nor Hoffman flinched. Sirens could now be heard in the background.

"What's this all about?" Hoffman repeated.

This time, Schreiber answered her. "Do you have a beige overcoat, ma'am?"

"I think so, why?"

"Will you take us to the coat, please?"

"Not until you tell me why."

The squad car pulled up. Two large, well-built cops alighted the vehicle, and walked up to the porch. "What's the problem, Detectives?" one of them queried.

"Please subdue and handcuff this woman. She is interfering with the execution of a valid search warrant."

"Okay, Detective . . . what's your name? I will step aside," Judy conceded.

"Too late, Ms. Hoffman. The time for that was *before* you forced me to call for back-up. Boys, handcuff Ms. Hoffman and take her down to the station, please."

"Come on, Detective! There's no need for that. I'll be good."

Eddie ignored her, motioning the officers forward. They approached Hoffman. Each grabbed an arm, forced both behind her back, and applied the handcuffs. "Take her to the station," Eddie repeated. "Ms. Hoffman, last chance to help yourself here. Where will I find this beige coat and are there more than one?"

"Either in the front hall closet or in my bedroom. I've also got some clothing in the spare bedroom. Can we dispense with the cuffs now, please? I'm cooperating."

"Again, Ms. Hoffman. You should have cooperated from the start. We'll see you down at the station."

The officers hauled Judy Hoffman to the squad car, forced her into the back seat, telling her to watch her head, closed the doors and drove off. Eddie and Jerry entered her home and began ransacking the place. *Never piss off a veteran detective.*

The search hit pay-dirt; the detectives found three coats that might fit the description of the beige overcoat and placed them in separate sealed garment bags to avoid cross-contamination. They documented the find, where they found the coats, the date and time, and what they had to do to gain entry into the home.

Jerry wanted to take Hoffman's computer, but a computer or computer search was not authorized by the very limited search warrant, so Eddie ruled it out. He wanted to leave nothing to chance. If Hoffman was the murderer, Eddie did not want some warrant snafu setting her free. Truth be told, Mia as the murderer never sat well with Eddie. He could not get her reaction to the body out of his head. *A murderer does not go into shock at viewing her own handiwork*, he kept telling himself. But, until Hoffman was identified, Mia was the only logical suspect.

The two detectives left the residence and returned to the station where Jim Sawyer awaited the coats.

"Here you go, Jim. Take good care of these. Dot all i's. Cross all t's. Observe strict chain of custody protocol. If this one is the murderer, and I think she is, I don't want her getting off on some crime lab technicality."

"I've got your back, fellas. Let me go do my thing." Jim walked away with the three garment bags. Eddie called Bruch.

"We've got the coat. Actually, we have three coats. We had to arrest her because she wouldn't cooperate. She's in holding at the station. Sawyer has the coats. He'll be running tests shortly," Eddie advised.

"Thanks, Schreiber. Nice work. Thank Kramer for me. Let me know as soon as you hear from Sawyer."

"Will do. What do you want me to do with the woman?"

"Hold her. Let's see what Sawyer comes up with."

"No problem."

CHAPTER TWENTY-EIGHT

Jim Sawyer and his team worked diligently on the three coats. The garments were labeled, simply: 'Hoffman One,' 'Hoffman Two,' and 'Hoffman Three.' One and three yielded inconclusive results. Jim personally handled the final coat. Based on his conversation with Schreiber, the Southfield Police now believed that Hoffman was the murderer. However, they had no forensics to prove her involvement.

Eddie Schreiber voiced George Bruch's concern that a failure to confirm Hoffman as the killer might result in both women being set free. Each created reasonable doubt for the other. Sawyer carefully examined every inch of the coat under a high-powered magnifier. He found traces of a red or rust substance on the left pocket flap. *Blood?* He took high res closeup pictures of the stains, then scraped at one of the three spots he observed. He deposited the scrapings in a sterile container and sent them off to the lab, with a special request for a blood stain expert to analyze and compare the blood, if that's what the substance was, to Congressman Crawford's. He also cut a piece of cloth from the other pocket flap and sent that piece to the lab for comparison with the beige coat fibers found at the murder scene. He used combs, tweezers, and a vacuum cleaner to collect any possible hair or other fiber on the coat. He put those materials in separate containers and shipped those off to the lab. He requested the lab to also do a DNA and fibers comparison between residuals found on the coat, and routine fibers and DNA found in Crawford's apartment. If all else failed, perhaps he could still place her at the scene. He put a rush on all three samples. *This will keep those guys busy for a while*, he thought to himself.

***

Zack Blake convened a breakfast meeting at Little Daddy's with Shari Belitz, Micah Love, and Reed Spencer. The topic of conversation was Judy Hoffman and the search warrant. Zack wanted to always be two moves ahead of the police and the prosecutor.

"Can we all agree that if there are crime scene DNA or fibers on that coat, it's game over and Mia will be released?" Zack posed.

"Yes," Shari concurred. The other men nodded their affirmation.

"What happens if there is no match?" Zack speculated.

"Why don't we wait to see what the lab comes up with?" Reed suggested. "They're damned good, you know."

"I'm not disputing that, Reed. But what if there are no positive findings or the results are inconclusive? What then? The judge isn't going to postpone the hearing while we try to develop more evidence. Bruch seems to prefer Mia to Hoffman—bird-in-the-hand, I guess. He's not going to drop the case unless he's handed an airtight case on Hoffman." The foursome paused the conversation, all eyes on Zack.

"What are you thinking, Zack?" Shari inquired.

"Not sure, just thinking," Zack replied, his mind elsewhere.

"If the judge continues the hearing, we follow the previous protocol and script, get her on the witness stand, and you do to her what you've done to every other witness in this case," Shari rallied the troops.

"I agree, Zack. If you can poke enough holes in her story, even if there is no physical evidence of her involvement, perhaps you can create enough reasonable doubt for the judge to dismiss," Micah suggested.

"That's the problem, Micah. Right now, Mia is the defendant, not Hoffman. Bruch is prosecuting *Mia*. Remember, the standard at the prelim is not reasonable doubt, it is more likely than not. I'm concerned we won't have enough to prevent prosecution."

"So what? You try the case on reasonable doubt and win it. What's the difference?"

"The difference is that a vicious killer remains free, perhaps for years, until Mia is well enough to handle a trial."

"How is Mia?" Reed wondered.

"I heard from Rothenberg this morning. She's more alert, writing notes, even uttered some words. Doc's encouraged."

"That's wonderful, Zack! Mazel Tov!" Shari exclaimed.

"Thanks, Shari. I don't know where we'd be in this case without you."

"I appreciate the compliment, Zack, but you are the man who suggested and implemented the plan. I am your lowly servant," Shari replied.

"I've been paying your bills. These are *servant's* wages? And I thought Micah was expensive!" They all laughed.

"Okay. How about your lowly, high-paid consultant?" Shari suggested with an angelic smile.

"More like it. Back to our next steps. Shari, how does the psychological protocol work if we don't have the fiber and DNA? Does she still cave?"

"I would have to tweak the profile a bit. I'm not sure I can answer that one yet. Let me talk with Lauren and we'll get on that, with your permission, because you will be billed, sir," Shari quipped.

"I don't doubt it."

"I may have an idea, but it involves trusting the cops," Micah thought out loud.

"Trust the cops?" Reed laughed. "You?"

"Cops aren't the bad guys, Reed. They usually try to get these things right. The problems come when they become so fixated on a particular suspect, they dig their heels in and won't see the forest through the trees. I think I can work with Schreiber and Kramer. Can you handle Bruch, Zack? And we need to get the fabulous Ms. Belitz involved, too. The more I think about this, the more I think it might work."

"My professional psych advice is let's wait and see what happens with the samples," Shari suggested.

"Shari, my dear, how would you like to leave New York and come to work for the Blake firm, full-time?"

"You can't afford me."

"I can afford you, but it might upset the apple cart. A paid consultant is one thing. An employee that makes more than my law partners? That would be a problem," Zack groaned.

"More than your partners? Ms. Belitz? Can you train me to do what you do?" Reed exclaimed.

"Sure, Reed. And you can bill Micah for your new expertise."

"Hey, cut the crap, Belitz, biting the hand that feeds you. All this talk about money is making me hungry." Micah picked up his menu.

"When are you not hungry, boss?" Reed inquired.

"All three of you on my ass, now? I may not share my idea."

"We're sorry, Micah. Allow me to make amends. Go ahead. Order your usual three breakfasts," Zack schmoozed.

"That's better. I'm an important cog in the Blake machine. Don't you forget it."

"Never crossed my mind."

***

Sawyer called Schreiber with bad news from the lab. What he thought might be blood evidence was, in fact, paint splatter. Apparently, Hoffman was a freelance artist. The fiber and DNA comparisons were inconclusive and required more testing. For now, they could not confirm a match to the crime scene fibers. Hair and additional residual DNA analysis was negative for anything that matched Mia or her husband.

Schreiber contacted Bruch, and the prosecutor seemed pleased with the news. Apparently, he still held out hope for Mia to be bound over for trial and a courtroom victory over Zachary Blake.

Bruch immediately called Blake to gloat about the new developments. He would call the court and request that the judge reconvene the hearing. Zack requested he hold off for a day or two while the lab continued its analysis. Bruch saw no harm in a short delay. He had no problems letting the miserable Ms. Hoffman cool her jets in a cell for another day.

Following his conversation with Bruch, Zack called Shari into his office and both phoned Micah with the news.

"No match, Micah. Time for plan B," Zack advised.

"You might still get a match, Zack. If it was conclusive, the lab would have indicated that," Micah tried to reassure.

"Quite possible, I suppose, but we don't have the luxury of time if the hearing continues without positive DNA or fiber matches. Again, it's time for plan B," Zack concluded.

"I wasn't resisting, Zack. I was being positive and reassuring," Micah sighed.

"I will be reassured when you call me and tell me you've implemented plan B."

"On it, boss. I'll keep you informed."

Zack hung up the receiver and turned to Shari. "Okay, professor, it is time for you to work your magic."

"What do you need me to do?"

"Here's the plan . . ."

CHAPTER TWENTY-NINE

Micah Love paid a courtesy call to Eddie Schreiber and Jerry Kramer. He drove to Southfield Police headquarters, walked up to the sergeant's desk and asked to see the veteran detectives. They kept him waiting awhile but, after forty-five minutes, Jerry Kramer came strolling out of the bullpen. Micah was a former cop; the two detectives did not know him well, but knew he was former police. Micah guessed correctly that his former status would make a difference. Once a brother-in-blue, always a brother-in-blue.

"Micah, Eddie's on a telephone call. What can we do for you?" Jerry greeted him without a 'hello'.

"Is there some place where the three of us can talk privately?" Micah requested.

"I'm not sure what time he'll be done."

"I'll wait. This is important."

"Suit yourself. Can I get you anything? Coffee, tea, a coke?"

"Coffee, black, thanks."

Kramer left the waiting area, returned with a cup of coffee, and handed it to Micah.

"You sure you want to stick around? Could be a while."

"I really need to talk to you guys. I need a favor and I have a message from Zack Blake."

Kramer was intrigued; Micah could tell. "What kind of message? I can take it to Eddie."

"I need to discuss it with both of you. Blake's orders. He's the one paying my bill."

"Okay. I'll be around. Eddie knows you're here."

"Thanks, Jerry."

Micah pulled out his cell phone, sent a few texts, reviewed some emails and returned a couple of phone calls. Twenty minutes later, Kramer returned and invited Micah into the bullpen. They walked through a maze of workstations over to a small conference room at the end of the pen. Eddie Schreiber was seated in the room. As Kramer and Micah walked in, Eddie rose and greeted Micah warmly. "Good to see you again, Love. How's it hanging?"

"I'm doing okay. I've got a favor to ask you guys."

"Jerry filled me in. Said you wouldn't talk until you got both of us in a private room. Well, here we are. What's up?"

"Can anyone hear our conversation in here? Is this room monitored?"

"No, Micah. This is totally private," Schreiber promised.

"First question: Do either of you believe that Mia Folger is guilty and Judy Hoffman is innocent?"

"Off the record? This discussion won't come back to bite us in the ass?"

"You have my word as former police."

"Good enough for me. I can't speak for Jerry, but I was never comfortable with Mia as the killer. Her reaction made no sense," Schreiber confessed.

"Jerry?"

"Ditto. What he said. Why, Micah? What's up? It's not like we can do much about it," Jerry lamented.

"Zack Blake and I have an idea, but we need your help to pull it off. Will you help us?"

"Is this legal . . . totally kosher?" Schreiber demanded. "I'm willing to help, but I will not do anything shady, like private eyes do."

"I resemble that remark," Micah responded with a smile. "This is a bit around the edges, but it is legal and ethical in Michigan."

"I guess we have to hear it to decide now, don't we? Spill, Love. What's going on?"

"Bruch would rather bind Mia over than arrest the true perp. He saves face, at least for now, and gets to boast that he beat the great Zack Blake in court. He is not going to go along with this. You guys must agree to work the plan without him—behind his back, so to speak. He'll be pissed when he finds out. Are you willing to risk the wrath of Bruch?" Micah asked.

"How convinced are you that Hoffman is the murderer?" Kramer wanted to know.

"One hundred percent. Hoffman is guilty; Mia is not," Micah confirmed.

"Then we'll risk it. We're in, Micah," Schreiber consented. "You have my word as *current* police."

"Good enough for me. Here's the scoop." Micah repeated every word Zack and Shari told him to repeat. Eddie and Jerry listened intently, nodding their heads, glancing back and forth at each other as Micah laid out the plan. Micah wrapped up his pitch and awaited a response.

"Are you sure about the law on this, Micah? I've heard about this technique in certain cop circles, but I've never tried anything like it before." Eddie was dubious.

"Zack says the case law supports us. You can't get away with it in some jurisdictions, but Michigan is not one of them. It is perfectly kosher in Michigan."

"Can you send us some case law?" Kramer suggested.

"I'm sure Zack can send you something. If you see some case law and it supports what I am saying, are you in or out?"

"We're in," Schreiber promised, turning to Kramer who nodded. "Let's nail the bitch."

"How much time do we have? When do you have to charge her or let her go?"

"We've got another twenty-four hours. More, if we charge her with obstruction or something."

"Good, let's keep that in our back pockets. Zack and Shari are scripting the scenario as we speak. All you guys will have to do is stick to the script. Zack, Shari, and hopefully, Hoffman will do the rest."

"Who's Shari?"

"Jury consultant from New York. She got forensic psychology training. She will know what buttons to push to get results."

"Right, the podcast lady mentioned her. Let's give it a go, then," Schreiber urged. "Hoffman is a smug little shit, and I want her in prison for a long, long time."

"This plan represents the best chance we have of that, and of clearing the name of an innocent woman."

"We feel terrible about that," Eddie conceded.

"Mia hasn't spent any time behind bars. No harm, no foul, but let's get her exonerated, shall we?"

"We shall," Kramer replied.

***

After hearing from Micah that the cops were in on the plan, Zack and Shari went to work on refining the script. Shari weighed her team's psychological profile, buzz words, and button-pushers, and devised language that virtually guaranteed the proper result. If Kramer and Schreiber stuck to the script, the plan would work. When they completed what Zack called "Shari's work of art," they arranged a private meeting with Jerry and Eddie at the Blake law firm. They did not want to meet with the cops at police headquarters; such a meeting would raise eyebrows, cause suspicion, and, potentially, get back to Bruch.

"Thanks for coming, gentlemen. Here's your script. But I can do this one better. Micah has some very expensive microphones and recorders. Shari Belitz over there is a whiz at these scripts. I would be happy to set you guys up with Micah's listening and recording devices, and you can have Shari in your ear, the whole time, asking the questions for you to repeat."

"We only have one shot at this, so if she's as good as you say, put her in my head," Eddie consented. "Jerry?"

"Same here. I don't want to screw this up."

"Take us through the law on this, will you please, Zack? I know our department frowns on this kind of stuff."

"Sure Eddie. Here's some background. Some is obvious, stuff you see every day, some is not. Please bear with me."

Zack advised that the United States Constitution afforded any suspect the right to refuse to talk to the police. Miranda warnings advise them that anything they say can and will be used against them in a court of law. However, if a suspect chooses to talk, with or without counsel, the police have the right to use lies and deception to coerce a confession. From a criminal defense standpoint, obviously, it is not a good idea to cooperate with a police interrogation.

Shari's profile and research indicated that Judy Hoffman was too arrogant to exercise her right to remain silent. Shari was also convinced that Hoffman believed herself smarter than the police, smarter than Congressman Crawford and his wife, and smarter than the great Zachary Blake. With the right questions, Judy Hoffman would be unable to resist trying to deceive the police by answering their questions. Once that happened, Shari believed, the floodgates would open, and Judy Hoffman would incriminate herself.

Zack confirmed what the cops already knew. During a criminal investigation in Michigan, it is perfectly legal for cops to lie to suspects. Hopefully, the suspect will be coerced into saying something incriminating, or offering a complete confession in exchange for leniency.

There are multiple techniques. Sometimes a cop will tell a suspect that he or she was implicated by someone else. If the suspect thinks someone 'ratted him out' he may admit culpability and indicate that the snitch was the more culpable of the two. The cops might also tell a suspect that jail time will be excused or reduced. While the cops may lie, a suspect may not. It is a crime to lie to the police. Shari's plan was to appeal to Judy's ego, her assumption that she was superior to or smarter than the police. Under those circumstances, Hoffman would be unable to resist cooperating.

While it is always wise for a suspect to keep his or her mouth shut, it is also wise to realize that Michigan police are highly trained law enforcement officers and employ numerous techniques to solve crimes. The cops have virtually unlimited resources, high-tech equipment and expert operators, funded by taxpayer dollars. The plan was to chat

Hoffman up, appear friendly, perhaps clueless, indicating that they were looking for Hoffman's help in nailing Mia. Shari suggested they disclose the preliminary DNA and fiber results, reveal they were negative, and dupe Hoffman into believing she was about to be exonerated. The plan was to catch her off-guard, over-confident, and then spring false documents that would cause her to make harmful admissions.

Toward that end, Micah's team of experts prepared stunning false positive DNA and fiber findings. The documents were brilliant forgeries that linked Judy's overcoat to DNA and fiber trace evidence found at the crime scene. These reports confirmed a blood match between Crawford's blood and samples found on Judy's overcoat. Once confronted with this evidence, Zack suggested, and Shari agreed, the cops could then offer a lighter sentence in exchange for a confession.

"These documents are incredibly accurate forgeries, people. I've been a cop for over thirty years, I couldn't tell the difference between the real deal and these. Unbelievable!" Eddie remarked.

"I understand the other stuff," Jerry Kramer indicated. "Cops lie all the time in interrogation. But forged documents? Are you sure about this? I don't want this thrown out on a technicality."

"We'd actually like you to use both. I'll explain that later. For now, though, to answer your question, whether or not you guys dislike this level of deception, it is perfectly legal in Michigan. There are multiple Michigan cases where the police intentionally fabricated laboratory reports and exhibited them to the defendant during an interrogation to secure a confession.

"In one recent rape case, the cops suspected a particular person, but felt their evidence was insufficient to press charges. In cooperation with the prosecutor's office, the cops fabricated two scientific reports which they intended to use as ploys in interrogating the defendant. One false report was prepared on crime lab stationery; the other was prepared on the stationery of a testing organization. These false reports indicated that scientific tests established the semen stains on the victim's underwear came from the defendant. The cops showed the defendant these reports during interrogation, and the suspect confessed. The court of appeals upheld the confession and the conviction. The case is a carbon copy of what we intend to do here."

"Sounds like a solid plan, as long as it's legal," Eddie responded, still concerned.

"There's more. After we present these phony documents that say DNA and fiber analysis is positive for Crawford's blood and consistent with the fibers already found in the apartment, we advise her that if she cooperates, we'll take murder one off the table. Did she go there intending to kill him or just talk with him? She just wanted him to stay away from her girlfriend. He refused—things got out of hand. She meant to hurt him, but not to kill him. She didn't think he'd bleed out. She temporarily lost control. We've all done it. Probably looking at manslaughter, maybe even involuntary manslaughter. She could be free in five years or less, which beats a life sentence.

"That's the plan, gentlemen; what do you think?"

"If it's legal and ethical to use these phony documents, I'm on board. I don't love the idea of her getting out in five years. As to the rest, may I check with municipal counsel?" Eddie inquired.

"As long as the lawyer is not from the prosecutor's office and agrees not to snitch to Bruch."

"He's a good guy. He'll do what we ask," Jerry promised.

"Good to go, then?" Blake posited.

"Yes, we'll set it up for tomorrow. She'll be ripe by then, almost sixty hours in the pen. I like the part where this beautiful lady whispers sweet nothings in my ear," Eddie joked.

"Aw, shucks, Detective. I'm blushing. But it won't be sweet nothings. It will be a whole lot of somethings. If you follow the script, she will sing like a canary," Shari boasted.

"Looking forward to it," Eddie replied.

CHAPTER

THIRTY

The following day, after Judy Hoffman was fed breakfast, she was taken from her cell and placed in a holding cell at police headquarters. After a short wait, she was retrieved by Jerry Kramer, brought to the small conference room near the bullpen, and handcuffed to the table. Jerry's instructions were to leave the room and let her stew.

Forty-five minutes later, her wrists aching from being handcuffed, Judy Hoffman was bristling. Eddie Schreiber opened the door, walked in, and sat across from her. Shari's voice was in Eddie's ear, quietly saying 'testing, testing.' If Eddie began the conversation with "is there anything I can get you before we start?" he could hear Shari. He started with that request. Judy politely declined. Eddie Mirandized her; she declined, "for the moment," to remain silent or request a lawyer.

"You may request an attorney at any time, Judy. Understand?"

"Yes, dammit. How long are you going to hold me here?" she demanded. "I know you can't hold a suspect indefinitely."

"That's true, but we can do so for seventy-two hours; you are at sixty with twelve to go before we are required to charge you. The purpose of this little meeting is to decide the charges against you. We'd like to talk to you, talk some sense into you, and hopefully, you can avoid a long prison sentence."

Shari planted several seeds in that paragraph. Judy learned that she had to stay in a cell for another twelve hours. Apparently, the cops were about to charge her, and she was being offered a lifeline. The seeds were working—Judy was intrigued.

"If you had anything on me, you'd have charged me already," she blustered.

"Not true. We told you when we brought you here; your coats were being tested for fiber and DNA. As it turns out, we also tested blood samples we found on the coat," Eddie dangled. Shari floated the idea of blood on at least one of the coats.

"Blood? What blood?" Judy was visibly shaken.

A decision was made to tell the truth as often as possible. Therefore, Shari prompted Eddie's next comment.

"The crime tech discovered a mysterious red or rusty substance on one or more of your overcoats. We sent it to the lab for blood analysis and a comparison to blood taken from the crime scene." Another blow to Judy's inflated ego. She had mistakenly believed this would be a walk in the park. After only two questions, she was reeling.

"I see. And the results?"

"They haven't come back yet. We'll have them soon. Perhaps there's room to talk before blood results come back," Eddie repeated Shari's prompt. He could see the wheels turning in Judy Hoffman's brain. *Is there a deal to be made?*

"They will come back negative," she falsely claimed. Two can play the lying game. The problem for Judy was that Shari was much better at the game.

"Are you willing to take that chance?" Eddie asked. "You see these?" He waved the phony reports in her face. "These are preliminary fiber and DNA analysis. Two out of three tests place you at the scene. The blood will represent the trifecta, the final nail in your coffin. Best to get out in front of this, Judy, don't you think?"

Eddie did not want to show her false reports unless she insisted. He was still uncomfortable with the technique—ethical and legal or not. But if she was never shown the false reports? He liked that scenario much better. For the moment, she wasn't asking to see them. 'Are you willing to take that chance?' was another Shari prompt, providing Judy with the potential option of confessing, cooperating, and pleading to a lesser charge before the final nail was hammered.

Shari's theory concluded Judy was the murderer, and unless she was a psychopath and incapable of rational thought, she was a rational person. She knew she was guilty. She wore the coat. It was logical the coat had blood spatter.

Only her arrogant conclusion that the police would never identify her had prevented her from destroying the coat. She cursed her stupidity. A deal was sounding better and better. *What do they really have?* She remained silent, listening to Schreiber's review of the evidence. She couldn't believe how much he'd pieced together.

"The good news is that Mia Folger's DNA is all over the place, too," Eddie continued to float Shari's words. As Judy visibly brightened at the news, Shari and Eddie brought the hammer down. "But, of course, this was Mia's apartment. Her DNA is *expected* to be present. The surprise was the presence of *your* DNA and fiber. You didn't know Mia or Bradley Crawford. You weren't even casual friends. You never had dinner at each other's houses. How did your DNA and fiber end up in their apartment, Judy? You see the problem? We won't even *need* the blood." Shari gave her temporary hope only to have it immediately come crashing down. Yet another nail in Judy's resistance.

"Want to know what I think, Judy? What I am willing to take to the prosecutor? Would you like to hear it?"

"Not particularly," she bluffed.

"Okay. I won't tell you what I think or what I'm willing to recommend," Shari and Eddie retracted. Shari knew that a person guilty of murder who knows the police are on to her would want to hear about the best possible deal to be had.

"I'll listen," she conceded, her defenses beaten down as predicted by Shari's psychological profile.

"Are you sure?" Eddie teased. "Why don't we take a break? You want anything?" He rose and began to leave the room.

"No! I don't want a damn break! I want to hear what you're thinking and willing to take to the prosecutor!" she snapped.

Shari had created desperation. The plan was working to perfection.

"Calm down, Judy. We can work this out. Here's what I'm thinking. You went over to the Crawford place to talk to Crawford.

You wanted him to go back to his wife and stop screwing your girlfriend, correct?" Judy said nothing.

"You get there, that day, and Crawford tells you to pound sand. He treats you like an insignificant nobody . . ."

"That's right, he acted like a total asshole," Judy blurted, her first admission. She *was* at the Crawford residence

"Asshole, indeed. Anyway, you ask him nicely to leave your girlfriend alone. What does he do? He threatens to call security to have you forcibly removed from the premises. He asks: 'How did you get up here, anyway?' You tell him how you disabled the cameras and snuck up on the freight elevator. You're wearing gloves, correct?"

"How do you know all this?" she asked, softly, shaking her head. "Were there cameras that I missed?"

Admission number two—Judy Hoffman was the person who disabled the cameras at 5000 Town Center. Shari was on a roll.

"We've pieced a lot of it together, Judy; with good old fashioned police work. Anyway, here's where I can help you, if you'll let me. The more he talks and mocks you, the angrier you get. You just came there to talk to him, to reason with him, am I correct?"

"Yes, I told you before, yes."

"You asked for a glass of water or something and ended up in the kitchen. No prints because of the gloves. He said something like 'drink your water and get the hell out of my house.' You saw a serrated knife sitting on the counter. You had an out-of-body experience. You picked up the knife. You didn't mean to do it—hell, you probably don't even *remember* picking up the knife."

"I really don't. I don't know where I got the knife."

Admission number three—Judy picked up the knife.

"Crawford started to panic, didn't he? Maybe he challenged you—gave you a choice—put the knife down and get the hell out or he'd call security or the police."

"That's exactly what he said."

"You panic. You've disabled the cameras. You're in the apartment, holding the knife. If he calls the police, you're in trouble! You've got to stop him. You start waving the knife around, ordering him to put down the phone. You don't want to kill him."

"I didn't, I don't, but he won't put the phone down."

"What happened next? You hit him with something and knock him out or to the ground. You find some zip ties and bind his hands and legs. Now he's your prisoner. You're afraid the wife is going to come home, right?"

"Yes, she could have come in at any moment. I was terrified."

"You are now temporarily insane. He's still unconscious. You are a strong woman. You pick him up and throw him over your shoulder, take him down to the basement and into that storage room, where no one will disturb you."

"It was quiet down there, that's for sure, until that asshole woke up."

Admission number four—Judy subdued and bound Bradley Crawford, and took him to the basement storage room where the murder took place.

"He does wake up and he starts screaming. He's defiant. He tells you that you will not get away with this and that he can screw anyone he wants. You swing the knife . . ."

"It wasn't intentional," she lied. "I just lost my cool and started to swing. I didn't mean to hurt him, let alone kill him."

Admission number five—Judy Hoffman swung the knife, which penetrated Crawford's body.

"Crawford begins to scream. He tells you he'll turn you in, the first chance he gets. He tells you how much power a congressman has. He promises to ruin your life. He says he will own your ass and fuck your girlfriend whenever he wants. He orders you to release him and get him to a doctor. You say, 'you'll never fuck her again, asshole', or something like that. You swing the knife and slice off his pecker."

"I just swung. I was shocked at what happened."

"You mean his death, or his missing penis?"

"At that point, just the penis. I didn't know he would bleed out. I tried to stop the bleeding. It wouldn't stop bleeding. I couldn't let him call the police, could I?"

Admission number six. Game, set, and match. It was Judy, not Mia, who severed the congressman's penis.

"Of course not, Judy. What did you do next?" Shari, through Eddie, was now testing how committed Hoffman was to tell the story. As predicted, Judy needed no additional prompting.

"I don't know, I panicked . . . thought about calling the cops myself. Call 9-1-1 and get him treated. Maybe they can sew it back on. I couldn't bring myself to do it. I was so angry. I carried him back up the stairs, laid him down in his bed, staged the apartment to make it look like a robbery. I didn't know Mia would be charged, but Elyssa said she was a stone-cold bitch. Poetic justice, I figured, when she got charged with the murder. I snuck out down the freight elevator and out the back door."

"And you were wearing that beige coat, weren't you?"

"Yes. Enough already. I told you what happened. It's temporary insanity, right? An attorney like Blake could take care of this and get me a good deal, right?"

"Not as good as you can get right here, right now. An insanity plea is not going to work. Maybe involuntary manslaughter, maximum fifteen years, out in two to five, if you behave. That's a lot better than life in prison."

"I can't serve time. How about probation? I'll sign anything you want."

"You can't get probation, Judy. You murdered a public official, a United States Congressman. You will have to serve time. How much time depends on the charges and how compliant a prisoner you are. Are you ready to put all this in writing? I need a signed confession to go to the judge."

"I'm so sorry." She burst out crying, the weight of the world leaving her shoulders. "Please tell Mia and Elyssa how sorry I am. I didn't mean to hurt him. I certainly didn't mean to kill him. I'll take anger management classes. I'll do anything you want. I'm so sorry."

"I will draft the confession, you can sign it, and I'll take it to the judge with my recommendation. I can't guarantee what she'll do, but I'll give it my best shot."

"Thank you, sir. I appreciate everything you're doing for me." Eddie began to feel guilty for deceiving her. But he followed all the rules and used very little deception. The confession would hold up on appeal. He was pleased he did not have to use the fake reports.

"Let's get you back to a holding cell." He uncuffed her from the table, cuffed her hands in front of her, and led her out the door. A uniformed officer escorted her to a holding cell.

Zachary Blake and Shari Belitz watched and listened to the whole interview. They developed a plan, obtained the support of the police, and executed the plan flawlessly. They embraced and high-fived each other when Hoffman confessed. Mia would soon be a free woman. The real murderer was in custody, the innocent victim and widow was exonerated. All that was left was to put it on the record.

CHAPTER
THIRTY-ONE

Dr. Harold Rothenberg knocked on Mia Folger's open hospital room door. Mia invited him in. To Mia's surprise, Dr. Rothenberg was accompanied by two strangers. The strangers hung back as Harold approached Mia's bedside.

"How are you feeling today, Mia?" Harold inquired.

"Better, thank you. Ready to go home. Sad that my husband will not be there."

"You've made remarkable progress, Mia. I'm so pleased, but also terribly sorry about your husband. He was a good man. I have some news for you, though. I would like to introduce you to two people who had a lot to do with this. Mia, I want you to meet Zachary Blake and Shari Belitz. Zachary's a lawyer. He's been defending you throughout the trial. Shari is a very talented jury consultant. She's been of invaluable assistance to Zack throughout the process. As I indicated, they have some very good news for you. Zack?" Harold motioned for Zack and Shari to come forward.

"Hello, Mia. It is nice to finally meet you. Several weeks ago, Harold asked me to handle your criminal case. I'm not sure you know this, but you were accused of killing your husband, and the Oakland County Prosecutor's office brought murder charges against you."

"No, I didn't know that. What makes them think I would murder my husband? I *loved* my husband."

Zack turned to Harold. "Are you sure she's up to hearing about all this?"

"She's doing fine, Zack. I would rather she hear about the past few weeks from us than from the press or the public," Rothenberg suggested.

Zack turned back to Mia. "You found out your husband was having an affair. Do you remember?"

"Yes, I do. I remember everything. It was Elyssa Naylor. He promised me it was a stupid, harmless fling and that it was over."

"That must have been after you sent him a few angry texts and told Dr. Rothenberg that you wanted to dismember a certain body part of your husband's. Do you recall the texts?"

"I do. I'm so embarrassed!"

"No need to be embarrassed. Are you aware that your husband was murdered the exact same way you threatened in the texts?"

"No, I was not aware of that."

"Someone got ahold of your texts, leaked them to the press, and made it look like you dismembered your husband and killed him, just like you said you would."

"Oh, my God! And the police actually believed I killed him?" Mia exclaimed.

"Yes, Mia. Shari and I have been working on your case ever since, trying to get you exonerated."

"Oh my God! I had no idea! Where do things stand now? It's like an out-of-body experience. I'm suddenly dealing with some sort of breakdown, the death of my husband, and now I must defend myself from a murder charge on top of it all?"

"That's where we have good news, Mia. We have identified the actual murderer. She has confessed and is negotiating a plea, as we speak. She will soon be formally charged and will plead guilty, probably to manslaughter or second-degree murder. After I leave here, I am going to court to have the prosecutor formally drop all charges against you."

"That is such a relief! Wonderful news, under the circumstances. I am familiar with your career, Mr. Blake. How is it that I landed the great Zachary Blake as my attorney?"

"Ask the doc, here." Zack nodded toward Harold. "He's believed in you from the start."

"Why? I gave him nothing but a hard time. I was quite the shit."

"No, you weren't. You were angry. Your husband had an affair, anger was an appropriate and rational response. Unfortunately, your anger reached a boiling point at the same time your husband was killed. That made you the perfect patsy," Rothenberg explained.

"For who? Who killed my husband? Was it that Naylor woman?"

"No, it was her former lover, a woman by the name of Judy Hoffman," Zack advised.

"Naylor is *gay*? What did she want with my husband? I'm confused."

"Naylor is bisexual. Hoffman is gay. Hoffman blamed your husband for her break-up with Naylor. When you posted those texts, Hoffman decided to kill him the exact way you threatened."

"You mean she . . ."

"Yes, Mia. I'm afraid so. Bradley was dismembered as you described in your texts. In fact, you found the body and that is what sent you into hysterics and into your recent catatonic state," Rothenberg recounted.

"I don't remember any of it," Mia confided.

"Probably a good thing, Mia. Your mental status is still quite fragile," Rothenberg suggested.

"And where do you fit in to all of this, Ms. . . ." Mia addressed Shari.

"Belitz, Mia, Shari Belitz; it's nice to finally meet you. I am a jury consultant. Zack retained my company to do focus groups and other work on the case. It has been my pleasure to contribute to a just result."

"Wow! Sounds expensive. Thank you for all that you did. Speaking of which, Mr. Blake," Mia began.

"Zachary. My friends call me Zachary," Blake interrupted.

"I owe you guys my life, my freedom; I owe you *everything.* I'm not a charity case, Zachary. I can afford an attorney. I want to pay you. In fact, I must insist on it."

"We can talk about my bill after you are well, fair enough?" he proposed.

"Let me have your email or, better yet, your cell number. I'll send you a reminder text," Mia promised.

A text from Mia Folger? No thank you. That's what got us all into this mess, Zack mused.

"Get my number from Harold," he suggested. Right now, I'm off to court to officially make you a free woman."

"Freer than I ever wanted to be. My dear Bradley . . ." Mia sniffled.

"Let's get these people out of here and get you some needed rest," Rothenberg ordered.

"Zachary, Shari, again, *thank you*, from the bottom of my heart," Mia gushed.

"You're welcome, Mia. Truly, it was our pleasure," Zack replied, nodding at Shari.

Rothenberg gave her a mild sedative to help her sleep. He walked out with Zack and Shari.

"She going to be okay, Doc?" Zack inquired.

"I think so, Zack. This has been a very traumatic experience. But she's a strong woman. She'll rebound from this."

"I'll call you from court and let you know the final outcome."

"Thanks, I appreciate it."

Zack and Shari walked out to the hospital parking lot. "Nice people," Shari observed.

"Yes, I've known Doc a long time. He's been treating my boys. He's a good friend."

"You and Jennifer both told me what a good friend he's been. Obviously, he's also a great doctor," Shari observed.

"What else did Jennifer tell you?"

"My lips are sealed. What happens between two women on salon day stays at the salon and between the two women."

"I respect the sanctity of salon day. What time's your flight?"

"Three o'clock."

"Let's head to court. I'll handle the final details and get you to the airport."

"I can take an Uber."

"Not on my watch."

"A limo?"

"I'll drive you myself. It will give us a chance to talk and me a chance to thank you, from the bottom of *my* heart. I could not have done this without you."

"Yes, you could. Maybe not as effectively, but you are one talented lawyer, Zachary Blake. The justice system and our citizens need more attorneys like you out there fighting for the people."

"Quite a compliment coming from you, Shari. Thank you. Let's get to court."

***

"All rise! Forty-Sixth District Court is now in session, the honorable Jordyn Bolton presiding," shouted the clerk.

Jordyn Bolton appeared from a hidden door, took the bench, and uttered, "Please, be seated."

"Today, we were scheduled to continue the preliminary examination in the case of *People v. Folger*. I understand there has been a development. Mr. Bruch? Do you have a motion?"

"I do, Your Honor. The People move to dismiss all charges against Mia Folger Crawford, with prejudice and without costs."

"Mr. Blake?"

"The defense, obviously, has no objection, Your Honor."

"Well, thank you, gentlemen. This is indeed a surprise. Nice to see justice done. Congratulations to both of you for getting this done right."

"Thank you, Your Honor," the two lawyers replied in unison.

The judge slammed her gavel and left the courtroom. Blake and Bruch shook hands.

"I agree with the judge, George. It's not easy to admit you're wrong. You should have a much easier time prosecuting the Hoffman woman. Thanks for doing the right thing when we showed you the evidence."

"You're welcome, Zack. I didn't do much. It's my job to put *criminals* away, not innocent citizens. It's easy to dismiss a case when you have compelling proof of innocence. You did a terrific job for your client. Congratulations. How's she doing, by the way?"

"She regained consciousness yesterday. Doc says she's got a long way to go, but she should be okay."

"That's great. It was nice working with you. Hope to meet again with a better case."

"Looking forward to it. What's the story with Hoffman?"

"I'm looking to charge her with murder two. Should be murder one, but Schreiber promised her manslaughter. It's up to the boss. I guess I'm good with either. She is one vindictive bitch. She needs to be off our streets for a long time."

"Put her down, George, like the rabid dog she is," Zack laughed.

"I'll do my best. Hey, Zack? Do me a favor, would you?"

"What's that, George?"

"If she calls you for representation, please say no."

"George! Was that an attempt at a joke? You have a sense of humor, after all? Will wonders never cease!"

"Fuck you, Blake. See you next time." Bruch turned and walked away

"Bye, George," Zack called out.

Bruch gave him the one-finger salute, without turning back.

CHAPTER

THIRTY-TWO

Judy Hoffman was pissed as hell. The best offer she received from the prosecutor's office was murder two. She had given up trying to obtain an agreement for the involuntary manslaughter charge that Eddie Schreiber promised her. *I should have chopped off* ***his***.

Judy hired a lawyer and railed on about a system where the cops can make false promises to obtain a confession. She alleged that the cops used falsified DNA and fiber analysis reports to create the impression that they had concrete evidence of her guilt.

The attorney filed a motion to have the confession set aside. The motion was heard in front of Judge Jordyn Bolton. Bolton quickly disposed of the first issue. Schreiber testified that he never promised her an involuntary manslaughter plea. He told her he would *recommend* an involuntary manslaughter plea. When the lawyer asked Hoffman which was true, the promise or the recommendation, she had to admit that he'd only promised to recommend the plea.

The second issue was more troubling and controversial. There is a split of authority about whether the police can produce false documents for a suspect to read. Some cases view this tactic as merely a written version of the oral lies or promises cops make every day in interrogations all over the United States. Other courts opine that a document has more authority and can be placed in someone's file, making the person look guilty when he or she has not been *proven* guilty. Bolton was not a fan of the practice.

Again, Eddie saved the day. He testified that he and Kramer had, indeed, prepared false reports, demonstrating positive DNA and fiber analysis found in the Crawford condominium. However, he never *showed* the documents to Judy. She never read them. He held the fake docs in his hand, told Judy that they contained positive findings and that he had the evidence in his hands. However, Judy never asked to read the reports.

Judy called Schreiber a liar, recalling clearly that she had been shown the documents. Jerry Kramer was called to verify a video recording of the entire confession. The video backed up Schreiber's claim that he never showed her the documents. As a result, the lie was verbal, like the lesser offense promise. Bolton denied the motion to suppress the confession.

All Judy's lawyer could do now was get her the best deal possible to avoid a trial. Trials are expensive—Judy was willing to spare the state the expense, but she wanted the involuntary manslaughter plea that Schreiber promised. The prosecutor argued for murder one. He was obviously blustering, because Judy had zero incentive to accept a plea to the highest offense to which she could be convicted. Negotiations continued, and the offer was reduced to murder two.

The prosecutor argued that manslaughter required provocation or some type of fear. Judy, through her lawyer, countered that anger in manslaughter cases is the same as fear and that there was insufficient time between her anger and the killing for any reasonable person to calm down. She argued that her inability to calm is what caused the murder, and that made the crime manslaughter. The prosecutor countered with what he referred to as 'troubling aggravating factors.' The crime was particularly brutal. Judy had an opportunity to save Crawford and, instead, allowed him to bleed out. She also dismembered him after rendering him completely defenseless.

Judy counter-argued what her lawyer termed 'mitigating factors.' Judy accepted responsibility for the crime and confessed. She had no prior criminal history, no criminal record of any kind. She also argued that Michigan was one state where the penalty for manslaughter is more severe than most states.

In many states, manslaughter carries a three-to-ten-year sentence, depending upon various mitigating or aggravating factors. However, in Michigan, according to Michigan Penal Code § 750.321, manslaughter is a felony, punishable by fifteen years in prison and a seventy-five-hundred-dollar fine. This was hardly a minor penalty for a first time, cooperative criminal who acted in the heat of the moment and lashed out in anger.

The prosecutor reached out to Zachary Blake and asked if he could speak to Mia Folger, fresh out of the hospital. Mia agreed to the meeting. The prosecutor preferred to try the case rather than cave to Judy's demand. She recognized this was a first-time offender. However, she also found this crime far too savage and brutal to reduce to manslaughter. She offered Mia the opportunity to decide whether a manslaughter conviction was sufficient justice for her late husband or whether she preferred a trial.

Mia had been where Judy was. She was the angry spouse, betrayed by her husband. Judy was an angry lover, betrayed by her significant other. Mia wouldn't or couldn't kill anyone, but she certainly understood the level of betrayal experienced by Judy. She also wanted to put the entire episode behind her and move on with her life. A public trial, her relationship with her husband, salacious details of the participants' sex lives would be broadcast daily everywhere. This would be a terrible environment in which to heal.

In the end, Mia consented to the manslaughter plea. Judy was sentenced to the maximum, fifteen years and seventy-five hundred dollars. She would serve her sentence at the Women's Huron Valley Correctional Center in Ypsilanti, a penitentiary that housed female prisoners at all security levels. At her sentencing hearing she apologized to Mia and demonstrated genuine remorse. She also praised and thanked Mia for her "incredible generosity and compassion" in allowing her husband's killer to plea to a lesser crime and serve a shorter sentence.

***

That evening, Libby Curry posted her final podcast on the Bradley Crawford murder case. She ate humble pie, apologized to her listeners, and heaped praise on Zachary Blake, Micah Love, and 'newcomer' Shari Belitz:

"In what turned out to be anything but a *Slam Dunk*, dear listeners, all charges against Mia Folger have been dropped by the

Oakland County Prosecutor's office. Super-lawyer Zachary Blake continues his incredible winning streak. *Slam Dunk* should have realized, from the minute Blake appeared on the scene, that things would not play out as expected.

"In our defense, the Southfield Police and the Oakland County Prosecutor, sparked by a few salacious texts made public by this broadcast, were guilty of an unfortunate rush to judgment. While we here at *Slam Dunk* leaped to the same conclusions, we are not trained police officers. In such an important, high-profile case, discretion and careful consideration of *all* the evidence should have been law enforcement's number one priority.

"Mia Folger was lucky that her doctor is long-time Blake family consultant, Dr. Harold Rothenberg of Birmingham. Not only has Mia been exonerated from all criminal charges, she has also emerged from her catatonic state, been released from the hospital, is on the mend, and can finally begin to mourn the loss of her beloved husband, Congressman Bradley Crawford.

"Unless you've been hiding under a rock, dear listeners, you now know the incredible true story of a tryst gone horribly wrong. Ms. Folger and Congressman Crawford are public figures. As such, both are fair game to the press. Crawford's decision to have an affair with an employee, his legislative assistant, Elyssa Naylor, turned out to be fatal. Naylor, to the surprise of everyone in Washington and Southfield, was a bisexual woman—while she carried on with Crawford, she was also very privately intimate with another woman.

"*Slam Dunk* proffered, in one of its previous podcasts about this case, that Hell hath no fury like a woman scorned. We were correct.

Unfortunately, we targeted the wrong woman. Judy Hoffman, Elyssa Naylor's 'other woman', was the woman scorned in this salacious triangle. *Slam Dunk* has learned that Naylor dumped Hoffman for Crawford, which enraged Hoffman and spurred her decision to terminate the congressman. My listeners are all too familiar with the grisly details of how Congressman Bradley Crawford met his maker—we shall not repeat them here tonight.

"Thanks to the valiant efforts of the latest legal and investigative dream team, Zack Blake, Micah Love, and newcomer Shari Belitz, both the affair and the murderer were exposed, and Mia Folger was exonerated. Kudos to Blake, Love, and Ms. Belitz, the hotshot jury consultant from the Big Apple first identified right here on *Slam Dunk*. Belitz, as previously reported on this podcast, was retained by Blake to conduct a focus group, which led to alternate theories of the case and, ultimately, to the conclusion that Hoffman was the perpetrator. A special tip of the hat to this tenacious lady who, according to our exclusive sources inside the focus group, developed the theories that cracked the case.

"*Slam Dunk* has also developed a source inside the prison where Hoffman will begin serving her fifteen year sentence for manslaughter. We have learned, exclusively, that she can expect a rather harsh initiation into the sorority of prisoners at the prison facility. As more details are known, *Slam Dunk* will update you, dear listeners.

"Finally, as this unfortunate saga comes to an end, we wish to sincerely apologize and offer our deepest condolences to Mia Folger, who not only lost the love of her life, but was treated horribly by the media, the police, the criminal justice system, and this podcast. *Slam*

Dunk prides itself on getting it right and, in this case, we got it wrong. The United States Constitution declares all suspects innocent until *proven* guilty, and this podcast determined that Mia Folger was guilty well before all the facts were known. For that, we are truly sorry. We will try to do better in the future. We are pleased to report that Ms. Folger is on the road to recovery. We wish her well.

"Dear listeners, as the global pandemic rages on and Detroit faces numerous political, medical, and legal challenges, *Slam Dunk* will continue to report on the latest news and events that shape our city, our state, our country, and our world. Thanks for listening. That's all for now. Have a great evening. We'll talk soon."

***

Later that evening, Zack's cell phone rang. Caller ID flashed 'Shari Belitz'. Zack pressed the 'accept' button.

"Hey, Shari. How are things in the Big Apple?"

"Wonderful, Zack. Great city. It's not Detroit, but it's a great city," she cracked.

"I knew I'd convert you. Calling to come work for me?"

"No. I like being my own boss. You know that. I'm ready to work *with* you, as a consultant, anytime you call."

"Thanks, Shari. I was dubious at first, but you made a believer out of me. We will work together in the very near future. One caveat, though. I do mainly plaintiff's work. I researched and discovered you do mainly *defense* work. I need to lure you away from the dark side," Zack kibitzed.

"Insurance companies pay very well and always on time."

"So do I."

"True, but many of your brother and sister plaintiff lawyers live case-to-case and hand-to-mouth."

"That's an overstatement, but I get your drift. Did you call for a particular reason?"

"I wanted to find out what happened with the plea deal. Did Hoffman get the voluntary manslaughter deal?"

"Yes, Mia was given the choice of a trial or plea and she chose the plea. She claimed she understood the emotions that led Hoffman to kill. Isn't that something? It has been wonderful getting to know Mia. I'm not used to representing clients I can't communicate with until *after* I win their case. This was a strange one."

"Are you going to pursue a wrongful arrest and prosecution case? I just worked on one of those. The payouts are decent."

"I know. I've done a few in my time, too. I will probably pursue a case, with Mia's permission, to get my fees and costs paid and relieve Mia of the burden."

"That would be a nice gesture. I've got to hand it to you, Blake. You are one of the most compassionate, caring people I have ever met. Call me any time. Better yet, look me up the next time you're in New York. My husband and I will take you and your lovely wife out for a meal you'll never forget."

"It's a date. I've got to run. Take care, Shari. Talk soon."

"Bye, Zack."

Epilogue

Judy Hoffman was transported in a secure van to the Huron Valley Correctional Center. She was checked in and classified as a level two prisoner because her sentence was less than twenty years. Her transport restraints were removed; she was placed in a holding cell and served a pre-packaged meal. She underwent a full body and x-ray scan to detect any ingested or hidden contraband. A thorough strip search was performed. Judy was examined, head-to-toe, and instructed to squat and cough to ensure she had inserted no contraband up her rectum.

She was issued a set of 'R & D' clothing: t-shirt, socks, underwear, elastic waist pants, and a pair of slip-ons—something they called 'bus shoes.' She was required to wear these clothes until she received her prison uniform.

Next, she was fingerprinted and photographed for the purpose of issuing her an inmate identification card with her prison number and a bar code on it. The bar code was scanned every time she received meals or purchased items from the commissary. She was interviewed by three separate professionals: a physician's assistant asked her questions about diseases, especially COVID, and any other communicable disease. She was asked whether she routinely took medication, because the staff had to assure the availability of medications necessary to maintain the health of the inmate. She also interviewed with a psychologist to ascertain her general mental health status. Was she a risk of harming herself and others? Was she mentally fit for Huron Valley Correctional?

Finally, she met her case worker. She was advised what to expect or not expect from various staff members and what those staff members expected from her. She was provided a pamphlet of prison offerings in education, recreation, programming, work assignment, and other aspects of prison life. The pamphlet also detailed penalties for rule violations.

Judy received a clean bill of health and was assigned to general population. She was issued a bed roll consisting of two blankets, two sheets, a towel, washcloth, and some basic hygiene items. When all the preliminaries were completed, she was escorted to her assigned housing unit by a prison guard. She was shown to her bunk and rolled out the bed roll and blankets. As she worked, two large inmates stared at her—one, a light-skinned black woman with tattoos all over her body—the other, a white woman with a deep scar across her cheek and huge biceps. Judy was a strong, fit woman, but looked small compared to these two.

The guard finally left Judy alone, and the two women approached her.

"What's your name, hon?" the white one insisted.

"Judy Hoffman."

"Judy Hoffman . . . Judy Hoffman . . ." the black one repeated. "Why does that name sound familiar?"

"I dunno," Judy responded, wondering if this was some sort of initiation or scare tactic. It was working—she was scared shitless.

"Any of you guys heard of Judy Hoffman?" the black one shouted to everyone in the room.

"The woman who killed the congressman? *That* Judy Hoffman?" someone hollered.

"Whoa, bitch! Are you *that* Judy Hoffman?" the black woman asked.

"What's it to you?" Judy mustered a small level of courage.

"Well, Judy, let me tell you the way things are around here. We got a shitload of nasty bitches in this house. Emily here, and me, see? We's the nastiest of these bitches. We's the house managers. Name's Katrina, like the fuckin' hurricane. Understand? Whatever you want, anything you do, goes through us. Is that understood?"

"Got it. Anything else?"

"You never want to get on our bad side. The last few people that got on our bad side ain't here no more. Get my meaning?"

"Loud and clear. I don't want to be on your bad side."

"Now, we don't tolerate lying in here. The truth is everything. Get my meaning?"

"Yes."

"Good. Now answer my question, bitch. You the Judy Hoffman that killed Congressman Bradley Crawford? That why you're here?" Katrina huffed, waiting for the answer.

"Yes," Judy finally admitted.

"Well shit, honey. That's too bad for you. Bradley Crawford was *my* congressman. He wrote a letter trying to get me leniency." Katrina got right in Judy's face, nose-to-nose. "He was a wonderful man. In fact, I *loved* that man . . ."

THE END

Acknowledgements

As always, special thanks to my family—my wife, the Fab 4, and the 9 Grand—for their support. Thank you to Amy Lignor and others (you know who you are) for reading, critiquing, and making this a better novel. A special shout out to Shari Belitz for teaching me the ins and outs of trial/jury consulting and permitting me to insert her as a character in this 8th Zachary Blake legal thriller novel. Yes, Shari is a *real person* with a trial consulting firm in New York City. She asked to "speak" to my readers, so, here's her spiel:

To Mark M. Bello's Zachary Blake Legal Thriller Readers:

This is brash, fast-talking, curse dropping, trial consultant Shari Belitz popping in to say hello! This was a great challenge and a lot of fun matching wits with Zachary Blake in a high-profile criminal trial. Usually, I work cases on the civil side of litigation, representing companies which have been sued, so this was cool!

Trial consulting is a relatively new profession which traces its roots to the early 1970's during the Vietnam War when social scientists volunteered their time and expertise to defend a group of anti-war protesters who were prosecuted for conspiracy to raid draft boards.

What a long, strange trip it's been! Our professional backgrounds are as varied as the cases on which we work. We are psychologists, lawyers, communications experts or a combination. I first discovered I was fascinated with the intersection of law and psychology as it relates to human behavior, in college. However, it was after practicing law for many years, that I took a leap of faith and went back to graduate school to study forensic psychology with a concentration in jury research and science. The only thing more exciting to me than the study of individual human behavior is how individuals make decisions in a group setting.

People ask me what a "day in the life" of a trial consultant is like. Sometimes it is the glamour of the courtroom, or even conducting a focus group like the one featured in this novel, but mostly this is tedious grunt work. "Cases are won in your sweatpants!" is what I like to say. I often spend my days dissecting files to construct themes for a case, working with a witness to give strong, compelling deposition or trial testimony, or moderating a deliberation group in a mock trial, collecting qualitative and quantitative data. The work may be tedious, but it is exciting to test themes, watch them come alive in a courtroom, and having the satisfaction of seeing a once anxious witness shine in the witness box, while enduring a brutal cross-examination. I also select, or as we like to say in this biz, deselect jurors at trial.

I hope you enjoyed this little slice of my professional life as portrayed in the world of Zachary Blake. Thanks to Attorney/Author Mark M. Bello for this amazing opportunity. Everything depicted is close to my true character other than that Mark's decision to make me a sloppy eater for comedic effect. I assure you, if we ever work together I will exhibit my best table manners!

I hope you enjoyed "You Have the Right to Remain Silent" as much as I did. I never dreamed I'd be a featured character in a full-length novel—I'm so excited! To get in touch:

MY LINKEDIN:
https://www.linkedin.com/in/sharibelitz/

VISIT MY WEBSITE:
https://www.sharibelitz.com/

JOIN MY MAILING LIST
https://www.sharibelitz.com/connect

xo
Shari

About The Author

Mark M. Bello is an attorney, social justice advocate, and award-winning author of the Zachary Blake Legal Thriller series. Mark also writes for legal and political content sites and hosts the legal themed podcast, ***Justice Counts,*** on the *Spreaker* network. A Michigan native, Mark and his wife, Tobye, have four children and nine grand-children. For more information, please visit *https://www.markmbello.com.*

Books In The Zachary Blake Legal Thriller Series

L'DOR V'DOR –From Generation to Generation
(A Prequel Novella)

Betrayal of Faith (1)
Betrayal of Justice (2)
Betrayal in Blue (3)
Betrayal in Black (4)
Betrayal High (5)
Supreme Betrayal (6)
Betrayal at the Border (7)

The **Zachary Blake Legal Thriller Series**
is also available in audio book format.

Books in Mark's Social Justice/Safety Series for Children

HAPPY JACK SAD JACK—A Bullying Story

OTHER BOOKS BY MARK M. BELLO

L'DOR V'DOR –From Generation to Generation II

The Blake-Lewin Family Cookbook of Traditional Jewish Recipes

Connect With Mark

Website: https://www.markmbello.com

Email: info@markmbello.com

Facebook: MarkMBelloBooks

Twitter: @MarkMBelloBooks

YouTube: Mark Bello

Goodreads: Mark M. Bello

LinkedIn:

https://www.linkedin.com/in/markmbello

Subscribe to our mailing list and receive your free copy of

L'DOR V'DOR -From Generation to Generation

and other giveaways and other surprises.

To request a speaking engagement, interview, or appearance, please email info@markmbello.com

Made in the USA
Las Vegas, NV
01 November 2022